ACT OF TERROR

ACT OF TERROR

MARC CAMERON

PINNACLE BOOKS
Kensington Publishing Corp.
www.kensingtonbooks.com

PINNACLE BOOKS are published by

Kensington Publishing Corp.
119 West 40th Street
New York, NY 10018

ISBN-13: 978-0-7860-2495-7
ISBN-10: 0-7860-2495-X

First printing: May 2012

10 9 8 7 6 5 4 3 2 1

Printed in the United States of America

For Ben: the real deal

Washington Post, Front Page,
Sunday, September 24:

Security Concerns High For American 'Royal' Wedding

Specifics regarding a wedding of the vice president's daughter and Secretary of State Melissa Ryan's son remain a closely guarded secret. Dozens of world leaders are expected to be in attendance and analysts predict a multimillion-dollar price tag for security alone. . . .

NSA Flash-Intercept/Cellular
TS/ORCON (Top Secret/Originator Controlled)
Translated: Tajik/English—#HF5648
1732 hours ZULU:
Begin Translation [A: . . . DID YOU SEE IT? B: YES. IT IS PERFECT. A: SO . . . WE ARE TO BEGIN? B: PASS THE WORD—THE BITTER TASTE OF GALL WILL SOON BE A MEMORY. THE TIME HAS COME TO ACT. . . .] Transmission ends.

A murderer is less to fear. The traitor is the plague.

—Marcus Cicero, Roman statesman

WEDNESDAY
September 27

PROLOGUE

Quis custodiet ipsos custodes?
(Who will guard the guards?)

—JUVENAL

George Bush Center for Intelligence
Langley, Virginia

Wednesday, September 27
0710 hours

Seth Timmons would have made a remarkable spy—if that had been his mission.

The fact that the authorities would kill him and search his car after he was dead didn't bother him at all. It would do them no good. He'd left nothing but fingerprints—and Human Resources already had those in his file. They knew who he was—or thought they did. Americans tended to call notorious killers by their full names. At the time of his birth he'd been *Tum-afik Pedram,* but before the day was over he'd take his place in history as Robert Seth Timmons.

The dumbfounded investigators who scrutinized his past would find he was a twenty-six-year-old white male from Dayton, Ohio, with no surviving relatives. They would see he had an above-average intellect, with a graduate degree from MIT and a fluency in three Persian languages including Tajik. His present assignment at the Central Asian desk would reveal he knew far more than he should have about American intelligence.

Timmons's willow-thin build made him appear taller than his six feet. Wild eyebrows, bushy as ripe heads of wheat, shielded twilight-blue eyes. A prominent Adam's apple displayed the swollen knot of a goiter, something rarely seen in the well-fed youth of North America. The CIA security personnel who'd done his background investigation had been much too polite to mention such a thing. They had been comforted by his sandy hair, had gazed into his familiar face and seen a pleasant reflection of themselves.

Timmons switched off the slapping windshield wipers. Rivulets of water zigzagged down the glass as acres of employee parking filled up around him. Many had been at their cubicles for more than an hour. Flanked by armed guards and cloistered behind multiple layers of cameras and motion sensors, these early birds were lulled into a sense of security as sure as a mother's embrace. Timmons counted on the fact that they would be at ease among their own. Relaxed sheep were all the easier to slaughter.

A brutal, gray rain pelted his face as he hauled himself from the stuffy confines of the Taurus. He chanced a quick glance over his shoulder at the hazy tangle of dark woods beyond the employee parking lots, past Colonial Farm Road. Mujaheed would surely be hidden there, watching from the shadows, ready to kill him if he backed out before the job was done. There was no need. Timmons found himself looking forward to the end. He'd waited, it seemed, so very long.

He slung a canvas messenger bag over his shoulder

and began the soggy trudge across the parking lot toward the main entrance of the Original Headquarters Building—OHB to CIA staff. Dozens of other early arrivals slogged silently along with him, umbrellas, book bags, and wilted newspapers held above their heads against the incessant hiss of rain. Timmons studied them with his peripheral vision, wondering which ones would be alive to walk back to their cars at the end of the day.

The gathering herd of employees slowed and bunched at the bottleneck of security screening aisles they often called the *cattle chutes*. Timmons swiped his ID card, and gave what he hoped was an easy smile to the black uniformed guard who stood at parade rest eyeing the incoming tide of workers. CIA analysts were not allowed to bring weapons into the building and there was the outside chance the officer would search his messenger bag.

It didn't matter. The items Timmons would need for his mission were already inside, waiting.

On the elevator he had to force himself to stop tapping his foot. He paused at his cubicle at the Central Asian Desk long enough to log on to the computer. He stood, stooping in front of the keyboard, the empty canvas messenger bag still draped over his shoulder.

No emails. That was good. Everything was still moving according to plan.

He looked at his watch—7:24.

Alex Gerard was waiting inside the supply closet off the back of the mail room. Everyone called it a closet, but in reality it was a ten-by-eight room packed with reams of computer paper, toner, and everything else one might need to run an office.

"Are you excited, brother?" The redhead leaned against a stack of paper boxes, tapping an unsharpened yellow pencil against a cardboard lid. Gerard's birth name was Yazad Kabuli. He'd been with Timmons from the beginning, since they were filthy, starving boys.

"Of course I'm excited," Timmons said. "Who wouldn't be? Have you got them?" He tried to keep his hands from trembling.

At this early hour everyone who was at work would be settling in at their desks or making their way down to the food court for coffee. Even so, Timmons made sure to pull the door shut behind him.

"I do, indeed." Gerard nodded smugly. He was six inches shorter than Timmons and two years younger, but he always acted superior. He insisted on being the one who dealt with the go-between. He had to be the one who distributed the weapons.

"We have over a hundred rounds each," Gerard continued, his face turning passive, thoughtful. "I suppose that will be enough." He took a shiny blue-black pistol from his own messenger bag, racked the slide so it locked open, and pushed it toward Timmons—

The supply room door yawned open with a sickening creak at the same moment Timmons's fingers closed around the butt of the weapon. Both men looked up, shoulders slumped, eyes shining like rats caught in a bright light.

"Hey, Seth." It was Ginger Durham, the IT specialist responsible for the computer network in their department. Her jet-black hair was braided into cornrows and festooned with gold extenders and colorful beads. Timmons had been on several dates with her, the last four of which had ended up at her apartment. He found her ebony skin and easy laughter a pleasant distraction.

She smiled, showing her perfect teeth. "What are you guys up t—?"

Her eyes fell on the gun at the same moment the door swung shut behind her. She froze.

Gerard, who was closer, lunged forward, slamming his palm over her mouth as he drove her against the door with the point of his shoulder. He used his free hand to punch her hard in the stomach, knocking the wind out of her.

"Grab her legs," he hissed.

Timmons stuffed the handgun in his waistband and took the terrified girl around her thighs like a football player on a low tackle. She had the muscular legs of a sprinter and her stiletto heels could have done some real damage had she fought back. Amazingly, she allowed the men to lower her to the floor without a struggle.

Gerard lay across her chest, pinning her arms with his body, his hand still across her mouth. Her hair spread out on the tile around her face like a beaded fan.

"I could use some help here," Gerard grunted.

Timmons released the girl's legs and maneuvered himself higher so he could trade places with Gerard and straddle her belly, pinning her arms with both hands. He could smell the familiar, breezy scent of hyacinth perfume.

"Have you got her?" Gerard pressed the blade of a box cutter to the quivering vein on the side of the girl's throat.

"I have her," Timmons said. It was strange to see her lying there this way, helpless, frightened as a trapped bird.

"Not a sound," Gerard threatened as he raised his hand an inch.

"Seth," she gurgled. "Why—"

Gerard's hand slammed back down on her face. "I told you to keep quiet." He pressed the box cutter deeper so it drew a trickle of blood from her neck.

She nodded quickly, eyes round and white with terror.

Timmons spotted a roll of clear packing tape on top of the counter.

"Ginger," he whispered, in the same voice he'd whispered much more personal things. "You've got to stay still so he won't hurt you. Do you understand me?"

She nodded again, blinking away the tears that pressed from her thick lashes. Mascara ran in black streams down her cheeks.

"Okay . . . I'm trusting you. . . ." He let her hands go long enough to get the tape. Once her mouth was covered he took several wraps around her ankles and her wrists.

When he was satisfied she was well restrained, he looked up at Gerard. "It's done."

"Finally," Gerard said, shaking his head as if disgusted. He breathed a long sigh of relief. "That was just about the end of us."

"How are we going to do this?" Timmons looked down at the terrified woman's face. Ten minutes before, she would have called him her boyfriend. They'd even joked about starting a family together.

"Good question," Gerard said. "She'll bleed all over everything if we cut her throat—and I only have this one shirt here at work. It would be pretty hard to break her neck without making too much noise. . . ." His nostrils flared with all the talk of killing. Such things had always excited him.

"Well, we can't leave her alive," Timmons said. "Everything won't be in place until one-thirty. . . . That's over five hours away."

Ginger looked back and forth; her chest began to heave uncontrollably. She clenched her eyes as if closing them might drown out their words.

"We can hide her body behind these boxes," Gerard stared down in thought. "But someone will report her missing if she just disappears." Ginger's denim skirt had hiked up during the assault and he seemed transfixed by the dark, chocolate flesh of her thighs and snow-white glimpse of her underwear.

Timmons shrugged. "I'll tell Selma she got sick and had to run home. She knows we've been dating. It'll seem a plausible story coming from me. . . ."

Ginger's eyes flicked open. She stared up at Timmons, heartbroken.

Her muffled sobs turned into angry screams beneath the tape. She began to pitch and squirm, pounding her head against the floor and kicking out with her bound feet.

It was too late.

Timmons lay his full weight across her writhing chest. He pressed his palm over her mouth to help dampen the sound as Gerard reached in to slide a plastic garbage bag over her head. Timmons slipped his hand out quickly, then replaced it again while Gerard sealed the bag around her neck.

Her silent screams buzzed against Seth's palm. Dark lashes, soaked with tears, fluttered against the plastic.

Though he'd seen it done many times, Timmons had never actually killed anyone himself. He was surprised it took Ginger Durham such a very long time to die.

The others would go much more quickly. He would make certain of that.

Situation Room
The White House

1315 hours

Secretary of Defense Andrew Filson had the pinched mouth of someone who woke up angry every day. He was a man constantly in motion, and the tail of his starched French-cuffed shirt was generally flapping over his belt ten minutes into any meeting.

He tossed a navy-blue folder onto the long polished oak table surrounded by thirteen fellow members of the National Security Council. Six muted flat-screen televisions flickered along the walls of the cramped, subterranean room. Five were tuned to major media outlets. One glowed in vibrantly blank blue screen, attached to a laptop computer for the very few times a cabinet member was foolish enough to bring in a PowerPoint presentation for the commander in chief.

Winfield "Win" Palmer, the former director of national intelligence, and newly appointed national security advisor, sat to the immediate right of his boss—President Chris Clark. Sometimes brash, often outspoken, and ever devoted, the ruddy, stone-faced

Palmer had been Clark's right-hand man from the time they'd been assigned to the same company in the United States Military Academy at West Point, too many decades before.

Two seats away, SecDef Filson had reached nuclear-option-only mode more quickly than usual. Palmer shot a furtive glance at the commander in chief to see if he wanted the retired three-star reined in a notch or two.

Clark's gunmetal brow arched almost imperceptibly. Their time together in the military gave Palmer the edge when it came to reading his boss's unspoken cues. POTUS liked a robust discussion among his cabinet, sometimes allowing things to heat dangerously close to an all-out brawl before offering any sort of mediation. The White House Situation Room was code-named *Cement Mixer* for good reason.

Filson raged on with all the wind and fury of a true zealot. He waved another navy-blue folder in the air before tossing it on the leather desk blotter in front of him.

"The three yesterday make five," he said, black reading glasses perched on a bulbous nose as he consulted a hand-scrawled note on his legal pad. "I'm sure you have seen the markets this morning. Dropping like a glass-jawed boxer at our inability to protect our citizens." He looked at the folder in front of him, shaking his head in disgust. "Look at this. A rogue policeman working off-duty security in Oakland takes his service pistol and guns down fifteen at a Raiders game. Fans tackled the son of a bitch, but he was able to get away and blow the head off a young father in front of his wife and two kids before a sniper from his own department pops him between the running lights. . . .

"And how about this one?" Filson's eyes flicked up and down the document, pressing on with his grim news. "A TSA screener sneaks a bomb inside the secure area at Miami International, managing to turn the thirteen innocents nearest him into pink mist. Twenty more injured in one way or another." He scanned the last folder in his pile. "There was one tiny shred of decent news," he snorted. "A flight attendant out of Detroit tried to strong-arm a Delta pilot into crashing their 767. Luckily for the souls on board, the copilot happens to be a flight deck safety officer. He shoots her in the eye at thirty thousand feet. They had to do an emergency landing in Philly to wipe her brains off the instrum—"

"All right, Andrew," the president cut him off. "I know everyone here appreciates your vivid descriptions, but we do have our own copy of the files. The real question before us is the connection. All of these people were under thirty." He flipped through his executive brief. "What makes Americans with not so much as a parking ticket suddenly go berserk?"

"These people may have looked American." Filson jammed a thick index finger against the table. "But witnesses at three separate events heard the actors whisper something in another language shortly before each killing. Mark my words Mr. President, an outside group is behind each and every one of these incidents. My money is on al-Qaeda—"

"Someone heard a whisper in something they think was an unknown tongue?" At the far end of the table Jamal Ramidi, the president's assistant for economic policy, threw up his hands. He was a tall, birdlike academic who looked fragile enough to snap in a strong wind. Doctorates from Stanford in international trade and macroeconomics made him the perfect choice for dispensing executive advice on bean-counting. "For crying out loud, Andrew, just once, might it be possible that our troubles are domestic?"

Filson wagged his head with a curling sneer. "I'm not pulling this out of my ass, Jamal. These are coordinated acts of terrorism with Sandbox fingerprints all over them and you know it."

"Way to generalize, General." Ramidi pursed narrow lips. "I suppose you advocate a wholesale roundup of all us towel heads at once—?"

"Believe me." Filson clenched his teeth, leaning across the table. "I love this country enough that if—"

"Oh," Ramidi snapped. "And I suddenly hate my country because my grandparents are from Lebanon?" He threw his pen on the table, exasperated. "Mr. Secretary, you do not know Hamas from hummus."

"You know I'm not referring to you, Jamal." Filson did a poor job of masking his disdain for the man. He looked around the room. "Doesn't anyone but me see we are at war here?"

Secretary of State Melissa Ryan, who sat on Palmer's immediate right, looked across the table at her archrival in matters of foreign policy. Palmer caught the flash of indignation in her eyes. The product of an Irish boxer and a Roma, Ryan's sultry features and penchant for keeping the top two buttons on her Cavalli silk blouses unfastened had the power to befuddle the wisest man during a debate. At fifty-one, she'd graced the cover of *Vogue* only a month before. A former U.S. senator from Maryland, she'd been plucked from a prestigious job at the Brookings Institution when Clark took office. Many thought she would run for president when his tenure was over.

Filson blustered on, unaware he was about to be attacked. "Don't be so quick to take offense. Americans are dying. It is our duty to find those responsible and stomp them out—"

"The problem with that rationale, Andrew"—Melissa Ryan leaned back in a black leather chair to steeple her fingers in front of her chin, a condescending gesture everyone knew enraged Filson—"is that you've got to have a target or you'll find yourself merely stomping around looking foolish." She tapped the pile of crime scene photographs on her desk folio with a perfectly manicured hand. "Whom do you suggest we stomp first?"

Filson rolled his eyes.

Ryan turned to address the president. "As Dr. Ramidi points out, each and every one of these actors was an American citizen—all white for that matter."

"She's right, Andrew," President Clark said, pushing back from the table. It was a clear indication this meeting of the National Security Council was drawing to a close. "The Bureau is already knee-deep into this investigation. They believe there is a domestic terrorism connection." He looked at FBI Director Kurt Bodington, who sat in one of the chairs along the outer wall. As a guest of the NSC, he didn't get a seat at the table. "Am I correct there, Kurt? You're still thinking domestic?"

The man flushed. More lawyer than cop, he hated being pinned down on anything, especially in front of the Situation Room. Near the middle of his customary ten-year term as the FBI top boss, he was an inheritance from past administrations and Palmer had a list of possible replacements on his desk for the president's review.

"To be clear, Mr. President," he blustered, looking like he might cry. A bully to his staff, Bodington folded quickly when someone of greater authority challenged him. "Insomuch as my people have briefed me, I believe that to be correct. . . ."

Clark stared at him for a long moment, then shook his head. "Well, there you have it," he said. "The definitive bureaucratic answer."

There was a flutter of shuffled paper and the clatter of chairs as the rest of the room rose along with the president.

Filson and Ramidi carried on their animated argument at the far end of the table. The other council members milled together with their deputies in pods of three or four, following up on action items. The spirited conversations seemed to mingle and collide in the small room, statically charged with decisions that affected the entire world.

Palmer stood, waiting for a chance to talk with Melissa Ryan. A widower, he'd become the envy of single men in Washington by seeing her socially for the past four months. He found her charming, intelligent, and extremely athletic.

The president flashed his Midwestern schoolboy grin and cut in, taking Ryan's hand.

"So," he said, "that son of yours talked the vice president into giving up his one and only daughter?"

"You know Garrett, Mr. President." The SecState twirled tortoiseshell reading glasses in delicate fingers that belied her inner strength. "He's got a silver tongue."

"Just like his mother." The president nodded. "See that your boss gets an invitation, will you? It'll piss off my Secret Service detail, but I'd love to attend.

"We'd be honored, Mr. President."

Palmer's BlackBerry began to buzz. He was one of a small handful of people who kept his phone on in the Situation Room. Only a week before, Clark had relieved Palmer of his duties as the director of national intelligence to name him the new president's national security advisor. Over the years he'd been a key confidant and counselor. The new position just made it official.

"Go ahead and take that, Win," the president said. "I'll entertain Melissa for another minute."

Palmer nodded, taking the BlackBerry from his belt. "Winfield Palmer."

It was Millie, his personal secretary. "Mr. Palmer. I'm sorry to bother you, but something terrible has happened out at Langley. . . ."

At that same moment, FBI Director Kurt Bodington walked back into the Situation Room, a cell phone to his ear. His face had gone pale.

Sally Portman, the president's iron-fisted chief of staff, came striding in from the direction of the Navy Mess. She was flanked by two dour-looking Secret Service agents.

"Mr. President," she said, her mouth a tight line. "I need you to come with me. There's been an incident at CIA Headquarters. . . ."

Clark shot a glance at Palmer, eyes flashing like the fighter that he was.

"You know what I know, Mr. President," Palmer said. "I'll brief you as soon as I get more information."

"They're hitting the CIA now? I have had enough of this shit," Clark spat. "Call him in."

Portman and the two Secret Service agents hustled Clark through the door. They would take him to the subbasement bunker until things got sorted out. Palmer told Millie to get Director Ross from the CIA and call back when she was on the line.

Ryan moved in as close to Palmer as White House decorum would allow. She kept her voice to a hoarse whisper. "I know that look, Win," she said. "Who's the old man calling in? Everyone in the cabinet knows he doesn't trust Kurt Bodington."

"For this . . ." Palmer gave a sly nod. "The president has someone . . . special in mind. . . ."

CHAPTER ONE

Be polite, be professional, but have a plan to kill everybody you meet.

—RULES OF ENGAGEMENT, USMC

Between Wasilla and Anchorage, Alaska

One hour earlier
0815 hours, Alaska time

Jericho Quinn rolled on the throttle, leaning the growling BMW R 1150 GS Adventure into a long, sweeping curve under the shadow of the Chugach Mountains. Birch trees decked in full autumn colors flashed by in a buttery blur. Behind him, riding pillion, his ex-wife twined her arms tightly around his waist, leaning when he leaned, looking where he looked. It was the first time they'd been in sync in over two years. The weather was perfect, bluebird clear and just crisp enough to feel invigorating. The grin on Quinn's face was wide enough he would have gotten bugs in his teeth had it not been for the helmet.

It had been Kim's idea to make the half-hour ride out to Wasilla. She'd suggested they catch an early lunch at the Windbreak Café before scooting back to Anchorage to watch their daughter's youth symphony debut matinée. After months overseas, Jericho had been hesitant to let the little girl out of his sight—even for the morning. A nagging feeling that he needed to be there to protect her pressed against his gut like a stone.

The thought of being in the wind with his ex-wife won out over his nagging gut. He couldn't remember the last time she'd climbed on a bike behind him. Now, her thighs clasped at his hips. The press of her chest seeped like a warm kiss through his leather jacket, reviving a flood of memories from better times—memories he'd tucked away, just to keep his sanity.

He took the ramp from the Parks Highway to the Glen at speed, shooting a glance over his left shoulder before merging with the thump of morning traffic. Picking his line, he checked again, taking the inside lane to avoid a dented Toyota Tundra. The ditzy driver wandered into his lane as she chatted on her cell phone with one hand and held a cup of coffee in the other, steering with some unseen appendage. Quinn tapped the bike down a gear before accelerating past the rattling cage to relative safety.

Riding the highway reminded Quinn of combat. The whap-whap-whap of his brother Bo's 1956 Harley Panhead in the next lane was eerily reminiscent of a Browning fifty-caliber on full auto—and, everyone on the road seemed bent on trying to kill them both.

Kim began to administer a slow Heimlich maneuver, crushing his ribs as the motorcycle picked up speed. For a fleeting moment, Jericho considered slowing to keep her from squeezing the life out of him, but Bo's bike chuffed past, pop-pop-popping like a fighter pilot on a strafing run.

When the Quinn brothers got together, some sort of

competition never failed to erupt. They each had the broken bones to prove it.

Kim pressed in even tighter. She'd known him since high school and must have sensed what was about to happen. Pouring on the gas, Jericho felt the welcome buffeting of wind against his helmet as the speedometer flashed past eighty miles an hour and kept climbing.

The brothers rode their "Alaska" bikes, the older, more seasoned motorcycles they left in state for visits home. Stationed at Andrews Air Force Base, ostensibly with the Office of Special Investigations, or OSI, Jericho kept his newer BMW R 1200 GS Adventure there. The national security advisor to the president—his real boss—had added a few modifications that made the bike belong more to the American taxpayer than it did to Quinn. He stored the older GS in his parent's garage where his dad could take it out in between commercial fishing seasons to keep it exercised.

The Beemer wasn't the Rolex of motorcycles, but it wasn't the bottom of the rung either. Like the TAG Heuer Aquaracer on Quinn's wrist, the BMW was high-end, classy, without flouting too much bling. Bo rode the flat-black '56 Panhead the boys had rebuilt when Jericho was fifteen and Bo was eleven. Loud as a wronged woman, the smoke-belching Harley could scoot.

Kim gave a little squeal of delight, squeezing less with her arms and more with her legs as the bike screamed through ninety with plenty left to go.

They all wore leathers to protect against the chill of Alaska's fall weather—and road rash in the event of an accident. Bo, riding single, and to Jericho's chagrin, now well in the lead, wore a Vanson Enfield jacket in heavy cowhide. The angry eye of a black octopus glared above a white rocker with three-inch letters across his broad back. The cut identified the younger Quinn as a DENIZEN—a motorcycle club from Texas that dabbled in what Bo called the "lucrative gray edges" of the law.

Where Bo's Vanson all but shouted that he was a member of the Denizens, Jericho's Aerostich gear was unadorned. The supple Transit Leathers were made up of a black jacket and matching pants. Micro-perforated, they were completely waterproof and cooler than most protective gear right off the rack. The formfitting leathers came standard with durable TF armor inserts, but his new employer had added a few extras. A wafer-thin recirculating personal cooling system developed by the Defense Advanced Research Projects Agency and panels of level III-A body armor were sandwiched into the material. A Kimber Tactical Ultra ten-millimeter pistol, a forty-caliber baby Glock, and a Japanese killing dagger all hid beneath the innocuous black jacket.

Kim, wearing a beautifully skintight set of her own black leathers, discovered the second pistol about the time they hit ninety-five. Her entire body tensed like a coiled spring. She was funny that way. One pistol was acceptable, part of the job. Ah, but two guns—that was over the top in her estimation. A person carrying two guns had to be spoiling for a fight. If she found Yawaraka-Te—the Japanese dirk hidden in the ballistic armor along the hollow of his spine—Kimberly Quinn would surely reach an entirely new level of berserk.

The light at the Airport Heights intersection turned yellow. Bo shot through and continued to weave in and out of traffic on his way downtown. Riding double with an angry woman made it impossible to catch up. Quinn let off the gas, knowing he was about to get an earful.

Kim flipped up her visor the moment his left boot hit the pavement.

"Really, Jericho? Two guns?"

Holding the clutch, he rolled the throttle, listening to the old BMW's Boxer Twin engine. He closed his eyes to feel the familiar horizontal right-hand torque.

He loved the bike and, even when she was nagging, he was still in love with Kim. She'd been the one to divorce him, saying she couldn't stand the constant threat of his violent death and his long deployments to the Middle East. After two years, she'd hinted that there was a tiny chance for them to get back together—up 'til now.

She bumped the back of his helmet with the forehead of her own—it was the way she used to get his attention. They wore matching black Arai Corsairs, remnants of happier times when they'd ridden everywhere together.

"Seriously, why two guns? Are you expecting some kind of trouble?"

Jericho stared ahead, hands on the grips. He thought of what he'd just been through, the things he'd never be able to tell her, or anyone else. In truth, he always expected trouble—and found himself pleasantly bewildered during the moments when none came his way.

"You know me, Kim." He cursed the impossibly long red light. Gabbing about the harsh realities of his job had never been his strong suit. "If I was expecting trouble, I'd have brought my rifle."

Her arms gripped him as though she thought he

might try and escape. Quinn shuddered at the prolonged closeness of her body after so many long months. The fact that she'd let him spend the night had more than surprised him. Even her mother, who was devoutly religious and opposed to such things, had openly cheered when she called early that morning and discovered he'd not gone back to his hotel.

"You know what you are?" Kim shouted above the revving engine. "You're one of those samurai warriors I saw on the Military Channel. I don't know why I ever believed you would quit this job—"

Quinn craned his neck around to stare back in genuine awe. "Since when do you watch the Military Channel?"

"Shut up and listen." She bumped his helmet again. "The show said the samurai class felt this moral superiority—just like you. They all carried a couple of big honkin' swords. You carry a big honkin' pistol . . . or two. You both practically worship your weapons, and to top it off, you get to carry them around where others aren't allowed to. And just like those samurai, you get paid a handsome salary to lord over us common folk."

Thankfully, the light turned green.

"You got one thing wrong, sweetie." Quinn put a black glove to his helmet, ready to flip down his visor. He turned to catch a quick glimpse of his ex-wife's beautiful blue eyes. "I'd lord over the common folk for free."

A half a block later he tapped the Beemer into fourth gear. A Piper Super Cub came in low and slow to his left, as if racing him to land at Merrill Field. He was still chewing on Kim's observations of his moral superiority as he passed Fantasies on Fifth strip club and the iconic Lucky Wishbone restaurant coming into Anchorage proper.

As an Air Force OSI agent who spoke Arabic and Mandarin Chinese, he had plenty of opportunity to fight for those weaker than himself. Now, he was an OGA—an other governmental agent—working directly for the top adviser to the president. His particular skill set was put to use in ways he'd never imagined.

He was a protector, a blunt instrument—a hammer. His job was indeed superior, but there was very little about it that was moral.

Chapter Two

Anchorage

0920 hours

Every doting parent believes their child to be a prodigy at something. The Quinns just happened to be correct.

"Seriously? Bach's Chaconne?" A freakishly tall woman in stiletto heels that made her tower above Quinn twisted her face into a lipstick and mascara question mark. She was first-chair violin in the Anchorage Symphony—and not at all amused that some arriviste six-year-old was on the cusp of upstaging her. She patted Kim's arm. "Of course you know what's best for her, my dear," the woman said in a husky voice that matched her height. "But the Chaconne is an awfully difficult piece, even for an adult." She gave a condescending shake of her long neck before moving on to work the crowd.

Kim shot Quinn an exasperated look. She tugged at the arm of his leather jacket, chastising through gritted teeth. "Stop staring at everyone. You're giving them the look."

"What look? Don't be mad at me because she-man is jealous of our kid."

His back to the brick wall, Jericho's eyes played across the faces of hundreds of milling patrons. People of all shapes and sizes lined the stairs, coffees in hand, crowding all three floors of the lobby. Watching for threats was like trying to play multilevel chess.

From the corner of his eye, he caught an olive-skinned man peering at him from the railing of the floor above. The dark face pulled back as Quinn met his gaze.

"Stop it!" Kim punched him in the arm. "I mean it. You know exactly what I'm talking about. You are the only one here who looks like a terrorist.

Indeed, the bronze complexion of his Apache grandmother and his father's heavy beard that grew in by noon gave Quinn a Mediterranean look. A single glare from his whiskey-brown eyes had a tendency to part the crowds inside the Performing Arts Center like the Red Sea.

Kim told him he was paranoid, but he couldn't shake the feeling that something was about to go very wrong. Worried as he was, he gave his *look* to virtually everyone who met his gaze.

The Chinese called it *zhijue* or straight sense. To the Japanese it was *haragei*—the art of the belly. Whatever he called it, in Quinn's experience the feeling was something to heed, real as the sense of sight or smell. With Kim on the warpath, he decided to keep his wits about him and his worries to himself. He tried to affect a smile but was sure it came across, at best, like a wolf with indigestion.

Apart from her dark hair, little Mattie Quinn was a

miniature version of Jericho's ex-wife, complete with accusing blue eyes. His heart caught hard in his chest every time he looked at her. Shimmering ebony curls spilled happily over a velvet dress of midnight blue. White tights, black pumps, and a robin's-egg sash with a cockeyed bow she'd insisted on tying herself completed the outfit.

The packed confines of the Performing Arts Center—the PAC to Anchorage locals—only added to Quinn's anxiety. He had to admit the patrons were mostly harmless. Bo called them the Subarus-and-comfortable-shoes crowd. All were eager to hear the six-year-old prodigy.

Kim had been first-chair violin for years and had only just hung up her bow to try her hand at composing a symphony of her own. Everyone supposed Mattie's amazing talent had come from her. Quinn had never said so, but he believed his daughter's gift might have had some link to his uncanny ability with languages. He was fluent in four other than English and semi-conversant in a half dozen more. What was music if not another language?

For Mattie's part, her debut in front of eight hundred fans seemed the furthest thing from her mind.

Miss Suzette, Mattie's gregarious music coach, stood beside the backstage door holding a small violin case. Even as a prodigy, six-year-old Mattie couldn't handle a full-size instrument. The half-size nineteenth-century Paul Bailly fit her little hands perfectly. It was horribly expensive, costing more than Quinn's brand-new BMW—but Mattie was that good. She'd named the little violin Babette, after a favorite teacher.

Case in hand, Miss Suzette rolled up the cuff of her

matching blue velvet dress to check her watch every two minutes. Mattie ignored her, hanging on her Uncle Bo's muscular forearm with both hands as she swayed back and forth.

Bo had traded his customary T-shirt and leather vest for a freshly pressed white button-down. Even in Alaska semiformal called for men to wear a tie. Bo could only go so far—even for his only niece. The Quinn brothers had agreed early in life that wearing a tie was like being strangled to death by a very weak man. Only Bo was brave enough to go against Kim's orders and show up with an open collar. He'd not only forgone the tie, but rolled up the sleeves of his shirt to reveal the last few inches of the black DENIZENS octopus tattooed on his forearm. He tucked the heavy Vanson jacket under his elbow while he let Mattie do pull-ups on his outstretched wrist.

"Sick tattoo, Uncle Boaz." Mattie swung easily, as if the performance wasn't minutes away.

Fearless, Jericho thought. *That's my little girl.*

"Thanks, Sweet Pea." Bo flexed his arm, hoisting her high off the floor and bringing a giddy squeal. His eyes shifted to Kim, who frowned like a brooding raincloud next to Jericho. "But I don't think your mama approves. I do believe she's afraid if you hang around with guys like me you'll end up with a ring in your nose and a hand grenade tattooed on your back."

Miss Suzette held up her wrist so all could see her watch. "We should get our young star backstage and make sure Babette is tuned before the performance."

Kim nodded. "She does need to warm up."

"Okaaaaay." Mattie let go of her uncle and grabbed Jericho's hand. "But it's still a half hour. . . ."

"We'll be right out front," Quinn said. He dreaded the thought of letting her walk through the door and out of his sight, even for a moment.

Mattie leaned against her father's outstretched hand, swaying and batting her wide eyes. "Can I please ride home with you on your bike? Uncle Boaz has an extra helmet that fits me. . . ."

Quinn's eyes shifted to Kim. "Let's see what your mom says about that."

"Great," Kim groaned. "Put it off on the mean old mom. A hand grenade tattoo. That's my little girl. . . ."

Quinn kissed his daughter on top of the head, drinking in the smell before shooing her toward Miss Suzette. "You're my besty," he whispered. Every ounce of his being told him to go with her, but Kim was on the verge of stealing one of his guns and shooting him with it, so he let her go without a fight. He had, after all, virtually abandoned them both to fight terrorism. How much more out of his sight could she get?

Quinn found the packed concert hall inside the PAC suffocating. "There's not enough air in here for all of us," he said as they made their way to their seats.

The front two rows were roped off. Kim worked her way to the center when they reached the third row back from the stage. Quinn followed, knowing he should insist on an aisle seat with a better tactical advantage, but saying nothing.

Kim gave an exasperated sigh, reading his mind as she so often did. "Sorry we can't get your back to the wall, honey. All the gunfighter seats are up in the balcony if you prefer to sit back there."

She took the seat on his left. Bo sat to his right, beside an attractive Alaska Native woman in a long green dress. Bo struck up a conversation easily, leaving Jericho with the nagging in his gut and a disgruntled ex-wife's elbow digging into his ribs.

The Atwood Concert Hall's cushioned green seats were filled to capacity, even up to the nosebleed section. The curtain opened to thunderous applause. Anchorage had plenty of musically talented youth, but six-year-old prodigies were very rare indeed. Alaska's social elite—Quinn called them the NPR crowd—wanted to witness such an event firsthand.

A full youth orchestra sat on risers behind a single chair out front in the middle of the stage. The youngest members were over twice Mattie's age. Most were in their late teens. Miss Suzette sat at a baby grand piano a few feet from the chair, stage left.

Babette cradled in her tiny hand, Mattie Quinn walked onto the stage with all the poise of a woman five times her age. She curtsied toward the audience, saluted the conductor and Miss Suzette with her bow, and daintily took her seat.

A hush fell over the hall and Mattie began the hauntingly perfect notes of Bach's Chaconne. . . .

Quinn closed his eyes, listening to the music. He knew something was wrong before he opened them.

The first man appeared from the flowing shadows of the side curtains left of the piano. He was tall, with close-cropped black hair and the wispy beginnings of a black goatee. White socks stood out against an ill-fitting brown suit and ratty dress shoes. A youthful face glistened with sweat under the harsh glare of stage lights. He stood motionless for a long moment, as if frozen by stage fright—half on, half off. His right hand was hidden in the dark folds of the heavy curtains.

The conductor, a heavyset man in his fifties with a sweating bald head, attempted to wave the intruder off with white-gloved hands.

Music continued to pour from Mattie's bow as she played on, sticking her tongue out in rapt concentration, unaware of the scene unfolding behind her.

Quinn's blood ran cold as the man broke from his trance to stride haltingly toward Mattie. The curved blade of a scimitar hung from his right hand, glinting in the lights.

A murmuring buzz coursed through the packed auditorium as patrons worked to puzzle out the scene before them.

Quinn jumped to his feet. He'd allowed himself to go against his instincts, and now he was hemmed in. There was no way to get to his daughter before the attacker reached her with the flashing sword.

Kim choked out a scream when she realized what was happening.

If properly trained, the brain is capable of processing an amazing amount of simultaneous information under pressure. However, the body, unable to truly multitask, resorts to gross motor skills. Even as Quinn's right hand swept the tail of his leather jacket he knew his shot would have to be perfect. The twenty-yard distance wouldn't be the greatest problem. Lead bullets had a tendency to keep going after punching a hole in a human body. With a backdrop of fear-paralyzed teenage musicians, his rounds not only had to stop Mattie's attacker, they had to stop *in* him.

Quinn squeezed off two quick shots as the Kimber's

front sight came to eye level. The hundred-and-eighty-grain slugs slammed into the man's pelvis, shattering dense sections of bone into jagged shrapnel, tearing flesh and ripping through major arteries. He fell like a sack of wet sand.

"See one, think two," Quinn whispered his mantra, scanning both sides of the stage.

"Watch Kim," he snapped, passing the ten-millimeter to his brother. He still had the baby Glock.

"I've got her." Bo grabbed the pistol and as he too scanned the stage.

Kim screamed again and Quinn shot a glance over his shoulder just in time to see the silver flash of another blade in the row behind them. He sprang backward, throwing himself between this new danger and Kim. He felt a sickening thud as something heavy struck his shoulder. Thankful for the armored leather of his Transit jacket, he pressed toward the attack, bellowing like a bull as he grabbed a fistful of hair. He used the chair back as a fulcrum and yanked the attacker over the seats.

The glint of a blade flashed across the sleeve of Quinn's jacket. He lunged, trapping the wrist, twisting, turning the blade and the hand that held it back against itself. Tiny bones snapped as the full weight of the man fell, writhing and screaming across Kim's lap just as the house lights came up.

Quinn freed the blade and drew it straight up the attacker's throat in a fluid arc, killing him and splitting his chin and then his nose up the center like a butterfly.

Kim's chest heaved in disgust and fear. She tried to push away, but the man's weight and the closeness of the seats penned her in. A crimson spray dripped from her pallid cheeks. Her blouse was drenched in the dead man's blood.

She screamed at Quinn, reaching for Mattie. "Go get her!"

Jericho vaulted the seats in time to see Miss Suzette throw herself in front of a third attacker. A bewildered Mattie now stood frozen in front of her chair, bow and violin clutched to her chest.

Quinn recognized the sunken eyes and narrow face of the third man at once. Ratib Jabiri, right hand of Sheikh Husseini al Farooq, the Saudi mastermind behind the terrorist plot to smuggle weaponized Ebola into the United States. He would have succeeded had it not been for Quinn.

Chapter Three

Jabiri shot Miss Suzette in the stomach and shoved her cruelly out of the way. The brave woman lashed out with a foot as she went down, connecting with the terrorist's legs. The pistol flew from his hand as he tried to break his fall.

The Saudi's knees hit the wooden floor with a sickening crack. He cried out, but scrambled to his feet in an instant. Scooping up a startled Mattie as he ran, he hoisted her tiny body in front of him as a shield.

Quinn moved up the aisle with the superhuman speed of a terrified father, arms pumping as he shoved his way through the paralyzed crowd.

Mattie in tow, Jabiri dove behind black side curtains and disappeared into the shadows.

Quinn vaulted up onto the stage, using the hollow thud of the Saudi's footsteps and his daughter's muffled screams to guide him. Just yards ahead, past a series of heavy ropes and counterweights, Quinn caught a glimpse of black hair as Jabiri ducked down a narrow flight of stairs that led beneath the stage.

The Saudi was high enough up on the sheikh's food chain that he was used to a life of pampered leisure. Running was something done by servants. Quinn caught him at the entrance to the men's dressing room in the under-stage catacombs of music stands and prop tables.

Jabiri turned like a cornered animal, panting through bared teeth, his back pressed against the dressing room door. A thin shaft of light from the orchestra pit cut across the harsh angles of his face, adding to the menace of his sneer. A cheap black suit bunched at narrow shoulders. His white shirt was rumpled and loose at his heaving waist. A thin arm snaked around Mattie, pulling her close to his chest. The other hand gripped her face like a claw, pinching her cheeks between bony fingers. Her little legs, still in the frilly white tights, hung loosely in front of him. One of her patent leather shoes had fallen off during the run.

Quinn slid to a stop—just out of reach, heart pounding in his throat. He raised both hands to show he had no weapon. Mattie's lips quivered, but she didn't cry. Her blue-gray eyes focused hard as if trying to send a message.

"Stay back!" the Saudi hissed. "I will break her neck if you come one step closer. . . ."

"It's me he wants, Jabiri. You know that." Quinn's eyes flicked methodically, taking in the scene, deciding his next move. "Let the girl go."

The Saudi laughed maniacally. His eyes narrowed to black slits.

"So . . ." His lip pulled back into a snarl. "You know who sent me? Impressive."

"Whatever you say. Just put down the girl."

"I think not, Mr. Jericho Quinn." The muscles in

Jabiri's face twitched as he spoke. "I am ordered to make you suffer defeat, even as the sheikh has suffered—"

"Okay." Quinn nodded. "I will suffer. Do to me what you will. Just put the girl down." He swallowed back the panic rising in his chest. He'd seen too many children die horrible deaths in the mean streets of Iraq. None of them deserved it, but the guiltless often died in far greater numbers than the guilty. Mattie didn't deserve the violence. Quinn's life had brought it crashing down around her. Deserving had nothing to do with it.

"Oh, brave Mr. Quinn. You are an intelligent man." Jabiri's words dripped like poison from twisted lips. "How do you believe this will end? You want so badly to kill me. I see it in your eyes." He cocked his head to one side, as if teaching an important point. "The question, Mr. Quinn, is not if I will die, but how you will live after you watch me take a life of one so precious to you. . . ."

Mattie's eyes suddenly brightened as if jolted with electricity. She began to pedal her legs as fast as she could, her heels slamming into Jabiri's unprotected groin. That same instant, she turned just enough to sink her teeth into the base of his thumb.

The Saudi threw his head back, screaming at the sudden onslaught of pain. He shoved the girl away as if she was on fire, twisting his hips to protect his groin.

Quinn grabbed Mattie's hand and pulled, passing her back behind him. In the same fluid movement, he drew Yawaraka-Te from the scabbard along his back. Rushing forward, he drove the length of the Japanese blade into the startled Saudi's throat, nailing him to the dressing room door.

"You're right, Jabiri," Quinn whispered, leaning against the hilt as the Saudi struggled and gasped. "There was never any question that you would die."

Jabiri's hands fluttered momentarily at the blade, then fell to his side like a puppet whose strings had been cut. Quinn turned and dropped to his knees beside his daughter. The ruffles on her blue dress fluttered like a frightened bird. Gently, he turned her head away from the dead man.

Bo came sliding up behind them, gun in hand.

Quinn looked up, still holding Mattie. "Kim?"

"She's okay. Anchorage cops have her."

A sob caught in Mattie's throat as she gazed up at Quinn with doe eyes. "They killed Miss Suzette." She buried her face against his neck. "They didn't even know her. Who would do that?" She pushed back to look at him again, crying with abandon now. "What about Babette? I dropped her on the ground. . . ."

Quinn patted her head, smoothing her mussed curls. Sirens blared in the background. Hollow shouts echoed beneath the stage. All this had happened because of him. He'd gone away to fight a war—and now he'd brought it home.

Chapter Four

CIA Headquarters

1324 hours Eastern Time

Veronica "Ronnie" Garcia stood naked and flushed outside the shower stall, scrunching wet toes on the rubber mat. Dripping tresses of coal-black hair mopped the coffee-and-cream skin of her muscular shoulders. She grabbed her towel from the hook along the wall, enjoying the coarseness of the cloth after the rigors of her workout.

Garcia's Russian father had blessed her with broad shoulders and a strong jaw, but in a roundabout way, he'd also given her the reason she needed to consistently hit the gym. Peter Dombrovski had been attracted to women he described with the Yiddish word *zaftig*. While Veronica was by no means fat, her Cuban mother had been a round woman, passing on her own ample hips. They were perfectly suited for birthing babies but gave her a tendency toward what Ronnie's ex-husband referred to as "ghetto booty." To spite the jerk, she ran twenty miles a week and did a kick-butt kettlebell workout on the days she didn't run.

Garcia blotted at her hair with a second towel and looked down past the hard-earned collection of tomboy scars on bronze knees. She considered her somewhat stubby toes against the puddle of water and shook her head, sighing softly to herself. As a member of the CIA's uniformed Security Protective Service, she hardly had time for shaving her legs, let alone the niceties of painting her toenails. Her dark complexion made much makeup unnecessary and her busty figure put her at constant risk of not being taken seriously in the law enforcement world.

Jane Clayton, a svelte marathon runner from Human Resources, stood ten feet away at a bank of stainless-steel sinks. She fluffed her mousy pageboy hairdo with a blow dryer, wearing only a sensible gray skirt and white sports bra. The lunchtime workout crowd had all gone and she was the only other person in the locker room. The two women were acquainted, but not well, and in a place where trust was a seldom-traded commodity, not knowing someone well was tantamount to being total strangers.

They'd finished their workouts at roughly the same time, but Clayton didn't have to bother with all the weapons and gear Ronnie was faced with. She finished dressing and stepped into a pair of shiny black Danskos while Ronnie still wrestled to mash her boobs—which were proportionally in perfect harmony with her hips—into the impossible space provided by her female-cut ballistic vest.

"Time for a coffee?" Ronnie asked, securing the wide straps of her vest under her armpits.

"Gotta have my double almond latte." Clayton shrugged smallish shoulders. Her eyes darted to the locker room door, as if she'd said too much already. Overly talkative people didn't do well at the CIA.

"Maybe I'll see you there then." Ronnie smiled.

"Maybe." Clayton picked up her gym bag. She tipped her head toward the pile of gear arranged on the bench next to Ronnie. "My boss needs a staffing report, like, ten minutes ago. You still have a half an hour worth of crap to put on. . . ."

"I suppose so." Ronnie's heart sank as she watched Clayton scuttle out the door. She looked down at the bench in front of her. Just putting on her patrol boots would take a couple of minutes. There was a wide gun belt, the heavy leather retention holster for her Glock forty-caliber pistol, two extra magazines of ammunition, handcuffs, a wad of keys, pepper spray, a brick-sized radio, a flashlight, and an X26 Taser. It was no wonder her lower back ached. Even with her tendency toward a ghetto booty, there was hardly enough room around her waist.

Garcia had set a goal to make at least one friend outside her law enforcement circle. She'd have to hurry if she wanted to share a coffee with Jane Clayton.

Eight minutes later Ronnie walked quickly past the Manchu Wok and the Sbarro Pizza, weaving in and out of scattered tables of late-lunch diners. Tables of "heritage speakers"—second-generation citizens, each having passed the stringent background requirements of the CIA—sat in small, ethnocentric groups scattered throughout the food court. Ronnie said hello in Spanish to three dark-skinned girls she knew from the Cuban Desk and smiled at a round table of Sudanese women chattering in Arabic under black hijab headscarves. She kept an eye open for Jane Clayton and thought idly about how young everyone was at the CIA. It reminded her more of a college campus than a hard-nosed intelligence agency.

With no sign of Clayton in the crowd, Ronnie gave up and stopped at the Starbucks to order a tall Americano. When she'd first joined the uniformed ranks of the Agency, it had come as a surprise that Starbucks had found its way into the nation's clandestine stronghold.

She smiled at Martha Newman, who worked alone behind the counter.

Newman was a kindly granny of a woman with a blue-gray sweater to match her hair and a face that held a map of lines as enigmatic as the Kryptos sculpture outside CIA Headquarters. According to Agency legend, Ms. Martha had ridden a motorcycle through South America with her arms wrapped around Che Guevara and had, on more than one occasion, shared a bed with Fidel Castro. When asked, Martha would only smile and utter a few romantic Spanish phrases about her heart.

Martha spoke to her patrons in any of several languages. She seemed to particularly enjoy speaking thick, guttural Russian to Ronnie, who was obviously Hispanic.

"*Dobry den*, *Veronica*," she said, ringing up the coffee.

"And a good afternoon to you, Ms. Martha." Ronnie pushed aside the radio on her belt to fish a ten out of her hip pocket.

"Got a date tonight?" Martha asked, counting out Ronnie's change.

"You never forget anything, do you?" Ronnie grinned. She picked up her cup and focused on the old woman's sparkling eyes. "They should have kept you in the Clandestine Service."

"That's the truth." The old woman narrowed steely eyes. "*If* I had ever been—"

A sharp crack, like a backfiring car, echoed around the corner column where the food court made an L turn beyond the sandwich shop next to Starbucks.

A gunshot.

Ronnie crouched instinctively at the sound. Her hand dropped to the butt of her Glock.

Martha Newman's long face tensed in the hypersensitive way of someone who'd experienced violence firsthand. "Browning Hi Power," she whispered.

A series of five more pops came in quick succession followed by a pitiful mix of bewildered shouts and terrified screams.

"Yep, Hi Power," Martha muttered grimly, confirming her first assessment. "I count two shooters," she said. "One at the other exit off the main dining area with some kind of forty-five. The closer one has the Browning." Her head snapped around to stare at Ronnie. "Go on, girl. Call yourself some backup."

Glock in hand, Ronnie moved in a half crouch toward the staccato crack of gunfire. Going toward the danger area was standard procedure with an active shooter. She kept her eyes on the corner support column, listening to the shots and a rising tide of frantic wails. Weapon tight against her side, she reached with her left hand to key the radio mike clipped to her shoulder.

"Thirty-six to dispatch," she whispered, certain the shooters could hear her pounding heart.

"Thirty-six."

Ronnie willed her breath to slow. "I have at least two active shooters in the food court. Number One—somewhere near the south east exit, Number Two—about twenty yards east of Starbucks. Request Emergency Response team ASAP."

"Ten-four, thirty-six." The dispatcher's voice came across louder than Ronnie would have liked. She held her hand across the speaker to muffle the noise.

"I'm closing on Number Two shooter now. They are active . . . repeat, they are active. Request medical be put on standby."

Four well-spaced shots cracked around the corner—echoing in the open court. Fitful silence followed, then another shot. A gurgling whimper, as if someone was being strangled, rose amid mournful screams.

Two women wearing white hijabs and indigo dresses ran past, half stumbling, bent at the waist to avoid being shot. Neither was armed and the abject terror on their faces made Ronnie shoo them on, toward Ms. Martha and safety.

Ronnie counted twenty-seven pops before the shooting slowed. She did the math. The Browning had a thirteen-round magazine. Most forty-fives held seven or eight.

"*Maldita Sea!*" she spat, slipping into her native Spanish. She gathered herself to make a move.

Both shooters were reloading at the same time.

* * *

Seth—*Tum-afik Pedram*—Timmons pressed the release on the side of his Browning. The empty magazine clattered to the floor as he fished a fresh one from the waistband of his blood-spattered slacks. The world around him seemed a whirling image of pink gore and the whites of wide, pleading eyes.

His first targets had smiled like fools when they'd seen him approach. Don, a bald man with a graying goatee and the stomach of a fat toad, hoisted his paper cup as if to offer a toast. Seth pressed the gun to his face and pulled the trigger. There'd been no reason to single out the soft-spoken Don. Meeting Timmons's gaze had been enough to get his brains blown all over the slender woman sitting alone at a table behind him. Seth ran with her sometimes at lunch. Her name was Jane Clayton. She flinched at the shot, put a hand to her cheek in dismay, wiping off bits of Don. Her eyes blinked rapidly as she tried to make some sense of what had just happened.

Seth walked up and shot her in the neck, watched her topple like a bowling pin, and then moved on to shoot another victim.

He didn't look up from his work, but could hear the flat crack of Gerard's pistol. They stuck to a well-rehearsed plan: stay on opposite sides of the food court to make themselves harder targets, shooting one or two on each side of a larger group, then picking off the ones in the middle as they milled around like frightened deer.

Some, like Marcia Dubois, mouthed Seth's name in quiet shock. Her cubicle was across from his, covered with photographs of her three teenage daughters. She cowered, turning her head to one side, begging for mercy.

Timmons showed none.

Firing with one hand, he reached into the messenger bag at his side and brought out an olive-green object the size of a baseball. Before he could move, a tall African American woman held her plastic tray in front of her like a shield and rushed at him with a desperate scream.

Caught by surprise, Timmons shot from the hip, wasting three rushed rounds before he finally stopped her attack. The woman's bravery incensed him and he shot her twice more in the chest just to watch her body jerk.

Gritting his teeth, he pulled the cotter pin from the grenade and lobbed it into a knot of people huddled in the center of the food court. The flat metal spoon flew away from the device and fell against a dining table with a metallic, bell-like tinkle. . . .

Ronnie watched the M67 grenade sail toward the cowering group. She surely knew some of them, but had no time to process their faces before she dropped to the floor, plugging her ears as best she could against one shoulder and the heel of her left, non-gun hand.

The detonation flung tables, food, and chairs skyward, kicking the air out of her lungs. Showers of white dust rained from the high ceiling like fissures of venting steam. Smoldering napkins fluttered amid smoky silence. Charred bits of noodle and French fries stuck to walls and columns.

Ronnie wiggled her jaw, trying to clear the jumbled mess of thoughts in her head. Even absent shrapnel wounds, the sharp concussion from such an explosion had a powerfully stunning effect on the body's soft tissues.

The blast left an eerie void, punctuated by whooshing stabs of pain in Ronnie's ears. She pushed up slowly from the floor, staggering to her feet.

The greasy smell of gun smoke and blood stuck to the roof of her mouth. She shook off the urge to vomit, took a deep breath, and moved to the corner that loomed in front of her. One more step would bring the shooters into her view—and put her in theirs.

Ronnie Garcia wasn't the best shot on the force, but she was consistent, even under the pressure of a screaming, spit-launching line coach.

Ninety seconds after the killing began, she stepped back from the corner and brought her Glock up to eye level in both hands. With slow deliberation, she began to sidestep, inch by slow inch—*cutting the pie*, they called it. Her heart beat like a kettledrum as the first assailant came into the picture formed by the glowing tritium sights of her Glock.

She struggled to control her breathing and mouthed the words her instructor had drilled into them on the range: " 'The key to life is front sight and trigger control.' *Focus on the front sight. . . . Press the trigger, front sight. . . . Press . . . front sight . . .*"

A young, redheaded analyst she recognized from the Central Asia Desk pushed his way through overturned plastic chairs toward a group of three women huddled under the edge of a round table. Even at twenty yards, the bloodlust was palpable in the kid's wild eyes. He flung a chair out of the way and loomed over his cowering victims, grinning maniacally.

Front sight . . . press—

Ronnie shot him twice, center mass. She prayed he didn't have on a vest.

Watching him crumple, she took another half-step to reveal not one, but two shooters working their way between the long tables less than ten yards away. She took the one in the lead first, a tall, quiet man with a bobbing goiter—Timmons was his name. She'd always liked him. . . .

She rushed her first shot. It went low, slamming into the man's groin. He staggered back, eyes thrown wide in surprise, struggling to keep the gun in his hand. Her second round caught him square in the chest. The Browning slipped away. A wan smile crossed his face as his body toppled across the screaming woman he'd been about to kill.

Ronnie processed the identity of the third shooter a split second later. Her breath caught hard and painful in her throat.

Surrounded by a melee of screams and gunfire—and surely deafened by the grenade blast—the third man walked from table to table, finishing off the wounded with another Browning Hi Power. Up 'til now, he'd not even noticed Ronnie's presence. It was a man she knew well, someone she'd called a friend. Her stomach lurched. She had to force herself to stay aimed in.

Dressed in the maroon polo shirt of CIA Academy staff was a decorated veteran of the Clandestine Service—and the firearms instructor who'd supervised her and countless others at the range.

Ronnie put her front sight over the chest of Marty—Mags—Magnuson, the newly appointed CIA deputy director for training. When he looked up from his bloody rampage, she demonstrated his old mantra with two center-mass shots. The key to life was indeed "front sight and trigger control."

Chapter Five

The White House
2025 hours Eastern Time

"Please sit." President Clark flicked a hand toward the green Queen Anne couches on either side of his larger, olive-colored chair. His back was to the fireplace, facing the Resolute Desk and the floor-to-ceiling windows overlooking the Rose Garden. The first lady had redecorated the Oval Office to be reminiscent of Theodore Roosevelt's stint in the White House, with rich, dark evergreens and bright whites. The painting of the former president on horseback had been moved from the Roosevelt Room to a spot of honor to the right of his desk above the Remington roughrider bronze.

Palmer sat to the right of the president in a matching chair. Apart from advising on matters of national security, his self-appointed secondary duty was to sit nearest the president when anyone else was in the Oval Office—including most members of the cabinet. The directors of the FBI and CIA sat across from one another, each on an opposing couch. DCIA Virginia Ross smoothed her dark skirt and sat to the president's right. On the heavy side, she constantly tugged and adjusted her clothing.

A Navy steward brought a silver tray of coffee and set it on the oval cherrywood table in the center of the furniture. The cups were already poured and made to the specifications of each guest.

Clark took his mug—bone white with the presidential seal—and nodded toward the door that led to his secretary's office. "Eric," he said. "Please ask Mrs. Humphrey to show in our guest."

"Of course, Mr. President." The steward shut the door on his way out.

The president put the cup to his lips, then set it back on the table without drinking. A stab of dark emotion creased his normally smiling face.

"I'm not sure who we can trust," he said, glaring at both directors. "Frankly, I'm not at all certain I want to bring *either* of you in on this."

Both Bodington and Ross tugged at their collars.

There was a confident knock at the door. The matronly Mrs. Humphrey entered, leading an attractive Hispanic woman with broad shoulders and the athletic, corn-fed look of a college softball player. Her dark hair was pulled up in a wooden comb, giving her a slightly disheveled look. She wore the navy-blue slacks of a CIA security officer and a pressed white polo shirt that highlighted her maple complexion. She wore no sidearm, but the outline of her Kevlar ballistic vest was visible under her polo shirt. Her arms swung slightly away from her body like someone who wore a gun belt for a living. Brown eyes, holding a glint of sparkle, even in abject fatigue, flicked around the room, taking it all in. The distinctive Green A identification badge of one who was allowed into the West Wing hung around her neck.

Palmer caught a glimpse of movement outside the door—Secret Service personnel who'd moved even closer than normal to the president over the last eight hours. A trained observer in his own right, the new national security advisor noticed the distinct outline of submachine guns under the loose coats of agents who normally carried only a pistol. Interior White House posts, particularly those outside whatever door the president happened to be behind at the moment, had double the number of usual agents.

Jack Blackmore, the agent in charge of the presidential detail, appeared at the threshold. He looked like a male model from a hunting magazine with his chiseled features and splash of gray at his temples.

"We can be relatively certain about Ms. Garcia, Jack," Clark said with a smiling nod.

"Very well, Mr. President," Blackmore said, shutting the door with what Palmer knew was the anxiety of one who safeguards the life of another.

Clark stood, as did Palmer and Bodington. "Please have a seat, Ms. Garcia."

Palmer studied the young woman as she thanked the commander in chief politely, then perched herself at the edge of the couch, nearest Virginia Ross. Since the other woman was technically her boss, Garcia undoubtedly saw her as an ally. For the time being, Palmer was sure Ross cared little one way or the other about her valiant security officer.

"Well." The president picked up a light blue file

from the coffee table. "Ms. Garcia, it appears we owe you a debt of gratitude."

Garcia's round cheeks, already flushed, turned a darker shade of crimson. "I was just doing my job, sir."

"A fine job of it too." Clark smiled. He leaned forward, cutting to the chase. "Ms. Garcia, we've read your report and I have to say, the thing that intrigues me the most is your discretion. Not once do you mention Deputy Director Magnuson as one of the shooters. Care to tell me why?"

All eyes fell to the CIA officer. Palmer smiled at her composure. He wasn't sure if it was pure naïveté or something deeper—something he looked for in those he hired for special duties.

"Well." Garcia nodded, biting her bottom lip before taking a deep breath. "The idea that senior management at the CIA could be involved in a terrorist act might be a little disconcerting to the American people. I knew Director Ross would release that information if she thought it prudent."

Clark nodded. "Something like that gets out, it could cause a lot of trouble," he said. "That goes without saying. Particularly after we took the time to reexamine Mr. Magnuson's background."

Now it was Ross's turn to flush. As director, it was her responsibility to see that her employees, and more importantly her division deputies, were properly vetted. Magnuson had passed no fewer than three periodic security clearances over the course of his career and double that number of polygraphs. The fault really couldn't be placed at her feet, but everyone in the room knew responsibility could not be delegated.

Clark tilted his head, looking at Garcia. "Would it

surprise you to know Magnuson made three unreported trips to Peshawar, Pakistan?"

"After what I saw today, sir," Garcia said, "nothing would surprise me."

"All three shooters had a calendar in their respective homes with today's date colored in red and the same Chinese character." The president paused, glancing up at Palmer. "What is it again, Win?"

"*Dan*," Palmer said. "It means *gall*—bitterness."

"Chinese . . ." Garcia mused, almost to herself.

"Oddly enough, yes," the president said. "Chinese."

He gave Director Bodington a hard look. "Other than that, the Bureau has found precious little evidence to connect them. No emails back and forth, no phone records . . ." He paused for a long moment before raising the blue file folder again. "Young lady, I hope you don't have any plans for the near future. What I'm about to tell you is really going to screw up the next few months of your life."

Garcia smiled, giving a shrug that, to Palmer, seemed utterly beautiful and free of guile. The poor kid obviously no idea what she was getting into. "I'll make it work, Mr. President," she said.

"Outstanding." Chris Clark wasn't one to stop and linger over the details. "Here's the deal then, Ms. Garcia. I need to know how much I can trust you."

Garcia flushed, recoiling as if the question were a slap. "Well, completely, sir."

Clark caught Palmer's eye. It was his cue that the national security advisor should do his job and dispense a little advice.

"In the end," Palmer said, "we have to trust someone, Mr. President. Veronica Garcia has demonstrated her loyalty as well as her valor in stopping the CIA shootings—"

Bodington weighed in—though he wasn't willing to interrupt the president, he would interrupt Palmer. "Sir, you're suggesting we share highly classified material with—my apologies to Ms. Garcia—but essentially a security guard. Is it not just as plausible that Deputy Director Magnuson was trying to stop the shootings and she killed him before the response team arrived?"

Garcia went from sweet to seething in the flash of her dark eyes. "I've never met you before, Director Bodington, but I'm sure you know it'll take about two seconds for ballistics to confirm the DD's weapon murdered at least half a dozen of my coworkers."

Bodington tried to wave her off, all but ignoring her to make his case to the president. "Please, sir, listen to reas—"

Garcia's shoulders began to tremble. "I realize we have an extreme situation here. Frankly, I don't even give a damn if you call me a security guard. It's what I do. Someday, I hope to work for the Clandestine Service—and when I do, I hope to have the sense to look at a little evidence before I accuse someone of being a cold-blooded terrorist."

Clark gave a quiet smile, sucking on his front teeth the way he did when he was particularly amused. "Kurt, I think the fact that she didn't call you a son of a bitch shows incredible restraint. Two points here: First, as Win points out, we have to trust someone. Second, I'm not suggesting you share anything. From what I've seen, you have damn little to share. I'll do the sharing. So, do your boss a favor and sit still for a couple of minutes."

Bodington clenched his teeth, but said nothing more.

"Win." The president tipped his head toward Palmer. "Would you be so kind?"

"Of course, Mr. President." Palmer turned in his seat to face Garcia, who calmed immediately from her confrontation. "Plainly speaking, late yesterday evening, intelligence sources in Pakistan confirmed a problem we had suspected for some time. Foreign agents placed within our government—moles."

The director of the CIA shook her head. The muscles in her face clenched, but she kept quiet. It was obvious she agreed with her FBI counterpart. Briefing such a low-level employee was just not done. Palmer decided to address that from the beginning, since it was, after all, a plan he had endorsed to the president.

He moved to the edge of his chair, leaning in to close the distance between himself and the young woman. "We have to assume these agents . . . these moles could be anywhere and that they—like Deputy Director Magnuson—have passed various backgrounds and security checks. An in-depth review of both Timmons's and Gerard's files found several glaring holes in their backgrounds—facts that when take separately mean nothing, but in light of what they did, mean everything."

Garcia sighed, pushing a lock of hair out of her eyes as she processed the information.

It was a lot of information to dump on her, but

Palmer plowed ahead. "Both men are the sole survivors in their families. Neighbors who were interviewed for previous backgrounds admit they really knew the parents better than the boys. Neither have a single friend that remembers them earlier than the seventh grade. According to their supervisors at the Central Asia Desk, both were fluent in Turkic, but when we looked into it further, other than some Internet courses, there's no record of them ever studying that particular language."

"You believe them to be foreign born then?" Garcia mused.

"We do," Palmer continued. "And we missed it in their initial backgrounds. Essentially, everyone in the government needs to be re-vetted—and that includes the ones doing the vetting."

"Ah," Garcia said, deflating slightly. "And since you feel you can trust me, I get to begin the process."

The president held up the blue file folder containing the background investigation on Garcia. Palmer himself had completed a review only two hours before. "Except for your load of good old American credit card debt," Clark said, "you come out smelling like a rose, my dear. Who would admit to having a Soviet father and Cuban mother if they wanted to hide something?"

Director Bodington folded his arms tight across his chest, looking toward the Rose Garden as if to distance himself from events unfolding before him. Palmer never had liked the man, finding him a bureaucratic bloviate without concrete facts to back anything up. All hat and no cattle.

Garcia's eyes remained worshipfully attentive to the president, ignoring Bodington altogether. "I assume I'm being assigned to a team," she said.

Palmer smiled. "This is the team," he said. "Director Ross, Director Bodington . . . and you."

"And we are to vet government employees?" Garcia went pale. "All government employees?"

The president laughed, sucking his front teeth again. "All two million of them—not counting the Postal Service—but we've prioritized the list. As you clear people, they will begin to assist with the background investigations."

Garcia sat perfectly still.

"You in particular will focus on those with direct access to the president," Palmer said, hoping to calm her fears.

She turned her head to one side, hands folded quietly in her lap. Her eyelids drooped with exhaustion. "If I might ask . . ."

Palmer's chair began to chirp softly. Each piece of furniture in the Oval Office was equipped with a secure phone line so presidential guests could carry out pressing directives on the spot.

President Clark nodded. "Go ahead and take it, Win."

Palmer slid open the upholstered drawer hidden below the seat cushion and took out a white handset.

"Sorry to trouble you, Mr. Palmer," the voice said. It was Millie, his secretary. "You need to turn on the news, sir. The president will want to see this. . . ."

CHAPTER SIX

Joint Base Elmendorf-Richardson
Anchorage

Canadian cousin to the more ubiquitous government Gulfstream G5 business jet of Hollywood spies, the luxurious Bombardier Challenger CL 601 sat sleek and falcon-like on the ramp. Just as Quinn was an OGA—other governmental agent—the executive jet was an other governmental aircraft. Registered to the Federal Aviation Administration, the pilots were former Special Operations and reported directly to the national security advisor. Palmer had dispatched the plane to get the Quinns out of Alaska. If the sheikh had sent one team, he was likely to have sent two.

A low fall sun cast a pink blush on the snowy Chugach Mountains to the east, shining through the oval windows of the jet. Jericho knelt in the aisle, looking down at Mattie, who lay sideways in a soft leather seat, head resting in her mother's lap.

Two seats back, Kim's mother reclined with a damp washcloth over her eyes. Her head lolled from the effects of exhaustion and the Valium government medics had given her when they'd all been hustled away from an extremely curious Anchorage Police Department after the attack. Bo stood at the rear of the plane. Broad shoulder against the bulkhead, he chatted up the female Air Force staff sergeant who acted as safety officer and attendant. Brother Bo wasn't about to let a little bloody ambush on the family cramp his ability to hit on cute women.

Quinn's parents were out fishing for Pacific cod, the sheer danger of capricious Alaska waters protecting them from attackers.

Mattie looked up with a wan smile. Framed in a halo of her dark curls, the features of her perfectly oval face were drawn from fatigue. Her eyelids sagged. She blew him a kiss.

"You're looking at me funny, Dad," she said after a long, feline yawn. "I think I can trap you with my eyes."

Jericho kissed her forehead. "Oh, sweetheart," he said. "If you only knew . . . Now, you better get some rest."

Kim ran trembling fingers through their daughter's hair. She affected a smile for Mattie's benefit, but the tightness of her breath and the set of her jaw made it clear to Quinn she held him accountable for the attack on their family.

He didn't blame her.

She jumped at the sudden buzz of the secure phone on his belt. He groaned and stepped across the aisle to take the call.

"Listen, Quinn . . ." Winfield Palmer rarely waited for the person he was calling to say a word beyond hello before he moved straight to the business at hand. If you answered, it meant you should be ready to listen. "There's something I need you to see. Are you on the plane?"

"Yes," Quinn said, eyes locked on Mattie as he spoke. "We're fine, by the way. Thanks for calling."

"Yes, of course," Palmer said. "I mean . . . good. I'm glad. . . . Anyway, I need you to take a look at the news."

Quinn shot a look at his drowsy daughter. The last thing he wanted was to have her wake up to whatever catastrophe Palmer wanted him to witness on the news. He made his way down the aisle to the back of the plane, beyond Bo and his new girlfriend, to a teak cabinet on the galley bulkhead. "Any channel in particular?" he asked, turning on the seventeen-inch flat-screen satellite television.

"Won't matter," Palmer grunted. "This dumb son of a bitch is all over the place. . . ."

Quinn left it tuned to CNN. He used the remote to turn up the volume as he swiveled the nearest seat to face aft, sinking back into the cool leather.

The red Breaking News ticker at the bottom of the screen introduced the speaker as Congressman Hartman Drake of Wisconsin. He stood alone, a dark silhouette in front of the brightly lit Capitol dome. A veteran of the first Gulf War with a Purple Heart to prove it, he'd served in the House for over a decade, working his way up to the powerful but slightly boring Transportation Committee. Chiseled, Ivy League good looks and a propensity to wear a bow tie over a starched white shirt made him instantly recognizable. He was well known as a stridently outspoken isolationist, and his handlers made certain he hit the talk-show circuits at least once a month.

Quinn yawned, wondering what Drake could have done to infuriate Palmer since they were both from the same party. The Canadair's engines began to spool up without so much as a word of safety briefing from the flight attendant, who was still busy with Bo across the aisle.

Quinn bumped up the volume on the television with the remote on his armrest.

". . . among us. And so we find ourselves in the midst of what can only be called a national crisis." Drake leaned into the camera, a master at connecting with his audience. The glowing dome of the Capitol gave him the perfect patriotic backdrop for a nighttime press conference. ". . . a crisis of epic proportions. There are those, even in these hallowed halls of government, who will, no doubt, seek to discredit me, to call me a crackpot or accuse me of being . . . a hater. Well, my fellow Americans, I am a hater—a hater of those who would destroy this great nation." Drake paused for effect—gazing into the distance as if imagining a round of applause.

"I have in my possession," he continued, "a heretofore secret list. The eighty-six names on this document represent men and women within our own government who, it pains me to say, support the cause of militant Islamist terrorism. Further, we have strong reason to believe that certain names on the list were complicit in this morning's horrifying attack perpetrated on CIA headquarters. . . ."

The sleepy crowd around the congressman suddenly

erupted in a display of camera flashes and muffled shouts as reporters awoke to the smell of a real story.

Drake raised his hands to silence them.

"I am not prepared to go into detail at this time," he said. "Suffice it to say we have a cancer growing within us. I pledge to you, my fellow Americans, to do everything in my power to root out this malady. To this end, I have asked that the speaker of the House convene immediate hearings."

With that, he paused, put both hands on the lectern and mugged straight into the camera.

"My fellow Americans, I give you my word that I will not rest until I have rigorously examined each and every person on this list to ascertain their loyalty—or their disloyalty—to these United States. May God bless us in our cause, for it is just. Thank you for your time."

The congressman paused for a beat, taking time to gather his notes as cameramen got a few more seconds of B roll, before turning to walk back up the hill toward the Capitol. His entourage of staff hung back so the cameras could catch his darkened silhouette, trudging up the hill, alone.

Quinn had to stop himself from laughing out loud.

A slender brunette, one of CNN's pretty talking heads, took over, providing color commentary. Quinn used the remote to mute the sound.

"Did you get that?" Palmer said on the other end of the line. His voice dripped with unbridled disgust.

"I did," Quinn said. He moved back up the aisle, unwilling to be away from Mattie any longer than he absolutely had to. "Any truth to what he says about the CIA shootings?"

"There is." Palmer gave him a thumbnail sketch, including the CIA deputy director's involvement. "We've got a real situation here, Jericho. I could use you back ASAP."

"I need to get my family situated first," Quinn said, shooting a quick glance at Kim.

"Oh, yeah, I get that," Palmer answered, but it was clear in the clipped timbre of his voice he didn't.

Kim shook her head, catching Jericho's side of the conversation. "Go ahead," she said in a dismissive whisper. "We'll be just fine." The "without you" was implied in the frigid blue of her eyes.

Quinn rubbed the stubble on his face with his free hand, sighing deeply. "I can be at Andrews by . . . oh-eight hundred your time." Cell phone against his ear, he stared at his daughter, drinking in the sight. He wondered if Kim would ever even let him see her again.

"Very well," Palmer said, his voice hanging on the edge of another word for a long moment. "Jericho," he finally said, "I wouldn't call you back unless it was urgent. . . ."

"I understand, sir," Quinn said, looking across the aisle at his ex-wife, who wouldn't understand at all.

Chapter Seven

Quinn ended the call and returned the secure BlackBerry to his belt. He leaned back to stretch in the soft leather seat as the Canadair jet lumbered down the runway on its takeoff roll. It was the first opportunity he'd had to close his eyes since the attack, even for a moment.

The damp cold of Kim's fuming across the narrow aisle pushed away any thoughts of sleep. He could feel her stare, heavy, like a pile of bricks dumped on his chest. He opened his eyes, glancing sideways without turning his head. He'd been right.

"Who are you, Jericho Quinn?" Her voice was hushed, pitiful.

Quinn pushed the button to raise his seatback. Some things you couldn't take lying down.

Kim leaned across, whispering so as not to wake Mattie. "You know the worst part?"

Jericho sighed, defeated. "I can only imagine."

"You've ruined me for any kind of relationship with normal guys." Tears pressed from her lashes. It would have been funny had her words not been so deadly serious. "I tried to date Bryce Adams, the manager at the credit union," she sobbed. ". . . but he bored me out of my skull.

He'd never been the particularly jealous type, but the thought of his ex-wife dating another man made Quinn want to kick Bryce Adams in the nuts and beat him over the head with an axe handle.

"And then it dawned on me—" Kim smacked herself in the forehead with an open hand. "I suddenly realized I'm only interested in cops and firemen. . . . It's like I have some sort of battered-woman syndrome . . . but I'm the kind who goes for adrenaline junkies instead of bullies." She sniffed, hanging her head. "What the hell have you done to me . . . ?"

"Come on, Kimmie." Quinn moved across the aisle. She stiffened when his hand brushed her shoulder. He was sure she would have pulled away but for fear of disturbing Mattie, asleep now in her lap.

Kim's head suddenly snapped up, eyes probing like a CAT scan.

"I mean, seriously, Jer . . ." She threw up her hands. "What kind of OSI agent gets picked up in an unmarked jet and ordered back to Washington the same day someone tries to kill his family?"

"I—"

"Oh, please . . . just shut up." Kim's voice was a whispered hiss. "You'll only lie. It was hard enough before—seeing that look in your eyes, only guessing how cruel you really were. . . ." Her lips trembled as she spoke. "Now I've seen the things you're capable of firsthand . . . and so has Mattie."

Quinn opened his mouth to speak, but Kim's hand shot up, shushing him.

"Look," she said with an air of clench-jawed finality that shocked even Quinn. "I know we owe you our lives. I know if it wasn't for you, we would be dead. . . ." Her voice trailed off, but her eyes grew cold and seething. "But, if it wasn't for you, this never would have happened."

Quinn wanted to explain, to tell her there had to be people like him in the world, but it all seemed too trite to say out loud. Instead, he just sat there and took it.

"Stupid, stupid, stupid . . ." Her chest began to heave with bitter sobs. "I . . . I don't know what I was thinking, letting you back in."

"Kim," Quinn said softly, staring at her tiny hand. "Don't . . ."

She turned away to stare toward the flight deck, sniffing into a tissue. He'd lived with her long enough to know that when she looked away like that no amount of talking would get through to her.

"I don't know what it is you're up to," she whispered, still facing away. "I'm certain it's something important—and I'm just as certain you're good at it. . . . But do me a favor and leave us out of it."

She spun suddenly, her lips set in a tight line. "We're divorced, Jericho. You need to start acting like it."

Chapter Eight

Gaithersburg, Maryland
2310 hours

The two goldfish that were Ronnie Garcia's sole dependents had miraculously figured out how to survive in a half a bowl of cloudy water feeding on their own poop. She sprinkled some shrimp flakes in the bowl and promised to change their water when she had a free minute. The fish tore after the food like little bug-eyed piranhas.

She stripped off her polo shirt and threw it in the corner. She'd not been close enough to the men she shot to get any back splatter of blood on her, but the smell of gunfire and human pain hung to the dark blue fabric of her slacks. She loosened the straps of her ballistic vest, feeling the sudden lightness as she lifted the bulky panels over her head. She threw the vest on top of the laundry pile and took out the wooden comb she'd worn to the White House, shaking loose her hair.

She, Veronica Garcia, had actually sat on a couch in

the Oval Office and chatted with the president of the United States.

"Oh, Papa, if you could have seen me . . ."

The thought of it still sent a shiver down her back.

Then she remembered the killing.

She wished there was someone she could call, someone she could confide in. She gave a fleeting thought to calling her ex-husband, but quickly realized he would only make her feel worse in the long run.

In the end, she settled for a scalding shower. She stood under the water for a long time, leaning against the tile with both hands, hoping the heat would beat the memories of the day out of her body. She finally realized she really felt bad for not feeling bad enough and turned off the water.

The night was warm for Maryland in late September and she left her hair wet, hoping it would help her sleep a little cooler. She brushed her teeth, happy to feel clean again, and slipped into her favorite pair of stretchy yellow terrycloth sleeping shorts. She found a white tank top wadded up at the base of her dresser, sniffed it, and pronounced it clean enough to wear to bed. Collapsing back against the pillow, she flipped out the lamp . . . and stared up at the darkness, wide-eyed.

Memories of the day whirled inside her head like a cyclone. Gathering witness statements and after-action reports for the joint investigative team from the CIA and the FBI had taken hours after the last shot had been fired.

When she'd completed her reports, a trio of CIA shrinks had summoned her to a stark, white room to gauge her level of emotional and physical trauma. With just over seven years on the job, she'd never been involved in a shooting. It came as a shock to her interrogators that she wasn't more bothered by it. It was a surprise to her as well, but the men she'd shot had deserved to die. They had been killing the very people she'd signed on to protect, so she'd killed them. It was that simple. She would never brag about it, but she would do it again if faced with the same circumstances—and then move on with her life. The Agency shrinks had looked at her sideways when she explained the way she felt, but in the end, they signed off, pronouncing her sane as anyone else at the CIA.

One doc in particular, an older, Freudian-looking man with a twitchy right eye, appeared to be genuinely disappointed she was not pulling her hair out and running off screaming into the woods.

The grilling had ended shortly before 7 P.M. Her supervisor sent her home on three days' paid administrative leave—standard operating procedure after a shooting. She'd not even made it to her car before he called her cell to tell her to come in and put on a clean shirt. She'd been summoned to the White House.

Ronnie's job at the CIA made her no stranger to important political figures, and she'd become extremely hard to impress. But a personal meeting with the president, where he sat, legs crossed and smiling, to offer her coffee and tell her how much he needed her help? That was so very different from watching him walk down the marble halls at Langley.

Now, locked awake in the darkness, she flipped on the light and kicked the down comforter off her feet. Even for a girl raised in the Caribbean, the evening was much too warm. She sighed, beating her head against the pillow. If her father could see her now, he'd roll over in his regulation communist grave.

As a child in Havana she'd grown up immersed in a hodgepodge of cultures. Her father, a math professor from Smolensk, had known the importance of English and made certain his only daughter was fluent in that along with the tongues of her parents. Three languages, he said, gave her a good base from which to begin—

"Someone who speaks three languages, *milaya*," he would coax, using her pet name, "is said to be *trilingual*. And what do you call someone who speaks only one language?"

"An American." She would giggle at his little joke and he would tickle her as good fathers were supposed to do.

After the collapse of the Soviet Union, Russian support for Cuba had faded, pressing their family into near starvation. Her idealistic parents had been brokenhearted at governmental indifference toward those who had worked so hard to support the cause. They died within weeks of each other and she'd been sent to Miami to live with an aunt. She'd taken her mother's maiden name because it fit the darkness of her looks—and made her less of a target in south Florida than Veronica Dombrovski.

When she was still in high school, she'd watched a plainclothes Metro Dade police officer arrest a couple of gangbangers at a shopping mall and decided that was something she could do. Later, a friend in college had suggested she look into the CIA because of her language skills and she thought, yes, that was definitely something she could do. The semester before she graduated with a degree in psychology Ronnie had gone to the Agency website and sent in an email stating her qualifications and interest in the Clandestine Service. By then, Arabic and Chinese had nudged Spanish and Russian off center stage as strategic languages. She received a polite but curt reply, suggesting she complete a master's degree in economics or try the uniformed division and get her feet in the door. Her father had been right. Three languages were a good beginning. The uniformed security police weren't the Clandestine Service—but she was still CIA.

Ronnie rubbed her eyes, picking up the stapled document of forty-one pages from her nightstand. If she couldn't sleep, she might as well make a plan. She looked around the cluttered bedroom, littered with laundry and dry-cleaning bags. Boxes from takeout pizza and Chinese restaurants perched on stacks of books and magazines. Housekeeping definitely wasn't her strong suit, but she was a hell of a planner.

Palmer had set her priorities, beginning with the circle of employees closest to the president—and that put the United States Secret Service at the top of her list.

Ronnie was instructed to pay attention to key personnel, particularly the protective details of the president and vice president. Between the special agents and the Secret Service Uniformed Division, the lists contained over two hundred names. At first, she'd suggested it would take her a week per background. Palmer had countered, kindly but firmly, that she needed to review two per day, clearing these to assist her in her efforts. If she came across something out of the ordinary, she was to call him—and him only.

He stressed the fact, at least a half dozen times, that there were very few people she could trust.

The special agents in charge of each protective detail had been cleared already by Palmer himself. They would conduct personnel reviews of their own. Ronnie would provide an independent analysis as an extra precaution.

Scanning the entire document before she made a concrete plan, her eyes fell to a name at the bottom of the seventh page—Nadia Arbakova, a special agent in the Protective Intelligence Division at Secret Service Headquarters in D.C. Arbakova listed a Special Agent James Doyle as her emergency contact. Ronnie remembered the name and flipped back through the previous pages until she found it. Just as she suspected, Agent James Doyle was the whip on the vice presidential detail. An experienced agent, the whip wasn't a supervisor but took charge when the shift leader wasn't around. Doyle's connection to Arbakova and his relatively powerful position made the two agents a natural place to begin. She could knock two investigations out in half the time and give herself a little breathing room.

"You just got yourself moved up to page one, Comrade Arbakova." Ronnie did her best to imitate her father's thick tones. A note beside Arbakova's name indicated she was a second-generation American who spoke fluent Russian. Her home address was in Rockville. Ronnie would pass right by it on the way into the city.

With a more concrete plan, Garcia gave a shuddering stretch, raising both arms high above her head. Maybe sleep wouldn't prove so elusive. She'd stop off tomorrow morning and chat with Nadia Arbakova, catch her while she was getting ready for work and wasn't suspecting a visit. Maybe she could practice a little of her rusty Rusky. And, if everything in Arbakova's background came back clear, maybe they could even become friends, even if she was in law enforcement.

THURSDAY
September 28

CHAPTER NINE

Rockville, Maryland
0130 hours

A predatory expedition. Turcoman slavers—the bane of Central Asia in the 1800s—called it *alaman*. Russians had been their favorite prey. Mujaheed Beg took a comb from his shirt pocket and ran it through thick black hair, making certain the high, Elvis Presley pompadour was in place. He smiled at the notion that he was up to the same work as his Turcoman ancestors—on American soil. A heavy black brow over a hooked nose gave him the air of an extremely dangerous man. An American professor at Berkeley, where he'd received his undergraduate degree in marketing, had dubbed him Evil Elvis. Instead of taking it as an insult, Beg reveled in the reputation.

He had been born near the ancient Silk Road city of Merv, and Turcoman blood coursed through his veins. Predation came as naturally to him as it had to his merciless forbearers. He smiled when he thought of the old Silk Road axiom: *If on your path you meet a deadly viper and a man from Merv—kill the Mervi first.*

Beg drove his rented Saturn past the row of untrimmed shrubs and trees in front of Nadia Arbakova's house for the third time. The whitewashed brick appeared to glow under the hazy sliver of a crescent moon. It was set well back from the road, providing the perfect cover. Had his attack been destined for a trained CIA operative, he would have been more careful. Counter-intelligence agents were, as a rule, much more wary than law enforcement. Even the potbellied bureaucrat handcuffed and lolling in and out of unconsciousness in the seat beside him had installed CCTV cameras and a decent security system in his home. Spies, even the fat ones, took precautions against people like Mujaheed Beg—but they were never quite good enough.

Nadia Arbakova was no spy. What's more, her personnel file ranked her as only a mediocre police officer. At heart, she was an analyst, much happier working puzzles than arresting criminals.

Her scant record showed she qualified twice a year with her handgun, but her shooting skills were average at best. She would be easy to kill.

Beg gave the unconscious boob in his passenger seat a lopsided smile. There was yet much to do before he killed anyone.

The cell phone in his jacket pocket began to buzz.

"It's the boss," Beg muttered to the drooling Arab beside him. "He always bothers me when I'm working."

He answered curtly. "Yes?"

"Peace be unto you," the voice said with the rapid

click of Pakistani English. "I trust God has preserved you. . . ."

"Peace be unto you as well, sir," Beg said. He held the phone away from his ear and whispered to the unconscious man beside him, as if giving an explanation. "The boss always has to be so forward. . . ."

There was a pause on the line. "Are you with someone?"

"I am," Beg said.

"Very well." Dr. Nazeer Badeeb continued clicking away. He never seemed to care if Beg was busy doing his work or not. "I am concerned about this woman. She is beginning to share her theories. I fear she will . . . up some eyelashes."

The doctor firmly believed American intelligence services were less likely to eavesdrop on conversations in English—though, Beg thought, what this one spoke could hardly be considered English.

"Eyebrows, not eyelashes," Mujaheed sighed, correcting his employer's idiom. "You mean to say *raised* some *eyebrows*."

"Of course," Badeeb rambled on. "As you say. But I am nervous nonetheless."

"I will take care of that very soon." The Mervi's eyes shifted to the fat Arab, who snored fitfully in the pale green glow of the dashboard lights.

There was the distinct metallic clink of a lighter on the other end of the line as Badeeb lit a cigarette before he continued his staccato whining. "We wish them confused and frightened. Disorganized, not fortified. They must not connect too much too soon."

"I understand," Beg said. "I should begin my work then."

"Of course." Dr. Badeeb released a long sigh, sounding like a windstorm over the phone. Mujaheed envisioned the cloud of cigarette smoke enveloping his employer's sweating face. "You will find out how much she knows?"

"With great pleasure," the Mervi said. He looked through the foliage at the pool of yellow light spilling out Arbakova's bedroom window and put the car in gear.

Parking in a deserted alley behind the house, Beg roused the snoring Arab next to him with a stiff elbow to the floating ribs. A heavy dose of Rohypnol—roofies—had made the man pliable, but dazed. It had also caused him to spill the contents of his bladder all over the passenger seat. The man, whose name was Haddad, yowled in pain. His cry trailed off in a pitiful whimper.

"What do you want from me?" he sobbed.

"Whoa!" Beg said, tossing his head in a passable impression of Elvis. "You're all shook up. . . . What do you think I want?" Beg sneered. "Half the world knows what you do for a living. It is not the secret you believe it to be." He turned, holding up a black box the size of a garage door opener. Haddad's eyes flew wide. He began to fling his head from side to side.

"Nooo!" he screamed. "Nooo—"

Relaxed in the driver's seat, Beg depressed a white button on the box. There was a faint beep and the dazed Arab suddenly arched backward, driving thick legs into the floorboards as if stomping on the brakes. He slammed his head against the roof of the Saturn.

Teeth crunched, giving way under the convulsive tension brought on by forty thousand volts from the stun-belt over flabby kidneys.

It was such a fine show Beg wanted to clap.

Eight grueling seconds passed before the man's body fell slack. An acid stench filled the car's interior as he vomited in his lap.

Beg reached across with a pair of pruning shears and snipped the plastic zip ties around the Arab's wrists. He shoved him a roll of paper towels.

"You disgusting pig," he spat. "We are going to meet a woman. Make yourself presentable. You will walk beside me to the front door. Try to keep from defecating on yourself. Say nothing . . . and remember, I will have my finger on the button at all times." He tapped the black box. "If you do as I tell you, this will all be over soon."

"You . . . haven't . . ." the man panted. He tore off a wad of paper towels and working feverishly to sop his lap dry. His breath was ragged. His eyes darted from Beg's face to the box in his hand. White spittle pooled at the corners of his mouth. "You . . . haven't . . . even asked me any questions. . . ."

"Ah." Beg smiled, showing a mouthful of crooked teeth. "I am not interested in what you know," he hissed. "Only who you are." He opened the door, certain now the pitiful man would follow his every command. He was a slave. "Come. This will take much of the night. I am sure you will find it quite . . . interesting. . . ."

CHAPTER TEN

Maryland
0930 hours

Jacques Thibodaux's gumbo-thick Louisiana drawl broke squelch on the speaker inside Jericho Quinn's helmet. The Cajun was in the lead, broad shoulders eclipsing the low morning sun across the thumping I-495 Beltway.

"Say, Chair Force," the big Marine said. He rode a red and black sister bike to Quinn's gunmetal-gray 1200 GS Adventure. "I got me a Tango Tango Charlie situation here."

"Okay . . ." Quinn had only known the monstrous Cajun for a matter of months. Violent circumstances had thrown them together—made them closer than brothers—but there were still many idiosyncrasies he had to learn.

"Tango Tango Charlie?

"Turd Touchin' Cloth, l'ami. My protein and oat-meal shake is scootin' through me quicker than I'd reckoned on. I need to take a tactical dump before you get me involved in some hellacious gun battle."

Gunnery Sergeant Jacques Thibodaux was Corps to the core. A square-jawed, thick-necked fighting machine, he'd been recruited to Win Palmer's Hammer Team along with Quinn. Like Quinn, he now operated as an OGA, an other governmental agent, working under the guise of Air Force OSI. The Marine still couldn't get used to the idea he was detailed to the Air Force, a branch of the service he generally referred to as Wing Waxers—or worse.

Rather than answer, Jericho looked to his left, giving Thibodaux a thumbs-up. He pointed with his gloved hand to a little "stop and rob" convenience store just off the 495/270 interchange going toward Rockville. Their helmets were outfitted with sophisticated communications gear that connected via securely scrambled Chatterbox Bluetooth, but he hated to clutter up his head with talk while he was riding unless it was an absolute necessity.

Quinn activated the turn signal with his thumb, then glanced over his right shoulder to take the lane. An elderly couple in a red Hyundai sedan slowed, and then veered to fall in behind him rather than pass. A dark blue minivan laid on the horn when the old folks cut them off, but the move allowed Quinn room to move over as surely as if they were running a blocker car. Quinn watched the terrified face of the gray-haired woman in the Hyundai's rearview mirror. She kept both hands on the wheel, eyes glued to the road ahead.

Quinn waved a thank-you and chuckled to himself. He and Thibodaux wore black leathers and rode big, aggressive motorcycles. It was obvious they were wanton killers, on the hunt for an elderly couple in a Hyundai to murder. He had basically the same effect whether he was on a motorcycle or not. It was a feral look he'd been born with and it drove Kim crazy.

Quinn needed fuel anyway so he pulled in to wait behind a guy with a trailer full of lawn equipment and three five-gallon gas cans. He stayed on the motorcycle but took off his helmet and kangaroo-leather gloves. Jacques all but vaulted from his bike and trotted inside the little convenience store to take care of his Tango Tango Charlie.

The day was warm for late September and Quinn unzipped his jacket to let in some air. The recirculating coolant was great, but Quinn found he liked fresh air when he could get it.

Once the lawn guy was finished, Quinn rolled his bike forward and put it up on the center stand. The BMW's 1200cc motor didn't exactly sip gasoline, but the beast sported a nine-and-a-half-gallon tank that gave it long legs for a motorcycle—and let it live up to the *Adventure* designation. Unlike filling up a car, Quinn found he had to keep a careful eye on the nozzle to keep a geyser of gasoline from shooting into the air once the tank was full. He took his time, feeding a little gas slowly while he looked around the parking lot.

He had never been one to relax completely when he was in public, but the attack by Farooq had made him even more watchful.

Three Hispanic kids in their late teens put fuel in a tricked-out Dodge Neon at the next island of pumps, in front of Jacques's bike. They made fleeting eye contact with Quinn, mumbling something in Spanish about his bike. All were dressed in baggy jeans and covered with tattoos that identified them as members of MS-13—Mara Salvatrucha—a brutal street gang springing from El Salvador who earned their bones with robbery, rape, and murder. A paunchy kid wearing an open flannel shirt over a white wifebeater gave Quinn a curt nod, eyeing the Beemer and sizing him up.

Jericho nodded back. Too much attention could instigate a fight, but ignoring the guy completely would have been seen as a sign of disrespect.

One eye on the gangbangers, Quinn watched a rusty blue minivan pull in from the service road. It creaked to a stop beside the coiled air hose off the wooden privacy fence at the edge of the parking lot. It continued to idle. The driver, a heavyset man with dark, thinning hair and a wad of tobacco the size of a golf ball in his jaw, got out and kicked the back tire. Another man came around from behind the van, stopping for a moment to talk to the driver, who'd bent down as if to study the tire. The second man was bigger than the driver, with a close-cropped head of bleach-blond hair and aviator Ray-Bans. Both men wore loose-fitting western shirts—the sort that made it easier to hide a pistol.

Quinn recognized the vehicle as the same van the elderly couple had cut off in their little red Hyundai. His mind began to work through the possible scenarios, none of them good. They must have circled back from the next exit. He watched the men for a few moments, alternating his attention between them and the tattooed gangbangers to his right.

As he replaced the filler cap he noticed his windscreen was filthy with bug guts. Thibodaux was taking his own sweet time inside, so he decided to give it a once-over before they got back on the highway.

He reached around the concrete post next to the gas pump for the squeegee as the passenger from the minivan began walking toward him.

People with ill intent had a look about them that was impossible to hide. Quinn's eyes flicked to the gangbangers at the nearby island. They were dangerous men, each with at least one gun and probably an assortment of blades. But their mouths gaped half-open as they went about the business pumping gas and wiping down their little car. On the other hand, the bald man with the Ray-Bans had set his jaw like he was biting on a stick. He stared at the ground as he walked, conspicuously ignoring Quinn to peer up every few steps to maintain target acquisition.

The potbellied driver got back in the minivan. Brake lights reflected off the wood fence and there was a loud clunk as the transmission slid into gear.

Quinn reasoned that the guy in the sunglasses wasn't going to try and kill him. He could have done that from the window of the van. No, this would be a classic snatch and grab. There would be a couple more in the van, ready to fling open the door so Ray-Ban could shove him inside. Quinn had used virtually the same technique many times to pick up high-value targets from danger areas in Iraq.

He bent on the opposite side of his motorcycle as if checking the oil. Ten feet out, Ray-Ban's right hand darted behind his back, coming back up with the unmistakable yellow and black of a X26 Taser.

Quinn stayed low, behind the bike, pretending to be

oblivious to the oncoming attack. Ray-Ban moved closer, obviously hoping to dart Quinn while he was still kneeling. The minivan crunched across the gravel, moving in for the grab. The side door slid open with a loud, metallic thunk.

Quinn rose to his full height as the van pulled alongside the pump, crowding the surprised gangbangers. A man in a black ski mask leaned out the open door as the van rolled, one hand hanging on to a seat belt, intent on grabbing Quinn when he went down. A second man, also wearing a mask, stood next to the other holding a black assault rifle attached to a nylon sling across his chest.

Quinn swung the squeegee like a war hammer as Ray-Ban raised the Taser. The cover man inside the van panicked, bringing up his weapon to unleash a deafening string of machine gun fire. Bullets smacked the pavement, zinging into the air. The grab man in the van screamed something unintelligible and shoved his gun-wielding partner sideways.

Quinn's squeegee hit a home run and Ray-Ban's jaw gave way with a satisfying crack. He crumpled, never feeling the rounds from his partner's machine gun that struck him low in the spine. As he pitched forward, the twin darts from his Taser buried themselves into the lead gangbanger's pudgy belly. Both men hit the ground at roughly the same time, Ray-Ban dead from friendly fire, the gangster writhing in pain as fifty thousand volts coursed through his body.

Quinn rolled, keeping his BMW between himself and the oncoming van. He came up again in a low crouch, firing his Kimber at the open door. He squeezed off four snap shots. At least one of them hit the gunman, who let the rifle fall against its sling. The wounded man slouched, pounding on the driver's headrest, and screamed: "Go, go, go!"

The minivan careened out of the parking lot, bald tires spewing a plume of angry gray smoke. Thibodaux exited the store at a run, dropping protein bars and water bottles as he took in the sight of the ambush.

"You all right, l'ami?" the Cajun said, his own pistol now in his hand. He eyed the gangbangers, who were helping their wobbly leader to his feet.

"I'm fine." Quinn knelt beside the dead Ray-Ban. "I'm not sure what that was all about, but they wanted to get me in the back of that van."

"You recognize him?" Thibodaux toed the dead man's face with his heavy riding boot.

Quinn shook his head. When he stood up he had the man's wallet in his hand. It contained a Virginia driver's license. "Walter Schmidt," he read. "Mean anything to you?"

"Can't say that it does," Thibodaux mused. "But, he's got a face only his mama could love. Bet he's got a record for all sorts of evil doin's."

Quinn tucked the wallet inside his jacket and zipped it up. "I'm not too keen on waiting around for the coppers on this one," he said, imagining all the time it would take to explain things. Since going to work for Palmer, both men had taken a more liberal view of what and what not to report to the local constabulary. "Palmer wants meet us right away. You okay if we don't wait?"

Thibodaux rolled his eyes. "I'd prefer it if we didn't."

"Good enough, then," Quinn said. "Give me a sec."

He walked over to where the gangbangers huddled

around their pallid leader, who was now propped up at the door of the Dodge Neon. He spoke with them quickly in hushed tones. The fat one nodded and they shook hands like old friends. Quinn turned to walk back toward the store.

"Where you goin'?" Thibodaux yelled. He gave his GS an impatient twist of the throttle. "I thought you said we were outta here, brother."

"We are." Quinn grinned, hooking a thumb toward the wobbly gangbanger. "I just gotta grab the surveillance tape and get some cash from the ATM. I promised Hector I'd pay him three hundred bucks if he'd dump the body for me."

Chapter Eleven

Quinn briefed Palmer as they rode, letting Thibodaux watch his back, in case the blue minivan had a partner. The Cajun was linked in to the call via the Chatterbox.

"We'll do some checking into your guy," Palmer said. His voice was oddly distant for someone who'd just learned one of his men had been ambushed. "How far out are you?"

"Not far at all," Thibodaux came back. "Be there in fifteen if we don't get hassled by the Man."

"I'll clear the way for you with the state police. Just get here as soon as you can. Don't know if it's connected to your recent adventure, but we've got two more bags." Palmer ended the call.

Quinn dropped the bike into fifth gear and began to work his way in and out of traffic. The towering GS flicked easily for something that was a two-story building of the motorcycle world. Still riding on the adrenaline of the attack, Quinn had to force himself to stay off the throttle. He opened his face shield a crack and let the cool air wash around him—calming and exciting at the same time.

When someone asked him why he rode, he often told them, "The same reason a dog sticks its head out the window of a moving car."

"Two *more* dead guys?" Thibodaux shook his square head in disbelief. He straddled his bike as he peeled off his gloves. Every rider had a system of order to remove their gear. Jericho was helmet, and then Held Phantom kangaroo-skin gloves. Thibodaux was gloves, then helmet. Towering over six-four, the Marine could straddle the BMW GS Adventure and still flat-foot the ground with both feet. Broad shoulders and a back that resembled a pool table strained at the leather jacket, dwarfing the tall motorcycle. His hair was cut high and tight with just enough in front to call it a flattop.

"Palmer says two," Quinn grunted, still thinking about the dead man who'd tried to shove him in the moving van. He'd seen months of action working outside the wire in Iraq, but an ambush was a difficult thing to shake off—particularly after the recent attempt on his family. There was no way they were connected. Walter Schmidt and Farooq were worlds apart when it came to causes. Still, Quinn didn't believe in coincidence.

He pushed away a nagging thought and hung his helmet on a hook below his right handgrip. Airbrushed war axes, their blades dripping in blood, stood out brilliantly in the sun on each side of the gray Arai.

He swung off his bike and maneuvered it up on the

center stand. The drive out front of the modest white brick house was made up of crushed oyster shells, not the best footing for a motorcycle. He and Thibodaux had found a spot of packed clay at the edge of the ratty grass yard to park their bikes. Over three decades of riding had seen him dump more than one bike because of soft parking. The protruding engine heads on the warhorse GS were protected by brushed aluminum covers and if the bike tipped, the crash bars and aluminum luggage boxes would absorb much of the damage if it did fall. Still, the powerful motorcycle had several new additions courtesy of DARPA and he took special precautions to make sure he didn't walk out to find her lying on the ground.

Once the bike was parked to his satisfaction, he tugged off the reinforced Sidi riding boots and slipped into a more comfortable pair of black Rockport chukkas. He could ride in them if he had to, but running in the heavy Sidis could be a problem.

Both men nodded to Palmer's limo driver. As the president's national security advisor, Palmer rated a small Secret Service detail of his own. His driver, a special agent, stood with his head back, soaking up the fall sun beside a black armored limo. Arnold Vasquez was not as tall as Thibodaux, but the muscles and Sig Sauer pistol under his loose suit coat made it clear he had been hired for more than his ability behind the wheel. As fellow Marines, he and Thibodaux had hit it off immediately. Each time they met it was a contest to see who could bark *semper fi* first and loudest.

"Uuurrrrah!" Vasquez snapped when Thibodaux made his way around the limo. "Hey, Captain Quinn." The Cajun was a brother in arms; Jericho, as an Air

Force officer, was worthy of little more than a polite nod.

"Urrah, Arnie." Jacques grinned. "How you been gettin' along, beb?"

"Fine, fine," Vasquez said. He hooked a thumb over his shoulder. "The boss is inside with Bodington and Ross."

Quinn raised an eyebrow at that. "FBI and CIA Bodington and Ross?"

"The very same." Vasquez nodded.

"Don't tell my child bride," the big Cajun mused. "But I always thought Virginia Ross was sorta cute from her photo. Too cute to be the boss of the CIA, that's for damned sure. . . ."

Agent Vasquez rolled his eyes and leaned in, as if with a secret. "*Mucho jamon por dos juevos*, buddy," he said. "That don't show up in no press photo. . . ."

Quinn understood the words, but not the colloquialism. "*Mucho jamon*?"

"Too much ham for two eggs," Thibodaux chuckled. "Guess Arnie's sayin' the director of the CIA is a little easier to jump over than walk around. . . ."

The kid slouching just inside the half-open front door had an unruly mop of sun-bleached hair and an attitude that made him look like he'd only just graduated from his skateboard to a government job. He lowered mirrored Oakley sunglasses to give both Quinn and Thibodaux the once-over. Black motorcycle leathers and the hard-put gazes of men who had seen more than their share of extreme violence had a way of earning them scrutiny from the authorities.

At first glance it was impossible to tell if the young sentry was FBI or CIA.

"You superheroes looking for someone?" Skater Boy said. He stepped up to block their way, holding up the flat of his hand as if it was a bulletproof shield.

"FBI," Thibodaux whispered, turning to give Quinn a pained look. "No doubt about it."

Quinn couldn't help but smile. "Air Force OSI," he said. During his freshman "doolie" year at the Air Force Academy he'd learned to deal with overbearing people by picturing a red dot in the center of their foreheads. It was a trick he'd failed to mention during all his psychological interviews. "Special Agents Quinn and Thibodaux here at Mr. Palmer's request."

"Let's see some ID." Skater Boy snapped his fingers in the overly officious way of one new to the world of badges and guns and a little drunk on the terrible cosmic power.

Quinn sighed, imagining the red dot at the bridge of the kid's nose. He reached for his creds when a familiar voice cut the silence from a long hallway to his right.

"Let them through, Reagan." Palmer stepped out of an alcove at the end of the hall. He wore khaki slacks instead of his customary suit. The sleeves of a starched white shirt were rolled up to his elbows.

"Thank you for coming so quickly." He handed Quinn and Thibodaux each a pair of blue nitrile gloves to match the ones on his own hands, then dismissed Reagan the skater boy with a curt nod.

"Hope the double extra-large are big enough for those shovels you call hands, Jacques," Palmer said as he turned to walk back down the hall.

Quinn unzipped his leather jacket and took a deep

breath. Putting on the gloves flooded his mind with memories of the near miss they'd had with weaponized Ebola less than a month before.

Palmer raised his own gloved hand as he walked, appearing to read Quinn's mind. "These are more to protect the crime scene than your health."

Thibodaux groaned. "Since when do you use your hammer teams to go all CSI?" The mountainous Cajun was fine when it came to killing bad guys or bashing heads together, but he was known to have a bit of a weak stomach when too much time had passed from the point of violence.

"Since someone started torturing American spies." Palmer stopped at the gaping doorway at the end of the shadowed hall. A white refrigerator stood a few feet beyond the door at the edge of the kitchen. It was covered with photos of what looked to be three separate young families. Each bore enough of a resemblance to the other to suggest they were related. The absence of any male influence in the house led Quinn to believe a single woman lived here. The photos on the fridge were likely her siblings, nieces, and nephews. A framed diploma hung in the hall to the right of the doorway proclaiming the graduation of Nadia Arbakova from the United States Secret Service Training Academy in 1998.

Palmer pointed to the doorway with an open hand. "They're through there."

A single lightbulb tried feebly to fight away the darkness. Thin tan carpet did little to absorb the sound of their footfalls on the creaky wood. The walls to the stairway were painted glossy white and adorned with a cluttered mix of more family photographs. The broken frames and glass of two lay shattered on the steps, indicating a struggle. The moldy, metallic smell of terror and urine met Quinn on a wall of dank air from below.

"So, the woman who lived here is one of the victims," Quinn said, half to himself. The air grew moist as they made their way single file down the stairs—it was cooler, but no more comfortable. Even surrounded by people he knew, the heaviness in the house made him grateful for the familiar bulk of a pistol under his jacket.

"Brilliant police work." Kurt Bodington stepped around a concrete block wall at the bottom of the steps. "I suddenly find myself surrounded by crack investigators." A sneer dripped from his voice. Quinn had never met the director of the FBI but found it easy to dislike him instantly. The man was, after all, a lawyer.

Palmer stepped closer to a silent Hispanic woman who'd come around the corner behind Bodington. She was tall, with an athletic build that reminded Quinn of a lifeguard. A shimmering dark blue blouse accented the light tan of her suit. Sensible shoes, as black as her hair, made Quinn think she might be FBI. The hint of humility in her amber-flecked eyes made him wonder.

"Agent Veronica Garcia with the CIA," Palmer said. "She's the one who discovered the bodies this morning."

"Has an uncanny habit of being at the wrong place at precisely the right moment, if you ask me," Bodington grumbled.

Garcia shrugged off the insult, but her eyes flashed daggers. She kept her hands clasped behind her back, as if to restrain them from slapping Director Bodington.

"Pleasure to meet you, Ms. Garcia." Quinn raised his blue glove. "I'd shake your hand, but . . . anyhow, anyone who Director Bodington dislikes is a friend of mine. . . ."

"Let's get to the yolk of the egg," Palmer said, jaw muscles clenching as he glared at both men. "You two can duel at high noon after this is over."

Virginia Ross stepped around the corner of an unfinished Sheetrock wall. Thibodaux gave Quinn a tiny nod, agreeing with Arnie's earlier assessment. More academic than clandestine operator, Ross wore fancy blue pumps, navy slacks, and a yellow blouse. Smallish shoulders and broad hips made her look like an inverted blueberry ice cream cone.

Operator or not, she was more savvy in the ways of politics than Bodington, and enough of a spy to project a measure of tense civility.

"Officer Garcia was conducting a background check on Agent Arbakova. She stopped by a little after seven this morning and stumbled onto this interrogation site—"

"Interrogation site . . ." Quinn mused as they rounded the corner into the stark light of the open basement. It was interesting that Palmer had introduced Garcia as an agent, but her boss had called her "officer."

Bodington breathed in quickly through his nose, mouth clenched in a tight line, as if disgusted at having to discuss such things with anyone outside his own realm of control.

"Interrogation site?" Thibodaux whispered, swaying like a giant tree as he took in the gruesome sight in front of them. "Is that what we're calling this now?"

Chapter Twelve

The nude body of a dead man hung upside down in the center of the ten-by-twenty-foot unfinished basement room. His swollen feet were tied together by rough cords draped over a fearsome metal hook in an exposed rafter. Bare copper wires looped around each big toe, then ran to a small, gas-powered welding generator on a folding table a few feet away. The dead man's fingertips were raw and bloody from clawing at the rough concrete floor. His head-down position had caused his belly to distend horribly. His face was puffed and unrecognizable. Pooling fluids leaked from his nose and gaping mouth to the bare concrete below. A closer inspection revealed circular electric burns to his groin and wrists as well as his ankles. The wires around each big toe sunk deeply into charred, blackened flesh.

Quinn had seen this sort of thing before. A colonel in the Afghan KHED had suspected a teenage goatherd of involvement with the Taliban. The evidence against the kid had been overwhelming, but many Afghans like him had been pressed into service. Few possessed the zeal of their Saudi and Chechen compatriots and gave up information easily.

Quinn had arrived too late to stop the interrogation. The colonel had hung the nude boy from a rafter by his feet, run copper wires to his big toes and increased the voltage until he twitched like a marionette. "The Dance of Death," the colonel had called it.

The colonel had been from Hazara—a tribe particularly mistreated by the primarily Pashtun Taliban. The boy was Pashtun—and that had been enough to kill him, no matter what he'd known or hadn't known.

Quinn studied the man hanging from the hook in front of him. Like the KHED colonel, whoever had done this had had an agenda beyond interrogation. The depth of human cruelty never ceased to amaze him, even though he himself had caused the death of more than a few enemies of his country—and even a certain amount of pain.

This was not an interrogation. This was someone's entertainment.

Quinn stepped closer to the hanging body, studying the scorched flesh behind the dead man's knees. There came a point in any "enhanced" interrogation when the subject would say anything to stop the pain. That point had come and gone with this one long before the torture had stopped. Anyone trained by an American intelligence agency would know that—if they even cared.

"We know who he was?" Quinn said.

"One of ours," Virginia Ross said, eyes darting nervously around the room. She took a tentative step closer to the body. Her eyes suddenly locked on the congealing pool of fluids under the dead man's yawning mouth, she seemed not to know where to put her feet. Her words came in short spurts with a hard swallow in between each phrase. "Tom Haddad . . . he was an analyst . . . assigned to the Middle East desk."

"Is his name on Congressman Drake's list?" Quinn asked, knowing the answer before it came.

"It is," Ross said, swallowing again. "He transferred back to Langley from Cairo three months ago."

Quinn turned to look at Bodington, but said nothing.

The FBI director returned his glare for a long moment before shaking his head. "We weren't looking at him for anything, if that's what you were thinking."

Quinn didn't know whether to believe either director. It wasn't unheard of for the Bureau to watch Agency assets without informing their bosses—or vice versa, though the CIA wasn't supposed to conduct operations on American soil. Quinn did a lot of things he wasn't "supposed" to do, so he naturally assumed the CIA did what was necessary to get the job done.

"If he's not on anyone's radar, how'd he get on the list?" Thibodaux asked. "Maybe he really was a mole."

"We've yet to figure that one out," Palmer said grimly, nodding toward an empty chair with shreds of duct tape at the arms and legs. "There's one more."

Someone had been tied there, likely made to watch.

"Worse than this?" Thibodaux moaned. He turned to Quinn. "I'm gonna need one of my grandmama's good-luck gris-gris bags to protect me. This place is chockablock full of evil, beb."

"It's a woman." Palmer held open the door to a small unfinished storeroom. "This is . . . was her house."

Quinn stepped through the narrow doorway to find a small room awash with blood.

As a younger man, just starting out in the business, he'd been amazed at the amount of fluid inside a human body. There was a reason they called it "wet work."

The pallid corpse of an amber-haired female was thrown back over a collapsed stack of cardboard boxes. She looked to be in her late thirties—maybe Quinn's age. Her throat had been cut, all the way to the bone—Quinn guessed with some sort of wire. She was naked but for the beige bra that was bunched up cruelly under her armpits. A high-school yearbook and a small wooden music box—presumably things precious to the woman—had fallen out of the boxes and lay below the ashen white of the woman's trailing wrist. Droplets of coagulating blood pooled below the tips of curled fingers. High cheekbones and the steep angle of her jaw made Quinn guess she might have a hint of Asian blood. Her storm-gray eyes were thrown wide in a silent scream of terror.

Quinn turned away after he'd taken in as much as he thought he needed. Each time he saw a woman who'd been hurt or killed—and he'd seen far too many—he couldn't help but think of Kim. "Anything I can learn from this one?"

"FBI techs say she was raped," Palmer said.

Bodington leaned a hand against the door frame. "Too early to tell if there'll be any DNA. Son of a bitch bit a chunk out of her shoulder though—probably trying to subdue her. My guys can get a good cast of his teeth from the wound. Looks like the old girl put up a fight." He nodded to the tip of a female finger, complete with oddly untouched pink nail polish, lying on the concrete floor. "Killer probably used a garrote. Old girl must have gotten a finger inside the piano wire before he yanked it tight—"

"The old girl's name was Nadia," Veronica Garcia interjected from the doorway, behind Director Ross. She was icy, detached. "Nadia Arbakova. She worked for the Secret Service in their Protective Intelligence Division."

"Was she on Drake's list?" Thibodaux asked.

"No," Palmer mused, almost to himself. "Oddly enough, she was not."

"She's on my list," Garcia offered.

"Oh." Bodington gave a sarcastic smirk. "You've been in the field a half a day and you already have your own list?"

To her credit, Garcia ignored the pompous attempt to keep her in her place.

"She has a relationship with an agent on the vice presidential detail. He's one of the priorities you gave me." She looked at Palmer, who gave her a reassuring nod. "I'd planned to review her background information with her this morning."

"So," Bodington mused, "you just happened to drop by at exactly the right time to find two dead bodies in the basement?"

"I decided to stop off and chat with her this morning," Garcia said. "Her house is on the way in from mine. Thought I'd kill two birds with one stone, so to speak."

"Damn appropriate metaphor." The FBI director smirked, nodding at Haddad's body. "Maybe that's exactly what you did."

Quinn had had enough. "You need to shut your mouth," he hissed, suddenly losing patience.

The FBI boss blustered, rising up on the balls of his feet as if he might actually get physical.

"Calm down, Kurt." Palmer held up a hand. "He'd kill you before you could make a fist." He turned to a grinning Garcia. "Please continue, Agent Garcia. What's the boyfriend's name?"

"James Doyle," Veronica said. "He's working day-shift at the Observatory today. I have an appointment at three-thirty to talk to the agent in charge of his detail."

"Very well," Palmer muttered. "One victim on the list and one not . . ." He walked back toward the stairwell door as he thought, ignoring the grotesque, bag-like figure of Tom Haddad's bloated body. When he reached the base of the stairs, he turned to face the rest of the group. "It goes without saying we have a cold-blooded son of a bitch at work here, maybe more than one. This idiot congressman has crossed the line by going public with the existence of his list."

"Has he released the names?" Thibodaux asked. "I thought he said it was a secret."

"Drake has his own version of WikiLeaks. The entire list blasted out over the Internet last night right after his show." Palmer reached in his shirt pocket and removed a folded sheet of white paper, looking directly at Quinn. "Take a good look."

"Think I'll recognize some of the names?" Quinn took the paper.

"I'm sure you will, son." Palmer sighed. "You're one of them."

CHAPTER THIRTEEN

Some men killed for pleasure. Some, like Mujaheed Beg, were blessed with a righteous cause. To hold another's life in one's hands was enjoyable enough, but to kill an American—that was such a pleasure as to be sinful, unless the cause was a holy one.

The Mervi ran an olive hand through his hair, combed back like a wood duck. He squinted at the sun. It was nearly noon. His target would arrive at any moment.

A cloud of insects hovered like pepper tossed into the air a few feet off the paved jogging trail. Cicadas buzzed in the thick foliage along the shore of a small lake, ticking out their last few calls of the season. A swimming beaver cut a long V in the brown surface, disappearing under a raft of lily pads.

A creature of the desert, Mujaheed had been unaccustomed to such an abundance of life. He swatted a mosquito that landed on his cheek. A striped lizard scuttled along the paved asphalt trail before darting into a tuft of brown grass.

A car door slammed on the far side of the lake, echoing off the water.

Beg looked at his watch. So predictable.

Lake Artemesia Park was a stone's throw from the Beltway and adjacent to the College Park Metro station. Though it was in the city, the little gem of a park was tucked in among the trees and connected to miles of wooded trail. A peaceful lake beckoned University of Maryland students like Grace Smallwood who liked to run in the woods.

Mujaheed leaned against the cedar post of a small gazebo off the trail, pretending to stretch his calf muscles. He was dressed in a pair of gray running shorts and a black T-shirt. Apart from a small cardboard box in his right hand, he looked like any other jogger.

Most visitors preferred the cool of the evening and the park was nearly empty. One other runner—a young Asian man with a South Korean flag on his T-shirt—and a gaggle of young black women pushing baby strollers had passed him a few moments before. Beg gauged his timing so he'd meet Grace Smallwood coming from the opposite side of the lake, well away from the mothers' gossip group and the other jogger. The sight of so many women out in the open with their heads uncovered disgusted him. They deserved the rewards they reaped.

Mujaheed counted to twenty, then fell into an easy trot along the trail. He went counterclockwise around the lake trail to meet Grace Smallwood as far away from the others as possible.

* * *

Mujaheed had found the Russian woman the night before bland as a wet cloth. She'd fought, but not as well as he had hoped, considering she was supposed to be trained in such things.

He'd changed his shirt after he'd finished with her, and then taken some time to look through her bedroom. When there was an opportunity, he liked to get a feel for the life he'd just ended. He'd found little but a few photo albums and an inordinate amount of sewing crafts. A small framed photo of Arbakova beside a Native American man sat on a bedside stand. They both wore Secret Service T-shirts. It was the only evidence that she had any sort of a social life.

Mujaheed had lain back for a time on the soft sheets of her bed, watching a news program with a volatile U.S. congressman named Drake. The politician spoke in inflammatory sound bites about the evils of the Islamic world and the dangers of the U.S. weakening its ties with Israel. Mujaheed pointed his finger at the screen as if it were a pistol. He turned the channel to *Jeopardy!* before drifting off, the scent of the woman he'd just killed lulling him into a deep, dreamless sleep.

The doorbell had awakened him with a start.

It took a few precious moments to get his bearings and remember where he was. There'd been no time to chide himself for his stupidity. He'd barely had time to slip quietly out the back door as a dark, intensely beautiful woman came down the hallway. She'd called for Arbakova by name, as if they were friends.

He'd paused to peer back in through the kitchen window, cursing that he couldn't stay and spend more time with this one. The slight bulge at the ankle of her tan slacks told him she carried a pistol. The danger of the weapon had aroused his appetite all the more. The sure way she moved, the hard gaze in her eyes, told him she possessed all the fighting spirit Nadia Arbakova had lacked.

He'd resolved to get to know this woman someday soon. But before he could do that, there was the matter of Grace Smallwood from Lincoln, Nebraska. He'd been watching her too, getting to know her and the little secrets that made her vulnerable. Smallwood's death had to be an accident, and though Mujaheed Beg preferred the more intimate work of the garrote, his specialty—the skill the doctor paid him for—was accidents.

The diminutive Nebraska native was a picture of intelligent perkiness. She'd graduated with honors from the University of Maryland and then stayed on as a Terrapin to work on her graduate degree in public policy. One of her professors had introduced her to a particular senator, who had, in turn made introductions to a particularly well-placed family within the government. It didn't hurt that she was as cute as she was smart and that the senator who'd introduced her had a thing for brunettes with pixie haircuts. She had the pizzazz and brains to write her own ticket in Washington.

It was up to Beg to see that Smallwood never got the job. Another student, one more friendly to the jihad, would be hired after her untimely death.

She was listening to music on her iPod when she rounded the corner, head bobbing to the decadent beat of her song. She wore red shorts and a loose U of M basketball jersey that showed far too much of her skin for Beg's moral sensibilities. A small black fanny pack hung around her waist.

Beg approached from an intersecting side trail, timing his entry onto the main path so he crashed directly into the startled girl. As they collided, he opened the tiny cardboard box in his right hand and dumped the contents down the loose neck of her jersey.

"I'm so sorry," he sputtered. "How clumsy of me."

He offered a hand as they pushed away from their awkward clench.

"I'm okay. . . ." She crawled to one knee before launching into a series of short screams, swatting feverishly at her chest.

"Bees!" she gasped. "I'm allergic to bees!"

She clawed at her waist for the EpiPen that would stop her attack.

"Is this what you're looking for?" Mujaheed smiled, still playing the innocent. He unzipped the fanny pack and retrieved the yellow plastic tube containing her epinephrine.

Smallwood fell back against the pavement. Clutching at her throat, she gasped for air. She nodded emphatically, groping blindly for the pen. "Hurry. . . . Can't . . . breathe. . . ."

Mujaheed looked up and down the path. When he was certain there were no witnesses, he pressed the pen into the trail, activating the automatic injector and emptying the medication onto the path. He dropped the pen on the ground beside the stricken girl. It would be found later by authorities, who would believe she had panicked and wasted the drug that could have saved her life.

The girl looked on in horror. Her mouth opened and closed like a fish out of water. Horrific red blotches blossomed on her face and neck. Eyes that had shone brightly moments before grew bloodshot and vague. Flecks of spittle frothed from swelling lips. Her head slammed against the pavement with a violent crack. She began to writhe, kicking so hard at the edge of the trail, she lost a shoe.

The black women walking with their children would find her in a few moments. By then Grace Smallwood would be past the point of rescue—and Mujaheed Beg would be gone.

Chapter Fourteen

The Mervi hardly made it out of earshot from the gurgles of the dying girl when the cell phone in the pocket of his running shorts began to buzz. He hadn't even had time to take out his comb and see to his hair. It had to be Dr. Badeeb. No one else had his number. He let it ring, wanting to put more distance between himself and Smallwood before she was discovered.

The very picture of impatience, Badeeb called again in a matter of seconds. Beg slowed to a walk in the shadowed, tunnel-like forest clearing along the heavily wooded Paint Branch trail. A gray squirrel chattered from the high limbs of an elm tree. Wiping sweat from his forehead with the tail of his shirt, he took a deep breath and answered curtly.

"*Al-salamu*, Doctor." He waved a mosquito away as he spoke.

"*Wa alaikum assalam*," Badeeb whined like the mosquito. "You are healthy, praise be to God. . . ."

"I am," Beg sighed, suddenly more fatigued than he should be. Nazeer Badeeb was his employer, but the

Mervi found himself too weary for the customarily endless rounds of telephone politeness. "Why do you call?"

"I trust all is well in Maryland?" Badeeb sounded like a Pakistani version of the film actor Peter Lorre. The wheezing brought on by his ever-present cigarette was audible over the phone.

"It is," Beg said, walking faster to outpace the mosquitoes that flung themselves from the surrounding foliage to swarm his face. "Our trouble in Rockville has been taken care of and that obstacle at the university has been cleared away. Your friend should have no trouble getting the job she wants."

"Excellent," Badeeb said, a broad smile evident in his voice. "Praise be to God that you are able to clear the path for so many."

"Yes," Beg said absentmindedly. "Praise be to God. What do you hear of Drake? Might we know anyone on this list of his?" The Mervi did not ask outright over the phone, but Badeeb would understand his meaning. Were they themselves, or any of their people, on the list?

Badeeb kept uncharacteristically silent for some time.

"I have not put eyes on it," he said at length. "But Drake does us a great service by producing such a list. The Americans will devour themselves out of fear and mistrust of each other."

"Maybe," Beg mused. "Still, I do not like this politician. He seems much too powerful to have such radical thoughts."

"He does, indeed," the doctor said. Badeeb was always brooding over one idea or another. It was what made him so dangerous. "We will take care of Drake when the time is right." The metallic sound of his cigarette lighter clinked in the background. "Right now we have larger fish to cook."

"Fry," Beg corrected, shaking his head. "You mean bigger fish to fry."

"Yes." Badeeb gave a forced laugh. "Of course. Much bigger fish. . . . You have done well, my friend. Praise be to God. Get some rest for now. I will call you."

Beg ended the call and stuffed the phone back in his pocket. It was rare that he had more than a few days without some sort of assignment. In Dr. Badeeb's world, there were always paths that needed clearing, loose ends to tie up. The doctor kept the details of his plans to himself, sharing them only when someone needed to be moved out of the way.

Suddenly hungry, the gaunt Mervi picked up his pace. He would eat some pancakes with lots of butter pecan syrup at the Denny's around the corner and then return to his apartment in Virginia for some much-needed rest.

When he woke up, he would learn more of the dark woman who'd surprised him at Arbakova's house.

CHAPTER FIFTEEN

Standing outside Nadia Arbakova's front door, one hip cocked to the side, Ronnie Garcia's throat tightened as she watched Quinn and Thibodaux gear up. Dressed in black leather, with stiff riding boots and full-gauntlet riding gloves, the men reminded her of gladiators straddling futuristic machines out of an *Alien* movie. They mounted their bikes without speaking and roared down the driveway back toward Highway 270.

Arbakova's murder had solidified everyone's workday. Garcia would pay a visit to Agent James Doyle's older sister, Tara, and see what the Air Force F-22 pilot had to say about her kid brother. The big boy biker with the Louisiana drawl and his darkly handsome friend would check out a couple of addresses on the guy who'd apparently tried to kidnap them that morning. They would all link up around 1500 hours at the Naval Observatory—the official vice-presidential residence—for an appointment with Nadia's former boyfriend, Special Agent Doyle.

Ronnie put the tip of her index finger against full lips, eyes narrowed in thought. It would take some time to understand this one named Jericho. The Cajun dude had muscles on top of his muscles. Some women would be into that, but there was a brooding violence in the dark one that felt familiar to Garcia, as if she'd known him for a very long time.

Palmer and the others were still inside, letting the crime scene technicians go about their business while Bodington, no doubt, pitched high-level plans that didn't involve Garcia doing anything more than carrying his briefcase.

Beyond the trees, the bikes threw up a spray of gravel, disappearing around the line of oaks along the deserted street. Ronnie sighed, jingling her keys in her fist. She looked at Arnie Vasquez, Palmer's Secret Service driver. "You know that one?" she asked.

"You talking about Quinn?"

"Hmm." She bit her bottom lip. "He married?"

"Not anymore."

"Hmmm."

"He's a dangerous man, chica . . . *muy* dangerous."

"Hmmmm."

"Something else you want to know?"

"I'm wondering how he likes his coffee. . . ."

Arnie smirked. "And just how do you want him to like his coffee?"

Garcia opened the door to her shiny black Impala and gave Vasquez a wink as she climbed in behind the wheel. "Strong, hot, and Cuban."

Chapter Sixteen

Province of Nuristan
Eastern Afghanistan
0700 hours Afghanistan Time

She was no diplomat—but Karen Hunt was a spy, and good spies knew how to be diplomatic when they had to be. Peering out the flat, elongated window of the concrete command bunker, she rocked back and forth on her feet, arms folded against the chill of the thin mountain air. She nodded toward the tiny window where she could just catch a glimpse of the gray crags that towered over the little copse of concrete buildings, sandbag bunkers, and double ring of concertina wire that that made up Camp Bullwhip.

"I mean, seriously," she said. "It's just like they told me it would be. This really is like living at the bottom of a Dixie cup."

First Lieutenant Bryce Nelson, the camp's ranking officer, glanced up from a table where he stood poring over a weathered topographic map. He was gaunt faced and world worn for a man in his late twenties. "Like I said . . ." He shook his head, then returned his attention to the map.

None of the soldiers wanted her here. They didn't trust spooks—with good reason. Spooks sent them off into the mountains based on analysis and guesswork. Soldiers liked their truths more black and white. Camp Bullwhip was definitely on the shady gray edges of what could be considered a sane place to stick an American forward operating base.

Three of her first four days saw mortar attacks from across the silt-choked river that formed the northern boundary of the camp. An enemy sniper had set up shop on the fourth afternoon, zipping in potshots from the rocky crags above. The shooter hadn't killed anyone, but kept soldiers pinned down for forty-five minutes until a couple of F15s dropped enough ordnance on the mountain to kill two dozen snipers.

The attacks had been halfhearted at best. They were testing, Hunt thought, like remote probes, methodically checking out the remote base's defenses and troop response.

She'd left Kabul the week before in a Chinook helicopter with supplies and a reinforcement platoon of forty-two soldiers from the Tenth Mountain Division. Once the athletic and youthful war fighters had climbed aboard and strapped themselves into his bird, the pilot had drawn a round of cheers when he'd announced he was honored to be flying an entire "can of American whoop-ass."

From the moment she saw the isolated combat outpost she'd understood why soldiers who lived there felt their position was too exposed. It was twenty miles from the nearest support base and surrounded by high foothills in the shadow of the jagged Hindu Kush. It was only by dumb luck—and the Afghani insurgents' general inability to shoot straight—that no one had been killed.

Lieutenant Nelson took a grease pencil from the sleeve pocket of his BDU shirt and made some notes on the laminated map. He was ready for patrol, dressed in full battle rattle except for his Kevlar helmet, which rested on the plastic folding table alongside the map.

"Our meeting with Mullah Muzari is when?" Hunt said, still gazing out the window. She was debating whether or not she should go ahead and put on her heavy flak vest to help ward off the bone-numbing chill. It had been cold in Kabul, but she found it almost impossible to get warm in the thin air of the mountains. Lieutenant Nelson, from Sweetgrass, Montana, seemed impervious to the cold. He kept the space heater at a low simmer when Karen felt a roaring boil should be the order of the day.

"Meeting is at oh-nine hundred," Lt. Nelson said.

Karen yawned, rubbing her eyes with a hand grimy from a week at the remote outpost. "That's what?" She looked at the Seiko dive watch on her wrist. "Two hours from now? The village is only two clicks away."

"It is," the LT said, his boyish dimples withdrawing into the worry lines of his face. "But we'll need to do a sweep of the village before we sit down for our tea party. I'll have to post guards and send a patrol into the mountains above us to keep an eye out for snipers. That takes a little more time than just a stroll into town."

Nelson was twenty-six, but the stress of a month in

command of an indefensible base surrounded by mountains and crawling with *Hezb-e-Islami Gulbuddin* had chased the youthful sparkle from his brown eyes.

The HiG was an insurgent group that had formed decades earlier to repel the Soviets. They were violently opposed the U.S. occupation and though fierce competitors with the Taliban, they could at least agree on their visceral hatred of the Americans.

Hunt had been assigned to the outpost with one mission: to find out if there was a viable chance for peace with Mullah Muzari, an HiG commander who'd been on the U.S. government's capture or kill list since late 2006. He'd recently been making noises about wanting to negotiate. The folks at Army Intel and the CIA had put their big giant brains together and decided Hunt should fly in and see if he was for real.

Clean water was always at a premium and, like everyone on the base, Lieutenant Nelson looked as if he'd slept in his clothes for the past month. Hunt didn't want to think about how she looked. She wore desert camo and a matching ball cap to cover her short, easy-to-care-for brown hair. She wasn't actually in the military, but the uniform kept her from presenting a more appetizing target to any snipers in the mountain hidey-holes that overlooked the camp. As one of the Agency's few female paramilitary intelligence officers, Hunt kept herself fit to the extreme. One might see a man in her position with the beginnings of a middle-age spare tire, but Karen reasoned women in her line of work didn't need that kind of scrutiny. She had the look of a healthy farm girl accustomed to hard work in the outdoors and the oval pink cheeks of a Rubens painting. At nearly five-ten and a hundred thirty-five pounds, she was blessed with long legs that helped her run the mile in just over five minutes. She took pride in the fact that she'd been able to do more pull-ups than all but two of the men in her basic agent class at Camp Perry.

When she'd signed up for the CIA she'd done so with what she believed to be full knowledge of what she was getting herself into. Her father had been a well-respected case officer in the Clandestine Service. He'd dragged Karen and her mother all over Central Asia when the countries were still fresh and beautifully raw with their recent independence from the Soviet Union.

Life had been austere when they weren't at the family's stateside base in Boston. Foreign travel hadn't just meant adventure. It had been bare lightbulbs, toilet tissue that resembled flimsy wax paper, and rude housing. But, compared to the way the locals had it, the Hunt family had always lived like comparative royalty. As far as Karen knew, no one had ever shot at them and she'd only had to eat one goat's eye to keep from offending someone. As a Boston girl and world traveler, the one thing she'd never really gotten used to was the cold.

She'd joined the Marine Corps for a short stint, training at Parris Island and moving into the Lioness Program before being redrafted by the Agency because of her father's connections. The fact that she spoke, at least to some degree, all of the major languages of Afghanistan convinced someone in the government that they should send her back to college and stick her in the CIA.

Nelson stooped over the map, resting both hands on the table. His voice brought her back from thoughts of her past. "It takes time to get this shit set up, you know."

Hunt held up both hands. "Understood, LT. Relax. The enemy's outside the wire. Not in here. I'm just asking questions, that's all."

"I know. . . ." His voice was a tight whisper. "My colonel says he's in contact with Mullah Muzari and that Mullah Muzari says things will soon be under control. And then some goatherd feeds me intel that it's Mullah Muzari's guys that are lobbing lead at us every day. . . ."

She suddenly felt sorry for the harried lieutenant. "I hear you," Hunt said, walking toward the window to get a clearer look outside. Something didn't look right. "When I send in my report I'll stress that it's not working with Muzari. You do what you need to. . . ."

Hunt's voice trailed off as she watched a young boy of nine or ten approach the front gate at the near end of the American-built wooden vehicle bridge across the Bandagesh River. It was the only way in through the maze of sandbags, ten-foot fencing, and razor wire that surrounded the five-acre base. Lt. Nelson moved to stand beside her.

Both watched in shocked surprise as the two soldiers standing post left their fortified checkpoint and walked to the gate for a chat with the child.

"No, no, no . . . what in the hell are they doing?" Nelson moaned under his breath. He reached for a radio on the table behind him.

Hunt stared in disbelief that two highly trained men, both veterans of countless violent contacts with the enemy, opened the only fortification between the base and the hostile surroundings.

"Are they really going to let him in?" Instinctive dread pressed at her gut.

Nelson let fly a flurry of curses. "That's exactly what they're doing. . . ." He craned his neck out the bunker window.

It wasn't uncommon for insurgents to use kids to play on the sentiments of American soldiers who were far from family and younger siblings—lull them into a false sense of security. Surely these men knew that.

"Foster!" Nelson barked across the radio. "Get that gate down on the double."

"It's okay, LT," Specialist Foster's voice came back in a wash of static. "You're not gonna believe it, but this kid speaks English. Says his name's Kenny—"

"Impossible!" Hunt snatched up a pair of binoculars from the map table. The boy loitered at the gate, preventing the soldiers from closing it without bringing the heavy steel beams down on top of his head. He wore faded blue jeans and some kind of ball cap with a logo on it she couldn't read. A red, white, and blue Pepsi T-shirt was just visible under a black fleece jacket. Streaked blond hair caught the heavy rays of afternoon sun over the sawtooth western slopes of the Hindu Kush. The boy certainly had American features, but Hunt knew such a thing was impossible. Even without the binoculars, she could make out the look of detachment on the kid's face—almost, but not quite, a smile—as if he'd just won a game but didn't want to let on.

Lieutenant Nelson found a fresh string of curses as he swept his M4 off a rack near the door. He headed toward the gate at a trot.

Hunt fell in beside him, wishing she had a rifle instead of her puny nine-millimeter handgun.

"Shut the damned gate!" Nelson screamed into the radio as he moved.

"Seriously, Lieutenant," Foster came back again, almost giggling. "This kid speaks English better than Nguyen. Can you believe this shit? He says he's from—"

They'd made it to within twenty meters of the gate when Foster suddenly pitched forward, his head exploding like a blossoming red flower. Chunks of him flew into his partner and the boy. The crack of sustained rifle fire followed an instant later, drawn flat on the thin mountain air.

Specialist Kevin Nguyen, the second gate guard, had just handed the kid a chocolate bar when the shooting started. He scooped the boy up in both arms and ran for cover behind the gate bunker as withering incoming fire began to pour from the mountains. On the American side, fifty-caliber Brownings opened up with a reassuring clatter from each of the three raised sentry posts, sending a fusillade of lead and glowing tracer rounds back toward the surrounding mountains.

Gray puffs of dust kicked up as bullets struck the ground around Hunt's feet. She crouched, doubling her speed to sprint for the relative safety of the concrete guardhouse. Nelson moved backwards, methodically picking off attackers with his M4 as they swarmed the half open gate.

Hunt made it to the guard shack and slid behind a concrete Jersey barrier, pistol clutched in her hand. She landed beside Specialist Nguyen, who now lay on his side, firing his rifle with one hand while he shielded the little boy who called himself Kenny. Hunt rolled up on her shoulder to watch in horror as a stream of insurgents in black turbans materialized from every mountain shadow. Pouring through the gate, the screaming Afghans engaged surprised pockets of soldiers, caught flat-footed in the attack.

Less than thirty feet away, an HiG fighter so young he was yet unable to grow more than a few sparse whiskers on his pointed chin, stood in the full open and pressed an RPG to his shoulder, aiming for the guardhouse. The look of jubilance on his face was unmistakable as he chanted the hollow, breathy "Allahu Akbar!" of a holy warrior.

Hunt shot him twice in the chest with her pistol as he pulled the trigger. He slumped and the RPG hissed past, missing the intended target but skittering along the rocks to blow the tires off a Humvee behind them.

Still firing, Lt. Nelson dove behind the concrete barrier to land beside Hunt with a heavy grunt.

"Anybody hit?" he said, his eyes still referencing the EoTech holographic sight of his M4.

"We're doin' just fine, LT," Nguyen snapped back, between well-placed shots from his rifle. An enemy fighter fell almost every time he fired.

Hunt rolled half on her side in the dirt so she could look Nelson in the face. "I'm sure you guys got a Predator up somewhere around here. What do you say we call and see if we can borrow it?"

The LT grunted in agreement, handing his M4 to Hunt.

"You give us cover while I make the call. . . ." Radio communication with higher command from the narrow Afghan valleys was impossible and Nelson never went anywhere without a satellite telephone on his belt. It took agonizing seconds for the link. When command finally picked up, the urgency in Nelson's normally collected voice was obvious.

"We're getting our asses handed to us!" he screamed above the din of gunfire. "We need air support ASAP!"

Another voice, shrill and broken, came across the radio Nelson had set on the ground. "AAF coming through the fence by the Afghan Army latrines!" It was Sergeant McCrary, two years younger than Nelson. AAF was Anti-Afghan Forces. "What's your location LT?"

Nelson snatched up the radio. "Stand by." He turned back to the sat phone. "Get us support as soon as you can," he said, a pained look on his beaten face. "Bring them in—hello . . . ?"

He dropped the phone. "Dammit. Lost the signal." He took up the radio again.

Hunt shot two more insurgents while she listened to Nelson give orders that chilled her to the core.

"Fall back, fall back," the lieutenant shouted into the radio while he surveyed their situation as best he could with a wall of bullets flying overhead. "All able, form a new perimeter around the command bunker. Watch your dispersement. We're gonna have to hold these guys off for a while. . . . Fixed wings are twenty minutes out, Apaches are forty."

Nelson had just ordered all his men to abandon his own position at the front gate. They were now nearly a hundred yards outside the new perimeter.

"Sit tight, LT," McCrary's voice crackled over the radio, nearly drowned out by gunfire and yelling. "I'll get a squad together and we'll come bring you in."

"Request denied," Nelson barked. "We'll hold them

off from our position. You see to your defenses. . . . That's an order."

Insurgent shooting lulled for a moment as the fifty-cals opened up to drive them back from the gate. Three black turbans popped up from the river bank fifty yards west of the bridge. Hunt and Nguyen shot got two of them before the third ducked out of sight.

"How many do you think?" Hunt said, more to herself than anyone else.

"Three hundred . . ." It was Kenny, peering from under the shelter of Specialist Nguyen's body. The look in his dull gray eyes reminded Hunt of a child that got his kicks from torturing animals.

The boy smiled as if he knew a deadly secret, raising his dirty brow slightly. "They've been watching everything you guys have been doing for two weeks, figuring out how to take the camp." He grinned up at Nguyen, who looked back in slack-jawed amazement.

"Thanks for the chocolate bar," the kid said. He gave a bored sigh, oblivious to the bullets zinging overhead. "Too bad they're going to cut your filthy head off."

With that, Kenny opened his fleece jacket. A black cylinder about the size of a can of deodorant rolled into the dirt toward Hunt. The boy's hands shot to his ears. He ducked his head against Specialist Nguyen.

"Grenade!" Hunt screamed, a half second before the blast slammed into her chest.

CHAPTER SEVENTEEN

7th Fighter Squadron
Langley Air Force Base
Virginia

A curt airman wearing green digital camo BDUs and a pencil-thin mustache had disappeared with Ronnie Garcia's ID what seemed like hours before. Now she stood outside the reinforced steel door, rocking back and forth from one foot to the other. Evidently, there was some concern about her level of need to be within spitting distance of a hangar full of F-22 Raptors.

Palmer had seen to it she was credentialed as a full counterintel agent for the CIA—but even in the shadow of the Agency's headquarters, so few people ever actually saw CIA identification that she was met with a tilted head and arched brow—the universal expression for ". . . Sure you are. . . ."

Garcia had stopped for a Diet Dr. Pepper on the drive in and was now sure some unseen Air Force security officer was having a dandy old time watching her do the potty dance outside the bunkered door. From the number of cameras and sophisticated satellite antenna arrays that bristled on the concrete block hangar, her misery was likely being beamed directly to the Pentagon.

The door gave a sudden electronic buzz and a metallic click. In a near state of panic, Garcia reached for the handle, but it was pushed open by a slender brunette in a green Nomex flight suit. The leather name tag above her right breast pocket identified her as Major T. Doyle.

The major winked a startling blue eye—a woman-to-woman wink.

"You know, they make us gals wear diapers when we fly," she said in a comfortable Texas drawl. "Haven't come up with a way to connect our lack of exterior plumbing to the relief tube . . . though they've tried some pretty uncomfortable dumbass ideas, let me tell you. Come on. The head is right down the hall here."

"Thanks," Garcia sighed, waving to the camera above the door. At least someone had been paying attention to her dance.

Her business taken care of quickly, Garcia met Tara Doyle outside the ladies' room door. She was immediately struck by the major's uncommon beauty. Thick hair, so black it shone blue in the stark light of the cavernous aircraft hangar, was pulled back in a loose ponytail. Glacier-blue eyes locked on Garcia and drew her down the side hall to a cramped office Doyle shared with another pilot.

Doyle dipped her head toward the vacant desk. "Speedo won't be back for a couple of hours. You can grab his chair if you want.

Garcia rolled the padded chair around beside Doyle's cheap wood veneer, DOD-issue desk.

The major kicked her desert-tan boots up on a stack of folders and leaned back with her hands behind her head. She was slightly built, a head shorter than Ronnie. Had it not been for the grace and maturity in the way she carried herself, the baggy fight suit would have made her look like a child in pajamas.

"All righty then," Doyle said, with the swagger of someone accustomed to commanding a hundred-and-fifty-million-dollar aircraft. "What does the CIA want with a little ol' jet jockey like me?"

"Just a few questions." Garcia leaned forward in her chair, resting her elbows on her knees. She hoped it made her look more earnest. "Have you ever met a woman named Nadia Arbakova?"

"Sure. My baby brother's lady friend. They both work for the Secret Service. I don't think much of her, to tell you the God's honest truth—she's a little too much of a shrinking violet for my blood. Awfully damned needy . . ." Doyle lowered her eyes. "But I'm guessing you already knew that. Does this have anything to do with that congressman's list of infidels?"

Garcia bit her lip. "There's really no delicate way to put this—"

"Well, hell, don't then," Doyle said. She let her boots slide to the floor. "I'm a female pilot in a sky raining testosterone. Folks don't sugarcoat stuff around here."

"Arbakova is dead," Garcia said. "Murdered."

Doyle folded her hands in her lap. "Does Jimmy know?"

"Not yet. I'm on my way to see him after this. I understand he and Nadia have a relationship."

"Had." Doyle shrugged. "Jimmy broke it off a couple of weeks ago. He said she was starting to see the boogey man. . . . Guess she had a right to."

"Did she ever talk to you about that?"

Doyle shook her head, staring off into space. "The three of us went to dinner maybe three or four times. She was always the quiet one. Jimmy and I did most of the talking."

Garcia glanced down at her notes. "Jimmy is Native American?"

"Northern Cheyenne," Doyle said. "My parents adopted him when he was eleven. I was nearly seventeen. Mother and Daddy died in a car wreck about six months later."

"Tragic." Garcia gasped.

"You're tellin' me," Doyle said. "The poor kid comes to us as an orphan, then we both end up parentless. I took care of him as best I could. I made sure he got through junior high and high school while I went to college on an ROTC scholarship."

"Did you ever meet any of his Native relatives? Cousins, aunts, uncles?"

"Yeah," Doyle said, tapping a pencil on the desk. "He had an aunt and uncle on the res in Montana. Anyhow, they couldn't take care of him."

"Can you give me their names?"

"I don't remember, but I can find out. I don't know if they're even still alive."

The major suddenly leaned across her desk, cobalt eyes focusing sharply on Garcia. "And that all leads me back to my original question. I'm smart enough to know the CIA doesn't investigate the murder of a Secret Service agent. Is my baby brother mixed up in something he shouldn't be?"

"I don't know yet," Garcia answered honestly. "Does the name Tom Haddad mean anything to you?"

"Nope," Doyle said, leaning back again, arms on the rests of her chair like a queen on a throne. "Sounds Arab."

"He used to be the CIA station chief in Cairo." She watched Doyle's eyes for any sign of a reaction. "His body was found with Ms. Arbakova."

"Listen, Ms. Garcia. . . ." Doyle released a long sigh. "I fly fighter jets for a living so I'll leave the spy-hunting shit to you. But no matter what he tells you, this is gonna be awful hard on Jimmy. He's always been a little on the sullen side. All he ever wanted to do was guard the president of the United States. Used to talk about it nonstop when he was a kid. To tell you the truth, I'm surprised the Secret Service even lets him near the veep. He can be kind of a downer to be around. Not a big one to demonstrate emotion. Neither was Nadia for that matter. Guess that's a side effect from being orphaned young."

"Wait a minute." Garcia sat up straight. "Arbakova was an orphan too?"

"Raised by a couple of older sisters." Tara Doyle gave a quiet little chuckle. "I guess Jimmy has an excuse to be sullen though. He gets himself orphaned twice—and then he has to be raised by the queen of West Texas bitches. Speaking of that, I have to get my bird ready for a flight. Are we done?"

Ronnie shut her notebook. "For now."

Tara Doyle shut the door behind the nosy CIA agent and took a cell phone from the pocket of her flight suit. She pressed the second number on her speed dial list.

"Jimmy?"

"Hey, sis. What's up?"

"Listen to me," Tara said. "I don't know what the hell you're mixed up in, but a lady CIA agent just came by to see me."

There was a long silence on the line. "And?"

"Nadia's dead."

"That's not funny." Jimmy's voice turned ice cold.

"I'm not screwin' with you. This woman is asking a lot of questions. You sure there's not something you want to tell me?"

"Are you serious? Nadia's dead? How?"

"She didn't say," Tara sighed. "Listen, Jimmy. I told her I'd met your aunt and uncle from the reservation in Montana."

"Okay."

"You understand what I mean?" Tara said. "When they come to talk to you, you just say you don't remember any family but you've heard me talk about them. I'm afraid this could screw up your career if you're not careful."

"Understood," Jimmy said. "Thanks for lookin' out for me."

"Listen," Tara said. "I gotta go. I'm sorry about Nadia."

"Me too," Jimmy said. It was difficult for her to read his voice. "Me too."

CHAPTER EIGHTEEN

U.S. Naval Observatory
Washington

Quinn sat on the vice president's porch and waited quietly. Where others might feel the overwhelming need to ask questions during an interview, he let silence do much of his work for him. Garcia was in the chair next to him, leaning forward, but following his lead. Thibodaux stood back, listening but giving the group some space.

James "Jimmy" Doyle stared out over the rolling green lawn as if in a trance. He wasn't a tall man, but what there was of him was built like a tree trunk. He had the slightly narrow eyes and Asiatic look of a Native American.

"You'll find out soon enough. . . ." Broad shoulders rose and fell with calculated breaths. "But she was starting to get really paranoid. I told her she was going to get fired. . . . I guess it got her killed."

Doyle had hung his jacket over the back of the white

wicker chair exposing his sidearm, expandable baton, handcuffs, and radio. His shirttail had come untucked and his dark tie hung loose and cocked to one side, like a silk noose around his muscular neck.

Palmer had called ahead to Sonny Vindetti, the special agent in charge of the VP's protection detail, to let him know one of his agents was about to get what might turn out to be devastating news. Nancy Hughes, the vice president's wife, had been delivering a tray of cookies to the small cottage below the residence that acted as the Secret Service security office. She'd seen the look on Vindetti's face when the call came in and demanded to know what was going on. It was a standing opinion with most detail agents that snowy-haired Mrs. Hughes was the best suited of anyone in the United States to run the country if anything ever happened to the president. She had the brains, the fortitude, and, coming from the old money of a father in the West Texas oil business, the family name to make her political royalty.

As Robert Hughes was happy to point out in the self-deprecating way that had served him so well, he was "no rocket surgeon, but he was, at least, smart enough to marry the right gal." Nancy could be as unforgiving as a concrete wall if she felt she was being wronged, but she cared about her agents as if they were her own children. The VP's code name was *Pilot*. Hers was *Peregrine*, but the Secret Service satellite detail that saw to her security referred to her as *Mother Hen*.

Quinn, Thibodaux, and Garcia had arrived at roughly the same time. Peregrine had met them at the driveway and ushered them up her steps, insisting Special Agent

Doyle hear the news from the comfort of her front porch. She personally brought him a glass of lemonade and a box of tissues.

He hardly even blinked at the news. His angular jaw tensed; he stared a thousand-yard stare.

"Tell us about her theories," Quinn said.

"That's the thing. I don't know. She was acting crazy, but I didn't know why. She started sleeping with a gun under her pillow, said she didn't know who to trust." Doyle rubbed a hand over a thick head of black hair. "I told her she needed to get some help and she went off on me."

Quinn's eyes shot to Garcia, then back to the stoic young agent. "But you have no idea who might have wanted to kill her?"

They'd agreed before leaving Rockville he'd lead the discussion. An interview would work better than a dog-pile interrogation—and Nancy Hughes would likely peck the eyes out of anyone she thought was bullying one of *her* agents.

Doyle gazed out over the hedges and flower beds of the manicured lawn. "Nadia was an agent and all, but she just did intel. . . . Paranoid or not, nobody should have wanted to hurt her." A single tear, the first sign of real emotion, pooled in the corner of Doyle's eye. He sniffed, using the back of his forearm to dab at his nose.

Quinn nodded to himself. One of the first rules of an interview was not to believe in tears unless the snot was flowing.

Garcia slid forward in her chair, leaning in slightly. "Do you remember what you talked about last?"

Doyle shrugged. "No . . ."

Good answer, Quinn thought. People who remembered too much were rehearsed—and lying.

"You know a man named Tom Haddad?"

"No," Doyle said. "Do you think he killed her?"

"We can't give you details at this point," Quinn said. "But whoever killed her probably killed him as well."

Doyle suddenly sat up and straightened his tie. "I need to get back to work. My boss wants to see me after this."

Mrs. Hughes cleared her throat and peered over the top of gold reading glasses, a clear sign that the interview should wind down.

Quinn got to his feet and stuck out his hand. "I'm sorry for your loss, Agent Doyle." He never carried business cards, so he handed his Moleskine notebook to Garcia so she could write down her contact numbers. When she was finished, she tore out the page and handed it to Doyle, who shuffled off toward the detached security office as if he was walking to the gallows.

CHAPTER NINETEEN

A stone's throw from the Secret Service motorcade that was always staged and ready to go in the event of an emergency, Ronnie Garcia leaned on the open door of her Impala. Thibodaux stood beside his motorcycle, fiddling with the strap on his helmet. Quinn had hung back to make a quick call from the Secret Service office landline.

"Can I ask you something?" Garcia said to Thibodaux, chin resting on the back of her hand.

The hulking Marine glanced up, nodding slightly before turning his attention back to the inside of his helmet. A robin hopped in the grassy shadows behind him.

"Knock yourself out."

"Director Ross told me you and Quinn haven't been working together much more than a couple of months. Seems to me like you've been friends forever. . . ."

"I assume you've never been in the military?"

"That's true." Ronnie felt a pang of regret for having to answer that way.

"Well, beb, you get a different sort of relationship with someone who you know you can count on—someone who's spilled blood to save your life. . . ."

Quinn came down the hill a moment later. Garcia found herself happy to see him, but disappointed that her conversation about him had come to a stop.

"Palmer wants us to get together in the morning and compare notes without the Bureau and Agency big dogs in the mix." Quinn looked at Garcia. "He'd like you there as well."

"Sounds good." She looked at her watch. "Not much more to do this evening. You guys ever eat?"

Thibodaux slid into his black leather jacket and checked his watch. "Well, hell, but don't a kidnap attempt and a double bloody murder make the day just zip by," he said. "I got a Lamaze class with my child bride in an hour and a half. . . ."

"Are you kidding me?" Quinn turned to Garcia, chuckling under his breath. "The guy's got six sons and he still has to go to classes. . . ."

"I know. Don't rub it in." Thibodaux hung his head like a dejected schoolboy. "I expect it's her way of making sure I come home for more than just the fun part of the process."

"Sounds like a smart girl," Garcia said. "How about you, Agent Quinn?"

"I could eat," he said. "But lose the Agent stuff. Plain old Quinn is just fine—or Jericho."

"Bueno." She smiled broadly, showing a mouthful of gorgeous teeth, startlingly white in contrast to her coffee-and-cream complexion. "If you like Cuban, I know a great place in Silver Springs. Best *moros y cristianos* this side of Havana. It's not too far from here."

"I suppose I'm game." Quinn shrugged, remembering what Kim had told him*: We're divorced. Start acting like it.*

Garcia nodded at his BMW. "I assume that's got a GPS."

Quinn tapped his helmet with an open palm. "I'll keep up."

"Cubano's. Tucked in just off Georgia Ave." She gave him the address. "I'll go ahead and get us a table." Apparently not one to futz around once a decision was made, Garcia shut her door and tore down the circle drive, leaving a whirlwind of fall leaves in the wake of her tires.

Thibodaux sauntered over to Quinn like an uncle bearing advice. He rested a broad hand on the smaller man's shoulder. "You mind yourself now, bro," he said as both men gazed down the road after the departing Veronica Garcia. "Take it from me—and I'm an expert on such things—that gal will suck a hickey on your soul before you can say batshit."

Quinn raised a wary eye. He wanted to change the subject so he reminded the big Marine of the tight rein Mrs. Thibodaux had on his language. "We're getting near the end of the month, Jacques—Camille only gives you five non-Bible curse words every thirty days. I'm no religious scholar, but I'm pretty sure *batshit* doesn't make the cut for the Good Book."

"You just watch yourself, l'ami." Thibodaux threw a thick leg across his bike. He turned the key, paused a moment to let the electronics run through their cycle. "I have to go meet Cornmeal at that baby-birthin' class, but you listen to me. I know a thing or two about bad women. I'm tellin' you, that sexpot Cuban is one bad *jolie fille*."

"Don't be such a pessimist, Jacques," Quinn said.

Helmet visor flipped skyward, Thibodaux looked Quinn square in the eye. "Oh, I'm being optimistic, brother. A bad woman can be a mighty good find." He pressed the start button and the GS growled to life. The opposing cylinders ripped happily as he gunned the throttle with a toothy grin. "I'm just not sure you're ready for such heady doin's."

Four blocks away, Nona Schmidt slouched behind the wheel of a faded maroon Nissan Sentra parked under a row of trees. She watched in disgust as a pompous-looking blond man in a herringbone jacket came down the white concrete side steps of the Norwegian Embassy to let his little fuzz-ball dog take a dump across the sidewalk, next to the street. Bastard. All that sovereign ground of Norway just inside the ivy-covered wall and he had to let his stupid dog tootle over to crap in America. Schmidt thought about getting out and hitting him in the head with the ball-peen hammer on the floorboard but decided against it, reminding herself that she had more important duties across the street. Her blue eyes homed in on the twin gates leading out of the Naval Observatory.

A shiny black Impala made the slow S turns around the concrete exit bollards, then stopped, waiting for traffic. The dark woman whom they'd seen earlier with Quinn was driving. To Nona's horror, she came straight across Massachusetts Avenue.

The sight of the woman brought on a wave of instant panic. No one had expected they would come out this way. They'd gone into the Observatory grounds on the Georgetown side. That's the way they were supposed to leave.

Nona picked up the radio from the seat between her legs. She wore extra-short cutoff jeans everyone called Daisy Dukes. Her pale thighs were bare—and now covered in gooseflesh that made the wispy blond hairs on her skin stand on end from worry. She turned the radio speaker-side up but kept it low in her lap and out of sight the way her boyfriend Scott had taught her. He was in the National Guard and knew everything about tactics. Her daddy liked him for that at least.

"I think they may be coming this way," she hissed, trying to keep her lips as still as she could, looking like a bad ventriloquist. "The spic lady in the Impala just drove by me, going"—she consulted the map in the seat beside her—"north."

"Sit tight and wait for the motorcycles," her brother, Bobby, came back. He was set up with Scott in the parking lot of the Whole Foods Market on the opposite side of the circle, a half mile away. "If you see them, sing out and we'll come runnin'. You stick close, but don't let 'em see you. Remember what those bastards did to Uncle Walt."

Nona nodded into the radio, then, remembering she had to speak out loud said: "okay . . . roger . . ." She was every inch the patriot but this tactical stuff gave her the heebie-jeebies.

Sitting off Embassy Row, where every other building belonged to some country besides America, filled her with righteous indignation. The Embassy of Finland was a half a block to her left. Azerbaijan was behind her. Nona didn't know if Azerbaijan was the good guys or the bad guys, but it pissed her off that they had their own little piece of sovereign real estate smack in the middle of the U.S.A. Iraq, Iran, Belgium, and even the papist Vatican had little cancerous toeholds. It made her sick.

American to the bone, she even hated driving the Jap car, but Scott had reminded her of the need for operational security. They had to blend in driving around D.C. She thought it an awful thing how in the nation's capital, you had to drive a foreign job not to stick out. Her brother's 1981 Ford Bronco, designed and built in the good old U.S.A.—now that was a truck. She drummed both hands on the wheel, wishing she was in the Bronco—

The unmistakable roar of an approaching motorcycle made her wish she was back at the safety of their little compound in Martinsburg. An instant later, she watched a slender man in a black leather suit straddling a silver-gray BMW wind his way through the zigzag exit barricades from the Observatory grounds. The man wore a gunmetal helmet and rode the bike in the easy, self-assured manner that could only belong to Jericho Quinn.

Nona sat transfixed for a moment, eyes marveling at the fluid grace of the menacing bike as it leaned this way and that going around the concrete blocks. It reminded her of a dancing horse she'd seen once at a rodeo.

She'd seen a photograph of Quinn. The man's gaunt looks and that dark, unshaven face made her go all melty inside. She'd read of IRA women running honey traps—luring young British soldiers into their homes for sex so they could be ambushed and have holes drilled into their knees by other faithful Irishmen. Nona had earned a slap from her daddy at suggesting she might try such a thing with Quinn.

And now he was riding his motorcycle directly toward her.

Her brother beat her to the radio.

"We got the big guy coming out of the gate now on our side. Looks like he's alone."

Nona chewed on her bottom lip, twisting and tugging at a curl of honey-colored hair. She knew she would have to follow until the others caught up.

"Qu . . . the other one just came out this way." She cussed herself for almost using Quinn's name over the radio. Scott had warned against that.

"Got it." Bobby's voice twanged with excitement. "We're on our way. Don't let that son of a bitch outta your sight."

Nona sank back in her seat trying her best to look invisible as the bike rumbled past her. When it was almost to the end of the next block, she made a quick, three-point turn like Scott had taught her and fell in behind. It was up to her, and though the thought made her shake so badly she could hardly keep a grip on the wheel, her face flushed with the pride of being a part of something so important. This time wouldn't turn out like the screwup at the gas station. If they couldn't capture Jericho Quinn, they would kill him.

Hunky or not, the country could use one less traitor.

CHAPTER TWENTY

Nancy Hughes couldn't help thinking that the quicker she got Jolene married to Garrett Filson, the quicker the two lovebirds could get around to the business of giving her grandbabies. She often said she was born to be a grandmother. Her naturally red hair had gone snow white about the time she turned fifty. And she certainly preferred the honesty of children over the adults in Washington. Jolene had come along late in life as it was, when the Hugheses had been married almost ten years. Then she'd taken a sabbatical from college for a three-year stint in the Peace Corps. At twenty-seven, the girl had waited long enough—and so had Nancy.

Hughes sat in a wicker chair on the long front porch of the vice-presidential residence, sipping her sweet tea and looking over the park-like lawns of the Naval Observatory. The house was nice enough, but it was a bit of a step down from their home back in Dallas.

Nancy Hughes had made a solemn vow to herself that—except for the mandated security detail—Jolene's wedding would not cost the American taxpayers a dime. Besides, she'd told her daughter, the taxpayer couldn't afford the kind of wedding she wanted. That had to come from their considerable family war chest.

She leaned back and put her feet up on a wicker ottoman that matched her chair. This wedding had monopolized so much of her time for so long—and now it was almost on top of her. So, so much to get done, and there was so little time to do it. This wedding was a gift to her daughter—and herself. It was the wedding she'd never gotten.

Ginormous, Garrett called it. . . .

The door opened behind her and she heard the heavy footfalls of her personal secretary, Gail Peterson. Nancy found it amazing that a woman barely five feet tall and the weight of a postage stamp could shake the entire house when she walked.

"Excuse me, ma'am," Gail said in her syrupy East Texas drawl. She waited to go further until given leave to do so.

Apart from her stomping around and overly timid nature, Gail was a fabulous secretary. Frumpy polyester suits and hair dyed a faded shade of blond, she'd worked for the family in one capacity or another for over thirty years.

"Have a seat, Gail," Nancy said. "I need someone to talk to anyhow."

"Oh, no, ma'am," Gail said, a little catch in her throat.

It was then Nancy looked up to see her red eyes. She'd been crying. Nancy moved to the ottoman and patted the seat where she'd been sitting. "Please. I insist."

Gail complied. "I just talked to her earlier this week. . . ." She broke into a series of ragged sobs, drawing a crumpled tissue from the cuff of her blouse to dab her eyes. "The poor thing's background clearance just came through and I was just fixin' to call her in when I heard. . . ."

More sobs.

Nancy bit her tongue. She patted Gail's knee. "Heard what? Whose background?"

"I'm so sorry." Gail dabbed at her nose with the tissue. "I saw those agents here and I thought they told you. I thought you knew already. . . ."

Nancy closed her eyes, praying for patience. "Told me what, dear?"

"The assistant . . . we hired to help with the last . . . minute . . . wedding stuff . . ." Gail began to weep as if a dam had broken inside her. Her words were punctuated by tremulous gasps for air. "Grace Smallwood . . . got stung by a bee . . . and now she's dead. . . ."

Chapter Twenty-one

Quinn was all too familiar with the road between the Naval Observatory and Silver Springs. The Army's Military Amputee Training Center was located off the same road at Walter Reed Hospital. He'd visited far too many of his friends there during their rehab. Riding down the quiet, park-like streets, he could smell the odors of antiseptic and adhesive tape common to amputee wards.

The night before his first deployment, Kim had rolled over in their bed to face him, tears streaking her face. They'd had dinner with a classmate from the Air Force Special Operations Indoc class. The poor guy had just come back from Iraq with a stump instead of a left hand. In hindsight, the dinner had probably been a mistake, but what do you say? *Hey, bud, we can't go out to eat with you because I'm about to deploy and your hook would scare the crap out of my wife. . . .*

Nobody deserved that.

The Bluetooth inside his helmet gave a soft chirp,

barely audible over the wind whirring through his half-open face shield. He tapped the side of his helmet.

"Quinn."

"Daddy . . ." It was Mattie. Her voice was drawn, tired like a frayed cord.

Quinn suddenly felt dizzy. He let off the throttle and coasted into a parking area along Rock Creek littered with fall leaves.

Two blocks behind Quinn, Nona Schmidt's chest tightened. She tapped the brakes on the maroon Nissan. "He's stopping!" she barked into the radio, forgetting to keep it in her lap and out of sight. "I'm almost on top of him. What should I do?"

"Just drive on by and find a place up the road to stop," her brother said. "Play it cool and pull over at the next parking area. We're less than three miles back."

Nona found it impossible to keep her eyes off Quinn as she sped by, faster than she probably should have.

"He's all by himself at the turnout," she spoke into the radio.

"Good," Bobby came back. Nona could hear the engine of their van roaring in the background. "We'll take him where he sits."

"What's wrong? Are you okay, sweetie?" Quinn watched a maroon Sentra drive by with a wild-eyed blonde behind the wheel.

"We're fine, Daddy. Mama says to tell you hello."

Quinn closed his eyes and sighed. "I sorta thought she was mad at me."

"She is." Mattie giggled. "Way, way mad. But I'm not, so she said I could call you." Her voice grew softer. "She says you're not coming home for a while."

Quinn had taken fists to the nose that hurt less. For a moment, his throat was too tight to speak. He slumped forward, resting on the handlebars. "Yeah," he said. "I have some important things to take care of at work. . . ."

"Important like those men who shot Miss Suzette?"

"Yeah," he sighed. "Kind of like that." She was awfully smart for a six-year-old.

"Okaaaay," she said, putting on her mosquito-whine. "As long as it's that kind of important."

"Can I talk to Mom?"

"She says she's busy."

"What's she doing?"

Mattie giggled again. "She's busy staring at me."

"Okay," Quinn said. "Tell her hi for me."

"Miss you, Daddy. You're my besty. . . ."

Quinn ended the call and sat, thinking. In the past when Mattie called, he'd suspected Kim may have put her up to it. Not this time. Watching your daughter snatched off the stage was bad enough. And then having your ex-husband literally butcher someone in your lap, it was enough to make anyone snap.

He'd seen the look in her eyes—a resolve stronger than he'd ever seen before. Maybe their marriage really was over. . . .

Quinn started the bike and pulled back onto the empty road. He tried to press the thoughts of such finality from his mind, thinking instead of Veronica Garcia as he leaned the growling GS into a series of smooth S turns along Rock Creek Park.

Though new to the anti-terrorism business, the Cuban woman understood very well what he was doing. The woman had a look deep in the crystalline amber of her eyes that at once startled and intrigued him. He'd caught a glimpse of it the moment they'd first met at Arbakova's home, and then saw again during the interview with Jimmy Doyle.

Outwardly, she was cordial enough, knew the right things to say and the right moments to say them. She was intelligent enough to keep up her end of the social contract when it came to niceties—but deep down, in a part of her brain most people don't like to acknowledge, there was a darkness—a darkness that made her an extremely dangerous human being.

Quinn knew that darkness all too well. He saw it every day when he looked in the mirror.

"He's moving again," Nona Schmidt whispered, half relieved that they weren't taking him on the road.

"Don't lose him," Bobby said, agitation buzzing in his voice. "We're nearly there. We'll get him when he stops again."

Chapter Twenty-two

Quinn had never eaten at Cubano's, but the heads-up display on the GPS inside his helmet visor brought him in like a guided missile. His stomach growled louder than his motorcycle by the time he made the turn off Georgia Avenue. It was a popular place and he had to park the bike halfway down the street in front of another restaurant. He unzipped the Transit jacket and pulled the tail of his black polo shirt over the Kimber ten-millimeter. Resting in the Galco inside-the-pants holster, the pistol would be invisible to all but the most experienced observer. Temperature-regulated or not, eating supper wearing a leather jacket on the warm fall evening was bound to draw more attention than he wanted. As was his habit, he let his elbow graze the butt of his pistol, reassuring himself. It calmed him to know the gun was there.

Garcia had found a table outside on the raised patio out front, separated from the street by a short rock wall and metal fence. She waved him over, virtually bouncing with excitement at showing off her favorite restaurant.

Quinn caught the eye of a waiter with a thin black mustache and a loose white guayabera shirt as he trotted up the steps. “I’m with the lady over there,” he said, pointing at Garcia with his raised motorcycle helmet.

Pungent smells of garlic and peppers mixed with grilling chicken. The sweet odor of plantain frying in butter enveloped him like the warm, fleshy hug of a buxom aunt.

“Of course, señor,” the waiter said, showing him to the table.

Quinn ordered a Diet Coke and pulled out a chair across from Garcia. To her credit, she’d chosen a table against the outside wall—a wall to protect his back. Kim had always known to give him the “gunfighter seat” when they went out to dinner. She made fun of him, but she did it.

The evening was warm and Garcia’s tan suit jacket was draped over the back of the chair beside her. Black hair hung thick and loose around the shoulders of a sleeveless blouse of iridescent blue. Cloth and curls shone like a butterfly wing in the low rays of an evening sun. She’d taken the time to freshen up with a new coat of plum lipstick. The color was perfectly suited to her caffè latte complexion—a fact not lost on Quinn.

“Sorry it took me so long,” he said, taking in the lay of the land as he sat down.

Nearly every table was taken both on the patio and, from the looks of things through the double picture windows, inside the restaurant as well. An older couple chatted at the table to Quinn's left, closest to the door. Both looked like academics with sensible, stand-around shoes and ratty cotton dress shirts frayed at the collars and cuffs. The slender man spoke to his enraptured female companion in hushed tones about past sailing trips to Havana and how much trouble they would be in if anyone in the U.S. government found out. Just beyond the conspirators, three tables had been pushed together for a birthday party. The blue-haired matron had the seat of honor, surrounded by her large Cuban family.

"Looks like a nice place." Quinn stuffed his Held kangaroo hide gloves inside the Arai. He hung the leather jacket, with Yawaraka-Te inside, over the adjacent chair.

Garcia reached to touch the helmet, running her finger over the crossed war axes dripping candy-apple blood. "Interesting art," she said. "I like."

"Frank Frazetta."

"Ahhh." Garcia's full lips drew back in an easy, plum-colored smile. "The Death Dealer . . ."

"Amazing." Jericho chuckled. "I knew I liked you."

Garcia leaned across the table, folding her hands in front of her breasts as they pressed against the edge. "My father was a toe-the-party-line Russian in Fidel's Cuba. He was supposed to be anti-American in all things—but get this. . . ." She looked to her left and right as if to make sure no one was listening in on her secret. "He taught me to be a closet Molly Hatchet fan. His favorite albums were that one with the Death Dealer. . . . And what was it? There was a guy with a red beard and a bloody axe. . . ."

"*Flirtin' with Disaster*." Quinn shook his head in

disbelief. She was dangerous *and* had good taste in music.

Garcia's eyes played up and down, studying him. "I'll bet you were the kind of kid who had Meat Loaf posters all over your walls. I mean, since you ride and all."

"Would have, but my mom didn't care for the blood-dripping warriors. She drew the line at half-naked women on motorcycles." Quinn sat back in his chair, taking a deep, slow breath.

"I can't imagine someone like you coming from a demure sort of mother," Garcia said, still eying him intently.

"Oh, my mom's an Alaska girl through and through," Quinn said. "She could fillet a halibut, field dress a moose, and birth a baby all the same day—but she's awfully tenderhearted. I supposed that sort of thing skips a generation.

Garcia still leaned forward, pressing against the table. "Mr. Palmer said you were a boxer at the Air Force Academy."

"I dabbled." Quinn shrugged. He would have to talk to Palmer about the depth of information he disclosed. "I did okay."

Garcia wagged her tan finger. "Okay? I hear you won the Cadet Wing Open your senior year and came in second the year before."

Jericho pressed an index finger to his nose, showing the lack of cartilage that went along with repeated blows to the face. "Those statistics are true, but as my kid brother is so fond of pointing out, if you come in second in a boxing tournament, it means you got your ass kicked at least once."

Suddenly uncomfortable with so much personal talk, Quinn cleared his throat and picked up a menu. "So, what's good here? You mentioned something called *moros* and . . ."

"*Moros* and *cristianos*—spiced black beans and rice." Garcia picked up her sunglasses from the table and began to toy with them. Her eyes sparkled with mischief. "Moors and Christians. You know, like black people and white people . . ."

"I'm so hungry a big bowl of that sounds good."

"It's a side dish."

He shut his menu and pushed back from the table. "I need to hit the head. Surprise me. Something spicy sounds good for the main course."

Garcia's full lips parted as if to speak, but in the end she only smiled broadly, keeping her thoughts to herself.

A half a block up the quiet street in the parking spot directly behind Quinn's motorcycle, a windowless white van sat in the evening shadows cast by the Mi Rancho restaurant. Nona Schmidt slouched behind the wheel and watched as her boyfriend, her brother, and her Uncle Frank walked under the blue awning and through the double glass doors into Cubano's. She'd abandoned the Nissan around the corner. Her job was to pull up front with the van when she saw the men drag Quinn outside. She never considered the idea that they wouldn't be able to handle him.

He'd gone in only seconds before. Probably to use the can. The Mexican woman—Scott called her the Spic Chick—still sat at their outside table. She looked like she was his date. Quinn was supposed to be dangerous, but Nona didn't fret over that. She'd seen her boyfriend fight mixed martial arts in Corbin, Kentucky. He'd whipped the everlovin' ass of everyone who came into the octagon—actually broke one guy's arm in four places. He was sure enough capable of beating the crap out of some bike-riding dude who was past his prime.

Nineteen years old, rawboned, and handsome, Scott Brady was tough as they came. And, every bit as important to Nona as his muscles, he had nearly perfect teeth. He'd have no trouble with Jericho Quinn, who, with any luck, would have his pants down when they shot him.

It seemed such a waste to Nona, but after the mess at the gas station, the boys had decided not to bother with a Taser. The plan was for Scott to take out both his knees with a .22 pistol. Scott said if the guy bled to death before they got him back to the compound to interrogate, well, that was his own damn fault.

Nona bit her lip. She hoped it didn't come to that too awful soon. . . .

Chapter Twenty-three

The overpowering scent of hand soap and toilet deodorizer hung in the men's room, where Quinn stood along the side wall at the single urinal. The air conditioner blew full force and condensation beaded on the chilled chrome pipes. His mind was occupied with the pleasant image of Veronica Garcia's purple lipstick. To his right was an empty toilet stall. Behind him and to his left was a double porcelain sink.

The three men filed in one behind the other. They gave off the energy of men in a rush, but had to slow down in the cramped space.

The hair on the back of Quinn's neck stood on end as soon as they came through the door. The one in the lead, a muscular kid in a white T-shirt, was nearly on top of him by the time the door swung shut behind the last man in line. There was no time to go for a weapon.

Sidestepping away from the urinal, Quinn closed the gap on the first attacker. He trapped the kid's wrist with both hands and forced his stainless pistol back against his belly. Keeping his hands centered and low, Quinn lunged forward with the full force of his legs, snapping the wrist and causing the kid's finger to convulse on the trigger. The gunshot was deafening against the steel and tile of the restroom. The kid's eyes went wide, blinking in disbelief at the blossoming red stain on the belly of his T-shirt.

A half second later the next man in line hit Quinn in the side of the head with a staggering left hook. His fist felt like a blow from a chunk of granite. Quinn shoved the bleeding kid out of the way, lunging for but missing the pistol as it clattered to the tile floor.

He kept his feet, throwing up a quick elbow to fend off another powerful hook. This guy was older but must have had some boxing training. He rained down blows as quickly as Quinn could block them. Dazed, Quinn saw nothing but fists, each coming fast on the heels of the last.

Roaring like an enraged bear, Quinn drove forward, shoving the older attacker backwards.

"Get off me, Uncle Frank!" the kid behind him yelled, smashed between the door and his companion.

Quinn pummeled Uncle Frank's midsection, keeping him pressed back against the guy behind him, buying time while his mind went into overdrive. All he needed was a moment to get to his own gun. He was in good enough shape; in most fights, the other guy tired out in a matter of seconds.

This wasn't going to be one of those fights.

Uncle Frank rolled sideways, absorbing Quinn's punches as if they were mosquito bites. Given the fresh opening, the younger man behind rushed forward, reaching with both hands for a takedown. He wasn't near the fighter his Uncle Frank was and Quinn met him with a fierce head butt for his trouble. He bellowed, spewing a spray of blood out the newly formed gap where his nose met his brow.

Uncle Frank tried a snap kick, but Quinn moved just in time, avoiding a crippling blow to the side of his knee. The kick hit him in the thigh, sending a wave of nausea through his gut. He exhaled hard, blocking a haymaker from Frank, while he kicked out to fend off the snot-blowing kid. It was like shooing away gnats inside a closet. No matter what he did, they kept coming.

Ronnie Garcia watched the three men disappear through the front door. The leader, a young man wearing a white T-shirt and faded jeans, carried a folded newspaper. The other two, similarly dressed but with more hair, followed closely on his heels. None of them looked the type to bring their own reading material into a restaurant. There was something about the way the men held their mouths that told her they were up to no good.

She'd spotted the white panel van about the time Quinn went inside. There was a girl behind the wheel, and though Ronnie couldn't make out her features, she felt sure she was involved.

To prove her point, Ronnie stood up from the table. Holding her cell phone to her ear, she pretended to be having an animated conversation and pointed directly at the van.

An instant later, the van's lights came on. Panicked, the girl backed into the car behind her, then sped forward, crashing into Quinn's motorcycle. Beefy as it was, the BMW GS was no match for the heavy van. Metal groaned and sparks flew as she dragged the bike along the pavement, before turning sharply to speed away in the other direction.

Jericho's bike was a twisted heap of metal—but if Garcia was right, that would be the least of his problems.

She reached the front door in three quick bounds. She flung it open to run headlong into their waiter. The tray of Diet Cokes crashed to the ground. He apologized profusely with his words, but his dark eyes cursed Garcia's clumsiness to the last drop of his Latin blood.

She smiled sheepishly, helped him to his feet, and apologized, explaining she had an urgent bathroom emergency. The waiter's glare softened some as she hopped over the puddle of ice and soda.

Never one to shy away from action, Ronnie bent quickly to draw the tiny Kahr PM nine-millimeter from the sheepskin holster inside her left ankle. She paused briefly in the dim alcove outside the men's room. Greeted by the heavy thuds of a fight in progress, she tucked the pistol close to her side, and shouldered open the door.

Something heavy hit Quinn in the back of the head just as he popped Uncle Frank in the jaw with an elbow cross.

Quinn staggered, sickened from the blow, fighting to keep on his feet. He grabbed Frank's shoulders and drove a knee repeatedly into the man's groin as a surge of adrenaline chased away his nausea. He spun before the snot blower could hit him again, shoving the older man into his companion.

As if revitalized by some voodoo zombie spell, Frank sprang back into action immediately, soaking up everything Quinn could inflict.

"I'm about sick of this shit," the kid said, pulling a black pistol from the waistband of his pants. "Get out of the way, Uncle Frank. We don't need to talk to him th—"

Ronnie Garcia exploded through the bathroom door. She took a split second to survey the situation, and then put two quick rounds in the kid's chest.

Distracted, Frank's eyes left Quinn long enough to allow him to draw his Kimber. Cursing under his breath, the older man lunged for the gun on the floor beside his dying nephew as Quinn shot him.

Garcia kicked the pistol away and played her own gun back and forth, assessing the situation.

All three attackers down, Quinn leaned against the sink, panting. The booming gunfire in the close quarters of the tiled restroom had rendered him momentarily deaf.

When he looked up, Garcia's plum lips made beautiful shapes. He heard no sound but the throbbing whoosh of his own heartbeat.

After a few seconds, he was able to make out partial sentences.

". . . hurt, Jeric . . . get . . . hospital . . ."

The disjointed words slowly began to register in his brain.

He grinned stupidly, feeling a little drunk, and took a moment to study this woman who'd just saved his life. Her face was calm, black hair in perfect order, belying the fact that she'd just shot her fourth man in half as many days. Amber eyes locked on him as she canted her head to one side.

"I'm okay," he said, dabbing at a bloody gash above his brow with the knuckle of the hand that still held his Kimber. He worked his aching jaw back and forth and began to do an assessment to make sure nothing was broken. "I've seen worse." He let go of the sink, felt his knees begin to buckle, and grabbed it again.

"That's hard to believe," Garcia said. She nodded at the three men on the bloody floor. Two were dead and a third was unconscious, blowing pink bubbles out a ragged gap of flesh in the bridge of his nose. The flimsy toilet stall lay smashed into pieces.

"Call Thibodaux," Quinn groaned. "And Palmer . . ."

"I will . . . of course . . ." Garcia's eyes darted from the porcelain urinal to Quinn and back to the urinal again. "But I . . . well . . ." She looked down her nose at his belt with an impish smile. "Looks like you were a little busy when these guys jumped you. You might want to . . . put away your . . . pistol. . . ."

CHAPTER TWENTY-FOUR

Somewhere in Afghanistan

CIA paramilitary officer Karen Hunt choked back a mouthful of bile as consciousness slammed into her like a kick in the head. She fought wave after endless wave of nausea, retching against something warm and coarse. Facedown, she blinked burning eyes and tried to stop the swaying motion in her head. She wondered for a moment if she might be on a boat. There was nothing around her but blackness and searing, bone-numbing pain. Rough cords bit deep into her wrists and ankles. Reality sifted back into her brain like grains of irritating sand. It took several seconds to realize she was on the back of a moving animal. The rough wooden packsaddle—and the slow, lumbering gait of the beast—sawed at the tender flesh of her belly just below her ribs.

A heavy blanket kept out not only light, but any semblance of fresh air. The sour stench of yak dung and wet wool cloyed at her throat. Sickened again, she suddenly realized her gaping mouth was pressed directly against the matted hair of the animal.

By slow degree, voices wormed their way in through the rancid blackness. She could make out the thick, phlegmatic tones of men speaking Tajik. Closely related to Persian, it was the common language of the high mountains of Central Asia. Hunt was fluent in Farsi and Pashto. Tajik was close enough she got the gist of what was going on.

Her captors were jubilant men, gloating as they recounted their recent bravery at attacking Outpost Bullwhip. It didn't seem to bother them that a handful of ragtag Americans had killed over eighty of them. They praised fallen brothers who had died as martyrs in the holy fight, and cursed the dead Americans to roast in eternal fire.

Memories of the battle and of Lt. Nelson suddenly rushed back into Hunt's fevered mind. She shivered when she recalled the strange little boy who loved chocolate and smiled ever so sweetly as he spoke of cutting off her head.

The yak stopped abruptly, its bony spine heaving with exaggerated breaths. Hunt tried to use the time to readjust but was strapped down too tightly. She was baggage and nothing else. Her hands and the backs of her calves, which must have extended beyond the coverage of the blanket, were numb with cold and lack of circulation. Karen found that if she strained her neck and pressed her cheek against the side of the beast, she could see a stone-covered path and a splatter of green manure beside a cloven black hoof.

Maybe she was dead and being carted off to hell by

the devil himself. It would stand to reason . . . if the devil spoke Tajik.

"Cut deep, my brother," a voice said somewhere to her right. "We reach Big Headache pass by nightfall. . . ."

A donkey suddenly filled the air with sorrowful braying. Years before, when Karen had first visited the mountains of the Hindu Kush, she'd seen a string of forlorn pack animals with their nostrils slit up each side in a cruel gash. Her father had explained the men who traveled with their pack trains in the highest passes often cut their animals like this. They believed it would help the beasts draw more air in this place they called the Roof of the World.

Karen groaned when the yak lurched forward again, stumbling into a bone-jarring gait. The air grew colder as they climbed and she found herself grateful for the musky layer of warm air that surrounded the animal under the coarse blanket.

When the trail became particularly steep and the yak slowed to catch its breath or pick sure footing, the man walking behind let fly a stream of oaths and curses. His heavy stick struck Karen in the spine as often as it did the yak.

Unfazed, the weary animal continued on, plodding forward at exactly the same gate as before. It had been beaten many times before. She knew her beatings were just beginning.

An eternity later, the yak stopped again, this time on command. Karen strained her ears as shuffling footsteps approached. She heard the thump and scratch of fingers manipulating the cords on the packsaddle.

A sudden blast of light and cold washed over her as the covering was jerked away.

Rough hands tore at the ropes across her back and thighs. At first she thought they'd stopped to give her a break, but one look at these men told her they were not the sort to waste time giving her a pit stop. They'd only paused along the scant excuse for a mountain trial to readjust the saddles before starting a major uphill push.

Towering walls of craggy stone rose into the gray sky. The thin ribbon of trail ahead, wet with heavy fog, wound its way upward disappearing into the same clouds.

Gray sky, gray rock, gray void.

Hunt squinted at the silhouette in a black turban towering over her. The smell of the yak was suddenly a bittersweet memory compared to the foul stench of the man. Only hours before, in the relative safety of Camp Bullwhip, she had joked about the "sweaty-outhouse" smell of insurgents. Now, it made her want to vomit.

As her eyes slowly became accustomed to the light, she could make out the raw, peeling face of her yak driver. He'd been badly burned and wore a rancid bandage that looped over his head and under his chin. The sickening smell came from some form of infection as much as his lack of hygiene. Karen guessed him to be in his late twenties, but he was already missing most of his top teeth.

"*Tik-brik*!" he commanded again in what she realized was English. He wanted her to take a break.

He raised a robed arm and pointed at an outcropping of rocks behind them, along the narrow excuse for a trail. To their right, gray stone rose up for thousands of feet. To their left, the thin band of rubble that passed for a path fell away into a gray nothingness filled with fog and the crash of a river far below.

"You go!" the man ordered again. He carried a roll of pink toilet paper on a leather cord draped over his shoulder. It was a sort of status symbol in a land where many still used a handful of stones to cleanse themselves.

He pointed with his Kalashnikov and tapped the toilet paper with the other hand to get his point across.

The yak heaved a shuddering sigh, relieved to be rid of its load. Hunt began to shiver uncontrollably, blinking to keep her balance on the narrow bit of rock and loose debris. They'd trained her for so many different scenarios back at Camp Perry—but being strapped to a packsaddle wasn't one of them.

She pointed at the toilet paper with a trembling finger. The man shook his head emphatically and shoved her, pointing his rifle at a pile of rocks that was presumably supposed to serve as her outhouse.

There were other men up ahead along the trail with a dozen other yaks and donkeys. Some of the pack animals bristled with guns; others had tarped loads she couldn't identify. The fog and the way the trail curved made it impossible to see more than twenty meters in either direction. She assumed there were even more men around the corner. The ones she could see were similarly dressed to her toilet-paper-wearing tormentor and, she had no doubt, smelled just as disgusting. They ignored her as if she wasn't there, tending to their animals or weapons.

"You make fast!" the blistered insurgent barked as Karen picked her way around the head-high rock pile fifteen feet away. She expected him to follow her, but was relieved when he stayed at his yak.

She had no idea when they'd give her another chance so Karen took the opportunity to try and relieve herself. Her time at Camp Perry—and other, less well-known sites—had trained most of the shyness out of her. More times than she cared to remember, she and the other students had been made to squat on a raised platform with a simple hole cut in the center to "do their business." Such acts had the effect of either stripping away hang-ups about privacy or pressing them so far back into the psyche that they were bound to cause some sort of mental illness in the future. No matter how many times a moderately well-adjusted woman pooped on a tower in front of fifteen classmates, such a delicate act would always be difficult with hateful men standing a few meters away.

Instead of resorting to stones, she ripped off the hip pocket of her BDU pants to clean herself. It was then she realized her captors hadn't done a very good job of searching her.

Folded in her back pocket, sealed in a clear plastic pouch, was a rayon scarf with an American flag printed on the back. On the other side were printed instructions in six of the local languages—Pashto, Arabic, Farsi, Tajik, and Dari—advising the bearer of the scarf that they were entitled to a handsome reward if they assisted the American who owned it. It was her *blood chit*, a token to the local populace that she was worth more alive than dead.

Karen searched the other pockets in her baggy BDU pants until she found the stub of an eyebrow pencil.

Praising herself for a shred of female vanity, she scratched out a hastily planned message.

"Make fast!" her captor chided again, moving close, but not coming around the rocks. It sounded like "*mek-fus.*"

"I'm done," she said in Tajik, hoping the man would revert to his native language. "Just cleaning."

She weighted the scarf down with a heavy rock so it wouldn't blow away, but left the bulk of it to flutter in the mountain breeze.

Hitching up her pants, she stumbled quickly around the rocks, working her way back along the edge of the trail before the stinking yak beater could come around and see her message blowing in the wind.

She climbed back on the yak without being told, biting her lip as her captor lashed down the heavy blanket.

She'd heard stories from local women about slavers. But they mostly preyed on young girls. Hunt was dressed in an American military uniform. That would surely make her worth something to someone. She supposed that was why she was still alive.

She shivered, despite the sickening warmth of the yak, and wondered which would be worse, getting her head cut off or living the rest of her life as someone's slave. All she could do now was pray that they were the last in the pack train and someone friendly—or at least greedy—would find her note.

FRIDAY
September 29

Chapter Twenty-Five

Mt. Vernon, Virginia

Thibodaux's BMW rested on its center stand in front of an eighteenth-century redbrick two-story. Quinn estimated the lot to be over five acres, much of that taken up by a fenced Japanese garden, complete with a gurgling stream, wooden footbridge, and stone Shinto *torii* gates. The nearest home was over a hundred yards away on either side. Thick hedges gave the grounds an added layer of privacy. Lofty oaks and huge silver sycamores threw the driveway into a near constant blanket of cool shade.

A beaked warhorse, the motorcycle was aggressive even in its idleness, coiled as if in anticipation of violent action. Quinn couldn't help but think it looked lonely, though, without his bike next to it. A few feet away, nearer the house's forest-green front door, was a Ducati 848 EVO painted a deep blood red. Thibodaux said it was the color of a Bourbon Street whore's fingernails, but he kept that between himself and Jericho. Shorter and more compact than the BMW, the

Ducati was a superbike—with a race fairing and a stock hundred-and-forty-horse Testastretta engine. With its pointed, upthrust sport-bike tail and humped gas tank, it looked like an angry red wasp. Like its owner, the Ducati was graceful, utilitarian, and dangerous.

Without a bike, Quinn had no reason to wear his riding gear. The black Transit jacket, leather pants, stiff Sidi riding boots, kangaroo-hide gloves, and Arai helmet lay in a forlorn pile near Thibodaux's GS. He wore faded blue jeans, Rockport chukkas, and a gray Under Armour T-shirt that kept him cool in the warm fall weather. Palmer had promised to get him another bike as soon as possible—but it wasn't happening quite soon enough to suit Quinn.

He busied himself by sitting on the curb and beating himself up over his divorce and prolonged separation from his daughter.

"Tell me why we do this again," he said, his voice glum.

" 'Cause we're good at it?" Thibodaux shrugged massive, rounded shoulders as he did a pushup in the gravel to eye the oil sight glass mounted low on the BMW's Boxer engine.

The owner of the red Ducati, Emiko Miyagi—Mrs. Miyagi to her two charges—appeared from around the corner of the house. She padded softly in the afternoon shadows of her crescent driveway as if floating an inch above the ground.

"I believe it is much more than that," she said. "Do you know *Ushirogami wo Hikareru*?"

Quinn stood, giving her a polite bow. "To have the hair on the back of your neck pulled?"

"That is correct," Miyagi said. "But the nuance is

much deeper. It much more correctly means having to follow a certain path but not quite wanting to do so. Devotion to duty often involves such a feeling . . . but, the blade must cut. That is what it is designed for. Is it not?"

"Now . . ." She pursed her lips and stood stoically with her hands clasped in front, a sure indication she was ready to take the conversation somewhere else.

Jericho sighed again, this time in relief.

"Palmer-san believes it is better for you to remain hidden," Miyagi said. She had the body of a gymnast, with short, powerful legs and muscular shoulders that belied the narrowness of her frame. Tan cotton slacks hugged the gentle curve of her hips. A black polo shirt hid a mysterious tattoo above her right breast, the edge of which was only partly visible, and completely unidentifiable, during their daily yoga lessons. Thibodaux thought it was some kind of snake. Jericho didn't hazard a guess. The three had just finished a rigorous two-hour session of cardio and yoga—a great deal of which involved head-low positions like *Sirsasana*, a forearm headstand that Miyagi appeared to favor over all other postures. She assured Quinn it would help heal the injuries he'd received in the men's room at Cubano's. Amazingly, she'd been right. After a few minutes of yoga, the full-bore thumper he'd woken up with had quieted to little more than a dull throb behind his left eye.

The men had it on good authority from Win Palmer; Emiko Miyagi was not a person to bet against in a fight. Quinn had yet to see her in any sort of action other than a yoga headstand, but he'd been around enough dangerous people to know this woman had a certain degree of what soldiers called "innate badassitude." She would not do to have as an enemy.

Luckily for Quinn, she seemed to like him. Poor Jacques Thibodaux was not so fortunate.

She continued her instructions. With Mrs. Miyagi, life was a lesson, and she was the teacher. "We have routed all your phones and the email accounts you provided us through a series of remote computers in vacant office space located in three states—all rented with cash."

Her lips turned up in just the hint of a sneer at the towering Cajun. "I have routed your phones through separate locations so those who wish to harm Quinn-san do not trace him back through you. . . ."

"Of course you did." Thibodaux shrugged, giving Jericho an I-told-you-so look. "No need to protect me. Just keep me from getting Quinn killed—"

"That is correct," the stoic woman said. She handed each of them a silver thumb drive Quinn recognized as an IronKey. "Please use this when you log on to any computer. It will hide your IP address and allow you to work on the Internet anonymously. Additionally, any intelligence you are able to collect will be protected with multiple layers of security." She glared hard at Thibodaux, turning her head to one side as if explaining something to an obstinate child. "If you input the wrong password ten times, the inside of the drive will be destroyed. There is no way to recover it."

"Noted," the Cajun said. He'd learned better than to argue with Miyagi.

"Now, I have something for you." She reached for a paper shopping bag behind the red Ducati.

"You mean for Quinn." Thibodaux couldn't help himself. He was only half joking. "I don't get anything, right?"

"Correct again," Miyagi said with a half bow. But for the mischievous glint in her black eyes, her expression was deadpan. "Perhaps when your life is in danger by unknown foes, Palmer-san will direct me to issue you such equipment."

Quinn couldn't help but chuckle. Though she had the apparent wisdom of a woman twice his age, her smooth skin and youthful physical ability suggested Emiko Miyagi was no more than forty. Maybe it was because he spoke Japanese, but for some reason, this mysterious, badass warrior woman had taken to him. For whatever reason, she bristled like a porcupine when Thibodaux got near her.

She held a polished wooden box in front of her, offering it to Quinn with outstretched hands. "Generally speaking, we will be able to track your whereabouts through your secure BlackBerry."

She motioned for him to open the gift with a half bow. The tiniest glint of excitement sparkled in her eyes.

"A Breitling Emergency," she said, rocking slightly in satisfaction.

Thibodaux rolled his eyes, but she appeared to ignore him.

Quinn lifted the stainless-steel timepiece out of the blue velvet lining. It was heavy, thicker than three silver dollars, with two crowns on the side, one larger and located just below the other on a cylindrical metal tube built into the watch in the six o'clock position. He'd known guys in his squadron at the Air Force Academy who'd purchased such "babe-gettin' " watches to use as conversation pieces in bars.

"I'm assuming you could triangulate on me if I were to unscrew this and pull out the wire antenna." He held up the watch and touched the lower crown.

"Exactly." Mrs. Miyagi smiled, showing perfectly white teeth. "But there is much more to it than that."

The Bluetooth device in her ear began to flash. She touched it and turned half away before speaking.

"*Moshi*, *moshi*," she said. Answering the phone was one of the few times she consistently spoke Japanese. She nodded silently, listening. "Of course," she said at length. "Right away." She tapped the earbud again to end the call.

"Palmer-san wants you both to meet him at the Alexandria office." Her voice was absent any trace of an accent.

Quinn nodded. He slipped off his comfortable TAG Heuer Aqua Racer and latched the heavy Breitling around his wrist.

"Seriously?" Thibodaux's mouth gaped open. "I don't get an electronic emergency watch?"

Mrs. Miyagi groaned as if having to explain a simple truth to a small child. "No, Thibodaux-san, you do not." She held a hand out toward Quinn, slowly opening her fist to reveal a set of keys. "In the meantime, you will need a bike. Please, take the Ducati . . . on loan. Careful though. She can reach ninety miles an hour in five seconds."

Chapter Twenty-six

Fort McNair
Washington

Congressman Drake's list had sent a shock wave through the military. Ranking officers from each branch had appeared on the list—and anyone who looked or acted out of place fell under immediate scrutiny from peers and superiors alike. All branches of the service took on an immediate shroud of darkness and mistrust reminiscent of Cold War Europe and the East German Stasi. Informants sat behind every desk. Old scores begged to be settled.

No one trusted anyone else.

Lieutenant Colonel Dane Fargo stood with both hands planted on the gray military desk, reading the top folder in the stack of file folders before him. The file, thick and dog-eared, literally made him want to sing. He'd cashed in every favor, called in every debt, and used the last drop of his political capital, but he'd gotten one more name added to Congressman Drake's list.

He knew in his heart that Jericho Quinn should have been on the list from the beginning. The man was too good to be true. He spoke Chinese like a native and his Arabic was flawless. Months of his life were completely unaccounted for. Even his dark complexion and heavy black stubble suggested he was of foreign blood.

Even now, when the veracity of all those on the list was in question, Jericho Quinn had gone completely underground. When they did find him, Fargo knew he'd be a tough nut to crack. But that would be the most enjoyable part of the process.

Fargo had traded his customary camouflage battle dress uniform for a dark blue business suit that hung awkwardly off sloping shoulders. A white shirt gaped around his neck as if he were a child wearing his daddy's clothes. Ill-fitting suit or not, Fargo couldn't help but feel that his time had finally come.

Congressman Drake's list of possible subversives had caused no small stir among the halls of government. Men and women formerly trusted as golden children by their superiors—civilians and soldiers alike—found themselves under deep suspicion. Men like Fargo with rock-solid backgrounds, who also happened to have a close relation in the U.S. Congress, had finally been given the opportunity to rise to the top of their respective heaps.

When he'd heard about the massive, government-wide vetting process, he'd called his uncle the congressman right away. A few handshakes and backroom deals later and Lt. Colonel Fargo had been given a special team of investigators stationed at Fort Lesley J. McNair along the Potomac River. It was altogether fitting, Fargo thought, that his task force was headquartered on the very same spot where Mary Surratt and her coconspirators were hanged for their part in the plot to assassinate Abraham Lincoln.

In reality, the men on his team made the flesh on the back of his neck crawl. Trained at Fort Huachuca at the U.S. Army's Interrogator School, these four were Senior Echoes, an unofficial subunit within the Five Hundredth Military Intelligence Group that called themselves the Boom Squad.

Military interrogators often referred to themselves as Echoes. Fargo needed rogues, men willing to bend the rules of civility. His rank and the suffocating air of fear that had enveloped the nation allowed him to handpick the harshest men from these ranks, men who would do the hard things no one talked about at parties. Self-taught in the tactics of the 1960s-era heavy-handed KUBARK CIA Interrogation Manual, all were NCOs, and none, as far as Fargo could tell, were used to taking any sort of order from a superior officer. They were perfect for what Fargo had in mind.

Psychology mixed with a liberal amount of thumbscrews was par for the course with these men. Spanish inquisitors had nothing on them. Pig-eyed and emotionless, they were extremely talented at what they did. A simple stare from any of them caused Fargo's flesh to crawl. They were a necessary evil, just the sort of men he would need to capture and interrogate the backstabbing son of a bitch Jericho Quinn.

Fargo relished the control that this newfound fear had given him over his fellow soldiers. He recalled the motto of the Stasi: *Schild und Schwert der Partei—*

Sword and Shield of the Party. He'd been a shield long enough. Being a sword was proving to be much more fun.

If it happened to get messy—so much the better.

Chapter Twenty-seven

Alexandria, Virginia

The national security advisor sat behind an expansive desk. Abnormally clean in Quinn's opinion, the shining mahogany surface was large enough to warrant its own zip code but had little more than a black leather blotter and manila file folder on top. Palmer turned a Montblanc fountain pen back and forth between his fingers, eyes playing between a pair of fifty-two-inch flat-screen monitors to his right that displayed CNN and Fox News. A third screen, separated from the others by an old-fashioned grease board, displayed a Google Earth map focused over the countries in Central Asia.

American paintings by Catlin and Remington hung on the dark cherry-paneled walls. A roughrider bronze identical to the one in the Oval Office sat on a small table to the right of Palmer's desk. Above it, in a framed shadow box, hung a Winchester lever-action rifle. Apart from the flickering glow of the three flat screens, there was no other light in the room. All the masculine art gave it the aura of a perfect man-cave. Just a stone's throw from the Pentagon, few knew of the existence of the office.

Quinn sat opposite Thibodaux on the burgundy leather button-tufted sofa. A rich Moroccan carpet that looked as though it were made from five kinds of chocolate stretched out on the wood floor between the couch and Palmer's desk. On the coffee table were two files containing a wealth of intelligence information on the West Virginia paramilitary group calling itself the Constitutional Sword.

Apart from their white supremacist and anti-Semitic views, the CS portrayed themselves as strict protectors of American virtue and freedom. They were working off Drake's list and had eight of the names, including Quinn's, highlighted. Three of those on their shortlist were missing. One, a DOJ attorney named Rosenthal, had been found that morning shot to death in his Volvo near Dupont Circle.

Now that Bodington's guys at the FBI had climbed up their collective rectums, they offered little threat to anyone but each other. Each CS patriot raced to out-rat their fellow zealots for the best plea deal they could get as the jaws of the Department of Justice slammed tight around them.

The real dangers were the other organizations, yet unknown, who might also have chosen targets on the list.

"Two pivotal calls today." Palmer peered at the men from behind his desk like a high school principal. He had a habit of doling out precious pieces of information one at a time.

"And?" Quinn said. He knew Palmer well enough to prod him a little just to show he was fully involved with the conversation.

"An old yak herder stumbled across one of our blood chits in southern Badakhshan Province. He turned it in to a platoon of U.S. Marines out on patrol."

"Any reports of aircraft going down in that region?" Quinn asked, accustomed to such documents being issued to pilots in the event they were shot down over hostile terrain.

"Bearer wasn't a pilot. Coding on the cloth indicated she's a CIA paramilitary officer attached to FOB Bullwhip in Nuristan."

"Badakhshan is north," Thibodaux mused. Collectively, he and Quinn had spent time in nearly all the *Stans* of the world. "She's on the move, but that's a long ways away from any of our bases."

"If we can believe the writing on the chit, she's a prisoner and heading deeper into the Hindu Kush. The note says there's a boy among her captors who speaks 'perfect English.' "

"No shit?" Thibodaux rubbed his chin. "This just keeps getting worse. You think they're holding an American kid prisoner?"

Palmer shook his head. "She indicates the boy is a hostile."

Jericho moved to the edge of his seat. "You mentioned two calls."

"I did," Palmer said. "SecState called about the time you were getting your ass kicked at Cubano's. You boys have no doubt heard of MSF—*Médecins Sans Frontières*?"

Both men nodded.

"Doctors Without Borders," Thibodaux translated the French.

"Ran across them all the time in Iraq," Quinn said. "I'm pretty sure it was one of them stitched my brother and me up in Senegal a few years back."

Palmer steepled his hands in front of his face. "In any case, Secretary Ryan faxed over a report from a certain doctor with MSF who's done a lot of work in the Hindu Kush. Seems this doctor . . ." Palmer leaned forward to consult the notepad on his desk. "Doctor . . . Deuben has been sending reports to the U.N. about child trafficking in Central Asia for years. The last report says locals tell of a hidden orphanage where the kids all speak English."

"Let me guess," Thibodaux said. "This orphanage is supposed to be somewhere in Badakhshan Province."

Quinn nodded. "Makes sense."

"We've been getting similar reports from Pakistani Intelligence," Palmer said. "But to tell you the truth, they all seemed like fables until recently."

"The same ISI who was helping bin Laden hide out? I'm not sure I'd trust Pakistani intel with directions to the crapper," Thibodaux scoffed.

"Touché." Palmer rubbed his chin, thinking.

"Where is this guy now?" Quinn asked.

"Tending to the health and welfare of prostitutes in Kashgar," Palmer said. "And it's Dr. Gabrielle Deuben, a female, not a guy." He looked directly at Quinn. "Your record says you've spent some time in Kashgar?"

"I have," Quinn said, instantly recalling the frenzied sounds and spicy smells. "Shortly after I graduated from the Academy. Program called Lieutenants Abroad. The place is about as Muslim as you can get in a hardfisted regime like China. It's untamed, like something out of an Indiana Jones movie."

"Yes, it is." Palmer put his feet up on the desk and stared at his ceiling with some obvious memories of his own. "I need you to talk to this doctor—find this orphanage if it exists. I could send in Special Forces, but it's impossible to know who to trust. The Pakistanis warn we could have moles in key positions of the military. POTUS wants this close-hold. The fewer people who know the better until you get your ass back here with some useful intelligence. We could chase our tails hunting sleeper agents all day long."

Palmer stood. "This Drake character is turning into a real pimple on my ass. His witch hunt hearings start tomorrow. People are starting to see ghosts where there aren't any. This is shaping up to be a hell of a lot like the McCarthy era. We have to find out the man behind this and stop him—fast."

"You think this is LaT?" Thibodaux offered. LaT or Lashkar-e-Taiba was a militant Pakistani group rivaling—and some said surpassing—al-Qaeda in danger to the United States. Their name meant Army of the Pure.

"Likely," Palmer mused. "Or some offshoot cell thereof. But while that link matters as far as an investigation goes, this sort of operation is personality driven. There is always some despot with a lofty goal. Bin Laden, al-Zawahiri, Hitler, Pol Pot . . . every group needs a driving force. That individual is our target." Palmer leaned forward at his desk, looking hard at Quinn. "I'm not clear yet on what their plan is, but you have to find out who that person is before their sleepers make us tear ourselves apart as a nation."

Palmer took a TV remote from the lap drawer of his desk and pointed it at the screen displaying Google Earth. The bird's-eye view zoomed in over the rugged confluence of three of the world's highest mountain ranges—the Pamir, the Himalayas, and the Hindu Kush.

"I want you in Kashgar ASAP," Palmer said, shining the red dot of a laser pointer on Western China. "But the Chinese would have a fit if we send you in on government business. I think it's time you took some shooting leave."

Jericho smiled at the notion. During the nineteenth-century spy/counterspy Great Game between England and Russia, British soldiers had often been given "shooting leave" so as to venture into neutral ground without official cover—or protection.

"Now wait just one damn minute," Thibodaux all but roared from his seat on the couch. "With all due respect, sir, I don't think Quinn should be sent over to Kashgar all by hisself to talk with this *fille* doctor and her string of Chinese hookers."

"Don't worry. He's not going alone, Jacques. He just won't be going with you.

"Roger that," Thibodaux said, shaking his head ever so slightly. He was a Marine, and Marines took orders whether they liked them or not. Quinn respected that, but he could also understand the big Cajun's disappointment.

Palmer produced two blue passports from his desk drawer and shoved them toward Quinn. "You and Miss Garcia will go over posing as a couple on a motorcycle adventure vacation. It's the end of the season, but you should still have a couple of weeks of good riding weather. See what Dr. Deuben knows and get her to show you this orphanage. Keep me apprised of what you find on the Secure Satellite Link."

"Adventure motorcyclists . . ." Thibodaux muttered, arms folded across his chest in a muscular pout.

"I get it, Jacques," Palmer said. "But you don't speak Chinese and with your bulk, you'd draw too much attention." Palmer grinned. "If I ever need someone to go undercover as a pro wrestler, you'll be our guy."

Palmer's cell phone gave a soft chirp. He looked at it and nodded grimly. "It's POTUS," he said. "Garcia will be here any minute. Let her in and play nice. I have it on good authority she carries a knife."

"I'm just sayin," Thibodaux sighed after they left Palmer's office and shut the door behind them. "I can't believe they're sending you over to Bootystan with nobody to watch your back but the new kid."

Quinn grinned. "There is that thing about her saving my life in the men's room. Besides, I thought you liked her."

"Yeah, yeah, yeah, she's hot as a firecracker and all that," Thibodaux said. "But have you looked in her eyes? She's got crazy-ass clowns in there with knives and meat cleavers and shit. . . . All of 'em do. . . ."

"Even Camille?" Quinn chuckled.

"Are you kiddin' me, beb?" Thibodaux threw up both hands and scoffed. "Hell yes, even Camille. I love her to death, but my little Cornmeal is the worst. Sometimes, when I'm lookin' down into those spooky eyes of hers, I can see her with a pair of scissors tippy-toein' up on me when I'm fast asleep. . . ." His broad shoulders shook with a full-body shiver. "Ohhh-weee, that little woman can bring some misère."

Chapter Twenty-eight

Spotsylvania, Virginia

Lieutenant Colonel Fargo kept to the paving stones as he picked his way across the yard. He stayed a half step back from his partner, wanting him to reach the door first. Piles of dog crap lurked like land mines, half hidden in the thick grass. Three overturned bicycles, a red tricycle with no wheels, and assorted cap pistols and water guns lay strewn from street to porch. A headless GI Joe doll hung by one leg from the dead branch of a lone elm in front of the modest gray two-story.

Dogs and kids . . . they both gave Fargo the creeps.

Both Fargo and his partner wore dark suits and Wiley X tactical sunglasses, looking every inch like the proverbial government men in black that they were. Though members of the American military rarely went armed on the soil of their own country, drastic times called for drastic measures, and each carried a Beretta M9 pistol in a shoulder holster under his suit coat.

First Sergeant Sean Bundy, a classic thug if the Army

had ever seen one, tossed a condescending look over his shoulder as the two men wove their way through the maze of toys and lawn clutter. The stinger of a three-inch scorpion tattoo stuck above the size-eighteen collar of his white dress shirt. Sunlight shone off the pink of his freshly polished scalp. "Tell me this guy's name again?" Bundy asked.

"Marine Gunnery Sergeant Jacques Thibodaux," Fargo said, feeling a touch superior as the words left his mouth. "You know, this is the second time you've asked me that. I thought you Echoes were keen on remembering the slightest details."

At the steps now, Bundy spun, his top lip pulled back in a quivering half snarl. "I'm not asking because I want to know," he snapped. "I'm asking to give you a concrete thought to focus on . . . sir. You've been whistling a bad rendition of a Rossini opera ever since we got into the car this morning."

The blood drained from Fargo's face.

"You need to calm your ass down . . . sir." Bundy glared. "I'll handle the gunny's blushing bride."

Any trace of superiority left Fargo as if a plug had been pulled. From the moment he'd met Sergeant Bundy his gut had felt as if he'd drank a quart of curdled milk.

A day ago, when they were putting together their action plan, it had seemed like a good idea to interview Mrs. Thibodaux while her gigantic husband was away. Now that they were actually standing on her front porch, Fargo wasn't so sure. He would have turned away had it not been for fear of looking weak in front of a man who was his subordinate. He bit his bottom lip. Had he really been whistling Rossini?

"His wife's name is Camille," Fargo offered, trying to save some semblance of dignity. "Maiden name was Bottini. Her friends call her Cornmeal."

"Cornmeal," Bundy chuckled, turning back to the door. "That's messed up."

Sergeant Bundy pounded with his fist, rattling the entire house. Fargo felt his flesh crawl.

"Maybe they're not home," he muttered, half under his breath.

Bundy looked over his shoulder again and shook his head. "I hear footsteps. They're home."

A shadow drifted across the glazed oval window and the door flew wide open.

"Help you?" A pregnant woman leaned into the narrow gap between the door and the frame. Mussed, coal-colored hair was pulled back in a faded blue bandana. Her white T-shirt stretched tight against the beginnings of a swollen baby-belly. A small child wearing nothing but a sagging diaper clung to the leg of her gray sweatpants.

"Gunny Thibodaux hereabouts?" Bundy asked, without introducing himself.

"Who would be askin'?" The woman glared with haggard green eyes under a furrowed brow. Fargo thought she might be attractive if she put on a little makeup and lost the baggy sweats. She certainly filled out the white T-shirt with more than just her belly.

Fargo stepped up next to Bundy, drawn forward in spite of his nerves. He opened his black credential case and held it at belt level. "Army CID. Actually, we're trying to find a friend of your husband's. Jericho Quinn."

Camille touched the corner of Fargo's credential case, looking back and forth from the photo to his face.

"Your picture don't favor you at all." She smirked.

The snot-nosed kid at her leg reached up and tugged at the case, trying to have a look of his own. Fargo yanked it back and slid it in his suit pocket.

Camille tossed her head, blowing dark bangs out of her eyes. "Listen, boys, if you'll excuse me I got baths to give and supper to cook. Leave your card and I'll tell Jacques you stopped—"

Without warning, Bundy shouldered his way inside the house. Fargo's gut lurched into his throat, but he followed dutifully.

Camille's look shot daggers as both men barged past.

"What the hell do you think you're doin?" she spat.

Bundy scooped up the little boy and rubbed the top of his head—as if he had the capacity for affection.

"Hey, kid." His smile was half snarl. "You look like a tough little guy."

"*Porca vacca*!" Camille's growled from somewhere low in her chest. The sound of it made Fargo's jaws lock up.

The woman's face twisted into a silent scream. Her shoulders began to shake. "You put my baby down right damn now or so help me . . ."

"After we've talked awhile," Bundy whispered, drawing the little guy to him. "I need something from you fir—"

"I said put my baby down!" Camille launched herself at Bundy, claws out, grabbing for the child with one hand and slashing out with the other.

Bundy kicked her hard in the belly, shoving her

away as he pushed the baby out in front of him as a shield.

Camille went down hard, falling flat on her bottom with a loud *whump*. Shaking her head, she sprang back to her feet in an instant, enraged past the point of seeing.

"Okay, okay, Mrs. T." Bundy grinned a savage grin, like someone who held all the cards.

She grabbed the squalling baby and backed away toward the wall, eyes smoldering with rage. Her face had gone pale and she kept one hand on her stomach. The kick had hurt her more than she was admitting.

Fargo felt his stomach churn. This was all getting so out of hand.

"I think you'd best calm down, Cornmeal," Bundy hissed through clenched teeth. "I'd hate to see your kid get hurt because you lost your temper."

"*Me ne frega*!" Camille screamed, flicking the fingers of her free hand under her chin in disdain. "I don't give a damn what you'd hate." Tears welled, but pride kept her sobs bottled up as if she might explode.

Bundy stepped sideways over a pile of folded towels, putting some distance between himself and the furious mama bear. His eyes shot to Fargo as if to say: "Your turn."

Fargo held up both hands, trying to gain control of a deteriorating situation. He couldn't help but think that if the gunnery sergeant came home now, they were dead.

He gulped. "You have to understand, Mrs. Thibodaux. This is a matter of national security. A friend of your husband's—Jericho Quinn—has vanished, along with his family."

Camille kept steely eyes trained on the men while she maneuvered her little boy behind her. "And that gives you leave to come in here and terrorize me and my kids?" She shook her head emphatically, her voice barely above a whisper. "I said get out of my house or I'm callin' the cops—"

Bundy clapped his hands together with a loud pop, causing everyone in the room, including Fargo, to jump. "Cornmeal," he sneered, wagging his bald head. "We are the cops. Now, it's important for you to know Jericho Quinn is wanted on some very serious—"

Camille snatched up an eight-by-ten photograph of her husband in his dress blue uniform and hurled it at Bundy. The heavy pewter frame caught him square in the shoulder, shattering the glass, then bouncing off the far wall.

"It's important for *you* to know," Camille hissed, "that I don't aim to let anyone come bargin' in my house uninvited! I am not gonna stand here and listen to a single word from you." She took a half step toward them with an aluminum baseball bat she'd grabbed from behind the door.

Bundy licked his lips. For an agonizing moment Fargo was afraid he might actually shoot the woman. Instead, the trained Echo simply raised his hands and walked toward the door. Once outside, he turned to look back. "Tell your husband we stopped by," he said, a little too smug for Fargo's taste.

"Oh, I'm gonna tell him, all right." Cornmeal Thibodaux's lips pulled back into a hysterical laugh. "And when I do, he's gonna shove this baseball bat up your ass." She patted her little boy on the head without looking down. "Don't worry, sugar. Ass is a Bible word. . . ."

* * *

The house shook when Camille slammed the door behind the two intruders. Brad, her youngest, stood beside her in a sagging diaper. Already rattled, he jumped at the sudden noise and threw back his head to bawl at the ceiling. The older boys were playing down the street. That was a blessing. Both took after their daddy. Only nine and eleven, neither had a smidgen of patience when it came to a bully. Camille was sure they would have done something stupid with the two suits. They probably could have taken the one named Fargo—but the bald one had a mean bone. He was dangerous. Camille had run into men like him when she was tending bar, before she met Jacques. They were men who had a rip in their moral fabric, men who not only lacked a conscience, but reveled in the pain of other folks.

The look he'd given her sweet little boy made her legs go weak.

"Mama." Denny, her seven-year-old—and the most sensitive of her boys—stood at the top of the stairs, flanked by his five- and three-year-old brothers. The three held hands, sobbing quietly as they looked down with their blinking doe eyes that always made her think of Jacques. They'd seen the whole horrible episode.

"Mama," Denny stammered, his little voice graveyard quiet. "Were you gonna really hit those men with my bat?"

"If I had to, sugar." Not much of a crier herself, emotion showed itself in crimson blotches on her neck.

"Why was he holding Brad?" Denny was the official spokesman, but all three boys stared down at her, demanding an answer.

A wave of nausea swept over her and she had to use the bat as a crutch to keep her feet. She caught her breath, patting the top of a squalling Brad's head. She was a Marine wife, and these were Marine sons. There was no need to lie to them.

"He was trying to scare me," she said.

"Why?" Denny demanded.

Camille suddenly thought of the other boys playing up the street. A stabbing pain shot low across her abdomen, arcing like an electric shock. A veteran of six pregnancies, she'd never felt a pain so severe.

Overcome with nausea, she dropped the bat and fell to her knees. She doubled over, cradling her swollen belly, trying to keep from throwing up.

Denny ran down the stairs to cup his mother's face in both hands. "Mama! What's the matter? Should I call nine-one-one?"

She pulled him closer, tears of agony streaming down her cheeks. "You gotta promise me something, sugar."

Ashen faced, the boy nodded quickly, but sounded unconvinced. "I'm gonna go call nine-one-one—"

Camille grabbed him by his T-shirt as he turned to get the phone. Of all her boys, Denny was the one most likely to obey her.

Her shoulders began to shake uncontrollably. Searing pain grew like a pool of hot acid in her gut. She pulled her son close to her, using him as a support to stay upright for just a little longer. "Promise me you won't tell your daddy about those men."

"But Mama . . ."

"Promise!" Camille screamed like a crazy woman.

"Yes, ma'am," Denny stammered. "I promise."

Camille fell back onto a pile of laundry, writhing, imagining she was in hell. She was vaguely aware of her son's voice talking to the 911 operator.

She prayed that her little guy would keep his word. Jacques could never know about the men. He was sure to kill them if he found out—and that would land him in prison.

"Oh, Jacques," Camille whispered, the pain growing more intense. She felt the room close in around her. He couldn't go to prison. She felt sure she was bleeding to death inside. With her gone, the boys would need him more than ever.

CHAPTER TWENTY-NINE

Washington

Congressman Hartman Drake sat against the edge of his desk, accidentally knocking a stack of loose papers onto the floor. He ignored them, focusing on the glossy photographs in his hands. In the great scheme of things they weren't half-bad pictures. Damning, sure, but the angles were incredible and did a wonderful job of showing off his physique.

He wasn't a tall man, barely five feet seven, but the two hours a day he spent in the House gym showed in the way his arms and chest swelled under the starched white shirt. He was particularly proud of the fact he'd been able to bench-press three hundred and fifty pounds for three clean reps on his forty-fifth birthday. His office was rife with photographs of him skiing, horseback riding, mountain climbing, and sky diving. If it was adventurous, he did it, took a photo, and put it on his wall. The lurid photographs he now held in his hands would have fit right in with the other trophies.

Drake peered over the top of the photographs at his aide, David Crosby. "Nietzsche had it right, you know."

"About what, sir?" Crosby sighed, pale eyes casting around the room like a cornered animal.

" 'The true man wants two things: danger and play. For that reason he wants woman, as the most dangerous plaything.' See?" The congressman glared, half grinning, across the top of his black reading glasses. "I'm normal. Anyone other than you see these?"

Crosby, a freckled Midwestern law school graduate with a sparse blond beard, shook his head emphatically. "I open all the mail myself."

Drake breathed a sigh of relief. If he could trust anyone it was his smarmy assistant. He'd helped the kid cheat on his bar exam. Crosby was bought and paid for.

There were three photographs in all, each showing Drake completely nude, getting athletic with the same busty brunette. They were of excellent quality and left little doubt as to Drake's identity. In a way, he felt bad for depriving others of a look at the pictures.

The congressman chuckled a little despite the situation. The bitch must have had one of those hidden nanny cams. He held up the bottom photo for Crosby to see. "Come on, Dave," he leered. "Tell me you wouldn't make the beast with two backs if that came along and threw herself at you. I mean, if these get out, who's gonna blame me? Besides Kathleen, I mean."

"Congressman." Crosby swallowed hard, shying away from looking too long at the photograph of his boss and the brunette. "It's obvious this is an attempt at extortion. And the timing could not possibly be any worse."

Drake nodded, almost absentmindedly. He couldn't seem to tear his eyes off that last photo. The girl was drop-dead gorgeous, there was no question about that—with bouncing, pixie-cut hair that made him think she might be Tinker Bell's evil twin. But this particular photo caught his quads at just the right flex. . . . At least if the photos got out on the Internet, he'd have nothing to be ashamed of in that regard. It was a crying shame Kathleen wouldn't allow a camera in the bedroom.

Drake shook his head, forcing himself to focus.

Crosby went on with his whimpering worry fest.

"Roger Grantham's test results came back positive for lymphoma," he said. "He's giving a press conference in an hour."

Drake slid the damning photographs back in the envelope. So, Grantham would step down as speaker of the House. The job was as good as his.

"You have unprecedented support from the public since you came out with the list," Crosby said. "Tatum Hanks wants the job, but you're the party's certain nomination for speaker."

"You think so?" Drake loosened his blue and silver bow tie and undid the top button of his starched shirt. Hanks was majority whip. In other circumstances would get the party nod. But Crosby was right. In the wake of all the terrorist killings, the public and most members of Congress were lined up behind Drake.

"So what are we going to do?" Crosby said, fidgeting with his hands.

"David." Drake smiled. "We are going to make certain I become speaker of the House."

"Sir, I mean what are we going to do about the photos? If they get out, we're screwed."

Drake chuckled. "Interesting choice of words, considering." He put a hand on the kid's shoulder. "There wasn't any note?"

Crosby shook his head, looking pale. "No, just the photos."

"Don't look so glum, David," Drake said. "Remember, I know this girl. I know where she lives."

"Do you want me to call someone in to help us . . . I don't know . . . take care of the problem?"

"Come on, Dave," Drake belly laughed. "I'll handle this myself. I step out on my wife once in a while. I'm not some mobster who has people whacked because they cross him. How would that look for the guy who's about to be the number-three guy in the line of succession for the presidency of the United States?"

CHAPTER THIRTY

New York City

Mujaheed Beg stood against the peeling yellow wallpaper of the crowded hotel room looking over his shoulder out the window. Six stories below, the clang and clatter of garbage trucks on Thirty-ninth Street helped to drown out the soup of angry voices in the suite with him. The Mervi brooded sullenly, keeping his back to the wall. It angered him that the doctor had insisted on his presence in New York when he was so close to finding out more about the dark woman who had almost stumbled onto him at Arbakova's house.

Still, the doctor was his employer. When he'd called to tell Beg to take the five-o'clock Acela Express out of Union Station for New York, the Mervi had grudgingly complied.

Now he found himself at the Eastgate Tower, standing in a room that was, as many rooms were in Manhattan, little larger than a closet. The hotel was just a short distance from the United Nations. Groups of foreign nationals were the norm, even in the day and age where men with dark skin and a Middle Eastern look were viewed as potential terrorists anywhere else.

Dr. Badceb sat on the edge of the queen bed. He lit his sixth cigarette of the evening with the butt of his fifth, grinding out the old one in a glass ashtray on the mattress beside him. He picked a bit of tobacco off his lip and waved away the plume of blue smoke that encircled his face.

Over the course of the last two hours, eight other men had slipped into the room one at a time, each with dark faces and even darker dispositions. Some smoked, sitting on the low dresser beside the television. Others squatted along the wall, peering sullcnly over black beards and thick mustaches.

The room smelled of old cigarettes, burned coffee, and body odor. Beg was a creature of the desert and yearncd for thc smell of wind, or at the very least, fresh blood.

"Brothers," Badeeb said, waving his cigarette in the air. "Please, we must remain calm. Think of all our young friends. They have become martyrs in our struggle. Do you not scc the news and what the Americans are doing to one another?"

Mustafa Mahmoud, a gaunt firebrand from Lahore, threw up his hands. He had the only chair in the room. "I must ask you the selfsame question, Doctor. Do you not watch the news? This infidel congressman, Hartman Drake, is to be the next speaker of the U.S. House of Representatives."

A murmur of consent hummed around the other men in the room.

Mahmoud continued, his words clicking off his

tongue. "Have you not heard what this man says about Pakistan or Palestine or the entire Middle East? He would bomb all Muslim countries off the map if given the opportunity."

Badeeb pressed the flat of his right hand to his chest. "I understand your worry," he said. "But we are compelled to continue with our original course of action. Assets are in place. We have traveled much too far to alter plans at this point in time."

Mahmoud stood abruptly and stared directly into Badeeb's sweating face. Beg moved forward a half step. Watching. The others in the room fell completely silent.

"My brothers," Badeeb said, waving Beg to stay back. "I promise you. I myself will take care of Drake when the time is right. I am certain he will be invited to the infidel wedding."

"Of course, you know best, Doctor," the skinny Pakistani muttered. "I am but a simple hotel keeper. But think on this. If we continue on your original plan, and Hartman Drake does not attend this wedding, he will have the power to do untold damage."

"I ask you to trust me," Badeeb whispered, bowing his head.

Mujaheed Beg held his breath. The doctor paid him well, but there was far more to his work than mere employment. He saw the doctor's dedication, saw the devotion the man gave to his jihad. Of all the men in the room, Beg was perhaps the only one who could have faith in the doctor's plan—and when it concerned Hartman Drake, such faith was proving difficult even for him.

The man needed to die.

SATURDAY
September 30

Chapter Thirty-one

Washington
0830 hours

Nancy Hughes sat in her favorite white wicker chair overlooking the rolling lawn of the Naval Observatory. The grass glistened from an overnight rain. A white porcelain cup and saucer rested on her lap, steaming peacefully in the quiet air.

She took a sip of her Earl Grey and tipped her head at her new assistant. “Mrs. Peterson is ill today. Think you can handle her duties along with your own?”

“Absolutely, ma’am.” Amanda Deatherage gave an impish smile that Hughes found unsettling. She was a small girl, not much over five feet tall, with narrow, girlish shoulders and piercing hazel eyes. Her stiff, red wool suit and large Wilma Flintstone pearls gave the impression of a child playing dress-up. She had a tendency to tug at her clothing as if it was bunching up and her stockings sagged noticeably above the heels of scuffed pumps. Her résumé was impressive enough and she possessed decent organizational skills. It was the rumpled appearance that had put her number two behind Grace Smallwood on the applicant list.

"Excellent," Hughes said, taking another sip of tea before setting the cup on the porch. She took up a small notepad and situated a pair of gold reading glasses on her nose. "So, how will I earn my keep today?"

Deatherage opened the burgundy leather appointment calendar and studied it for a long moment, pen poised above the pages.

"Let's see, ma'am. . . ." She scanned the schedule.

"Nine a.m., you meet with the head of the Kiva non-profit . . . uh . . . at the Smithsonian Castle." She looked up, mouth open in reverent awe. "That is, like, the coolest thing ever. Anyways, after that, at eleven-thirty, you have lunch with the first lady at Ben's Chili Bowl. . . ."

Hughes closed her eyes and leaned back in the chair. "Are you sure? For some reason I thought that was Monday."

Deatherage's auburn bangs bobbed as she shook her head. "It says right here: Secret Service notified . . . SLOTUS and FLOTUS—Ben's Chili Bowl eleven-thirty a.m."

Hughes made a face as if she'd just eaten something bitter.

"I prefer you don't call me that, dear."

It was common knowledge that *POTUS* stood for the president of the United States. The first lady got *FLOTUS*, a name that made one envision gliding gently above the ground. Nancy Hughes had no problem being the second lady, but the vice president and his wife were saddled with the *VPOTUS* and *SLOTUS*—

terms that her oilman brother said suggested an erectile dysfunction drug and some sort of skin disease.

"Yes, ma'am . . ." Deatherage looked quizzically at the calendar. "Oops . . . like, I mean the biggest *oops* ever. You were right, Mrs. Hughes. The dinner with FLOT . . . the first lady *is* Monday. After the Kiva meeting today, your schedule is open to work on the wedding."

"Excellent," Hughes said, resisting the urge to point out that Gail Peterson never had "oops" moments when it came to schedules concerning the first lady. "We have a great deal to do and a short time to get it done."

"May I ask a question, Mrs. Hughes?"

"Certainly, dear."

"I'm, like, all afraid I'm not working as hard for you as I should be. . . ."

Hughes lowered her reading glasses. "How do you mean?"

It looked as though the poor girl might actually be welling up with tears.

"I . . . I admire you so much, Mrs. Hughes. You, like, volunteer your time to all sorts of great causes. I just want to be a real help with this wedding."

"Of course you're going to help me, dear," Hughes scoffed, attempting to lighten the mood. "I wouldn't have it any other way."

"But you won't even tell me where the wedding is supposed to be." Deatherage sniffed back a sob, hand to her chest as she worked to regain her composure.

"You're to help with the guest list, dear." Hughes shook her head. "The vice president believes the fewer people know the location until the last minute, the better for everyone."

"I understand." Deatherage sniffed. "I'm sorry, ma'am. This is all, like, just such an honor for me." She turned to the back page of the appointment book. "So far you have sixty member of Congress and fifteen senators who have RSVP'd."

"We do expect a fair number of dignitaries," Hughes said. "Security and transportation are going to be a nightmare. At last count we had heads of state from Australia, the U.K., Germany, and Brazil. Have we heard from any others?"

"Tom Selleck's publicist called last night to say he plans to attend," Deatherage said, her mouth hanging open. "This is crazy—before she died, my mom used to watch old *Magnum, P.I.* reruns all the time. I can't believe Tom Selleck would come to your daughter's wedding."

"He's a family friend," Hughes said. She leaned forward, touching the girl on the knee. "I had no idea your mother had passed away, dear."

"I was fifteen," Deatherage sighed. "She and my dad were killed in a car wreck on a trip to the Grand Canyon. They left me with friends. . . ."

"That's just awful," Hughes said, about to cry herself. A sudden thought made her smile. She got to her feet, motioning Deatherage to follow her. Words spilled out as she walked. "I'll tell you what you need. You need a project to really sink your teeth into. There will be a gob of politicians at the wedding. The heads of state have security, so their details have been made aware of the location. The remainder of the guests will be in the dark until the last minute—to keep the terrorists at bay. We'll be making their transportation arrangements. It's a big job, but I'm going to assign you transportation coordination. Think you can handle it?"

Deatherage trotted along dutifully behind, pen and appointment book in hand. "I . . . yes, I'm sure I can."

Hughes stopped abruptly. "You're my wedding assistant, Amanda. The vice president will just have to realize I need the help. I'd have to tell you sooner or later. It may as well be now." She leaned in close. "But remember, this truly is a matter of national security. You have to promise to keep this between us." Nancy Hughes flushed. It felt good to do good.

Amanda Deatherage looked up at her with beaming eyes and grinned. "Of course, ma'am." Deatherage nodded. "Cross my heart and hope to die. . . ."

CHAPTER THIRTY-TWO

Western China

The wizened old Uyghur who picked them up at the Kashgar airport wheeled his lime-green VW Santana away from the chipped curb and onto Yingbin Avenue. The paved road would take them six miles to the south and into the city. He wore a ratty gray suit coat and a stained shirt, making his bright yellow four-angle traditional silk hat seem out of place. Wisps of thin gray hair peeked from the edges of the hat, hanging down in the old man's wrinkled face. He reminded Quinn of a moldy raisin.

"Have you and your wife come for the Sunday Market, *tovarich*?" The man knew Quinn wasn't Uyghur since he couldn't speak the language and he obviously wasn't Chinese. Proclaiming that no American could learn Mandarin so fluently, he decided Quinn must be a Russian and referred to him as *comrade* at the end of every phrase. Ronnie played along, speaking sultry Russian to Quinn in hushed tones. He had no idea what she was saying.

"We very much hope to see it," Quinn said, still in Mandarin. Memories of his previous trip to the Silk Road city flooded back to him as they drove. "They say one may find everything at the Sunday Market but the milk of a chicken. . . ."

"Everything indeed, *tovarich*." The old Uyghur laughed, showing his grizzled face in the dusty rearview mirror. The fact that he had only two surviving teeth made his Chinese slurpy and difficult to understand.

He laid on the horn, honking at a driver atop a two-wheel cart behind a placid donkey clomping patiently down the middle of the road.

As they neared Kashgar proper, Quinn was startled to find how much of the old city had been demolished in the years since his visit. It was as if the boxy concrete buildings commissioned by Beijing were a virus, consuming anything and everything with history or character. He looked out the window at the benign face of the cart driver as the taxi rattled past. At least some things about the place hadn't changed.

"I know of a place that sells vodka, *tovarich*," the old man said, working for a tip. "Perhaps you wish to stop?"

"I believe we'll just go to the hotel," Quinn said.

"A most excellent and noble choice, *tovarich*." The old man scooted forward a little in the seat, squaring his shoulders. "It is good to meet another upright man in the world. . . ." His eyes flicked up, looking into the mirror again. "But if you should change your mind, I will leave my number with the hotel staff."

A city bus belched black smoke in front of the *Chini Bagh* hotel. The taxi driver shot around to take them into the circular portico, narrowly avoiding an oncoming scooter truck. Now that was the old Kashgar, where every drive was a near-death experience, Quinn thought. A chorus of blaring horns, shouting men, and braying donkeys struck Quinn like a slap as he opened the taxi door and helped Ronnie step out onto the curb. She looked ravishing in her light khaki travel pants and airy cotton shirt—long sleeved so as not to offend Muslim sensibilities. Her big Hollywood sunglasses and modest silk scarf knotted at her chin made her look like something out of a 1960s travel poster.

Quinn gave the wrinkled driver thirty yuan—a little over four dollars—and assured him his services wouldn't be needed later for any vodka runs. Motioning for Ronnie to walk ahead, Quinn grabbed his waterproof duffel and walked toward the gaudy new hotel. During the days of Rudyard Kipling and the Great Game, the grounds had been the home of George and Lady Macartney, British consul to Kashgar. Though their orchards and gardens were gone, the old residence, home to no small amount of intrigue against the Russians, still stood on the hotel grounds, converted to a Uyghur restaurant.

The waifish Han Chinese girl at the front desk handed Quinn a handwritten message while she ran his credit card. It was scrawled on a sheet of lined paper torn from a spiral notebook and folded in half.

Welcome to Kashgar. Will call your room around four p.m. to set up a meeting.

Best—

G. Deuben

It was nearly five, but the desk clerk said there hadn't been any calls. She knew Deuben and rang up her office, passing the handset to Quinn.

Deuben's assistant, a woman named Madame Claire, refused to speak anything but French on the phone. Quinn was able to establish little more than the fact that the doctor was not in.

The *Chini Bagh* clerk, eager to help, happily pointed out that Deuben's office was just a few blocks away.

Ronnie wasn't happy about it but agreed to wait in the room for Deuben's call while Quinn ran up the street to try and speak with Madame Claire in person. They agreed to call each other as soon as either of them got a location on the doctor.

"Do you know Wash Feet Number Six?" Madame Claire was a withered French woman reminiscent of Mother Teresa. She wore a tattered purple and blue scarf over graying hair and tried her best to communicate in a fricassee of butchered Chinese, English, and French.

"Doctor, she is mop up trouble at Wash Feet Number Six. Easy from here."

"Trouble?" Quinn asked, fearful he'd open up a can of conversation Madame Claire was not able to handle.

"Bad men." A frown fell over the French woman's face. "Rough up Tina Fan. She is no terrible girl. Stupid, yes—no terrible."

Bad men roughing up women, Quinn thought, half smiling. At least he was heading in the right direction.

Madame Claire stepped out the clinic door and looked carefully up and down the teeming street as if fearful of getting run down by a passing donkey cart or motorcycle taxi. She pointed east with a bony hand, past street vendors selling spices, nuts, fall squash, and pottery under red and white canvas awnings. The odor of peppers and cumin filled the air.

"Walk by," she said, standing on tiptoe as if it would help her reach farther. ". . . *naan* . . . *pain* . . . bread cooker . . . go this." She held up her left hand to illustrate. "Wash Foot Number Six one block down . . ." She held up her right hand. "This side."

Quinn gave Madame Claire a two-hundred-yuan donation for the clinic and thanked her for her help.

He chuckled as he walked past a street vendor selling fragrant bowls of *ququ*, wonton mutton soup. "Wash Foot," he mused under his breath.

Xi yu—foot washing—was big business in China. Stalls could be found from the fanciest hotels to the seedy, red-light shops where considerably more than one's feet got a rubdown. Six was an auspicious number in Chinese since it sounded somewhat like the word for *happiness*. Wash Foot Number Six—*Happiness Foot Wash*.

Since the good doctor's medical ministry was bent toward downtrodden silk-road prostitutes, she'd located her clinic close to where they worked. Madame Claire's directions were choppy, but they were dead-on.

Quinn didn't have far to walk before he found Happiness.

A sullen Filipino girl looked up from a cell phone when Quinn stepped into the dim interior of Wash Foot Number Six. She sat on a tall wooden stool, her narrow back to a Chinese anatomical chart on the peeling wallpaper. Tight spandex shorts displayed everything she had to offer. A tired blue halter top hung off her bony chest. She wouldn't have been out of high school if she'd known the luxury of such a thing. The heavy smell of cheap perfume and talc hung like a toxic cloud beyond the beaded curtains dividing the cramped wooden vestibule from a set of stairs rising into the shadows of a sagging upper floor.

"I'm looking for Dr. Deuben," Quinn said in Chinese. He'd called Garcia with directions to where he was going, but if trouble was brewing, he didn't want to wait.

The Filipino girl's cloudy eyes fluttered when he spoke, her body flinching slightly like one who was accustomed to being beaten along with conversation. When she realized Quinn wasn't going to strike her immediately, she leaned forward, her red-caked lips twisted into a brazen smile. It was a terrifying thing to see on one so young. Quinn gucsscd shc might be all of fifteen.

"Maybe you don't need doctor," the girl sneered, running chipped nails through dull black hair that lay in strands on her shoulders. She was so small. He imagined her playing dolls with Mattie.

"I think you need Happiness girl. I give you damn good foot wash, no shit—fifty yuan." She quoted him the lustful foreigner rate. In a place like this, Quinn knew her normal price was likely not half of that—about three dollars.

"Anything else negotiable." She tossed her head in an effort to look cute, but only managed to look dizzy.

Quinn swallowed, trying to keep from getting sick. "No, I'm pretty sure I'm looking for Dr. Deuben."

The girl slouched back against the wall on her stool,

deflated. White lace stockings rolled down to her knees, leaving a gap of skin between them and the spandex and exposing a map of bruises at various stages of purple and yellow. She was obviously used to a rough clientele.

"Doctor not here," she sulked. "You not want Happiness girl, you go now. Gao come back. He beat shit from you like he do Tina Fan. "

"I was told Dr. Deuben was here right now," Quinn pressed the issue. He took a half step toward the beaded curtains over the wooden stairs.

"She no here!" the girl snapped in English. "You go now!"

Quinn tensed as heavy footsteps pounded down the stairs.

A dark hand, followed by a mountainous, turban-wearing Sikh, emerged from the curtains and into the vestibule. He stood toe-to-toe with Quinn, tut-tutting the girl with a pointed forefinger. He turned to Quinn and shook his head. "*Trust a Brahmin before a snake, and a snake before a harlot. . . .*"

"*And a harlot before an Afghan*," Quinn finished the sentence.

"Ah," the Sikh said. "Splendid to meet a man who knows his Kipling." He extended his hand. "I am Belvan Virk, Dr. Gabrielle's bodyguard."

"Jericho Quinn." He shook the offered hand.

Belvan Virk had a good three inches on him, and the broad shoulders and blocky, muscular build of a bare-knuckle boxer. His bloodred turban was wrapped tight and pinned in front with the swords and circle of a *Kahnda* or Sikh crest. Jet-black hair and uncut beard were tucked neatly beneath the edges of the spotless cloth. He wore dark slacks and a collarless white dress shirt. A curved dagger hung at his right side.

"The doctor has been unable to call because of these recent troubles." Virk parted the beaded curtains, pointing up the stairs with an open hand. "The . . . proprietor of Number Six went missing on a trip to Urumqi last week—likely murdered by bandits. In any case, the girls here are without pimp or protector. They have had a bit of trouble from a certain local."

"Gao?" Quinn mused.

"Yes." Virk nodded, amused. "You catch on very quickly."

"Gao come back too," the Filipino girl threatened, still perched on her stool, arms folded in defiance. "He my customer anyway. Tina Fan stole from me. She deserved, she got."

Quinn followed Belvan Virk up the stairs and along a windowless wooden hallway to a ten-by-ten chamber that looked more like a jail cell than a bedroom. The enormous Sikh had to stoop under the low ceiling. The odor of sweat, lamb grease, and cheap perfume hung heavy in the close air. An oil lamp only added to the darkness with a thin ribbon of black smoke.

A Han Chinese peasant girl, from Fuzhou, Quinn guessed by her dialect, lay facedown on a sagging mattress set directly on the scabby rug. She wore nothing but a dingy pair of panties that had at one time been white and trimmed in lace. The soles of her tiny feet were black from walking barefoot. Raw pink lines of flesh crisscrossed her shoulders and legs. Ribs pushed, cage-like, against sallow skin as she sobbed. The points of her spine shone through like a row of small stones above a pale yellow sea.

Gabrielle Deuben sat on the edge of the filthy mattress dabbing at the girl's wounds with a bottle of foul-smelling antiseptic. She wore a blue clinic coat over a pair of khaki slacks and a red T-shirt. Blue nitrile gloves and a silver chain completed her ensemble, accenting sensible brown hiking boots of the type worn by mountaineers. Flaxen hair was piled up on her head as if putting it there had been an afterthought. She kept it in place with luck and a couple of wooden chopsticks.

High, pink cheekbones stood out over a strong, Germanic jaw that clenched in marked concentration as she looked over the wounds. She wore no makeup, and appeared to revel in her plainness. Quinn guessed she was in her mid-thirties. A spartan life in Central Asia kept her a little on the gaunt side and added more than one streak of gray to her hair.

An earthenware bowl sat on the bed next to the two women, filled with pink water and soiled rags.

"There now," the doctor said in passable Chinese. "I think we've gotten out all the debris."

"You hurt me worse than Gao," Tina Fan sobbed.

"I know it seemed so, child," Deuben sighed. "But you risk infection from the filthy rope he uses as a belt. It's probably full of camel dung . . . or worse." She pulled a sheet up to gently cover the girl's legs, leaving her back open to the air. "Stay facedown for a few minutes and I'll put on a dressing."

Belvan Virk looked on with a sparkling eye. He had an easy smile, almost hidden under the massive black mustache. He seemed to revere the doctor to the point of worship and Quinn found himself wondering if there was more to their relationship than the Sikh had admitted.

Tina Fan sobbed softly as Deuben stood and peeled off the blue gloves.

"Mr. Quinn," she said in clipped but perfect English. "Thank you for coming. Forgive me if I am not too happy with the male gender at the moment."

"I understand completely," Quinn said. "Do you know why they did this to her?"

"Misogynists." The doctor shrugged, scratching her nose. It was not too big, but it looked as though she was the lucky one in a family of otherwise very large noses. "You know what misogynist means?"

"I do," Quinn said.

"It means," she explained anyway, "someone who hates every bone in a woman's body except his own. . . ." Her voice trailed off to watch his reaction before she continued. "More than likely these men wished to stake a claim since the owner and pimp of this lovely establishment has gone missing. Or maybe beating the poor girl excited them. I've long ago given up on understanding what men will do for a shake and a shiver." She suddenly turned to Quinn. "In any case, I've been writing to the United Nations for over a year and you're the first they've sent out to investigate my claims."

"I believe there may have been a mistake, Dr. Deuben." Quinn shot a look at Virk, half expecting the big man to try and grab him by the scruff of the neck if he delivered any unwelcome news. "I am from the U.S. government, not the U.N."

"Is that so?" Deuben studied him for a long moment, her slate-colored eyes playing over him in the smoke of the flickering oil lamp. She folded her hands together in front of her, chest moving slightly with each breath. At length she clapped her hands. "All the better," she pronounced. "The United Nations does little but talk. Your government actually has some teeth—if they would only use them. Are you prepared to bite with those teeth Mr. Quinn?"

Quinn considered his answer, but his thoughts were cut short by a pitiful yelp from the Filipino girl in the lobby.

Chapter Thirty-three

Heavy footfalls approached, clomping up the wooden steps. On the mattress, Tina Fan's bony shoulders began to heave so hard she retched, curling into a fetal ball.

An instant later, three Chinese men appeared, silhouetted against the open doorway by the naked lightbulb in the hall. All were thick-necked and brawny, dark and accustomed to hard labor under the sun. The apparent leader was bald but for a ring of greasy hair on his wedge-shaped head. Sneering with stained yellow teeth, he slapped a short, hardwood truncheon against his open palm.

Quinn's eyes shot from the newcomers to Belvan Virk. Men with clubs at the door of a brothel would not have good intentions. The massive Sikh let his hand fall to the dagger at his waist. He tipped his head slightly in answer to Quinn's unspoken question.

These were the same men who'd given Tina Fan the beating.

Without waiting for the thugs to speak—or even

move—Quinn closed the distance in one quick stride. Feinting with a quick right jab, he slammed the flat of his left hand into the leader's nose, then, twisting toward the thumb, wrenched the club away. He brought the heavy wood up hard and fast, catching its owner on the point of the chin. There was a satisfying crack as teeth crunched and gave way.

Wasting no energy on excess movement, Quinn used the downstroke to catch the second thug in the center of his forehead. Black eyes rolled back as wood smashed into bone. The third man raised his hands, but Quinn thumped him too, driving him to his knees. He'd come along for the whipping. It was a little too late to back out now.

All three thugs were facedown on the dirty green rug in a matter of seconds.

Virk smiled broadly, bright eyes dancing above his black beard in the lamplight. He clapped his hands softly, giving a respectful half nod.

"No need to answer my previous question, Mr. Quinn." Dr. Deuben knelt beside the unconscious attackers to check their pulses. A moment ago they would have been happy to beat her senseless. "I'm certain you will have no trouble biting whoever needs to be bitten on behalf of the American government. Now we just have to make sure the rest of Gao's crew don't cave in your skull before you can get out of town."

CHAPTER THIRTY-FOUR

Ronnie spoke a smattering of French and it was fairly simple for her to track Quinn to Happiness Foot Wash. She arrived while Gabrielle Deuben was still dispensing medication to a subdued and sheepish Gao.

The doctor had been completely won over by Quinn's methods and insisted on being their guide for the evening, escorting them around Kashgar. Belvan Virk led the way through the teeming streets, his red turban looming above the throng as he scanned for signs of danger.

Ronnie walked a half step behind, enjoying the opportunity to observe Jericho Quinn in his natural environment. She'd never met a man so self-assured. He walked by plate-glass windows without once checking himself out, and seemed somehow connected to the "now" of every situation. His uncanny ability at languages surely helped with that.

Though Uyghur spoke their own language, more closely related to Tajik Persian, most spoke passable

Arabic or Mandarin. Quinn slipped effortlessly from one language to another as he stopped to chat with this shopkeeper or that, inquiring about the price of a silk hat or a piece of yellow pottery.

Watching him, Garcia realized Kashgar was the perfect metaphor for Quinn. The more civilized, manicured part of him was somehow strained and unnatural. It was the haphazard, uncivilized nature—the feral labyrinth of instinct and uncertainty—that gave man and city endless possibilities.

"And here we are." Deuben clapped her hands in front of her waist as seemed to be her habit when she was pleased about something. She waved at a middle-aged Uyghur man using a piece of cardboard to fan away the smoke from a grill of sizzling lamb kabobs.

They were in Kashgar's famous Night Market—a sea of food and people. Mounds of saffron yellow noodles vied for space between tables piled high with baskets of naan that bore a suspicious resemblance to bagels, and platters of dumplings, vegetables, and boiled goat heads. A half carcass of mutton, split down the spine, swung from a metal hook ten feet from the table where Deuben had decided to sit. Knives, hatchets, axes, and swords seemed to be everywhere.

Quinn seemed fascinated by the frenetic sights and sounds of the place. It was as if he was coming home. Virk stayed on his feet, facing outbound behind the doctor.

Deuben patted the seat of a metal folding chair beside her, looking up at Garcia. "Come," she said. "You must sit. This place has the best *suoman* in Kashgar, I promise."

Ronnie's eyes shot to Quinn, looking for approval.

He'd promised not to let her accidentally eat any goat lung or other so-called delicacies without a warning.

"Not dog." He grinned. "*Suoman* is a sort of stir-fry with noodles, peppers, and meat. Pretty good stuff."

"Pretty good stuff?" Deuben pounded a glass bottle of red pepper sauce against the flimsy wooden tabletop, squashing a fat black fly. "Ali's *suoman* is heaven on earth." She held up four fingers to the man fanning smoke from the kabobs. He gave her an almost imperceptible nod, passing the cardboard fan to a teenage boy in a V-neck sweater so he could get to work on the *suoman*.

In the stall next door a young woman in a white bonnet pressed pomegranate juice into shot glasses. Beyond them three young male barbers gave as many gray-bearded men haircuts and vigorous face rubs.

"I love to come here," Deuben said. "The old cultures in Central Asia are all being . . . how do you say? *Zerstueckelt* . . . broken apart."

"It has changed," Quinn sighed.

"And so," Deuben said, clapping her hands together in her lap. "Did anyone tell you about this orphanage?"

"Only that you'd reported stories of a place that seemed to prefer blond, blue-eyed children."

Deuben took a deep breath. "I have not seen the place myself, but my work often finds me for some weeks at a time among the Kyrgyz horse camps in the High Pamir. They speak of such a place in hushed tones. So, so many of the Kyrgyz have succumbed to opium addiction. It's not uncommon to see women blowing opium smoke into their babies' faces to ward off hunger. Officials don't pay much attention to such women when they say their fair-skinned children are being carried away in the night. Most have been taken at gunpoint, their parents slaughtered . . . but even that draws little notice from the authorities."

"So kids are actually kidnapped?" Ronnie weighed in. "It's not just an orphanage?"

"The line is blurry out here," Deuben said, flicking away the dead fly. "It's a hard life. Infant mortality is so high parents often won't even name a child until well after it is walking. Some children are abandoned, some are sold by their parents or unscrupulous relatives. A pretty green-eyed girl can bring an incredible sum from the right millionaire in Dubai or some other place on the pipeline. Along with the missing children, I can name American petroleum engineers, teachers, a Peace Corps volunteer, and a newlywed couple who have all disappeared in the Pamir over the last decade."

"Is it common for women here to have fair-skinned babies?" Ronnie asked.

Deuben swept her arm toward the Night Market. Strings of electric lights cast a yellow glow over the crowds as twilight gave way to darkness. "Take a look. Tajik, Uyghur, Kyrgyz, Uzbek—the list goes on and on. Under the coat of grime from their hardscrabble lives, many have quite fair complexions. Some claim to be descendants of Alexander the Great and his armies." She tipped her head toward the kabob grill. "Look there, even Ali's son has green eyes and an orange tint to his hair."

"So," Quinn said. "You've had many reports of this place but have never been there?"

"No, but I have spoken with a Kyrgyz woman who has. She described it to me. It's not too far from here . . . how do you Americans say it? As the crow flies."

Virk leaned back a hair, twisting his neck so he could offer an opinion over his shoulder. "Unfortunately, such a crow would have to fly over the Pamir Knot—where the Hindu Kush, the Himalayas, and the High Pamir come together."

"This is true," Deuben conceded. "But I can tell you the back way in."

Quinn continued to study the crowd, eyes flashing this way and that. "I understood you would come with us."

"Oh no." The doctor stared down at the stained tablecloth, still fiddling with the bottle of pepper sauce.

"I see," Quinn mused. "Do we still have the bike rental set up?"

For a brief moment Ronnie thought the fact that the doctor wouldn't be joining them might jeopardize the mission.

"Of course," Deuben said. "They are ready to go, along with gear and supplies. The man who owns them will meet you at FUBAR tomorrow morning. It's near your hotel."

Quinn had briefed Ronnie on FUBAR. Once the famed Caravan Café, it was a favorite stop for adventurers who wanted to share a drink with other expatriates and check their email. Since the Chinese crackdown and near media blackout during the recent Uyghur unrest, email had been spotty at best. Those lucky enough to log on to the Internet experienced extreme government filtering, affectionately known as the Great Firewall of China.

Ali brought four plates of *suoman*—steaming mountains of noodles with red peppers, onion, and mutton arranged around the outer edge like the spokes on a yellow wheel. Garlic and cumin rose on the heady steam to tickle Ronnie's nose in the crisp evening air.

Deuben hung her head, twirling at her noodles with a pair of collapsible lacquer chopsticks she took from her vest pocket. "I do wish I could come along, but quite frankly, I would do you more harm than good. I had a bit of trouble with the Chinese military near the checkpoint at Tashkurgan a few weeks ago." Her face screwed into a distasteful sneer. "The intrusive pests are everywhere. One of their jeep patrols caught me trying to get over the Wakhan Pass into Afghanistan."

"I understand," Quinn said. "It probably would be best if you didn't come, then. What is your back way in?"

Deuben looked up from the table, gray eyes sparkling with mischief. "Over the Wakhan Pass into Afghanistan."

A sudden flurry of commotion above the normal chatter rose from a knot of street vendors across the adjacent walkway. Quinn looked up from his meal to see two men in dark suits and wispy, flowing white beards work their way through the milling crowd. Each smiled serenely, holding their hands palms forward, as if to say, "We come in peace."

Belvan Virk widened his stance as the men approached. He reached to tap Deuben on her shoulder. "Umar's men," he whispered.

"Umar?" Deuben's shoulders sank, deflated. "*Scheisse*! I was afraid this would happen." She pushed back from the table and stood, facing the two elderly men.

"*Asalmu aleikum*," she said, pressing her right hand to her breast.

Both men returned the greeting, hands to their chests. They looked at Quinn through amused, smiling eyes, narrowed into slits by their near-toothless grins. Each wore a fancy four-cornered hat in yellow silk, richly embroidered in geometric patterns. The spokesman, a shade taller than his partner, wore a thick pair of glasses in black frames that made his eyes loom larger than the rest of his wrinkled face. His lack of teeth gave him a handy gap in which to place his hand-rolled cigarette.

"Is this the one?" he said, gesturing to Quinn with an open hand. He smelled of cloves and motor oil.

"It is," Deuben sighed, as if she knew exactly what the men were talking about.

Quinn, already on his feet, introduced himself, his right hand to his breast.

The men nodded politely but continued to conduct their business with Dr. Deuben.

"Would he accept?" the old man with glasses asked, cigarette dancing between his lips.

Deuben nodded. "I feel sure he would."

The men smiled in unison at the good news. "Most excellent. Umar will meet him at the small enclosure off the camel pens at five o'clock."

Quinn started to speak, but Deuben held up her hand to shush him.

"I will bring him," she said. "What of the Chinese soldiers? They like to patrol the Sunday market. I'm certain they would not approve of such things."

"We will see to them." The old man grinned. "I have

made the garrison nearest the animal market a gift of two casks of plum wine. They will sleep late tomorrow morning."

"Very well." Deuben smiled tightly. "He will be there, *insh'Allah*."

The old men bid their good-byes to the doctor, eyeing Quinn as a curiosity, shaking their heads as they disappeared into the crowded night.

Deuben collapsed back in her chair, releasing a pent-up groan. She pushed a lock of blond hair out of her face.

Belvan Virk turned, brooding. "This is madness," he said. "Umar is a giant. . . ."

Ronnie had watched the entire episode with a string of noodles hanging from her chopsticks. "Would someone like to tell me what just happened?"

"I wouldn't mind that either," Quinn said, though he had a sinking suspicion he knew already.

Deuben pushed the plate of *suoman* toward Quinn, urging him to eat. "Umar is a local businessman who considers himself the best fighter in all of Kashgar. But for Umar, Gao and his little crew were some of the toughest men in town. At least until you came along. When you beat them, you took away some of Umar's street cred."

Quinn shook his head. It went against everything he stood for to run away from a fight, but he had the mission to think about. "We don't have time for this."

"I agree," Ronnie said.

"It doesn't matter." Deuben picked up a piece of grilled mutton and popped it into her mouth. "It is something you must do."

"I'm not sure you understand, Doctor," Quinn said. "I'm not frightened of this Umar. I simply don't have time to deal with him right now. My superiors are awaiting word about the orphanage."

Deuben swallowed her mutton and dabbed a bit of grease off her lips with a cloth from her vest pocket. "You simply don't have time *not* to deal with Umar." She pushed Quinn's plate of *suoman* closer to him. "He's the man providing your motorcycles and there's no one else in town who would rent to you if you snub Umar. Now eat up. He's a big fellow. You will need all your strength."

Chapter Thirty-five

Local hunters said the high valley was inhabited by *Pari*, beautiful female beings with supernatural powers. Dr. Badeeb had played on that fear, calling his school the Pari Children's Home—or simply Pari.

To an untrained eye, the face of the school looked like a pile of flat gray stones at the foot of a sheer rock face. Two similar peaks rose from the edges of a high alpine meadow surrounding the blue waters of a glacial lake. The peaks were covered with snow year-round, not quite tall enough to draw the attention of world-class mountaineers and much too dangerous to provide any negotiable pass for opium smugglers. Massive golden eagles soared unmolested in the rectangle of blue sky. A small herd of female ibex and their kids nibbled scant vegetation in the craggy peaks.

Flanking the hidden valley on three sides, these giant rocks formed the perfect palisade, protecting the high meadow from unwanted intruders. At the base of the largest mountain, almost hidden among the pile of flat stones, was a dusty wooden door framed by heavy timber supports. A closer inspection revealed a tiny, one-foot-square window, similarly framed a few feet past the door. Seven identical windows strung out along the mountain's base toward the apex of the valley.

A cluster of smoke-gray felt yurts dotted the valley floor. The protected Pamir provided excellent grazing grounds during summer months, and even now, well into the fall with a skiff of ice ringing the emerald lake, herds of yaks and scruffy sheep still munched on the frost-nipped pastures.

On the other side of the third window down, CIA paramilitary officer Karen Hunt sat in a clammy room carved into the bowels of the mountain. An oil lamp sputtered in a chipped hollow along the inside rock wall.

She'd thought her spine would snap before the caravan arrived at the valley. Two men, one on each arm, had dragged her on wobbly legs from her yak and into the dark twelve-by-twelve cell. When her eyes became accustomed to the flickering lamp, she'd been startled to find Lieutenant Nelson and Specialist Nguyen already lying on a pile of rags in the uneven corner of the cave-like room.

A plastic bucket sat on the floor under a constant drip from the carved stone roof. The water appeared to be clean, but smelled of sulfur. It was a small bucket for the needs of three people, no bigger than a table pitcher, but the dripping kept it full.

The concussion from the stun grenade, coupled with the rigors of the never-ending yak ride, had left Karen's skin raw and her body past the point of exhaustion. A knot from her beating throbbed behind her right ear.

Relieved just to be alive, she collapsed beside a similarly docile Nelson and Nguyen before passing into unconsciousness.

Karen stirred as a ray of pink light sifted in from the single window to paint the only flat wall of the cell. Her eyes were matted shut and every inch of her body felt as if she'd been dragged over an acre of broken glass. Moaning softly, she realized her head was resting in Lieutenant Nelson's lap. She forced open her eyes to see that he was leaning against the wall, looking down at her. Specialist Nguyen was curled up against her back, keeping them both as warm as possible against the damp stone floor.

"How long have we been here?" Karen blinked. She moved her neck from side to side, awakening the searing pain in the knot above her ear.

"I couldn't say," Nelson said. His eyes were glazed in the thousand-yard stare of someone lost in thought. "I'm hungry, if that means anything."

"Is anything broken?" Karen pushed herself gingerly into a sitting position beside Nelson, being as careful as she could not to disturb Nguyen.

"My collarbone is toast," he said through clenched teeth. "Won't be much use to you in a fight."

"We'll see ab—"

Karen's answer was cut short by the creak of the metal door. A Tajik guard with close-cropped gray hair stuck his head in and gave the cell a quick once-over. A moment later, three boys—none of them looked over twelve—brought in trays of dates, nuts, and rice along with three red cans of Coca-Cola. They were not the sort of cans with Arabic script that U.S. personnel called Abu Dhabi Cokes—these were American pop cans with English writing.

Karen felt Nelson's body go tense. They both realized the leader of the boys was Kenny, the same child who'd approached the front gate at Camp Bullwhip. The same one who'd so cavalierly thanked them for the chocolate while shrugging of the fact that they would soon lose their heads.

"Hey," Kenny grunted, a sullen preteen even in the wilds of . . . wherever they were. "You guys look like crap." He motioned for the other two boys, both younger and a few inches shorter, to place their trays of food on the ground and back away. For a child, he seemed to have a lot of experience dealing with prisoners.

"Go ahead." He waved at the piles of apricots and clumped rice. "You should eat when they give you food. One of you will need all your strength by the end of the day."

Specialist Nguyen rose up on one elbow beside Karen. "Hey," he muttered, rubbing his eyes. "How did you get here?"

Kenny smirked, glancing back at his two companions. "I told you," he said. "I'm from Milwaukee."

One of the boys, a freckle-faced kid of eight or so, bobbed his head and shoulders quickly, giggling.

Karen fought the urge to jump up and pound the little kid's face against the rock wall. "Listen, you guys, I don't know where they took you from. But we're Americans too. Kenny, just before we were attacked you said you were from Wisconsin. I'm from Boston. We're all on the same side here."

"That's where you're wrong," Kenny snorted. "After what the Americans did, we'll never be on the same side."

"What do you mean, the Americans?" Nguyen gasped, his voice wobbling like he might cry. "Why are you guys doin' this? We didn't do nothing to you but give you chocolate. Have they brainwashed you or something?"

Nelson held up a hand, shushing him. "Let's just eat something and see where that leads."

"I'll tell you where it will lead," Kenny said. "It'll lead to getting your infidel heads sawed off . . . but what do I know? You guys eat up."

The freckled kid's head moved like a bobbing dog statuette and he broke into a maniacal giggle.

SUNDAY
October 1

Chapter Thirty-six

Kashgar, China

0530 hours China Standard Time

"You cannot win. Do you understand?" A cloud of vapor enveloped Gabrielle Deuben's face in the pink-orange chill of early morning.

"I know," Quinn said.

Garcia rubbed her eyes and gave a long, feline yawn. "I've seen you fight," Garcia said. "I think you can take this guy. He's big, but he's fat."

Deuben shook her head. "That's not the point. If he wins, Umar loses even more face."

Garcia's eyes followed a potbellied Uyghur who looked more like a draft horse than a man. She'd been disappointed but not surprised last night when Quinn had slept on the floor, letting her have the bed. Even on the hard floor he appeared to have slept better than her. "And what if he kills you?" she asked.

"I won't let that happen." Quinn sat with his back to the wall. The eight-foot-high clay block enclosure was normally used to house livestock during the Sunday market. It was five-thirty in the morning and the camels would be arriving in a half an hour.

The fight would be long over by then.

"But remember," Doctor Deuben whispered. Her eyes, too, followed the Uyghur as she spoke. "You can't throw the match. That would be the worst of all for Umar's reputation."

"Don't win and try not to lose." Quinn nodded as if taking a mental note. "That should be easy enough."

Garcia wanted to scream.

Umar leaned against the same clay wall and did a press-up twenty feet away, stretching calf muscles the size of grapefruit. He wore a pair of dirty canvas pants and scuffed leather boots. A morning chill pinked the hairy skin of his bare back.

Garcia shook her head. The man's neck looked as big around as Quinn's waist. She'd spent no small amount of time wondering what Quinn might look like with his shirt off. Now her stomach was too tied up in knots to enjoy it.

"Shall we begin?" Umar's ancient gray-bearded assistant wheezed around his smoldering cigarette. Two lines of at least a dozen men each squatted stoically along the outer edge of the oblong arena.

Quinn turned to Garcia and smiled. "You think anyone's betting on me?"

Ronnie watched Umar flex his thick chest, bouncing his pecs as he ground a huge fist into an open palm. Quinn peeled off his white T-shirt to reveal at least a dozen puckered white scars on the tight copper flesh across his lower back. She wondered if maybe he'd been shot. His body was fluid and moved easily, seeming as much tendon and bone as muscle. He looked like a well-built ant about to fight a hippo.

Shivering at the sight of him, Ronnie gave Quinn a soft jab in the shoulder.

"Sorry, *mango*, my money's on Umar."

Quinn stood, stretching his neck back and forth to either side, hearing the cracks. But for the odor of animal dung and the sound of braying donkeys over the walls, he was taken back to his boxing days at the Air Force Academy. There was something about a pending fight that changed the very nature of the air and made it sweeter to breathe.

Umar the Uyghur had a jowly, egg-shaped face with short-cropped hair that reminded Quinn of Thibodaux's marine high-and-tight. A roll of fat around the man's belly said he didn't get much cardio exercise, but the rippling muscles in his arms and shoulders said there was a good chance he won his fights without even raising his heart rate.

Umar lumbered to the center of the camel pen, slapping his great chest with hands the size of dinner plates. He swayed like a mountain gorilla. Each scuffing step of his heavy boots kicked up a pink cloud of dust in the long rays of morning light.

He turned to Quinn, tilting his big head into the beginnings of a nod. Quinn returned the gesture, hands hanging relaxed at his sides. There would be no referee and no one to explain the rules. There were none.

Umar slapped his chest again, leaving a pink handprint on the undulating flesh. He flicked his fingers, beckoning Quinn out. His twinkling eyes all but disappeared behind a cheeky grin.

"I don't like this," Ronnie said through clenched teeth. "Here we are at the edge of the world and all the local police are passed out drunk. What if he decides he has to kill you to save face?"

Quinn gave her a wink. "I'm pretty skilled in the not-dying category."

He took a half step forward—and the giant Uyghur charged like a raging bull elephant.

Quinn stepped deftly to the side to avoid the oncoming freight train. A thick cloud of dust engulfed the Uyghur as he slid to a stop.

In general, fights with no rules lasted under a minute. Umar was over six and a half feet tall. Quinn knew one solid punch from this man and the fight would be over much quicker than that.

The Uyghur spun, dragging his left leg in an almost imperceptible gimp. His left shoulder sagged as he moved. Just a hair, but Quinn noticed. Big people tended to have big injuries. Sheer mass compounded any sprain, crack, or pull. Within ten seconds, Quinn was able to identify bruised floating ribs on the giant's right side, a strained AC ligament on each knee, acute plantar fasciitis of the left heel, and a badly torn rotator cuff. Collectively, the injuries were debilitating enough Quinn could have scored a decisive victory in a matter of moments. Unfortunately he wouldn't have that luxury. He'd have to drag out the battle—make Umar work for it. And both men would have to endure a considerable amount of pain.

Quinn dodged the direct effects of a crashing right hook, letting it graze his chest. He staggered backward, coughing as if it had been a devastating blow. For a man of his bulk, Umar could turn on a dime. Circling, he brought the screaming right fist around for another try. This time Quinn stepped past and gave him a swift cow-kick low on the left calf, an area sure to be painfully tight from the plantar fasciitis.

Umar turned again, nostrils flaring, panting hard. He gave a little shake of his leg and eyed Quinn through narrow slits. The kick had set his leg on fire; Quinn could see it in his eyes. Feinting with his left, the Uyghur followed with a growling bum rush. The crowd of squatting onlookers cried out in delighted surprise as they parted like the Rea Sea before the oncoming giant.

Quinn stepped aside again, a matador avoiding an enraged bull. He drove his knuckles into Umar's cracked ribs, and then slapped him in the groin as he bowled past so the crowd couldn't see what had just happened. Unable to stop in time, Umar slammed straight into the high block wall.

He pushed back, dazed and blinking. A trickle of blood ran from his nose and cracked lip where he had kissed the rough stone.

From the corner of his eye, Quinn could see the quizzical looks on the local men's faces. They'd clearly expected their champion to wipe the floor with the visiting American.

Umar wasted no time in rejoining the fight. In the

blink of an eye he rushed back to the center of the camel pen, now a boiling haze of pink-tinged dust.

Umar kept his left arm tucked tight, clearly protecting the injured rotator cuff. He threw another staggering right, but Quinn stepped under this time, landing a punch of his own in the soapy exposed flesh of the giant's armpit. The same nerves that made the area ticklish made it a perfect target to incapacitate the arm.

Umar's elbow slammed to his side, the entire arm flapping unnaturally as he moved. His round face fell into a slack-jawed stare and he slouched forward as if he might vomit.

Quinn knew he had to let the man win soon, or risk a victory himself.

He sprang sideways, giving the stunned Uyghur a perfect target for a left hook. Quinn took the punch on the chin, counting on the injured shoulder to take out some of the sting.

It did, but not much.

Quinn went down hard, slamming into the mixture of dirt and pulverized camel dung. Umar staggered over, trying to deliver a kick to his exposed ribs. Quinn rolled toward him, closing the distance and riding the leg up to wrench sideways against the torn knee ligaments.

A light of realization flickered in Umar's narrow eyes. His massive arms dangled like broken wings. In that instant, he realized Quinn knew all his weaknesses. He was an accomplished enough fighter to know when he'd been beaten.

Quinn rolled to his feet, rushing headlong into the giant as if he meant to tackle him. He bounced off, landing on his seat. Umar stood still, blinking.

Quinn scrambled up and rushed in again. This time, the Uyghur caught him up in a bear hug. It was all he could do to hang on with one arm partially paralyzed and the other shoulder torn and out of commission.

Hands at his sides, feet dangling, Quinn hoped the big guy had gotten his message.

The crowd of onlookers surrounding the camel pen shot to their feet when they saw Quinn had fallen into what they knew as Umar's crushing grip.

The giant Uyghur looked down and grinned—understanding.

Roaring, he squeezed Quinn tight against his chest and gave him a stiff head-butt to the nose.

Quinn's eyes rolled back as he fought to keep conscious. In the cloud of dust, Umar winked at him.

"Only a tap, my friend," he whispered. "You have my respect . . . and my thanks."

Quinn slid to the ground, landing flat on the seat of his pants. Blood streamed from his nostrils.

The crowd began to chant their beloved Umar's name.

Chapter Thirty-seven

Karen Hunt sat up with a start when the metal door clanged open. The three prisoners huddled close together for warmth as well as moral support. Specialist Tuan "Kevin" Nguyen had just been reminiscing about his parents making him study twice as hard as the white kids in his class.

As always, one of the adult guards peered into the room first before letting in the children. But this time, he followed them in, accompanied by three other men in knee-length *shalwar kameez* shirts and baggy pants. The men all looked to be in their thirties and forties with close-cropped black hair and dark beards. Two of them had strikingly green eyes.

Three of the men stood back against the wall, hands hanging loosely by their sides. The leader, one of the green-eyed ones, stepped forward.

Kenny stood beside him.

"You," Kenny said, pointing at Nguyen. "Get up."

"Why me?" Nguyen asked in a whisper like tearing paper. He didn't move.

"Why not you?" Kenny smirked.

Nguyen turned to look at Hunt, breathing faster through his nose. "I . . ."

"Take me," Nelson said, trying to push himself to a sitting position. He winced from the pain of his broken collarbone.

The kid folded his arms across his Pepsi T-shirt and gave an emphatic shake of his head.

"Nope," he said. "It's not your turn. Gotta be hi—"

Karen lunged, missing Kenny's neck by mere inches. She had no plan but couldn't let them drag poor Nguyen away without a fight.

One of the guards caught across the back of her neck with a heavy leather sap, driving her to the ground. A shower of lights blasted through her brain. Through the hazy shadows, she could hear the sounds of Kenny laughing and Kevin Nguyen screaming in terror as they dragged him away.

Chapter Thirty-eight

Umar held a blood-soaked cloth to his nose and pushed the paperwork across the counter. "Royal Enfield Bullet," he sniffed. "Only the best motorcycle for you, my friend."

Quinn signed the rental contract, written by some Chinese lawyer in poorly translated English. He worked his bruised jaw back and forth as he handed back the pen.

Umar tossed the rag on the counter and raised his beefy hand. His injured lip split back open when he grinned, dripping blood on the contract. "Four hundred and ninety-nine cc, four stroke, twenty-seven horsepower—best bike for you. Altitude no problem."

"Twenty-seven horsepower." Quinn nodded, thinking about the hundred-twenty-plus of his modified BMW. Still, the Enfield was a sweet little bike. Gaunt and skinny enough to show its ribs, it was a motorcycle that brought back memories of black-and-white newsreels from the war and dispatches that just had to make it through enemy lines. The Indian government had started using the Enfield bikes in 1955 and later bought the tooling equipment from the British in 1957. Little had changed over decades of production, but the new fuel injection would come in handy climbing the sixteen-thousand-foot passes leading into the High Pamir.

Umar knew his motorcycles. It a shame that these two little machines wouldn't make it back into his stable. Quinn made a mental note to see that new ones were provided as replacements as soon as he got home—if he got home.

Chapter Thirty-nine

Gaithersburg

Mujaheed Beg ran a chipped fingernail across the black-and-white striped pillow from Veronica Garcia's rumpled bed. Egyptian cotton. She had good taste. He held it to his nose and breathed in the musky floral scent of jasmine perfume. A pile of clothes lay strewn over the bed as if she'd dumped them out of a hamper. A small wicker basket full of lipsticks and eye makeup sat on the nightstand beside the bed. Two empty suitcases lay tossed on top of one another in the corner.

Wherever she'd gone, she left in a hurry.

Beg picked up a skimpy pair of leopard-print panties from the laundry on the bed and twirled them around his finger.

"It's now or never," he sang in a passable Elvis impression. His eyes wandered around the bedroom. "Show me her secrets. . . ."

He'd made a similar trip to Grace Smallwood's

apartment. It was how he'd discovered her allergy to bees.

Garcia's ballistic vest had been tossed unceremoniously on a pile of dirty laundry. A large-frame .40-caliber Glock and a smaller, more feminine Kahr nine-millimeter sat loaded and holstered on the top shelf of the closet. He slid the hangers over one by one, stopping at a sequined blue evening gown. It made him laugh out loud to think of this buxom woman trying to hide a pistol under the sheer gown.

"What has become of you, my dear?" he muttered, running his hands along the hanging clothes.

He found it unbelievable that the dangerous woman he'd seen coming into Nadia Arbakova's house would leave her weapons at home . . . unless she'd gone somewhere she could not take them. . . .

Veronica Garcia's bathroom revealed less than her bedroom. She took no medications but aspirin, used tampons instead of pads, and shaved her legs in the shower. Jasmine was her preferred scent for soaps and body lotions.

The familiar smell made him ache to meet her, to spend time with her alone in this house. He went back to the bedroom and shoved the pile of clothes on the floor to lie down on the striped sheets that smelled so strongly of her.

His phone began to buzz before his head hit the pillow. It had to be Badeeb.

He sat up, cursing in Tajik.

"Yes?"

"Allah be praised. Are you well?"

"Yes." He did not wish to waste time with the doctor on pleasantries.

"Are you nearby?" came the familiar clicky voice.

"How would I know if that is so until you tell me where you are?"

"Never mind," Badeeb said, snapping his cigarette lighter closed. "I have a job for you. I believe it will be straight up your street, so to speak. . . ."

Beg rubbed a hand over his hair. "I don't know what that means."

"You know," Badeeb stuttered. "Something you will enjoy—up your street."

"Right up my alley," Beg corrected. That such a witless man could accomplish so much of such great importance was surely a mystery.

"Yes, exactly that," the doctor continued. "This one will be quite enjoyable, for you. I need you take care of an issue with the congressman. There is a situation." Badeeb paused to take a long drag on his cigarette. "A situation I have been, of necessity, keeping from you . . ."

Beg picked up Garcia's striped pillow and held it to his nose.

"Of course." He closed his eyes and inhaled deeply, unwilling to leave the scent of Veronica Garcia so quickly for any reason. "I will meet you in two hours' time."

Chapter Forty

Xinjiang Province/Uyghur Autonomous Region
China

Dressed in matching olive two-piece Rev'it textile riding suits against the chill of high altitude, Quinn and Garcia reached the police checkpoint at Tashkurgan before lunch. They'd stopped on the way for a bathroom break along the Karakoram Highway at the black waters of Lake Karakul. Quinn paid a Uyghur man five *quai*—less than a dollar—to take a photo of Ronnie sitting on a camel. They didn't have the time for such things, but a tourist who rode by the high desert lake and didn't take stop for photos would be highly suspect. And, he had to admit, she looked pretty good sitting up there, snowcapped peaks in the background, her hair blowing in the wind.

The ramshackle outpost of Tashkurgan was little more than a faceless government building and a touristy hotel with a line of fake yurts. They would need a special permit to continue down the Karakoram to their ostensible destination of the Khunjerab Pass leading into Pakistan. Umar had assured them the police were used to letting people riding his motorcycles through. As it turned out, the three Chinese guards, who were barely out of their teens, offered to let Garcia get her picture taken wearing one of their hats for twenty U.S. dollars—each. Quinn gladly paid the sixty bucks and they were able to slip through as long as they promised to just "go and come back" to the Pakistani border.

"Not a bad fee all in all," Quinn said as they pushed the Enfields away from the concrete barricades and back on to the Karakoram heading south.

"That wasn't a fee." Ronnie wrinkled her nose. "That was a bribe."

Quinn swung a leg over his bike. "You say tomato. . . . We made it through without having to duct tape anyone and leave them in the closet. That's what matters."

Thirty miles south of Tashkurgan, they cut right, leaving the relative comfort of the paved Karakoram Highway to head west on an old jeep trail toward the sixteen-thousand-foot level marking Wakhir Pass and Afghanistan. Luckily, they saw no other traffic at the diversion from their promised route.

Garcia handled the rock-strewn road like Quinn had seen her handle everything in the short time he'd know her: by pretending she was an expert long enough that she became one. She was a strong woman, naturally athletic. Off-road motorcycling appeared to come easily to her.

As Umar had promised, the Enfield Bullets thumped along the rutted trail without complaint. Quinn had expected some drop in performance as they climbed near six thousand meters, but the bikes took Gabrielle's impossibly steep smugglers' trail along a sheer rock wall like metal mountain goats.

The only lag in performance was of the human kind. Both Quinn and Garcia were in excellent physical shape, but they were accustomed to living at sea level. By twelve thousand feet, even the act of horsing the motorcycles over gravel and dust forced them to stop for frequent breathers and sips of water. He'd read stories of ancient Buddhist monks who gave these places names like *Big Headache* and *Nosebleed Pass*. The throbbing killer at Quinn's temples made him understand why.

Garcia made no secret of the fact that she hated the dizzying heights, refusing to look down and urging Quinn to get going again shortly after they'd stopped. He was sure her knuckles were white under the thick leather gloves.

Fatigue wasn't their only problem. At thirteen thousand feet, they ran into a wall of blowing gray dust, ground fine as talc by the host of glaciers among the endless sawtooth peaks that stretched before them. The air was thin enough already and the dust made it nearly impossible to draw a breath.

Used for centuries by Silk Road travelers who wanted no contact with government officials, the hidden trail rose quickly, jogging around slabs of rock the size of houses and fields of gray boulders that fanned from snowcapped crags on all sides. Finally battling their way above the dust storm, they were able to make good progress until they were three miles from the pass.

Quinn saw the lone man from nearly a mile away, picking his way across a boulder-strewn side hill leading seven camels.

Quinn motioned for Garcia to pull off the trail alongside him on an uphill swell of gravel and dismount. There was just enough room for both bikes. It took his breath away when she shook her thick hair free of her helmet. He looked away quickly, back at the approaching camel herder, hoping she hadn't noticed his stares.

The herdsman's clucking and scolding could be heard for ten minutes before the little troupe crested the rise in the trail. Each camel had a barbed stick through its nose attached to a cord connecting it to the animal ahead. The man held a piece of rope from the nose of the lead beast. Only the baby trotted independently of the rest, even more knock-kneed and gangly than the adults.

"You have your camera handy?" Quinn asked.

Garcia tapped the chest pocket of her riding jacket. "Right here."

The copper bell on the baby's halter clanged happily as it plodded closer over the stony path.

"Go ahead and get it out," he whispered, smiling at the approaching man. "It's always some herder that trips you up. . . . He needs to think we're just tourists."

The herdsman raised his right hand to his breast, bowing his head slightly. He was young, still in his twenties with a flint-hard look in his eye the smile couldn't conceal. A FAM, fighting-age male, he carried a paratrooper Kalashnikov with a folding stock hung on a cloth sling over his shoulder. The Wahkir didn't see enough traffic for professional bandits, but if one smuggler happened to be better armed than another he met along the path, there was no honor among those in the black market. The collar of a wool suit jacket was turned up against the chill. The tail of his flimsy shirt hung out over stained khaki military trousers. Thin leather sandals did little to protect his cracked feet from the ravages of weather and stone.

Quinn thought it best to play dumb and gave an awkward Chinese greeting.

The camel man shook his head, grinning with a mouth full of indigo and snuff-stained teeth.

"No Chinaman," he said. He puffed up his chest. "Pashtu."

The herder eyed the Royal Enfields with a keen interest, dropping the rope to his lead camel. He patted the seat on Jericho's bike. "You sell?"

Quinn shook his head. It never surprised him when traders talked business in a whole multitude of languages. They might not be able to tell you the time, but they could barter, curse, and call you a cheapskate in the language of your choice.

Quinn shook his head. "Not mine. Umar's bikes. You know Umar?"

The herdsman's eyes went wide. He showed his blue-black teeth. "Umar's bikes," he repeated. He turned to stare at Garcia for a moment, took a deep breath, and stooped to pick up his lead rope.

Without a word of good-bye he clucked at his camels and started down the trail toward the Karakoram Highway. His animals trundled along after him bawling and farting until they fell back into their traveling jog.

"That was weird," Garcia said tucking the camera back in her pocket.

Quinn threw a leg over his Enfield, anxious to be moving again. "I'm pretty sure he was looking at you as much as the bikes."

Garcia paused. "What if he pulled the rifle?"

Quinn pretended to act incredulous. "And that from a woman who just witnessed my physical prowess at not beating Umar the giant. Come on, we should get going. That fight gave us a late start. We need to make it over Gabrielle's secret pass by nightfall."

"You afraid we'll run into Chinese soldiers?"

"Nope," Quinn said, starting his bike. "The big problem on smugglers' trails is smugglers."

CHAPTER FORTY-ONE

They rolled through the gap between two great, guardian-like boulders and into Afghanistan an hour before sunset. There was nothing to mark the nameless pass but for a stone cairn topped with the skull of a heavy-horned Marco Polo sheep. A half mile in, they were met by a crude, hand-painted and weather-worn sign showing a human figure with his leg being blown off by a land mine. It was a notice to all to keep to the relative safety of the trail.

Quinn stopped for a moment to check the map Gabrielle had drawn, comparing it to the topographic tour map Umar had supplied. The detail gave out thirty miles into Afghanistan. Quinn hoped that would be enough.

The next forty-five minutes saw them descend six thousand feet. A camp at ten thousand feet would be uncomfortable for flatlanders, but it would be infinitely better than one at sixteen thousand. Quinn slowed, turning back to Garcia, two bike-lengths behind him. It was impossible to tell behind her full-face helmet, but her eyes said she was grinning.

Ten minutes later they'd hidden both motorcycles behind a faded gray boulder, in a fold of the mountain of the main trail. Quinn removed his heavy armored jacket, setting up camp in the suspendered riding pants and a gray long-sleeved wool T-shirt. While cotton might be king in the south, growing up in Alaska had taught him wool was the way to go when things got wet and cold.

Garcia still wore all her gear against the chill and donned a Nepalese wool beanie with earflaps and braided cords.

"You've come a very long way from Cuba," Quinn chuckled. He situated the aluminum poles of their mountaineering tent over the flattest patch of rubble he could find. They'd told Umar they were married as part of the cover story—he would have been unhappy sending an unmarried woman out alone with Quinn. Wanting to save space on the smallish Enfields, the big Ugyhr provided only one tent. Luckily, it was a three-person, which in mountaineering terms translated as "tight for two."

Garcia squatted opposite Quinn and helped him thread the poles into the sleeves of the bright orange fabric. "Must be old hat for you," she said, teeth chattering. "I suppose this is a lot like Alaska?"

"In some ways." Quinn looked to his left at the sheer rock face that faded into a layer of clouds a thousand feet above. Fifty feet to his right an abrupt ledge fell away to nothingness for nearly a mile. Howling winds raced off hidden glaciers and the distant hush of a river whispered up from the valley floor. "Yeah, I guess it does remind me of home."

Quinn finished snapping in the last pole and looked up to see Garcia shaking her head and blinking as if she was dizzy.

"We should feed you and get to bed," he said.

She smiled weakly. "Not tonight, honey. I have a headache."

He took her by the shoulders and led her to the base of a car-sized rock, where he made her a sort of nest with their bedrolls and sleeping pads. "You sit here while I whip us up my two-mile-high specialty.

Garcia drew her knees to her chest, drawing her neck inside her jacket like a turtle and her hands into her sleeves. Only the pink tip of her nose showed above the collar of her coat.

"Seriously," she moaned. "I don't want to be a whiner, but I feel like someone may be digging my eyes out with a spoon. I couldn't eat a bite."

"It's the altitude," Quinn said. "I should have paid attention to it earlier."

"I'm a big girl, in case you haven't noticed." She let her head loll back against the boulder.

"You rest. I'll make supper," he said. He thought: *Oh, I've noticed all right.*

A couple of aspirin and Quinn's mutton noodle soup worked miracles. Ronnie went from feeling like she'd been trampled by a camel to aching as though she'd just been dragged by one. The pain in her head down to a dull throb, she was able to concentrate on Jericho.

"Hard to breathe up here," she said, wanting to make conversation.

"There's this sign on the wall above the swimming pool at the Academy," he said. "*The Air Is Rare*." He held a mug of soup under his chin. Steam curled around the stubble of beard that seemed twice as dark as it had only a few hours before. "We have an early start if we want to find the Kyrgyz camp tomorrow," he said.

The wind had died off with the sun. A thick layer of fog had settled in, rendering the orange tent almost invisible just a few feet away. They had to wear headlamps to keep from walking off the cliff.

Quinn played his light toward the tent. "Sorry about the cramped arrangements."

"No problem." She got up with a groan. "I've watched enough Bond movies to know this is the way things always work out. I only need to know if I'm the girl spy you end up with as the credits roll or the sacrificial one who has passionate sex with you, then dies halfway through the movie."

"Remains to be seen," Quinn mused over his mug, blowing away a plume of steam.

"Anyway," she added, "you look too beat to try anything tonight, Mr. Bond."

"Sex is messy." Quinn shrugged. "We'd probably knock the tent off the ledge—or your head would explode from all the exertion."

Garcia pursed her lips, thinking that over. She eyed him carefully. "I'm not sure if you're trying to talk me out of or into sleeping with you. . . ."

"Oh." Quinn grinned. "In Umar's infinite wisdom, he believed a married couple should have blankets instead of warm down bags. We're sleeping together all right. But that's as far as it goes."

"Because of your ex-wife?" Garcia went out on a limb.

"Maybe so." Quinn shrugged. "But don't necessarily expect the same resolve when I'm at altitudes below ten thousand feet."

"I'll make a note of that." She grinned.

Garcia stripped down to her black wool long johns before kneeling to crawl in the vestibule door. Exhausted or not, she hoped Quinn was watching her.

She wore the floppy Nepalese hat to bed. Using her rolled fleece jacket as a pillow, she tugged her side of the blanket tight around her shoulders as he maneuvered beside her. He piled the riding jackets over their feet but kept the blanket on his side turned down to his waist. Cuban versus Alaska blood, she thought. It made sense.

"Why did your parents pick Jericho?" she asked in the darkness.

Quinn sighed. He clicked on his headlamp and rolled up on his shoulder to stare at her. "I thought you were exhausted."

She batted her eyelashes, hoping she didn't look too much like a silly cow.

He snapped off the light and threw an arm across his forehead, seemingly oblivious to the cold. "My dad wanted to name me Gideon, but his sister stole the name for my cousin a month before I was born. I guess they figured Jericho was the next best name from the story . . . Gideon's trumpet and all."

Ronnie couldn't help but think he was in his element—hostile terrain in a hostile country.

"What's he do now? This cousin of yours."

"A big-shot banker in Anchorage," he said. "Pretty wealthy, as a matter of fact."

"Banker or secret government agent . . . let me see. . . ."

"He's home in a soft bed right now." Quinn rearranged the blanket, trying to situate his body between the rocks under the tent floor.

For a long moment there was no sound but distant wind and rivers.

"You know this really sucks," Ronnie said suddenly, not quite ready to give up Quinn's company to sleep.

"Why's that?" he said through a long yawn. She could just make out the outline of his chest, rising and falling in the shadows.

"Well, most couples have these sorts of sweet little conversations when they're breathless and spent. You have to lie there and listen to me snore and pass gas all night without any of the . . . you know, fringe benefits."

Quinn yawned again, longer this time, shuddering. "Could be worse. You could have night terrors and wake up trying to kill someone."

She scrunched up next to him, stealing the warmth of his body. Smelling the musky odor of his skin.

"Is that what you do?"

"Only when I'm extremely tired . . ."

Through the darkness, she thought she saw him smile.

MONDAY
October 2

Chapter Forty-two

Dawn took its time in the protected valleys of the High Pamir. The mist was gone, but the morning would linger gray and clammy-cold for hours before the sun finally peeked over the knife ridges high above. A brisk wind popped at the tent fly.

Quinn stirred under the blankets, feeling the familiar aches in his shoulders and hips from too many nights on the unforgiving ground. His hands felt like claws from gripping the Enfield's handlebars all day. The effects of the fight with Umar left him with a stiff neck and a wrenched knee that was sure to give him problems when he got older. He thought of the Chinese proverb: *When two tigers fight, one is injured beyond repair—and the other one is dead.*

During the night Ronnie had rolled half on top of him. Her arm flailed across his chest, the warmth of a long leg draped over his thigh. Quinn lay still for a moment, feeling the moist, fluttering puff of her exhausted breathing against his neck.

Bootystan, he thought. *Jacques, Jacques, Jacques. If you could only see me now . . .*

Trying not to wake her, he wriggled out of the tent, stifling a gasp as he stepped into his chilly riding pants and stiff Haix patrol boots. He munched a piece of naan from his day pack—courtesy of Umar's wife—and swung his arms trying to warm up. In the muted light, he could just make out the outline of a path he hadn't noticed the night before. Likely a game trail used by ibex or Marco Polo sheep, it ran at an angle to a small plateau about a two hundred feet above the camp.

"What do you see?"

Quinn jumped at Ronnie's voice behind him. She'd poked her head out the tent door.

"I'm thinking I'd like to take a look at what's up there. It might give me a glimpse of what's ahead of us."

"Take the bike." She yawned, catlike. "I'm awake. Anyway, a girl could use a little privacy first thing in the morning."

Quinn looked down at the Breitling. "Oh-seven-fifty Afghan time," he said. "I should be back in twenty minutes."

"Sounds good." She pulled her head back inside the tent. "I'll heat up some of that goat's head soup or whatever it was."

The trail up the mountain was strewn with baseball-sized rocks and steep enough Quinn had to keep the bike going forward or risk sliding back down. Umar had replaced the little bike's stock Avon tires with decent enough Chinese-made *Cheng Shin* knobbies suitable for the washouts and gravel roads of the western frontier. It climbed without complaint.

The trouble with the Enfield was that, being old-school, some parts were prone to break. The bolts that held on the muffler had sheared off somewhere along the way since they'd left Kashgar. Quinn knew he'd have to figure out a way to jury-rig the exhaust before it fell off or risk deafness and an avalanche from blatting engine noise.

The bikes had their flaws, but the simple beauty of the Enfield was its fixability. Every village from the southern tip of India to the Mongolian Steppe had at least one shade tree mechanic who was familiar enough with the thumper to repair it with little more than a metal file and a screwdriver. Quinn felt confident he'd be able to figure something out when he got back to camp.

At the top of the goat path he was greeted by row after endless row of jagged peaks and rivers of flowing glacier ice. The world seemed nothing but muted shades of blue and slate gray.

The trail he'd hoped to scout disappeared around yet another plateau. It was easy to see how someone could hide in such a forgotten place high on the roof of the world.

Disappointed, Quinn turned the bike, rolling it to the lip before starting the short but steep ride back to camp. His breath caught hard in his chest when he peered over the edge and he took a reflexive step back, out of sight.

Less than two hundred feet below, a pair of men in rolled Afghan *Pakol* hats and knee-length *shalwar kameez* shirts fingered through their gear. A third man

Quinn recognized as the young camel herder from the day before stood behind Ronnie, pinning her arms.

Adrenaline surged through Quinn's body as he realized he had no weapons. Each of the men had a rifle slung over his shoulder. In this part of the world, they were sure to have knives as well.

Every few seconds the camel herder craned his long neck to gaze up the trail, obviously expecting Quinn to return from that direction. He'd likely convinced his friends to travel all night in order to rob the rich tourists. The other two bandits tossed through clothing and camping gear as they searched for anything of value. It wouldn't be long before they realized the only thing in camp worth selling was Veronica Garcia.

Quinn formed his plan as he went, relying on instinct over intellect. Jumping from the Enfield, he found a rock and bashed at the damaged muffler where it joined the straight pipe coming directly off the engine. In seconds he was able to shear the remaining screw and rip the muffler away.

Moments later he sat aboard the silent bike. A soft wind blew in his face. Looking over the edge, he shifted into third. He kept an eye on Ronnie while he slipped the Breitling from his wrist and unscrewed the crown on the lower barrel that contained the emergency location transmitter. He stopped short of pulling out the wire that would activate the satellite beacon.

Gripping the watch between his teeth, Quinn made certain the Enfield's ignition switch was turned on. For his plan to work, he'd need the element of surprise and a hell of a lot of luck. The camel herder already knew he was unarmed—but he hadn't counted on the Breitling.

Quinn pressed the clutch so he could pop it when he wanted to start the bike, and released the brake. He was rolling.

A hundred feet above the bandits, the trail leveled before making the final drop to camp. Quinn popped the clutch here. The Bullet's 499cc engine shuddered, skidding the back wheel in the loose gray shale. Thankfully, it caught enough traction and thumped to life. Without a muffler the little bike rattled and popped like a fifty cal.

"*Made like a gun*," Quinn whispered the Royal Enfield slogan through gritted teeth. And that was just how he intended to use it.

Rolling on all the power he had, he yanked back on the handlebars, praying they didn't snap off in his hands. The bike rose to an agitated wheelie, bouncing over the rocks, rearing like an angry horse.

Two of the men dove for cover at the sound of a sudden attack. The camel herder shoved Ronnie to the side. He brought up the Kalashnikov and began to fire.

The Enfield's chassis and engine gave Quinn some protection from the gunfire, but he was thankful the guy used the regional "spray and pray" tactic with no attempt at aiming his shots.

Rocks and debris skittered down the mountain ahead of the bike. The deafening crack-crack-crack of rifle fire and motorcycle engine slammed off the cliffs and echoed through the canyons. Thirty feet out, Quinn used his teeth to tug the coiled antenna wire on the Breitling, activating the locator beacon. He tossed the watch toward the two bandits standing beside his gear and plowed the Enfield straight into the camel driver, sending him and the bike over the edge and flailing through empty space.

Quinn bailed off the bike a split second before the front wheel impacted the startled man in the chest. He grabbed Garcia by the arm.

"Run, run, run!" he yelled, dragging her over the edge.

An instant later the high clouds gave a piercing hiss and a Hellfire missile struck the men above with pinpoint accuracy. The entire mountain shook with the explosion.

On the narrow ledge below, Ronnie screamed. Her wrist slipped from Quinn's grip and they began to slide on loose shale toward the jagged lip of rock—and oblivion.

CHAPTER FORTY-THREE

Northern Virginia

Jacques Thibodaux paced the oblong tile floor in front of the bank of blinking flat-screen computer monitors and glowing digitized maps of China and Afghanistan. The whir of cooling fans gave the place the feeling of a giant white noise machine. Thibodaux had to keep his hands behind his back to keep from slapping the big-eared Air Force staff sergeant sitting behind a computerized instrument panel and beefed-up military version of a game controller. On the wall above hung a three-foot blue banner bearing the motto of his secret unit in ornate golden script: *hic sunt dracones*—"Here There Be Dragons."

A red dot pulsed on the tightly stacked topographic lines of the map, seventeen miles across the Chinese border into the Wakhan Corridor of Afghanistan.

An emotionless female voice, like the ones that warned military pilots to "pull up, pull up" and avoid low terrain, sounded the alarm of "Impact . . . impact . . ." followed by a repeated set of GPS coordinates.

Staff Sergeant Guttman, the big-eared object of the Marine's wrath, banged away furiously at the keyboard beside his game controller. His wide eyes blinked in teenage dismay at the instrument display on the panel before him.

A video game prodigy, he was one of a new generation of Air Force pilots assigned to Detachment Seven, the highly classified unit within the Fifty-third Test and Evaluation Group based at Eglin AFB. He was the primary pilot of the AX7 Damocles, a top-secret, Tier III—high-altitude, low-observable drone. Developed by Lockheed Martin's infamous Skunk Works project office, Damocles differed from the RQ-170 Sentinel in several ways, the most notable being that it carried a payload of weapons. Like the mythical sword on a single horsehair, Damo could loiter above the enemy for nearly two days at altitudes well over sixty-five thousand feet.

The emotionless female voice continued: "Impact . . . impact . . ."

Thibodaux stopped to rest both hands flat on the counter, breathing down the kid's neck. "Somebody wanna tell me what Bitchin' Betty's talkin' about?"

"I swear, sir." Guttman looked up, terrified. "It wasn't me. I didn't deploy anything."

Win Palmer sat in a leather office chair along the back wall of the narrow control room, across from Staff Sergeant Guttman. The windowless trailer was more like a submarine than an Air Force control center. The national security advisor's arms were folded across the chest of his white dress shirt, sleeves rolled up to his elbows.

"What deployed?" Palmer asked. "A Tomahawk or the Hellfire?"

"The one-fourteen, sir," Guttman chirped, his voice cracking from youth and fear. "The Hellfire."

"Very good," Palmer said. He leaned back, nodding as if relieved. "Damocles is normally armed with four Tomahawk missiles. We replaced one with a Hellfire to give Quinn close air support for this mission."

"And?" Thibodaux wanted to say, *What the hell does that mean?* But even he knew there were limits to ways you spoke to the president's right-hand man.

"The Breitling Mrs. Miyagi gave him," Palmer explained. "We programed Damocles to lock on to the watch when the ELT antenna was activated. The Hellfire would then deploy on a two-second delay. With travel time from altitude, that would give Quinn between five and seven seconds before impact."

"You mean to tell me"—Thibodaux's face burned red—"you just shot a Hellfire missile at Jericho?"

Guttman shook his head. He forced a sick smile. The kid was actually wearing multicolored braces on his teeth. "No, sir, at least not unless he told us to. The Breitling Emergency pings at two hundred and forty-three megahertz for your basic military frequency. Mr. Palmer's shop tweaked it to talk to Damo and Damo only. When your friend pulled the pin, the watch sent up a signal that went out like a giant cone. Damocles just had to lob one in the basket of that cone, so to speak. The Hellfire followed the signal down to the watch with less than one meter of error."

"Yeah, well," the big Cajun harrumphed, exhausted at being trapped stateside while Jericho was in danger, again. "Does Damo have a camera?"

"Multiple," Guttman said, puffing up his chest like a proud father. "Conventional and infrared—all mounted on a Gorgon Stare Pod—"

"Excellent," Thibodaux said. "Then get her zoomed in and let's make sure he's okay."

Guttman shot a terrified look at Palmer.

"Can't do that, Jacques." The national security advisor frowned. "The AX7 is a stealth platform, but it does leave some signature. With the Hellfire deployment, they'll be searching for us as it is. If we bring the drone lower to look through the cloud layer the Chinese will shoot her out of the sky. The Red Army has an air defense battery just outside of Kashgar. Too close."

Thibodaux rubbed his jaw. "You once said you wouldn't drop us in the grease without fair warning. Looks to me like Jericho is fryin' out there and you don't give a shit."

Palmer shook his head slowly. If he was offended, he didn't show it. "Quinn was fully briefed, Jacques. He knew how to deploy the weapon and how far away he had to be. He's alive now or he isn't. I'm betting he had an escape plan before he pulled the wire."

"We should at least look." Thibodaux rolled his shoulders, trying in vain not to let his temper get the best of him.

"No one wants to more than I do," Palmer said.

"I'll bet I do." The Marine stared hard.

"Easy to say, Jacques, when you only have your friend to consider . . ." Palmer studied him a long moment before nodding slowly, opening both hands. "But okay. You're in charge now. You say the word and

Sergeant Guttman will bring Damocles out of near orbit to check on our friend Quinn. Don't worry about the little dustup with China, Pakistan, and the rest of the world over our previously top-secret invisible armed UAV." The national security advisor turned to Guttman. "This man says the word and you bring her down."

"Sir . . ." Guttman stammered, looking like he might have already wet his pants.

"Just do it, son."

Thibodaux stood completely still, glaring at the ashen staff sergeant.

"Shit!" he finally spat, throwing up his hands. "Just forget it."

Across the room, Palmer released a pent-up breath. Guttman slouched in his seat, looking as if he might weep.

"There are damn few people in the world we can trust now, Jacques," Palmer said. "The last thing we need is for what we're doing to end up on WikiLeaks. We've got to believe Jericho knows what he's doing. . . . Give him a chance."

"I know." Thibodaux nodded. His neck burned with a mix of worry over Quinn and pity for men like Palmer who had so many layers of convoluted junk to consider. He preferred the heat of battle when it was kill or be killed. The political side of matters fatigued him. He turned to leave. Camille was in the hospital on bed rest and he hated to leave her alone too long.

"Jacques," Palmer called.

He stopped at the coded, metal door.

"Sir?"

"For the record, I wouldn't have made that offer if that had been another Marine out there."

Thibodaux grinned. "Shows how much you know, sir. I adopted Chair Force into the Corps about an hour after I met him."

Chapter Forty-four

Jericho clenched every muscle in his body. The veins on the side of his neck swelled as he strained with his left arm to hold on to Ronnie where she dangled five thousand feet above the hungry rocks below. He lay on his stomach, the crook of his right elbow clutching a nubbin of stone where they'd landed on the ledge roughly the size of a kitchen counter an instant before the Hellfire strike. The camel herder had fallen to his death and the two bandits left topside had been reduced to fine bits of ash.

The missile's impact had rendered Quinn partially deaf. He could hear snippets of Ronnie's frantic shouting, but her voice sounded like it was coming from the inside of a metal can. He couldn't see over the edge, but her hands clutched his forearm and he knew he had a good grip on some piece of her clothing. He could just make out the dust-covered crown of her head over the ledge.

Bracing with his legs against a thin fissure in the rock, he rolled backward, gaining inch by slow inch until he was able to haul her up like a fleshy, wriggling fish. She collapsed, wheezing on top of him, and he realized his handhold had been at the small of her back, on the bunched waistband of her wool long johns.

She looked down at his face as she rearranged her bunched clothing. "In some parts of Cuba, a wedgie like that would mean you'd have to marry me." Bits of gravel covered her lips. "Good thing I wore my big-girl panties. . . ."

"Yeah, good thing." Jericho was already working out a plan to get them up the sheer ten-foot face and back to the smoldering crater where their camp had been. He explained about the Breitling while he studied the rock.

"All this time you had an exploding watch and you didn't tell me?" She shook her head from side to side, her ebony hair a tangled nest of dirt and ash. "I *am* riding through China with James Bond."

"The watch just sent up a signal. The explosion was courtesy of the U.S. Air Force. And, technically—" Quinn grunted, trying to pull himself up with a shallow handhold, then slipping back down to hug it so he didn't fall backward into the dizzy drop behind him. "We're in Afghanistan . . . and now I won't even know what time it is."

"How far do you think—to the Kyrgyz camp?"

"If they haven't started their trek back out of the high pastures . . . maybe six miles according to Gabrielle's map."

Garcia faced the rock, raising her arms above her head. She arched her back and stuck out her butt.

"Come on," she said. "Give me a boost." Even under

their desperate circumstances, the stance took Quinn's breath away.

"As inviting as that looks"—he grinned—"you'll need to push me up first. That way I can pull you up."

"Okay . . ." Garcia shot a worried look over her shoulder toward the sheer drop. "But you know how I feel about heights. Don't leave me down here long."

CHAPTER FORTY-FIVE

The sounds of Nguyen's hoarse screams still rang in Hunt's ears when the kids came back in the room. Kenny was all grins, but he didn't mention the killing. They came and went at least five times a day. Both Hunt and Nelson talked to the other boys but refused to speak to Kenny again.

"What do you call it when a person likes to set things on fire?" A freckled blond boy of eight or nine asked Hunt from his cushion next to a sullen Kenny. His name was Sam and he had an earnest look in his eyes Karen found disarming.

"Pyromania," Lieutenant Nelson said, deadpan. He leaned against the curved stone wall of the cell. "Why? You know somebody who's into it? It usually means they wet the bed like Kenny." He'd talk sports or hunting with the other boys to pass the time, but he didn't pass up the opportunity to give the little jerk a jab if it presented itself.

The rest of the boys giggled until Kenny stared them down.

Little Sam scribbled in his spiral notebook, then looked up under blond bangs. "Don't you sometimes call them something else? I know there's another word. . . ."

Karen shrugged. "Just plain *pyro*." She'd decided to play along. Since the guards had dragged poor Nguyen away, a number of boys—all between the ages of eight and twelve—had come to the cell every few hours to talk. Karen counted seven different boys in all, but they came three or four at a time. Kenny was always with them and appeared to be their de facto leader. All spoke perfect English.

Sam seemed to be the most tenderhearted among them. He scooted his cushion closer, smiling up with the gap-toothed adoration of a kid brother. She tried to reach out to him a little, whispering in Tajik while the other boys were busy in a deep conversation with Nelson about baseball and the last World Series. He shook his head as if stricken, throwing a terrified look toward the door. He put a finger to his lips.

"The teachers will beat me if I talk like that," he said. All the boys called the guards *teachers*. "You should be careful so they don't hurt you."

"I see." Karen nodded. "I'm going to ask you something, Sam. Have you been taken from your parents? Are you American?"

He frowned, setting his jaw. "Americans killed my mother and sister," he said, tears forming in his eye. "I saw it."

She couldn't help but notice the hint of Boston in the boy's accent. The boy sighed, the weight of the world on his tiny shoulders. "I hate Americans . . . but you're a good lady, Miss Hunt. You sorta remind me of my mother. I wish . . ." His little voice trailed off and he stared blankly at the cell wall. He shook his head, stifling a sob.

"What?" Karen asked. She kept her voice calm and hushed so as not to alert the other boys just a few feet away. This conversation was something Kenny surely wouldn't approve of. "Tell me what you wish, Sam."

"Miss Hunt," the little boy said. "I should study."

"Sam." She gave him an exhausted smile. "I think you work way too hard."

"That sounds funny—'*ya wook* too *hod. . . .*' " He mimicked her Boston accent perfectly, dropping his Rs.

"Don't you see what they're doing?" Nelson had stopped his sports talk with the other boys and was now staring. "They're English bandits—learning how to speak like us. Copying our accents. That's why they killed Nguyen first. His parents came to the U.S. from Vietnam when he was just a kid so his accent wasn't perfect enough for them."

"Way to go," Kenny sneered. He stood to tower over the younger boy. "Idiot!" He knocked Sam off his cushion with a swift kick to the ribs. "Now they're on to us."

Hunt snatched Kenny's arm, yanking him down to face her. The guards might be able to push her around, but she wasn't about to let some runty kid get away with it.

"You didn't have to kick him, you little shit." Her fingernails dug into the flesh of his arm, drawing blood.

Kenny stared back at her with black pig eyes, breathing softly. "If you know what's good for you, you'll let go of me . . . you little shit."

Karen's entire body shook with rage. She shoved

Kenny away and reached to comfort a crying Sam. He buried his face into her shoulder, sobbing.

Kenny rubbed the nail marks on his arm, and then looked at the other boys. “Come on, guys. That’s enough lessons for the day.” He said. “Let’s go get a Coke. Come on, Sam. Stop being such a baby. You’re not in trouble.”

Sam sat up, nodding at Kenny, unconvinced. “Okay . . .”

“I’ll tell you what I wished for, Miss Hunt.” His solemn eyes glistened with tears. “I wish . . . I wish I could save you. . . .”

Chapter Forty-six

The surviving Enfield was cramped riding two-up, but they didn't have to worry about gear since most of it had been obliterated by the missile. The impact of the Hellfire had knocked the bike over and snapped the clutch lever, forcing Quinn to shift by feel alone. It was something he often did on the track, but the rough terrain made it touchy.

But for Ronnie's pants, the armored Rev'it riding suits had been blown to bits. The warmth of Ronnie's body pressed close behind him, unencumbered by heavy clothing, made it doubly difficult to concentrate on the narrow confines of the bumpy path.

He'd just warned her for the fifth time to stop breathing in his ear if she didn't want him to drive off the mountain when the Kyrgyz encampment appeared in the valley ahead.

After hours of nothing but rock and ice, finding the little congregation of smoky yurts and grazing sheep was like discovering life on the moon.

Nine felt yurts were strung along a small glacial

lake in a broad meadow. A handful of snot-nosed kids scampered out to meet them as the motorcycle chuffed into camp with two foreign devils aboard.

A stooped woman wearing a heavy wool sweater and a long skirt ducked out of her yurt to scold the gawking children. She was bent by years of childbearing and heavy lifting. Her face was so smudged with grime and soot that it looked permanently blackened. As soon as Quinn mentioned Gabrielle Deuben's name, the woman's eyes brightened and she motioned them inside.

"Ainura," she said, motioning for her guests to sit on the coarse piles of wool rugs against the wood lattice walls of the felt yurt. Her English was poor—just a few words, apparently taught to her by Gabrielle—but as a child she'd spent enough time in outpost towns that she spoke passable Russian. She bustled around the smoky yurt, preparing tea and bread as she introduced herself and asked for news about her friend, Dr. Gabby.

Quinn recognized the overly sweet, musty-incense scent of opium smoke as the woman gave him a chipped clay mug of tea. She was probably in her late thirties but looked fifty.

Her eyes narrowed, noticing his look. She turned to speak to Ronnie in Russian.

"She says she can tell you still smell the thief." Ronnie interpreted. Ainura sat on the rug beside them, hands folded quietly on the lap of a colorful, handwoven apron.

"She says her oldest son is addicted to opium," Ronnie continued. "She told him he could not smoke it in here so he went down the mountain to Sarhad."

Ainura's face remained stoic, but her eyes were

heavy with the misery of a woman mired in the hopelessness of a land where half of the children die before they reached their fifth birthday.

Quinn took a sip of his salt tea, nodding in genuine thanks. "Dr. Deuben told us of an orphanage somewhere in the mountains. . . ."

The Kyrgyz woman's green eyes flashed and the words began to spill out of her mouth.

Ronnie translated as she spoke.

"She thought perhaps that is why we were here. There are stories, she says, of soldiers who come in the night. They butcher the men and rape the women in front of the children before taking them away. . . ." Ronnie stopped translating for a moment and spoke in rapid-fire Russian, clarifying a specific point. She shook her head, but the old woman was adamant.

Ronnie looked at Quinn. "She says the soldiers are Americans."

Chapter Forty-seven

"Listen to me, Karen," Lieutenant Nelson said in a voice that made Hunt want to cry. "I'm not much help to you here. I don't know what the game is with these kids, but it can't be good. I'm thinking they must be using them to infiltrate American bases or something." He leaned against the gray stone wall of their little cell. Beads of sweat covered his upper lip. His fever had broken for the time being, but he had some kind of infection. She knew the fever would return soon and with a vengeance.

"Funny." Nelson gave a rattling chuckle. "I told my best bud back in Montana that I'd die over here."

Hunt put a finger to his lips. "We're not dead yet."

"It won't be long." He looked at her with sparkling eyes that belied the hopelessness of his words. "I broke up with my girlfriend before I deployed. Didn't want her to have to put up with worrying over my sorry ass. Wrote a death letter to my dad and left it with my brother. . . ."

"Shut up with the dying stuff," Hunt pleaded. "There's got to be a way out of this. I'm sure of it."

Nelson let his head fall back against the wall, wincing as the move wrenched at his collarbone. "Karen," he sighed. "Being sure isn't the same as being right. I envy your positive attitude, but you heard what they did to Nguyen. I don't know how far they brought us—and no one back home does either. We're MIA . . . very soon to be KIA. . . ."

"Don't give up," Hunt said. "I need you to stick with me here."

"I'm not giving up," the young lieutenant said. "I'm making a decision about how I go out. I plan to make them kill me quickly and you should too. Steal the joy of cutting my head off while I'm still alive."

Hunt scooted up beside him, shoulder to shoulder. If she was near death, she wanted a little friendly human contact before her time came. She rested her hand on Nelson's thigh, hoping it would provide some comfort.

He turned to look at her, smiling for the first time in days. "I'll tell you one thing—the next one of those little shits that gets close enough, I'm gonna rip his head off."

Hunt's laugh was cut short when the metal door flung wide. Five guards filed in and stood along either side. Two carried stiff rubber truncheons.

Nelson gathered himself up in a flash and charged the men head-on. Adrenaline pushed him past the pain of his broken bone.

Following his lead, Hunt rolled sideways, springing for the two men the lieutenant had already engaged.

The crushing blow of a truncheon caught her square in the back of the head. She staggered forward, slamming face-first into the rock wall. Stunned, she watched as two men dragged Nelson to the center of the room, where they dropped him unceremoniously on the rough stone floor.

Before Hunt could make sense of what was happening, rough, stinking men clawed like vises at each arm. The more she kicked and struggled, the tighter they held her. Soon, two more men had her by each ankle. She tried to kick free, but another dose of the rubber truncheon across the bridge of her nose brought waves of nausea and sapped her will to fight. Her head lolled back. Blood poured from her nose.

"Take me. . . ." Nelson whimpered from where he lay in a heap on the floor. "Please . . . not her."

The room spun around Hunt as the men dragged her toward the door. She wanted badly to fight, but was working too hard not to vomit from shock, pain . . . and what she knew would come next.

CHAPTER FORTY-EIGHT

Bethesda Naval Hospital
Maryland

Jacques Thibodaux crammed himself into the flimsy plastic chair that must have been meant to discourage hospital visitors. He'd already read the stack of *Soldier of Fortune* and motorcycle magazines at his feet and decided to click through the TV channels on the hardwired controller. It was all mindless game shows and pontificating celebrity judges discussing peoples' angst-ridden lives. Camille was resting so he kept the volume to a hushed buzz.

In the end it didn't matter. A male nurse with a blond goatee and green hospital scrubs came in to wake Camille up and see if she was resting properly.

Thibodaux bit his tongue and walked over to gaze out the window.

"You think you're foolin' anyone with that vest?" The nurse's voice surprised him. He should have been taking care of Camille, not quizzing Thibodaux about his clothing.

"Pardon?" He kept his gaze out the window in an effort to keep from getting confrontational. Camille had often said, only half joking, that one of his hateful looks could give a decent person chronic diarrhea.

"The vest," Nurse Greg said. "I mean, who wears a fisherman's vest in D.C. unless they're using it to cover up a weapon? You a cop?"

Thibodaux nodded, still facing away. He could see the nurse's reflection in the window as he placed a probe in Camille's ear to check her temperature. "In a word," he said.

"My dad's a cop," Nurse Greg said. "He wears a shoot-me-first vest too. I think you should just wear the gun in the open for everyone to see. I mean what's the point of wearing a vest where everyone knows you're a cop?"

"I bet your daddy's sure enough proud of you," Thibodaux muttered.

He watched as Camille reached up to touch the nurse on the elbow. Her voice was thick and hoarse from an exhausted sleep. "You should really go before he turns around," she said. "My husband isn't much for chitchat about his work with folks he doesn't know."

"Nearly done," the nurse chirped, not taking the hint. "Just need to check your blood pressure."

Camille coughed, clearing her throat. "Seriously, you need to go. Your being here is raising my blood pressure."

"Won't take long," the nurse said. He picked up her arm to put on the BP cuff.

Camille threw her head back against the pillow. "Jacques," she sighed. "I have asked this man to leave and he won't."

Thibodaux turned slowly to face the wide-eyed Nurse Greg. His jaw flexed, nostrils flared. The muscles in his neck tensed. Moving in close, he put his arm around Nurse Greg, eclipsing him with hulking shoulders. Leaning down he whispered a few words in the man's ear. Nurse Greg looked up, slack jawed, as if he'd just been slugged. He took one tremulous breath and left the room without even gathering up his kit.

"What did you say to him?" Camille narrowed her eyes.

"Not much." Thibodaux shrugged. "I told him he was gonna have a hard time picking up all his teeth with broken fingers."

"My man, the poet." Camille grinned, but he could tell she was hurting.

"How you doin', Sugar?" Thibodaux patted the back of his wife's hand. It was cool and the veins seemed to stand out more than he remembered.

"I'm okay," she said. "How's Jericho?"

"Quinn?" Thibodaux cocked his big head to one side. "He's . . . on an assignment. Why do you ask?"

"I don't know," Camille said. "I just haven't heard you talk about him much lately. Seemed like you were becoming pretty good friends."

"We are," Thibodaux said. "But let's us worry about you now. The doc says the baby is okay, but you were losing some blood. You'll need to stay on bed rest for a little bit."

Camille suddenly sat upright in bed. "The boys! Who's watching the boys?"

Thibodaux ran hand across his wife's forehead, easing her back against her pillow. "They're fine, Sugar." He shook his head. "Sandy's with them."

"Sandy's just sixteen." She turned her face away.

Jacques's mouth hung open. "Honey, Sandy watches the boys all the time. She knows how to handle them."

He was on the edge of the chair now, leaning over the bed so he could be on her level to console her.

Her hand began to tremble. She looked back at him. A tear ran down her nose.

"There's something I need to tell you," she whispered.

Camille spent the next ten minutes recounting what had happened with Lt. Colonel Fargo and the bald man who'd come with him. Thibodaux sat motionless, taking in every awful, heartfelt word. He struggled to remain calm while his wife told him how these men had been looking for Quinn and how they'd bullied her, kicked her in the stomach, and scared his little boys. They were the reason she was even in the hospital.

When she was finished, he stood and walked outside the room to use up his allotment of non-Bible curse words for the next decade.

CHAPTER FORTY-NINE

Fargo slouched in the passenger seat of a green Jeep Cherokee a block up the street from Thibodaux's house. Bundy sat behind the steering wheel, sipping on a Red Bull and gritting his teeth. They'd lost the suits for khaki slacks and black T-shirts. Bundy's ugly brown tattoo of a scorpion was now completely visible and appeared to scuttle every time he flexed the tendons on his thick neck.

Fargo found it obvious the man didn't like him. He hardly spoke unless spoken to and carried out orders with open disdain. The lieutenant colonel assumed it was because he hadn't actually been to interrogation training himself. He'd heard Echoes were a closed society. Still, they had a job to do and he intended to see it was done correctly. Responsibility could not be delegated, he told himself. And capturing Jericho Quinn was his responsibility.

He pushed from his mind the fact that no one would have been looking for Quinn had he not pressed his uncle to have his name added to Congressman Drake's list.

"He can't just have vanished," he said out loud, hoping to start a conversation with Bundy.

The first sergeant turned to look at him in the darkness of the Jeep but said nothing.

"Did you make the lookouts cover all uniformed branches?" Fargo tried to look stern, like an officer inspecting his troops, but he was pretty sure he just looked dyspeptic. Bundy had a way of tilting his head, just so, that made Fargo cringe.

"All of them," Bundy whispered, sounding like a bald version of Clint Eastwood. "Including the Girl Scouts."

"Have you . . ."

Three black sedans screeched down the street to park in front of Thibodaux's house. Two men in suits jumped from each vehicle. Four of them, armed with long guns, set up a perimeter around the house while two went to the door.

Fargo threw his binoculars to his eyes and watched as a moment later the men led a teenage girl and six pajama-clad boys out into the waiting sedans. He recognized protective custody when he saw it.

Something inside him felt like it broke and drained away. "Thibodaux knows," Fargo moaned, swallowing a mouthful of bile. "She told him."

"Of course she did, sir." Bundy smirked. "What did you think would happen? This is what we want—shake things up, stir the shit. See what they do."

"Oh," Fargo heard himself say. "If Gunny Thibodaux gets his hands on us, I know exactly what he'll do."

CHAPTER FIFTY

Karen Hunt, tough-minded paramilitary operative, slumped in the chilly stone room that served as her new cell. She'd been dragged away to face death alone, apart from the man who seemed her last friend on earth. Rocking back and forth, eyes clenched tight, she wondered how long she'd stay conscious while the men outside sawed her head off.

She'd seen videos during training—horrible things, images that wouldn't leave her mind. There was a time when soldiers and spies had been taught how to hold out as long as they could during torture—to keep from spilling vital information—but now, captives were rarely even interrogated. They were merely dragged in front of a cheap video camera and beheaded. She'd heard Specialist Nguyen's cries for help, down to his last gurgling whimper. These Jihadi bastards were more interested in a slow and agonizing death than an execution.

The guards had taken all her clothing, literally ripped it from her writhing body while they held her down. She'd thought they were going to kill her right then, but the children hadn't been allowed in the room and she knew they were supposed to witness such things. Fear gave way to anger as she decided they meant to rape her instead. They did neither, simply taking her clothes and leaving her a thin, white cotton robe. She supposed it was to be her death suit, but took some pride in the fact that it had taken five full-grown Tajik men to restrain her.

Ordinarily, Hunt was a woman of supreme self-confidence. "Virtually unflappable," her raters at Camp Perry had said. But the hopelessness of her situation, the certainty of violent struggle and a slow and painful death, was an acid test she was not sure she could handle. Her jaw felt slack, her stomach knotted until she could hardly sit up straight. The stark plainness in the stone cell spun around her like a gray cloud, formless and sinister.

"I'm not ready," she whispered to herself. The thought suddenly made her chuckle. Her face twitched in a pained half smile as tears dripped from the end of her broken nose to the stone below. Who was ready to die? Everyone had future plans, dreams, lists left uncompleted. . . . They saw themselves as the star in the little movie playing inside their head.

A jangle of keys outside the heavy timber door jerked her back to reality. She was thirty-three, not nearly old enough to be at the end of her own movie.

Hunt swallowed. They'd left her untied. She still had the skills from her training. Killing a man quickly was not as difficult as it sounded.

The hinges creaked as the door began to swing open, rusty from the constant drip inside the mountain. Hunt resolved to meet them head-on, to make them kill her more quickly than they'd planned. They expected her to be paralyzed with fear.

Kenny poked his head around the door, staying well outside her reach.

"How are you feeling, Karen?" he sneered.

She stared at him, saying nothing.

"I had to tell the teachers, you know." The boy's face brightened. "Sam's gotta pay for being weak."

Karen looked into Kenny's twisted face and decided that no matter what happened, she would see him die before they killed her. He was just cocky enough, he'd get too close to taunt her . . . and then . . .

"Anyhow"—he shrugged—"it's not you today."

"What?" She couldn't help herself. Relief, even guarded, trumped anger.

"Think about it." He howled with demonic glee and snatched his head back before slamming the door.

Hunt swayed, falling into a curled, fetal position against the cold, unfeeling floor.

A moment later, Lieutenant Nelson shuffled past the door. She pushed herself up on both hands, straining to hear.

"Hang in there, kiddo," he said, a catch in the whiskeyed timbre of his low voice. He wasn't fighting anymore.

A tear pooled on her cheek as she realized his inaction was to buy time for her.

"You're a good man, Nelson!" she screamed, giving over to sobs as she collapsed back to the floor.

But for the initial muffled growl at being subdued, the lieutenant made no sound. A jubilant cheer rose up from a group of excited children and Hunt knew it was over.

CHAPTER FIFTY-ONE

Quinn lay facedown on a gray stone outcropping overlooking a valley with seven felt yurts. A battle-weary Kalashnikov rifle lay on a tuft of frostbitten grass beside him. Ainura was an extremely poor woman and had little to give, but she'd been able to provide homespun wool coats for both Quinn and Garcia—and a beat-up old rifle that looked to be in working order. It was chilly out and though Quinn was appreciative of the weapon, he found himself more grateful for the coat.

Situated in a U-shaped valley, the gray-white mounds were surrounded by snowcapped crags that disappeared into the clouds. A ribbon of smoke curled up from an outdoor cook fire midway between the shelters. Three men stood around the fire while two women in head scarves stooped beside it, presumably cooking their dinner. A thin trickle of smoke escaped from the nearest two yurts. The rest stood lifeless in the chill of the valley floor.

Sweeping aprons of shattered boulders and stones

fanned from the mountain bases, giving way to a green pasture, nearly a mile long. Every few minutes another rock tumbled to the valley floor with a series of echoing cracks and thuds, forced away from the mountain by a freezing wedge of water in the cracks and fissures of stone. A hanging glacier, blue as the lapis from the mountains above, fed a large lake at the far side of the green pasture. It was from just such a valley the surrounding Pamir Mountains got their name. Lush and protected Shangri-las in the summer, these valleys, or pamir, were a favorite grazing ground for local herdsmen.

Quinn sniffed the air, tasting the familiar metallic scent of a storm. A brooding, guncotton sky hung close enough to touch. It was already spitting snow.

Garcia's shoulder rubbed against Quinn's as she lay beside him, peering through the single pair of binoculars that had survived the Hellfire strike.

"If there is an orphanage around here somewhere, the kids must sure hate Americans. . . . I mean, if they believe our soldiers murdered their families . . ." Her voice was breathy with the cold and altitude.

"I was thinking about that," Quinn said. "It would be pretty easy to dupe a bunch of terrified kids with a few American military uniforms. Plant a seed of hate strong enough that even living in the U.S. wouldn't be enough to root it out." He rolled up on his side. "Remember what the CIA shooters had written on their calendars the day they went on the spree?"

Garcia kept her eyes pressed to the binoculars as she spoke, her voice muffled against her hands. "A Chinese character."

"Right," Quinn said. "*Dan*. It means *gall*—as in *bitterness*. There's a story from ancient China about a ruler named Goujian. His armies were beaten and he lost his kingdom to a rival. He and his wife were captured. They swore allegiance to the new king, who treated them very well. So he would never forget the humiliation of his great loss, for ten years Goujian slept on a pile of uncomfortable brushwood instead of his soft bed provided by his captor—and tasted bitter gall before every meal.

"Eventually, Goujian conquered the rival king and took back his kingdom. *Wo Xin Chang Dan*." Quin emphasized the last word. "*To sleep on brushwood and taste gall*. If these kids are being prepared to come to the United States and hurt us, there has to be something bitter in them to keep them on track once they get there."

"Watching their families slaughtered would do that," Garcia said. "If one group of terrorists murdered their families posing as Americans, then another group staged a rescue to liberate the kids from the Great Satan. . . ." Still on her belly, she lifted her foot slightly, as a cat might flick just the tip of its tail to drain off excess energy while hunting. "Makes sense."

Quinn rolled back onto this stomach. "Now we just have to find them."

"The yurts are right where Ainura said they would be." Garcia played the binoculars back and forth. "I count a dozen horses, that many yaks . . . maybe a hundred sheep and goats. . . . No children, though. You think they're inside the yurts?"

"Not likely—"

"Maldita!" Garcia cursed. "Look at the size of that dog. At first I thought it was a horse." She passed him the binoculars.

"Nope," Quinn whispered, scanning the herds. "The horses are smaller. It's some kind of mastiff. Seems to be hanging apart from the men at the fire. Probably stays with the sheep to guard against predators."

"And intruding hit men from America," Garcia said under her breath. "I've honestly never seen a dog that big."

The guard dog presented a problem, but before Quinn could plan around it, he had to figure out where the kids were—if they were anywhere at all.

Convinced there was more to this valley than they were seeing, he began a visual grid search—looking near, then far, and dividing the valley into smaller increments. First he looked with his naked eye, then followed up with the binoculars. Five minutes into the search, he found the door leading into the side of the mountain on the other side of the glacial lake, a hundred yards from the yurts.

Once he pointed out the door, they were able to locate an uneven line of windows and vent holes pocking the mountain face. Low stone walls, nearly invisible at first glance, became clearer with every sweep of the binoculars.

"They'd need food if they stay here all winter," Garcia said, shaking her head.

"Look at the yurts closest to the horses," Quinn said. "There's no smoke coming out of them. What if they're used to store hay? As long as they keep the animals fed they'll have a ready food source all winter. . . ."

"So the kids are inside the mountain?"

Quinn nodded, still studying the layout.

"And how do *we* get inside the mountain?" Garcia rolled half on her side, resting her face against her hand. She was absurdly beautiful in her ratty wool clothes and grime-smeared face. "You got another Hellfire missile we can call in?"

"Nothing quite so sophisticated," Quinn grunted. He nestled down into the heavy quilted robe-like coat and gazed up at the brooding sky. Spitting crystals had given way to large flakes that floated lazily down to meet him. "It'll be pitch-black in two hours. This snow will dampen the sound of our approach. We'll just walk up and let ourselves inside."

Garcia's brown eyes widened. "Let ourselves inside? Me and you and Ainura's beat-up Kalashnikov?"

Quinn grinned. "I've seen you fight," he said. "We won't even need the rifle."

He closed his eyes, feeling the soft brush of snowflakes hit his face. If this kept up, they could be stuck in these mountains for a very long time. He pushed the thought from his mind, focusing on the tasks at hand.

Garcia cuddled in next to him, sharing her warmth. "And what about that giant dog?"

Quinn pulled her in tighter. "I'm thinking we'll have to make a sacrifice," he said.

The approach to far side of the valley floor took a painstaking three hours of picking through the shadows of a mile and half of rock. They had to cross three mountain streams. Shallow and braided, the crossings were made more difficult by near complete darkness and slippery, ice-slimed rocks.

By the time they made it all the way around, nearly six inches of snow lay on the valley floor. Quinn had explained his plan before they left, going over Garcia's job twice to make certain she'd have the timing down.

Timing, he knew, would be almost as critical as luck.

He held up his fist as they drew near the yurt farthest from the mountain face. It was one of the ones that he guessed held fodder for the milling herds of animals. The glacial wind hit them full in the face, bringing with it the odor of wet wool and the smoky bite of a cook fire. Though it chilled them to the bone, the wind direction was a blessing and made it less likely the big mastiff would pick up their scent.

"First contact is the trickiest part." Quinn leaned in close to whisper in Garcia's ear. "We have to make it happen on our terms."

"Okay," Garcia said, teeth chattering. "I'm ready to get out of this cold when you are."

Crouching, Quinn covered the open fifty yards to the white mound of the nearest yurt in a matter of seconds, sensing, more than hearing, Garcia on his heels. He kept the AK in tight to his side, hand around the pistol grip, ready.

He stopped, straining his ears for sounds of danger, sniffing the wind to make sure it still worked in their favor. Satisfied they were still relatively safe, he handed the rifle to Garcia, then took out his Benchmade folding knife. In darkness thick enough to feel, he began to slice at the thick felt where the yurt was tied to the base of its inner wooden frame. Five minutes of sawing brought him through the thick felt and able to cut enough lashing cords to pry a two-foot gap in the wooden lattice support structure.

The sweet, dusty odor of hay and grain wafted out into the freezing air.

"Bingo," Quinn said, reaching it to find a small bag of grain he could drag out through the opening. He sat upright, stretching his back from the effort of being stooped for so long. His ribs were still sore from Umar's crushing bear hug and he was pretty sure at least one was cracked.

He held the grain up to Garcia. The bag was about the size of a pillowcase but only partially full so it was easy to carry.

"You hang on to the rifle," he said.

"Ten-four." He could hear her body shaking from cold and tension. They had to get out of this snow one way or another.

Crouching again, they moved toward the grunts and baas of milling sheep bunched together in the darkness. Twenty feet out, the animals heard the shake of the grain bag and moved toward it as if called. The click and thump of hoofs over frozen ground grew louder and their gentle *baa*s became more excited at the prospect of food to warm them on such a cold night.

It was only a matter of time before the guard dog came to investigate the change in behavior.

Quinn stepped into the moving sea of animals, with Garcia close behind. In the darkness it was imperative they stay together.

"Gotcha!" Quinn grabbed a young lamb by the back

leg as it came to the grain. It wasn't much larger than a poodle. He turned away from the herd and used the Benchmade to cut the animal's throat, holding it tight until it ceased to struggle.

Garcia hadn't been happy about the idea of killing a baby sheep. He was thankful for the darkness so she hadn't seen him do it.

"You hear a growl?" Garcia said, moving in to give him the rifle.

"That would be our Goliath," Quinn said.

Garcia moved in behind, next to the milling sheep. The power of food kept them from panic.

The mastiff came in fast, galloping like a horse toward the smell of blood. Quinn braced himself, rifle in one hand with the lamb carcass in the other.

As the black shape of the dog launched toward him from the darkness, he pressed the muzzle of the Kalashnikov to the lamb's ribs and fired.

There was a muffled pop as the woolly carcass absorbed much of the rifle's report. A split second later, the huge dog slammed into Quinn, knocking the dead lamb and the AK from his hands.

Quinn rolled, bracing for another attack that never came.

"Pretty good at shooting by Braille," Garcia whispered as she helped him to his feet. "Now get my ass out of this snow. I'm from Cuba, for crying out loud. I'm not built for this."

"Okay, then," Quinn panted, slowing his pulse. "Let's go see if they lock their door."

Chapter Fifty-two

Quinn left the rifle hanging on a sling around his neck as they approached the door. He and Garcia were dressed as natives, and a native without some sort of weapon in the high mountains would stand out.

Quinn banged on the heavy door, snow piling up on his shoulders as he stood, hunched over against the building wind. Garcia stood next to him, a scarf pulled piously over her head.

A short man wearing a wool hat and carrying a black Makarov pistol answered the door. He motioned them both inside the dark cave. Quinn explained that they were travelers who'd lost their way and needed a warm place to stay. The man kept the pistol pointed at Quinn's chest, motioning them inside. He spoke irritated, rapid-fire Tajik, but Quinn spoke enough Dari, the Persian language of Afghanistan, that they were able to communicate.

He didn't shoot right away, saying he needed to speak with his boss.

A second man, younger, but much taller than the

first, appeared from around the corner and helped secure Quinn and Garcia's wrists with plastic flex cuffs.

Both men shook their heads and muttered in amazement that their stronghold had even been found in the darkness, much less approached. They left Quinn and Garcia in a small holding room, not much larger than a closet, and slammed a dented metal door. The place smelled of sulfur and stale water.

"That didn't go as well as I'd hoped," Garcia said as she leaned back against the rough granite wall. A single bare lightbulb cast a dull yellow glow on the tiny room. She'd heard apocryphal stories of spies caught in worse jams and somehow managing to escape—but more often than not, they ended up an unnamed star on the Memorial Wall at CIA Headquarters. She found some solace in the fact that she was finally living her dream—and living it with the most amazing human being she'd ever met.

"They didn't kill us first thing." Quinn, who seemed a man always in motion, worked his hands under his butt and past his feet as he spoke. "And we got inside. That's a win in my book." He tipped his head toward the exposed lightbulb. "They must have some sort of generator inside the mountain. It would have to be vented outside. That'll give us something to target when we get out of here."

With his hands in front he was able to remove the five-fifty-cord laces on his right boot. The Haix P9s were high-tops and the lace was nearly three feet long. Garcia watched as he tied a six-inch loop in one end of the cord, and then ran the free end through the inside of the plastic flex cuffs before tying another similar loop. He looked up and grinned like a schoolboy as he put the loops over the toe of each boot and began to pedal his feet as if riding a bicycle. The friction of the five-fifty cord sawed through the cuffs in a matter of seconds. Once free, Quinn quickly replaced the lace in his boot. "Never know when I might need to run without my shoes falling off."

"What about my cuffs?" Garcia said. She could see he already had a plan in the calmness of his eyes.

He reached inside the front of his pants. "These guys never do a good job searching the manly man areas." He produced a red knife no larger than his thumb.

"The Swiss Army teeny-weenie knife," she said, turning so he could cut her free. "Don't leave home without it. You got any more surprises?"

Quinn chuckled, his usual enigmatic self. "If I told you, it wouldn't be a surprise. . . ."

The lock on the cell door was a crude, pot metal affair and fell easily to Quinn's small knife blade. He peered out to find a long corridor cut into the mountain like a mine shaft. Bare bulbs, similar to the one in their room, hung on twisted wire along the stone ceiling. Water ran in inky black blotches down the curved walls. Every few yards, a thick timber beam had been knocked in place to help support the structure. Even with the bulbs, the tunnel disappeared into a vacant void at the far end.

As soon as he stepped into the hallway, he was met by children's laughter coming from the depths of the corridor. He motioned for Garcia to follow him.

"Wish we had the gun now," she said.

"Keep an eye on our six o'clock," Quinn said as he tiptoed down the tunnel toward the laughter. "If we need a gun, I'm sure there'll be one available."

Another eruption of laughter stopped him short. He peered through a six-inch-square cutout in the wooden door to his left to see a group of seven boys seated on thick cushions watching an episode of *M*A*S*H* on a color television. Ranging in age from what looked like seven or eight to their early teens, the boys were dressed in blue jeans and wool sweaters. They sipped on cans of soda and chatted to each other in perfect English. Across the room, slouched against the wall with her head between her knees, was a brunette woman in a white robe. Her hands and bare feet were bound, her face a bruised and swollen mess.

Quinn moved from side to side to check out as much of the room as he could. Relatively satisfied there weren't any guards inside, he took a deep breath and opened the door.

"Hey, guys," he said as the startled boys turned to see who was interrupting their program. "How are things?"

"Who are you?" A dirty-blond boy with heavy freckles and an evil sneer stood up from his cushion. Maybe eleven, he didn't appear the oldest, but the other boys stood back in respect as he spoke, deferring to him. "I haven't seen you before."

Quinn played a hunch.

"I'm from another school in Iraq. . . ."

The boys glared at him through narrow eyes, chewing over the concept.

"Another school?" A pimple-faced teenager with a gap between his front teeth whispered, as if in awe of such a notion. A hushed buzz ran through the group.

"We haven't ever heard of another school." The blond boy in particular remained stone-faced. He stared at them with hard green eyes.

"We've come to take a look around and see how things are going," Quinn added. He prepared to quiet the kid should he start to raise the alarm. "Are you well taken care of?"

"Dr. Badeeb tells us if we will have important guests," the glaring kid muttered.

"*Wo Xin Chang Dan,*" Quinn said in Chinese, taking a gamble. He shifted back to English immediately. "I was once a boy just like you. American commandos killed my parents, but I was rescued and trained at just such a school as this."

It worked. The group pressed closer, reaching to touch him. "Have you been to America?" A dusty boy no older than nine asked, haunting blue-gray eyes gleaming as if he'd just met a hero.

Quinn motioned Garcia up beside him. "We both have. This is my wife. She was trained in Chechnya."

Ronnie spoke a quick sentence of Russian to illustrate her origin. The boys, pressed closer, instinctively hungry for friendly female companionship. Tears filled the younger boys' eyes.

"You have a prisoner?" Quinn nodded at the woman in the corner. She stared back at him with a raised brow, as if trying to figure him out. "You have done well."

"She has a good accent but isn't useful anymore," the green-eyed blond boy snorted. He leaned in and gave a conspiratorial wink. "She refuses to talk with us after the teachers cut off her lover's head."

"Too bad," Quinn said, working hard to hide his disgust for the little tyrant.

"It's okay." The boy shrugged. "Dr. Badeeb gives us lots of music CDs and videos to watch."

"Your English is perfect," Garcia said, smiling as if she was really glad to meet him. "What's your name?"

"Kenny," the boy said, puffing his chest proudly. "I am small for my age, but I'm almost fourteen. Dr. Badeeb visited us a month ago and said I could go to America before winter is over. I cannot wait to go to the U.S. and begin to kill Americans. Have you killed many?"

"A few," Quinn said honestly. "I hope to be going back very soon." He took a step sideways so his back wasn't to the door. "Learning some good English from the television, I see. What else do they give you to watch?"

Kenny ignored him, his own questions gushing out like a river. "Tell me about America. Have you met any others like us? We have watched videos of the actions at the CIA. Seth . . . he became Seth Timmons—was my teacher when I was a small boy. He died as a martyr. Maybe you knew him. . . . Do you get to see others of us who have gone before? My sister was here—she is so very smart. Maybe you have met her." The boy grinned, showing huge white teeth. "You'd know her if you had. We kept an oil company worker here from Abilene, Texas. He would not shut up, but that was a good thing. My sister talked to him day and night for weeks . . . before Dr. Badeeb had the man's head sawed off." The boy smiled, lost in the memory. "I was young, but Dr. Badeeb tells me stories about her. I remember her face. She loved to practice her accent." Kenny grinned proudly. "She always told me she was going to go to America and be the queen of West Texas bitches—"

Quinn felt Garcia stiffen beside him. She opened her mouth to speak as the wooden door flew open.

Chapter Fifty-three

The three guards entered quickly, fanning out across the room. The apparent leader held his fire, screaming in heavily accented English for the children to move out of the way. Quinn knew they wouldn't take him prisoner a second time.

Grabbing Kenny by the collar of his heavy sweater, Quinn heaved the little terror like a screeching sack of sand at the nearest guard.

Garcia stepped into the guard nearest her, slapping away the barrel of his Kalashnikov to give him a well-executed cross elbow to the face. He staggered back against the wall, down but not out.

Somehow comprehending that things had changed with the new arrivals, the captive woman launched herself at the guard nearest her. With her bound hands and feet there was little she could do but roll and bite. But even that made a difference. The guard screamed in pain as she drove her shoulder into the side of his knee. His finger convulsed on the trigger, popping three rounds into the gap-toothed blond kid beside Garcia.

Quinn's opponent swatted Kenny out of the way. Before the man could bring his weapon up again, Quinn swarmed him with a quick round of percussive blows to his neck and throat. With both hands on the useless AK-47, the stunned guard was unable to defend against the onslaught. He slumped to his knees, gasping for air, as Quinn snatched the rifle, still hanging from the sling, and shot him in the chest.

Quinn put two rounds in each of the other two guards. The captive woman had managed to climb on top of a squalling Kenny. She bashed his head against the stone floor again and again before rolling off, exhausted.

Alive, but subdued to tears with his head covered in blood, the glaring boy crawled to the rest of his cowering group against the back wall.

Jericho did a quick peek outside the door. The hallway was empty for the time being, but it was sure to start raining guards soon enough. He'd counted at least seven when they'd first entered the mountain school—and that didn't count the men outside in the yurts.

He stooped to cut the woman free with his Swiss Army knife, taking stock of the room as he worked. Three guards and two boys lay dead. Kenny's scalp was awash in blood and Alan Alda still bantered away on the episode of *M*A*S*H*.

"Quinn, U.S. Air Force."

"Karen Hunt," she said. "Civilian, attached to the Army."

"Can you walk on your own?" he asked.

"I'm fine." Hunt rubbed circulation back into her wrists. "Your friend's not so good, though."

Quinn handed Hunt the AK. "Mind watching the door?"

The woman nodded, checking the weapon as if she had handled one many times.

Garcia stood, swaying slightly in the center of the room. A quizzical look crossed her oval face.

"Ronnie?" Quinn grabbed her by the shoulders. "Are you hit?"

She shook her head slowly, not sure herself. Blinking, she twisted, reaching over her shoulder to claw at her back.

Quinn's eyes fell to the dead boy who'd been killed by one of the guard's stray fire. To his horror, the grimy hand held a sharpened metal spike just larger than a number-two pencil. Garcia followed his gaze down to the weapon, realizing what had happened at the same moment as Quinn.

Her knees buckled and Jericho lowered her to the cushions the boys had been using to watch television. Gasps and muffled croaks escaped her trembling lips as she strained to speak. Frothy pink blood pooled on her tongue.

"How we looking at the door?" Quinn pulled Garcia toward him, rolling her on her side. He tugged up her coat. Her head lolled as he yanked the back of her shirt out of her wool pants and pulled it up over her head. She shuddered in his arms as he searched frantically for a wound.

Hunt shot a quick burst down the hall and got a string of return fire. "Doin' just fine over here," she said.

Quinn gave a withering look to the boys, who cowered less than ten feet away, backs to the wall. It occurred to him that more than one might have a homemade weapon.

"Are you all ready to die today?" he said.

They shook their heads emphatically. Even zealots need time to work up to the task of martyrdom—especially zealots in embryo.

He swore under his breath when he found the place where the spike had punctured her skin. Nearly the size of a dime, the wound was below her right shoulder blade in the pale flesh left by the tan line of her bikini top. Bubbles of pink blood oozed from the wound.

"Sorry, Ronnie," Quinn said though clenched teeth. "I have to leave you on your stomach for a minute."

Garcia nodded weakly. Her breath was reduced to shallow, labored croaks.

"Did it get a lung?" Hunt asked. She was barefoot and the translucent white robe did little to hide the swells and creases of her otherwise naked body. But she moved like a professional and the way she handled the AK was an intimidating sight.

"Afraid so," Quinn said. He fished a black Cordura wallet from the cargo pocket of his pants. It was a simple wound kit he'd carried with him everywhere since his first deployment. It contained just four items—a windlass tourniquet he could apply by himself, a foil envelope of QuikClot, a 14-gauge needle, and an airtight Vaseline bandage.

He ripped the seal from the bandage and applied it to the wound. It stuck well to the smooth skin over Garcia's back, sealing the entry point.

Her eyelids fluttered when he rolled her over on the

cushions. She struggled, mouthing something. Her eyes shot frantically around the room. Her hand came up and brushed his face, pulling him to her.

"West . . . Tex . . . Wes . . ." She swallowed, her windpipe arched unnaturally to one side. Her chest heaved in a futile effort to draw air.

Quinn touched her lips to shush her, then bent to put an ear to her chest. Her heartbeat was barely audible. Even with the seal, she struggled to breathe.

He'd seen it before.

"Okay, kiddo," he said, trying not to sound as grim as he felt. "You've got an air pocket building up in your chest. I have to give it a way out or it'll kill you."

She nodded. Glistening eyes stared up at the stone ceiling.

"We still good back there?" Quinn asked over his shoulder. He popped the top on the red plastic case containing the fourteen-gauge needle. Anything he did for Garcia would be short-lived if they were overrun by guards.

"We're good for now," Hunt said. "But they're working themselves up for an assault. We should move as soon as you get her stabilized."

Ronnie's eyes fluttered. A trickle of foamy pink blood dripped from blue lips.

"Stay with me, Veronica." Quinn held the three-inch needle between his teeth while he wrestled her sports bra over her breasts and under her armpits. He drew a mental line from her right nipple up to her collarbone. Staying outside that line to be sure he cleared her heart, he inserted the needle between the second and third rib.

It went against human nature to stab a friend—especially a wounded one—but an instant after he felt the tiny pop that indicated the needle had pierced the chest wall, he heard a hiss of escaping air. Ronnie drew a deep breath as if she'd just broken the surface from a long underwater dive. She smiled softly as the color returned to her face. Her head lolled to one side, exhausted.

Quinn withdrew the needle, leaving the plastic catheter in place to let air escape. He pulled her sports bra back down, praying the tight but breathable Lycra would hold the catheter in place long enough to get her out of the mountains.

Quinn hauled the unconscious Garcia over his shoulder, then looked up at Hunt.

"Ready?" he asked.

"One minute." She turned to a tall boy wearing a wool sweater and heavy sweatpants. "Gary, throw me your clothes."

The boy glanced sheepishly at Kenny's bloody face and stripped off his clothes. He threw them to her, sneering. "Bitch!" he spat.

Hunt snapped her fingers. "Shoes and socks too, kid." She slipped the boy's green army sweater over her white robe, tucking the flowing end into the sweats before putting on the shoes. She picked up two AKs, slinging one, and stood at the door.

"Now I'm ready," she said.

"CIA?" Quinn said. "You're the one who left the blood chit."

"That's me," Hunt said. She turned to stare at the remaining boys.

"Where is Sam?" she spat.

They stared back with the maddeningly blank faces that only preteen boys can muster.

She threw the rifle to her shoulder, aiming in.

"We don't know," Gary stammered, hands folded across the crotch of his dingy shorts. "Kenny told the teachers he was starting to like you and they took him away."

"We haven't seen him since," Kenny said, through swollen lips.

Hunt stood, aiming the rifle, chewing on her top lip. "These boys stood by and cheered while my friends were murdered. They're screwed up for life. I should shoot them all right now. . . ."

"Knock yourself out," Quinn said. "But whatever you're going to do, do it quickly. We gotta get out of here."

He was pretty sure she wouldn't shoot unless the kids attacked. As a CIA para, she'd been extremely well trained. From his experience, well-trained people didn't talk much about killing. When it needed to be done, they simply did it without wasting a lot of breath.

Hunt kept the boys covered as she backed toward him, taking up a position beside the door. "I sure as hell hope they follow us."

They made it down the hall as far as the T intersection where the side shaft and the main corridor connected. To their left, a row of metal barrels lined the dark tunnel that led deeper into the mountain.

"You think that's fuel oil?" Hunt whispered, nodding toward the barrels.

Quinn shrugged. "Could be. They're getting power from somewhere. Probably generators venting to the outside to diffuse any heat signature."

He stopped to readjust Ronnie's weight over his shoulder. She was facedown, buttocks in the air. His left arm wrapped around the crook of her knees. The posture pressed against her lungs and wasn't optimal for her injuries, but it was the only way he could move with her quickly and shoot. He not only had to carry her, but he had to check her constantly to make sure she was still breathing.

Another volley of gunfire rattled down the tunnel, zinging off the rock walls with yellow sparks.

"They're in the room on the left between us and the door," he said.

"I'm going deaf from all the racket," Hunt said. "But I think I hear footsteps."

She did a low quick peek, stooping to thrust her head around the corner for a split second before pulling it back again.

"I count three. They're inching along the wall trying to work up the courage to rush us.

"Think you can bounce a couple of rounds at them?"

"On it." Hunt set her jaw and nodded.

She held the Kalashnikov parallel to her chest, with the barrel angled slightly toward her. Thrusting it quickly around the corner, she fired three controlled bursts.

High-velocity bullets shot at such an angle tended to bounce away a few inches and travel in a relatively straight path down a flat surface. A muffled cry came from around the corner, along with the unmistakable clatter of a gun hitting the stone floor.

Seizing the moment, Quinn and Hunt rounded the corner, each finishing off a downed guard. Hunt paused long enough to grab a hand grenade from the belt of one guard as they ran past.

Heavy footfalls echoed up the corridor from the way they'd come. There were cries of protest from the boys, followed by a prolonged volley of gunfire.

"Can't say I'm sorry to hear that," Hunt sighed. She looked over her shoulder at the last few pops.

"Must have had orders to silence them if the place was compromised," Quinn said. Garcia was still draped over his shoulder, her arms trailing down his back. He reached to feel her pulse, inside her pant leg and above her ankle. It was weak, but palpable.

A screaming wind yanked the door from Quinn's hand as he pushed it open. He turned to Hunt.

"Ready?"

She pulled the pin on the grenade and held it in her hand. "Ready."

Quinn felt Ronnie stir at the fresh slap of cold air. "Stay with me, kid." He patted her tenderly on the butt, took a deep breath, and stepped into the darkness.

"We have a saying here in the Stans." Hunt tossed the grenade into the door behind them as they trotted away. "Caves are graves."

Quinn charged into the black storm, cutting left toward where he hoped the yurts and horses were waiting. Behind him, the mountain roared. Fire belched from the door. Tiny, slit-like windows glowed like rows of red eyes in the night.

Men poured from the yurts nearest the mountain. They scanned the blackness with feeble beams of battery-powered lights.

Quinn ran on, depending on surprise and night to help his escape.

The horses were right where he'd left them. Rumps turned toward the storm, they munched contentedly on a pile of hay Quinn had dragged from the feed yurt. He lay Garcia on the ground long enough to bring the horses to the leeward side of the structure out of the direct blast of wind. As gently as he could, he lifted Garcia's thigh over the larger animal's back. Hunt held her in place while he climbed up behind and let her slump back against his chest. With no stirrups and only a single lead rope from a leather halter for control, the going would be tricky—but at least they were moving. The driving snow would cover their tracks.

Hunt reined up beside him in the darkness on the other runty horse. "You're going to have to lead," she yelled above the wind. "I was under a tarp when I came in."

Two hours later Quinn's horse slipped. Both knees slammed into the ice with a sickening crack. They were already headed downhill and both Quinn and Garcia tumbled over the animal's head to land in a tangled heap on the snowy mountainside.

The raging storm and palpable darkness made it impossible to see more than a few inches. Heavy with worry, Quinn reached under Garcia's shirt to put a hand against her ribs. She winced at the sudden chill. That, at least, was a good sign. He checked the catheter. It was still in place. Her breathing was strained but steady. The biggest danger now was the cold. None of them was dressed for this sort of weather. Without movement to warm her, Garcia's body temperature was falling fast.

"Put her up here with me," Hunt shouted. She coaxed her little horse down the side hill below Quinn to make loading Garcia easier. "I'll try to warm her up while you lead the horse. Looks like yours is a goner."

The second horse collapsed a half an hour later. Past the point of exhaustion, Quinn stooped to muscle Garcia over his shoulder. He struggled back to his feet under the press of Garcia and the howling wind. Unsure if she was alive or dead, he'd resolved to get her out of these mountains or die along with her. Trudging forward, nearly blind on feet that felt like wooden stumps, he began to hear the sweet notes of his daughter's violin.

He remembered there was someone behind him, but who they were and why they were there escaped him. His world was one continuous stumbling movement, falling forward, catching himself, then repeating the process over and over again. He'd drawn his hands inside the sleeves of his wool coat, but his fingers were numb—likely frostbitten. He could only imagine what was happening to Ronnie.

Mattie's violin grew louder in his head. He saw her little face in the darkness, dark hair swirling in plumes of snow and ice. She shook her finger back and forth as if to scold him. Her little cheeks pooched into a disappointed frown. She looked so much like her mother when she did that. Heaven knew he'd done enough to disappoint them both.

Quinn stopped in the trail to stare at his daughter. The sight of her made him warm and sleepy. Something bumped into his back, knocking him face-first into the driven snow and shattering his beautiful vision.

"You smell that?" A voice rose up from the blizzard behind him.

He remembered now. There was another woman with him. Hunt. That was her name. He grabbed for the fleeting thought as he fumbled with Garcia's arms, trying to tug her limp body back up on his shoulder.

"I don't smell anything," he groaned.

"I'd know that stink anywhere. . . ." Hunt shouted. "It's yak."

CHAPTER FIFTY-FOUR

Arlington, Virginia

Thibodaux stood beside Palmer's leather sofa at parade rest, eyes intent on an angry-looking radar image on a flat-screen monitor. "So," the Cajun said, "we've found him then?"

Win Palmer sat behind his desk fiddling with a computer keyboard to zoom in tighter on the image. He put the cursor over a map of western China and the Wakhan Corridor of Afghanistan, where a red and yellow blotch marched across the screen. Beside the blinking arrow were the letters: LKP.

"His last known point was here." Palmer used the mouse to wiggle the cursor slightly. "This is where he called in the Hellfire strike. I sent another agent over to talk to Dr. Deuben. She sent them somewhere over here . . ." He moved the cursor three inches to the west. ". . . to talk to a Kyrgyz woman about the orphanage.

"And what does this Kyrgyz woman say?" Thibodaux moved up next to the screen, as if closer scrutiny might reveal his friend's location.

"That's the glitch." Palmer frowned. "That red blob there is the storm that's been dumping snow on the area since late yesterday. We sent a Blackhawk over Boroghil Pass from the Pakistani side. Those Kyrgyz migrate down from the high pastures every year about this time before the big snows hit. There was no sign of the camp Deuben sent them to. They could have already headed down to Sarhad to get ahead of the storm. The Blackhawk had to get back to base before it got caught in a whiteout—no time to do a thorough search. They can barely keep a bird in the air at those altitudes anyway."

"What about this spot here?" Thibodaux ran his finger along a band of light greens and blues on the map. "A break in the weather?"

"Bingo," Palmer said. "Not big enough to get an aircraft on the ground, but if we run it through time lapse on Damocles it does show us something interesting."

Palmer tapped that keyboard and brought up the same map with a time stamp of an hour before. The gap in the weather had passed over a mountain valley roughly ten miles from the spot the Kyrgyz camp was supposed to have been. Centered in the rocky scree along the mountain side was a small purple dot, nearly invisible to the naked eye.

"What am I looking at?" Thibodaux rubbed his jaw.

"Maybe nothing." Palmer shrugged. "Maybe a fire."

Thibodaux sighed. "I've been to that part of Afghanistan, sir. There's not much to burn in those mountains except yak shit."

"What we do know is that the dot wasn't there five hours before. It's some sort of anomaly and fire is the best guess."

"If it's a fire big enough to see from a satellite, it's likely Quinn's handiwork. Let's get someone in there to get him out."

Palmer leaned back in his chair, folding his hands across the flat of his stomach. "My thoughts exactly." The muscles in his jaws and neck flexed like taut cables. "But we can't. The next band of weather has moved in and stalled. All the technology in the world and we're stymied by clouds. Until they move, we're not getting anyone in or out."

CHAPTER FIFTY-FIVE

Near Gettysburg, Pennsylvania

"I need to talk to Bundy," Fargo said, walking through the back door of the remote farmhouse set in the middle of a twenty-acre parcel, five miles from the Gettysburg Battlefield. His collar was unbuttoned and a frayed red power tie hung loose around his neck. He was at the end of his rope and he needed answers.

Two young Echoes wearing black Doc Martens boots and sporting military buzz cuts sat at the kitchen table playing cards. Neither stood when he entered, though they knew he outranked them.

Castelleti, a big-eared kid with the beginnings of a beard, looked up with a sneer.

"I asked you a question, men," Fargo snapped. "Is he here?"

They grunted, nodding to the stairs leading to the basement.

The one named Jimenez peered up over his cards. "We got a new client who didn't show up for his hearings with the congressman." He suddenly began to look around the room as if trying to locate something out of place. "You smell that, Colonel?"

"Smell what?"

"That stuff that smells like piss." Jimenez sniffed. "You know what that is?"

"I don't know." Fargo took a long whiff. "What?"

"It's piss!" Castelleti smirked, red in the face.

Both men threw their cards on the table and broke into uncontrollable laughter, shaking their heads.

Fargo swallowed.

"Go on down, Colonel." Jimenez hooked a thumb over his shoulder, stopping to catch his breath. "Maybe you could help the sarge on this one. This new guy's givin' us zip so far."

Fargo had no stomach for interrogation, but the last thing he wanted was for a couple of snot-nosed subordinates to see him sweat.

"All right," he blustered. "I'll do that. It's important that I see him."

Fargo grabbed the wooden banister to steady himself as he made his way down the dark concrete steps to the musty basement. The smell of urine did indeed waft up to assault his nose. The movies he'd seen, no matter how graphic, were tame compared to the real thing. Graphic images had the power to alarm for a moment, but the mind became inured after a short time. The sounds of screaming, pleading, or even whimpering—which Fargo felt was the worst—added shock value, but even they made one numb after a time. But when sight and sound were combined with the smell of actual human misery, the sensations burned into a special place at the back of his skull where they would stay forever.

Fargo paused at the two-way mirror set in the wall of what had been a root cellar in the back corner of the basement. The farmhouse was surrounded by acres of vacant land so there was no need to soundproof the room. Bundy claimed the ability for one subject to hear another's woes, if they happened to have two clients, had a tenderizing effect.

The Echoes' latest subject was Steve Luttrell, number thirty-seven on Congressman Drake's list. Luttrell was a professional staffer for a powerful left-leaning lobbying firm in downtown D.C. He was in his late forties with a full head of snow-white hair that had once been red. He loved Mexican food to a fault and it showed in the prominent gut that folded over onto his lap. He was completely nude. Plastic flex cuffs secured pink shoulders, hands, knees to a gray metal chair in the center of the basement room. His back was to the door so as rob him of even the slightest notion of escape. Bright light glared in his face, causing him to squint through tearful red eyes. Strings of snot ran down the soapy white skin of his hairless chest.

Bundy sat in another chair five feet away, inside the circle of light, staring at the man with cold pig eyes.

Luttrell blinked against the assaultive light. "Why are you doing this?"

"You tell me," Bundy said, his voice a coarse whisper.

Luttrell threw his head back, howling at the ceiling. "I can't tell you anything if you don't ask me any questions!"

"What should I ask you, Steve?" Bundy said.

"I . . . don't . . . know," he sobbed.

"Why weren't you at your congressional hearings, Steve?"

"What?" He blinked. "I . . . I . . . what does that matter?"

"Are you a spy, Steve? A mole?"

Luttrell's chest heaved. "Noooo! Why does everyone suddenly think I'm a spy?"

"Okay. Let's talk about your wife," Bundy said. His voice sounded like the hiss of a snake. Pure evil. "Do you think you make her happy, Steve?" He leaned in close. "Because from where I'm sitting I don't think you could possibly make her as happy as I could."

A malignant smile spread over Bundy's face.

"You know, Steve," he said. "When we're in training, they teach us the three Ds—debility, dependence, and dread. . . . But you know what, Steve?" Bundy sighed, leaning forward in his chair. "I came up with a little something that works so much faster in my experience. I call them the three Ts. Can you guess what they are?"

"No . . . no . . . idea . . ." Luttrell's words came in breathless stops and starts.

Bundy reached behind his back to take out a pair of pruning shears. "Toenails, teeth, and testicles, Steve," he said. "Isn't that just brilliant? I think it's brilliant."

Luttrell began to blubber like a baby. "I . . . you . . . what . . ."

Fargo's cell phone began to ring. Luttrell's head snapped up, craning to see what was making the familiar noise outside the room.

Bundy's smile vanished.

"Help me!" the naked man cried. He rocked in his

chair until it tipped over, crashing against the concrete. "Somebody out there please help me!"

Bundy left the man lying on the damp concrete floor screaming until his voice grew hoarse.

"What the hell do you want . . . sir?" Spit flew from Bundy's lips as he slammed the door behind him. The scorpion tattoo flicked and danced as the veins in his thick neck throbbed purple.

"I need to talk to you." Fargo struggled to maintain even the illusion of control.

"You just set me back half a day there." Bundy glared as if about to strike. "This guy has got to believe the world is a vacant planet—no one else here but me and him. Hopelessness—that's what we're after. You just gave that son of a bitch a fresh dose of hope with your prancy little antelope cell phone tune."

"Would you shut up and listen to me for a minute?" Fargo tried to check the whine in his voice, but the words still came out more plea than order. He swallowed hard. "My source has found out there's a full-scale search being mounted for someone missing over the Chinese border into Afghanistan. This has Jericho Quinn written all over it. I need you to get your men together."

Bundy breathed in quickly through his nose at the mention of Quinn's name. "I wonder what he's doing over there. . . ." He rubbed his bald head with the flat of his hand, thinking. "You know, LT, this guy sounds like the only one among all the names on our list who would be a challenge to interrogate."

"We need to get on this right away," Fargo said, mistaking Bundy's calm for mutual understanding. "If he's still alive, I want us there to snatch him."

"You're an all-powerful lieutenant colonel in the U.S. Army." Bundy smirked. It was difficult to tell if he was being condescending or suggesting a plan. "You got some pull, right?"

"Damn right I do," Fargo heard himself say, though it sounded idiotic even to him.

"Quinn will have to come home to roost sometime. Let's bump up the locate we put out. We'll list him HVT."

Fargo felt hopeful for the first time in weeks. Listing Quinn as a high-value target would put the might of the entire military behind the search. "I could put him on the capture-or-kill list."

"Don't you want to talk to him, sir?" Bundy's black eyes churned, like something at the bottom of a polluted lake. "*I* want to talk to him—spend a little time getting inside his head. My advice—just list him HVT. Add a warning annex that no one is to have any communication with him whatsoever, per your directive. 'Gag immediately on arrest'—national security and all . . ."

WEDNESDAY
October 4

CHAPTER FIFTY-SIX

Afghanistan

The hollow chirp of a teakettle dragged Quinn out of a dead sleep layer by painful layer. His body glowed with the painful warmth of someone who'd suffered from extreme cold. A mound of heavy quilts pressed him against a hard hair mattress that smelled of alcohol, dried yogurt, and sweat. The pungent odor of smoke from a yak-dung fire mixed with a greasy smell of spiced meat that pressed against his empty stomach like a fist.

His mouth felt full of chalk. His head pounded from what he knew was severe dehydration. The clatter of metal pots and pans felt like kettledrums played against his ear.

Quinn knew he carried vital information, but he couldn't get his mind around it. He remembered the labyrinth of mountain caves, the English-speaking boys. They'd mentioned the name of a man who ran the school . . . a doctor. Dr. Badeeb. That was it. He and Garcia had to get the information back—

Garcia! The memories came flooding back.

He pushed himself up on one arm, shrugging off the quilts. It took a long moment for his eyes to become accustomed to the harsh lantern light inside the yurt. The events washed back over him in a crashing wave. Dizzy, he got to his knees.

Ainura, the Kyrgyz woman, stood beside her propane stove chatting with the female CIA agent they'd rescued. A rack of white yogurt balls dried on a tray above the stove.

"Ronnie," Quinn croaked, swallowing.

Ainura brought him a chipped cup of butter tea. He slammed it down like a man coming in from the desert. Nodding in thanks, he handed her back the cup.

"The other woman I was with." His eyes played around the interior of the yurt. "Is she all right?"

Karen Hunt knelt on a pile of felt cushions beside him. Patches of pallid, frostbitten skin covered her swollen nose and cheeks. Her lips were cracked and scabbed.

"She's alive," Hunt said, a grave look crossing her battered face. "For now. I'm afraid if we don't get her out of here soon . . ." Her voice trailed off in tight-lipped silence.

Quinn crawled to the mound of quilts nearer the stove. The warmest place in the yurt. He gently drew back the top blanket.

The Kyrgyz of the High Pamir were accustomed to treating injuries and illness without the immediate aid of a doctor. Ainura had rolled felt pads and cushions to prop Garcia up on her side. She'd been stripped her down to her long-john bottoms, but the Lycra sports bra was left in place to protect the chest catheter. Thick tresses of black hair matted to Garcia's gaunt cheeks. Her chest shuddered with each labored breath.

She stirred, moaning softly when Quinn picked up a hand. She was reactive—that was a good sign—but her nail beds were tinged a chalky blue. She was getting some oxygen, but not enough. He pressed an ear to her breastbone and heard what he'd feared he would—a wheezing, high-pitched rattle.

Exertion and cold from the extreme altitude were filling her lungs with fluid. He'd plugged the wound in her back, but a tiny bit of air aspirated from her punctured lung into her chest cavity each time she drew a breath, creating a pressure strong enough to press against her already-struggling heart. The catheter let the air escape, but it couldn't keep up.

Quinn kept his head against the warmth of her chest, listening for a time, thinking over his options. There were few. When he sat up, Garcia's eyes flicked open.

Chapped lips parted into a wan smile when she saw him. It vanished as quickly as it appeared. Her eyes shot around the room as if seized by a sudden realization. She opened her mouth to speak but managed little more than a breathy croak.

"Relax," Quinn said. "We made it out." He smoothed a tangle of hair away from her forehead, letting the back of his hand trail down the soft skin of her cheek.

She grabbed at his sleeve, pulling him to her lips. Her voice was like the slow release of air from a punctured tire. "Tar . . . Wesssst Texxxassss bih . . . bit . . ." Her eyes rolled back in her head and her hand fell away from his arm.

"You know what she means?" Karen Hunt stood off Quinn's right shoulder, a hot cup of tea in her hand.

"She's been saying the same thing over and over. Something about Texas."

He pulled the blanket back up around Garcia's shoulders. "No idea," he said. "But we have to get her to a hospital." He glanced at the felt-covered door of the yurt. "Is it still snowing?"

Hunt shook her head. "Stopped about three hours ago. Can I ask you something?"

"Sure," he said.

"How many of these kids do you think there are in the U.S. already?"

"I don't know." Quinn stared at Ronnie as he spoke. "Seven attacks over the last couple of weeks. That's if there haven't been more since we've been off the grid. The haphazard stuff feels wrong though. Anyone smart and patient enough to put a school like this one in place is planning something bigger than a few shooting rampages."

"I agree." Hunt nodded slowly. "They're brainwashing those kids young so that no matter how good their experiences are in America, they never forget their hatred. It all adds up. One of the boys—the one they killed for liking me—said Americans killed his mother and sister. If you can make a child believe you somehow rescued them from the evil Americans, it's not a far cry to pushing them to vengeance."

"Exactly," Quinn said. "I'm sure there are some details to get worked out, but I believe that's the gist of it."

He pushed to his feet with a long groan. He felt as if he'd been kicked in the head and rubbed down with heavy sandpaper. "My friends will be looking for me. I need to stomp out a distress signal in the snow."

Hunt took a sip of her tea and grinned. "And just what do you think us CIA types do for three hours while we wait for you to wake up? Already done."

Quinn collapsed back onto his quilts. He had to get the information back to Palmer about this Dr. Badeeb. The key to what was happening was sure to be with this guy. Quinn took a deep breath, struggling to remain calm. There was nothing to do now but wait and hope that Garcia could hang on.

CHAPTER FIFTY-SEVEN

Washington

Mujaheed Beg lay flat on his back on a piece of cardboard he'd found in a nearby Dumpster, staring up at the grimy undercarriage of his target vehicle. He much preferred killing people to killing cars.

Somewhere up the quiet street, beyond the CVS pharmacy, a dog barked in the darkness.

Over his years in America, he'd found he truly liked motorcars and cringed when he was forced as a last resort to shoot out a window or plant explosives under a hood. Badeeb had sent him to do a little mischief—make some necessary modifications as insurance. The problem with Congressman Drake would not solve itself.

Holding a penlight between his teeth, he inched his way deeper under the car before reaching up with a small Leatherman multi-tool. As always, it fell to Beg to take care of the doctor's problems.

Once he was finished, he slid out from under the car and brushed the dust of his jeans. He ran a comb through his thick hair and walked into the darkness singing "Love Me Tender" under his breath.

Chapter Fifty-eight

Afghanistan

Quinn's eyes snapped open at the familiar sound. He pushed back his quilts and was outside in an instant to watch the huge Boeing CH-47 Chinook settle into the whirlwind of snow. He raised his arm in front of him to ward off the flying ice and snow crystals from the twin rotors' hurricane-force winds.

Karen Hunt came up behind him and put a hand on his shoulder as a crew chief bailed out the forward starboard door and shuffled his way toward them in the deep drifts. His voice became clearer as the helicopter's engines wound down to a low, idling whine.

"You Captain Quinn?" he shouted, nearly falling on his face.

Jericho waved, relief washing over him. "I am. My partner's got a pressure pneumothorax. You got a medic on board?"

"We got a field kit," the kid said. He was close enough now Quinn could see the tab on the chest of his green Nomex suit that identified him as Crew Chief

Jorgenson. "No doc on board though." He took off his helmet and held it in the crook of his arm. He looked like a young Viking with his longish blond hair blowing in the cold breeze.

"You're to accompany me, sir," he said, all business. "We're supposed to get you back to Asadabad ASAP."

"I wouldn't have it any other way, Chief," Quinn said. "I need to get my friend stabilized."

Jorgenson nodded grimly. "We're on a quick turnaround, sir, due to weather. You'll have to do it on the bird."

Quinn used the Chinook's medical kit on Garcia as soon as they were all aboard. A new needle and catheter helped relieve the pressure. He put her on oxygen and had Hunt watch her while he went forward to meet the pilots.

Jorgenson handed him a green headset.

"Y'all are a long way from home." Quinn stood behind the cockpit watching the jagged, snowcapped peaks shoot by the windows in a vibrating blur.

"We could say the same thing about you, Captain." The pilot nodded. "Rod Jones, Eighty-second Combat Aviation Brigade. Bravo Company out of Kabul. Had to use the Fat Cow to get us out here and back." He nodded over his shoulder at the extended-range fuel tanks in the rear of the bird. "You must have some juice with someone for them to send us this deep."

Two desert tan Humvees idled on the ramp in Asadabad. One bore the red cross of a medical vehicle. The other had a fifty-caliber machine gun on top and bristled with soldiers dressed in full battle rattle.

"They don't look very happy to see us." Hunt's breath puffed a circle of condensation against the Chinook's round side window.

Quinn held Garcia's hand, studying the waiting men through a cloud of blowing yellow dust. The Humvees seemed absurdly small against the expanse of rock strewn landscape of desert and barren mountains.

Both vehicles rolled toward the rear of the Chinook as the rotors whined down.

"Can you remember a number without writing it down?" Quinn looked at Hunt as the helicopter's rear ramp began to lower.

"That's what I do." Hunt smirked. Her face went slack as she looked up and realized he was serious. "What's going on?"

Quinn rattled off two phone numbers. "Jacques Thibodaux. He's one of the few you can trust back home. Tell him what we found out about Dr. Badeeb. If you can't get hold of him quickly, talk to Winfield Palmer."

The ramp touched down on the desert floor and a squad of six men rushed forward, each with an M4 trained on the chopper's interior. A side glance out the window told Quinn the Chinook's pilots and crew had already exited through the front of the aircraft and waited outside to watch the show.

Hunt raised her hands. "The national security advisor? Why are you telling me all this?"

"Take care of Garcia," Quinn whispered. He opened his mouth to explain more, but the twin barbs of a

Taser struck him in the chest. He collapsed, writhing against the metal floor.

The voltage abated and his body fell slack. He was vaguely aware of the dark form of a soldier looming over him. There was a sharp pain in his neck—a rush of wind, then dreams.

THURSDAY
October 5th

Chapter Fifty-nine

Near Gettysburg

Quinn woke to nothingness. No light, no sound, no smell. He blinked, trying to clear his vision. Still nothing. Movement was hampered by some sort of harness around his waist. His arms were held wing-like by a similar strap, away from his sides. The faint taste of saline told him he was suspended in a warm-water bath—likely with Epsom salts to float him without effort.

A sensory deprivation chamber—an upright, coffin-like enclosure soundproofed and filled with enough warm water to leave only the victim's head exposed. He'd spent some alone time in one during training. Some in his element had fallen victim to hallucinations less than an hour after going inside the box. Their instructor had pointed out that the more well-adjusted they were, the more quickly they would succumb. Quinn had lasted almost six hours, three times as long as any other member of his training element.

Every prospective combat rescue officer was sent to

SERE—Survival, Evasion, Resistance, and Escape—training in at Fairchild Air Force Base near Spokane, Washington. As a trained interrogator, CRO, and OSI agent, he'd attended advance training at Fairchild and at the Navy's sister facility in Maine. Quinn was certain these two training cycles had taken at least a year off his life.

Having spent his youth in the wilds of Alaska, survival, escape, and evasion came easy to Quinn. There was little the enemy could throw at him during a pursuit that was more frightening than a nine-foot grizzly sow.

The R in SERE was a completely different story. The instructors had pointed out early in their training that the human mind was far more vulnerable to exploitation than the body. During times of extreme pain, the physical being simply shut down, in effect turning off its ability to feel inflicted stimuli.

Threaten pain and the mind takes over, filling in the blanks left by a skilled interrogator with all sorts of horrific details.

Quinn pressed his tongue to the roof of his mouth, listening for the sound and feel of his own heartbeat. It was a technique he'd used to stay grounded when he'd been "captured" by PRONA—People's Republic of North America—forces during training. There was a lot going on inside the human body and, with the mind turned inward, it was a pretty interesting place to visit.

Quinn had no idea how long he listened to his heartbeat and the gurgling of his own gut before the lid to the box came off. Harsh light clawed at his eyes and the heavy thump of a bass note assaulted his ears. Coming from an environment with no stimulation, the effect was like sandpaper on the skin. Hands grabbed at each shoulder and he was hauled out the top of the enclosure like a slippery fish only to be dropped unceremoniously on the ground.

Angry male voices barked opposing orders.

"Be still!"

"ON YOUR FEET!"

"Why are you here?"

"SHUT YOUR MOUTH!"

The shouting, combined with the pounding beat of the music, gave the impression of dozens of other men in the room. Quinn believed there were four. He recognized one of the voices and made a mental note of its position in the room.

Naked, he sat on the floor and did his best to ignore the screaming. He saw nothing but blinding white light. He focused, working to control his breath.

The blaring music suddenly stopped. A deep, disembodied voice came across some sort of loudspeaker.

"SIT!"

Quinn scanned the room and found a gray metal chair directly in the center of the glaring pool of light. Before he could move, the voice boomed out again.

"I SAID SIT DOWN!" Without warning a shadow strode from the wall of light and struck him across the thigh with a length of rubber hose.

Quinn scrambled for the chair, his leg on fire.

"TELL US YOUR NAME!"

Quinn coughed. Arms on the chair, he hung his head. If they knew who he was, he wondered why they hadn't restrained him.

"You know my name."

The rubber hose caught him across the left shoulder

this time, coming from another direction. Quinn didn't even try to deflect it.

"YOUR NAME!"

"Jericho Quinn. Captain, United States Air Force." He gripped the chair, swallowing hard as the nauseating effect of the blow seeped into his bones.

"See?" the voice said, normal now, without the aid of a loudspeaker. "That wasn't so difficult."

Quinn nodded.

"Is this about Drake's list?"

He heard a shuffle in the corner.

"Normally," the voice said, "you'd have been struck for unsolicited speaking. Consider this warning my gift to you."

Quinn nodded again, catching his breath.

"Now," the voice continued. "Let's get down to business—"

"Let's do," Quinn said, unsolicited.

When the punishing shadow appeared again, Quinn was ready. He grabbed the hose and wrested it from the attacker's grasp with a quick flip of his wrist. Striking quickly, he felt the satisfying thud as the hose struck home. There was a heavy groan as the man collapsed into the pool of light.

Quinn spun, launching himself wildly into the light. He crashed into the wall, falling back to the concrete floor. A Taser crackled from somewhere behind him and his body went rigid as a board. Molten heat shot up his spine. Fingers clenched around the hose in his hand. Toes curled inward from the pulse of fifty thousand volts that coursed through his muscles.

When it came to being Tased Quinn had the advantage of experience. The moment the shock ended he rolled, sweeping the hose behind his back to break the hair-like wires that connected the barbed darts to the Taser itself. He scrambled to his feet, roaring as he heard another crackling sound to his left.

Muscles spent, the second jolt of electricity affected him exponentially more than the first. He fell forward, his rigid body bridged on forehead and the tips of his toes. His face slammed against the floor once the shock was over. Saliva and blood dripped from his mouth and onto the gleaming concrete.

Naked and exhausted past the point of caring, he lay still.

"Foolish, Mr. Quinn," the voice said again from behind the light. There was almost a hint of pity in it. "I think this is enough for now. You should spend some time in the box."

Black boots tromped toward him. Strong hands pinned his shoulders while someone slipped a black cloth bag over his head. Lolling from the two bouts of Taser therapy on top of his recent battle with the weather in Afghanistan, he put up no more resistance as they secured him back in the box.

They pulled off the hood before closing the lid. Scowling down at him was a bald man, a scorpion tattoo running up the side of his thick neck.

"I want you give you something to ruminate on," the man said. "Before we turn out the lights, so to speak.

"We had a bit of a time locating Kim," the man went on. "Until she made a phone call back to some friends in Alaska." He grinned broadly. If evil had a face, this was it. "You should have trained her better than that, my friend. I am so looking forward to spending a little quality time with her and young Madeline. I know you'd like to stop me. . . . It must kill you that you're here . . . powerless. . . ."

The box closed leaving Quinn alone, floating in the dark with the screams inside his head.

CHAPTER SIXTY

Dr. Badeeb rested his arm against the cheap laminated motel dresser. Curling fingers of blue-gray smoke wafted around his sweating face as he puffed the last inch of his cigarette. He breathed deeply, screwing up his courage to talk to this dear one who'd come at his bidding.

Tara Doyle sat on the edge of the bed, her head covered with a drape of green pashmina. She wore a simple white blouse, unbuttoned at the collar, and navy slacks. She stared at the floor as Badeeb spoke.

He couldn't help but think that the brightness burning in her eyes might set the soiled carpeting ablaze at any moment. Perfectly suited physically, as well as emotionally, for the job with which she'd been entrusted. He could not think of a better student to come out of his school. Her birth name was Tara; it meant star in Tajik. She'd smiled when she found out she could keep it in America. It gave her something to hang on to.

"You have done well, my child," he said, lighting another cigarette. In truth, spending even a few moments with Tara set his nerves on fire, stoking his desire for tobacco—and other things—more than ever.

Badeeb moved to sit beside her. In the past, when she was younger, she had been a more willing participant in their meetings. She'd revered him when he went to visit, climbing up in his lap, taking his presents. Even later, when she'd become a woman at thirteen and their relationship had become physical, she would lie beside him and discuss politics, scheming on ways to cut the head off the American beast that had murdered her parents. She could never know that it had been his men, Tajik and Chechen fighters, who, dressed as American soldiers, had raped her mother and slaughtered her parents like goats.

"I am ready for this to be done," Tara said. "I'm sick of it here. It makes me tired."

"Soon, child," Badeeb said, turning his head to blow away a plume of smoke. "Very soon." He put his arm over her shoulder, caressing her with the hand that held the cigarette.

She shrugged him off.

"I cannot think of such things now," she said, still staring at the floor.

Badeeb took a deep breath, clenching his teeth. He was not used to rebuffs. He could have tried to coerce her. He'd done it several times before, but decided she would kill him if he did such a thing. She was different now, stronger. When he thought it through, that was exactly the sort of person he needed—wanted—her to be.

Still, it was such a shame.

He stood, putting some distance between them. His wife was old and smelled of raw melon and cold tea.

The scent of young Tara Doyle had enraged his passions. He could not be blamed for that. It was natural.

"The time has come then," he said.

"Good," Tara sniffed, getting to her feet. "I'm ready for this damn thing to be over."

"What of your brother? He will be on the island with everyone else. Does this give cause to change your mind?"

Tara dropped the silk scarf on the bed, and turned to go. "I have no brother in America," she hissed. "I need to go. Peace be unto you, Doctor."

FRIDAY
October 6

Chapter Sixty-one

Quinn fought to press unthinkable images of Kim and Mattie from his thoughts. He'd seen so much violence it was all too easy to insert their faces into the movie of his mind. Vivid colors splashed like fireworks in the blackness, pulsing then fading like multicolored campfire embers on an evening breeze. His father's voice scolded him, telling him to live up to his responsibilities as a man. His maternal grandfather—the man from whom he'd inherited his fighting nature—whispered softly about being prepared to die. The women in his life—Kim, Mattie, his mother, even Ronnie—came to him in turn to weep and plead for his help. Mattie was the worst. Her trusting eyes stung him like slaps to the face. He'd promised to protect her.

His rational mind told him what the man with the scorpion on his neck was doing. It was textbook brutality from the Cold War–era CIA KUBARK interrogation training manual. Strip away the clothing and all manner of identity, plant seeds of doubt.

Understanding the system did little to protect against it.

Quinn was shaking with rage by the time the box opened to let in a flood of light. Restrained, he could do nothing but wait for what happened next.

This time, they tied him down. Thick leather belts strapped his ankles and wrists to the gray metal chair. His naked skin was tender and wrinkled from hours in the saltwater chamber.

Across from him, the bald man with the scorpion tattoo on his neck sat in a similar chair, rubbing the point of his chin as he stared at his prisoner. A blue cordless drill hung from his other hand. The harsh interrogation light was gone, allowing Quinn to look around the windowless, gray room. He gave a silent nod of understanding when he saw the disheveled figure of Lt. Colonel Fargo slouching in the corner. A younger Hispanic man with muscular shoulders and a narrow waist leaned against the wall beside him. He was the one who'd hit him with the hose.

Squaring his shoulders, Quinn pressed his back hard against the chair and fought to regain his composure. The man with the scorpion tattoo was a professional. He knew the tricks, the subtle nuances of human behavior that displayed flickers of weakness. Quinn was pretty sure this one would be able to kill a weakling like Fargo with a prolonged stare.

"I have my doubts that pain will work on you," the bald man said, suddenly standing to loom over Quinn, his face just inches away. There was the hint of chocolate ice cream on his breath.

A milkshake. Quinn studied the man's solid muscles through the thin fabric of his gray Under Armour T-shirt. Someone this ripped wasn't the type to eat ice cream before bed. It had to be near lunchtime, which meant he'd been a prisoner more than twenty-four hours.

If Hunt had gotten the message out, Thibodaux would be looking for him by now.

The bald man smiled. "You're mulling over thoughts of rescue," he whispered. "I can see the pitiful flash of it in your eyes. They all think of rescue for a time." He pulled the trigger on the drill.

Quinn braced himself as the motor revved to a high-pitched whine. He kept his eyes open, focused on the twisted face of his captor.

The man released the trigger on the drill.

"No." He stood up straight again, taking a half step back from Quinn to study him, hand to chin, like an artist. "The pain of a drill bit going through your knee-cap wouldn't work on you." He took a quick breath and raised his eyebrows, wrinkling his smooth scalp. "But have you considered this possibility? Let's suppose you are rescued shortly after I ruin your knee. Where would you be then? On a government pension, making forty percent of whatever pitiful salary they're paying you now? And if you're not convicted of spying, do you think your friends overseas will prop you up?"

"Do you honestly believe I'm a spy?" Quinn whispered. "Is that what Fargo told you?"

The man shrugged. "I'll tell you what I believe," he said. "I believe you don't think I'll hurt you because we are both Americans."

With that, he handed the drill to Fargo and pulled a set of hooked pruning shears from his back pocket.

Quinn struggled against the restraints, trying to rock his chair, but found it was bolted solidly to the floor.

The bald man moved closer, nodding as his black eyes flicked over Quinn from head to foot, searching to find a suitable target. "You have taken remarkable care of yourself . . . considering how you've abused your body over the years. . . ." He touched the cool blades to a white scar on Quinn's shoulder. "Isn't it amazing the horrible things that run through the mind of a naked man when someone gets near him with a cutting instrument?" He turned to look over his shoulder at Fargo. "What do you think, Colonel? Shall we conduct a little operation?"

"You're the expert in these matters." Fargo nodded, staring at the floor. "Do as you see fit."

Across the room, the Hispanic man gave a scoffing chuckle.

"Quinn," Fargo spat. "You have to admit that you have an awful lot of explaining to do." The words fell flat, sounding like something one would say to a disobedient child rather than a prisoner about to be mutilated.

"So far," Quinn said, gritting his teeth as the bald man stooped beside him and pulled the little toe of his right foot away from the rest. "So far, no one has asked me any quest—"

He arched his back as the bald man clamped the shears around the toe, cutting skin and crushing bone in an agonizingly slow process. There was a sickening snap as the bone broke under the metal jaws. Quinn's breath came in ragged gasps. Excruciating pain shot up his leg from the jagged nubbin.

The bald man stood, holding the bloody toe in front

of Quinn's face. "This little piggy's going in the garbage," he laughed maniacally, throwing his head back.

A sudden pounding rattled the metal door behind Quinn. The bald man's eyes darted upward, he face creased with impatience.

There was another knock, followed by a muffled voice. "Someone wants to see the colonel." The voice was muffled, unidentifiable.

The bald man stared hard at Fargo, who let the drill hang limply by his side. "Did you tell anyone you were coming here?"

"I . . . er . . . I mean . . . no, of course not."

The bald man nodded. He raised his voice toward the door. "Jimenez, go see who it is." He turned back to Quinn. "I want to get to this messy business of softening our traitor so the Colonel can ques—"

It seemed to Quinn that the door exploded off its hinges. The limp body of another man tumbled forward on top of the startled Jimenez. A bright white flash, like a sudden bolt of lightning, filled the room, followed by the booming crack of a stun grenade. A moment later, a dark form hit Fargo like a cannonball to the chest, propelling him backward and into the wall.

Quinn recognized Emiko Miyagi as she shot by, wearing black BDUs. Her dark hair was pulled back in a short ponytail. A wakizashi, the Japanese short sword, flashed in her hand.

"What the hell?" Fargo held up the drill to ward off the woman's screaming attack. A moment later the revving drill and his hand, separated from his arm, lay convulsing on the concrete floor.

Jimenez growled, pushing away from Fargo in time to meet Jacques Thibodaux. The big Cajun ignored the attempted punches and scooped the startled Echo up by one arm and the seat of his pants. Jimenez weighed in at nearly a hundred and eighty pounds, but in his rage, Jacques lifted the man high overhead with a guttural roar before slamming him into the concrete floor. Leaving him where he was, the big Marine strode past to loom above the bleeding Lt. Colonel Fargo. Drawing his Kimber, Jacques put a ten-millimeter slug into the man's knee. Fargo screamed, clutched the amputated stump with his good hand, writhing in a rapidly growing pool of his own blood. Jericho's toe lay on the floor, inches from his contorted face.

"You all right, l'ami?" The big Cajun turned to free Quinn with a quick swipe of his Benchmade knife, before helping him to his feet.

"I'm fine, considering." Quinn's teeth chattered from shock. He looked down at the butchered, aching mess on the side of his foot. "Who really needs a little toe anyway?"

A slow dread crept into his body as he took stock of the room. "Where's the bald guy?"

"I was wondering the same thing," Thibodaux grunted, kicking Fargo in his wounded leg. "There's not a hell of a lot keeping me from putting another bullet in you. Where'd your cue-ball buddy go?"

Fargo craned his neck to look around the room. Sobbing, his face was contorted with unspeakable pain. Blood pulsed between his fingers "I . . . don't . . . know. . . . He was right here when you came in. I . . . I swear it."

"Well, he's not here now. . . ." Thibodaux said. "He didn't just vanish."

"Fargo's right," Quinn said, still looking around the room. "He disappeared the moment you guys breached the door."

"What's his name?" Thibodaux prepared to kick Fargo again.

"Bundy," he said through clenched teeth. "First Sergeant Sean Bundy."

"I found something," Miyagi said, Japanese short sword still in her hand. She used her foot to push at an elongated wooden flap that ran along the wall behind her. Six feet across and roughly a foot high, it was painted the same color as the concrete block that surrounded it. All Bundy had to do was drop to the floor and roll to escape the room in an instant.

"Dammit." Thibodaux glared, breathing through his nose as he focused all his rage on Fargo.

Quinn raised his hand. "Hang on a minute, Jacques." He limped over to stand over Fargo. "Why was I on the Congressman Drake's list?"

Fargo shook his head. "I . . . I'm sorry," he sobbed.

Quinn's voice hummed with tension. "Tell me how my name got on the list."

"I saw how much you traveled overseas. How . . . how good your Arabic was. . . . It just makes sense. I had you added after the fact so my team could investigate."

"Where can we find Sean Bundy?"

"He's . . . a senior interrogator . . . out of Fort Huachuca. Will someone pleeeeease help me stop this bleeding?"

Quinn nodded slowly. "I think the man from Louisiana is about to help you out with that."

Fargo's eyes snapped open as the big Cajun stepped forward.

Muscles and tendons on the side of Thibodaux's neck flexed. "Before you tortured my friend, you paid a little visit to my wife and boys. Remember that?"

Fargo nodded quickly. Sobbing so hard he could barely breathe.

Jacques raised the pistol level with Fargo's contorted face. "Lucky for you she didn't lose the baby or I'd have put you down a hell of a lot slower than this."

No one flinched at the shot.

"Sit down, Quinn-san," Miyagi said, sheathing the wakizashi. "I need to take a look at your injury."

Quinn sighed, realizing he was standing there in nothing but what God gave him. "First, I need some pants," he sighed.

Mrs. Miyagi gave him a stoic wink. "Do not dress on my account, Quinn-san."

"I'm about the same size as the guy you clobbered." Quinn nodded toward Jimenez, who lay unconscious on the floor. "Think you could help me out, Jacques?"

Chapter Sixty-two

Quinn limped to a chair so he could examine his mutilated foot. Just looking at it made white-hot fury rise like an angry phoenix in his chest. He shot a glance at Fargo, whose lifeless body slumped against the far wall, and thought about borrowing Jacques's pistol so he could shoot the dead man again.

"Garcia?" He almost hated to ask the question.

"She was still unconscious when I left the hospital." Thibodaux nodded. "I hear she's doing better now though. They got her on some IV antibiotics strong enough for a horse. Whatever she got poked with was pretty nasty."

"I'm assuming Hunt got the information to you about this Dr. Badeeb?" Quinn dabbed at the raw flesh around the shard of white bone.

"She did . . ." The Cajun gulped, grimacing. For someone as tough as he was, he had a weak stomach when his friends were injured. "Whoooeee, son! You are gonna need to put somethin' on that."

"Jacques." Quinn glanced up impatiently through

narrowed eyes. He was having trouble focusing and desperately needed something to wrap his mind around. "Badeeb. Could you get anything?"

Miyagi gave Quinn a small plastic packet. "Take this," she said. "It's honey. It will help with the shock." She shooed his hand away from the wounded foot and knelt to pick at it with a small needle. Quinn had no idea where she'd gotten the thing, but presumably carried one with her at all times. She glanced up at him with prodding brown eyes, as if to say, *Go on with what you're saying. I'll handle this.* Quinn relaxed and relinquished the throbbing foot to the mystical Japanese woman.

"We got lucky on this one, cher." Thibodaux's grimace perked into a full grin. "Dr. Nazeer Badeeb is a Pakistani pediatrician who has an apartment near Georgetown."

"We sure it's the same guy the kids at the orphanage were talking about?" Quinn winced as Miyagi poured some sort of noxious liquid over his foot. It burned as if she'd set him on fire. He threw his head back and gritted his teeth as he spoke. "For all I know, the name Badeeb is the Smith or Jones of Pakistan."

"I told you, l'ami," Thibodaux scoffed. "We got lucky. This Georgetown doctor Nazeer Badeeb is also licensed to practice medicine in Pennsylvania, Arizona, Ohio, and Texas. You remember Timmons and Gerard?"

"The CIA shooters?" Quinn said, mesmerized as Miyagi tapped a hair-like needle in the top of his foot, numbing the pain as surely as a local anesthetic.

"The very same," the Cajun said. "Your new CIA

friend, Agent Hunt, had the forethought to check their medical records. Turns out Nazeer Badeeb was each boy's pediatrician while they were in their early teens. He helped with the adoption exams."

Thibodaux pulled a notebook from the breast pocket of his black Nomex tactical shirt and flipped through the pages with fat thumbs.

"Badeeb immigrated legally back in 1980. Records show his first wife and two kids were killed in a dust-up along the Paki border between American operatives and Russian forces during the Soviet occupation of Afghanistan. Those that know him say he blames the U.S. for the deaths—though he didn't divulge that little factoid when he was trying for his citizenship."

"Keep your friends close and your enemies closer. . . ." Quinn mused. He got to his feet with a groan, feeling ten years older than he had only a week before. "So, have you picked him up?"

"Nope," Thibodaux said. "Palmer put a team on his clinic, but he hasn't showed. He's married again, this time to a Chinese Muslim gal named Li Huang. She's supposed to have a crash pad in Chinatown."

"In D.C.?"

"Nope." Thibodaux shook his head. "New York. And there've been a few more developments while you were off in Bootystan with your new girlfriends. They've announced the location of the VP's daughter's wedding. She's getting married off the south end of Manhattan on Governors Island at five o'clock."

"Tonight?" Quinn glanced at his wrist, remembering the Breitling had been reduced to molten bits by the Hellfire missile strike. "What time is it now?"

"Ten past eleven in the morning," Mrs. Miyagi said. She returned the vial of antiseptic to the cargo pocket of her BDU pants and took out a white pill, handing it to Quinn.

"Provigil," she said.

"Thank you." Quinn nodded, popping the pill dry. Provigil was a drug the military sometimes gave pilots to keep them awake during long missions. It didn't cause the jitters like caffeine or amphetamines and there was no crash when it wore off. It had yet to be determined if there were any negative long-term effects. After what Quinn had just been through, he didn't care. He had to keep moving. Sleep was not an option.

"Governors Island has to be the target," Quinn said. "Can we have them postpone it?"

Thibodaux shook his head. "Not a chance in hell. According to Palmer, the vice president and Mrs. Hughes feel safe enough since they didn't release the location to the public until a day ago."

"But many people must have already known," Mrs. Miyagi mused.

"And two can keep a secret," Jacques said. "If one of them is dead. . . ."

"I don't like it." Quinn used Mrs. Miyagi's shoulder to get to his feet. "We have to keep the president away at least."

"Palmer-san has advised him just so," Miyagi said. "But the president does not want to appear weak in front of the entire world. He has yet to decide what he will do."

"Secret Service has tripled the number of agents on-site. They're sweeping with Explosive Detection K9s and X-raying everything from the fruit baskets to wedding gifts."

Quinn nodded, his brain in overdrive. If he was a terrorist, he'd pick the wedding.

Killing so many world leaders along with the president would not only throw world economic markets into a tailspin, it would prove that the United States was touchable—weak.

The wedding was as ripe a target as they came. Still, the politicians were just that—politicians—and they were wont to do what politicians did while they depended on him to look after the dirty little details like keeping them alive.

Suddenly heady with the situation, Quinn looked down at Miyagi and smiled. She and Thibodaux had taken care of things with such explosive force and precision, he'd forgotten to thank them.

"I . . ." He took a deep breath, feeling energy flow into his system. The focusing effects of the Provigil were coming at him fast. "You both . . ."

Miyagi put the tip of her finger to his lips to shush him. Apart from picking at the bone of his butchered toe, it was the tenderest thing he'd ever seen her do.

"Warriors do not speak of thanks. We do our duty." She arched a thin black eyebrow. "Is that not so, Thibodaux-san?"

"I expect it is." The Cajun shrugged.

"Very good." She led Quinn toward the door. "Are you well enough to ride?"

Quinn flexed his shoulders, amazed at how good he felt. He took a deep breath and nodded. "As a matter of fact I am."

"Excellent," she said. "We haven't much time. I have already spoken to Palmer. Your bikes will be waiting for you in New York."

Quinn looked up. "The GS is fixed?"

"You will use my Ducati." Miyagi shook her head. "But see that it comes back in one piece."

Chapter Sixty-three

Washington

Hartman Drake turned the wheel of his black BMW 7 Series sedan and smiled as the luxurious vehicle accelerated up the GW Parkway toward Arlington Cemetery. He glanced at the navy-blue Suburban in his rearview mirror. Considering his past, it was difficult to keep a stupid grin off his face. As a United States Congressman, Drake wouldn't normally have rated a 24-7 security detail. But as the new speaker of the House, not to mention the leader of a public crusade against some extremely powerful—and now embarrassed—men and women within the government, he got dozens of threatening phone calls and hundreds of hateful emails each day. Civil liberties groups rallied outside the Rayburn House Office Building. Dark figures loitered in the shadows across Independence Avenue, photographing him as he came and went. Someone had even gone so far as to throw a brick through the bay window of his home in a gated community in Vienna, Virginia.

The Capitol Police had decided it would be prudent to assign a four-man detail.

Kathleen, sitting in the passenger seat, gushed over the fact that her husband warranted protection. She'd always been a little heady with power and prestige—ever since he'd been the editor of the college newspaper at Arizona State. Dumber than the box of proverbial rocks, she'd been fiercely devoted to him from the moment he got her into a game at the Sun Devil Stadium with his press pass.

He looked over at her with a contained smile. She was three years his junior, and her pale skin showed none of the pressures and anxieties of leadership that lined his brow like a washboard. He had to admit she was attractive in a stolid, hackneyed sort of way. She spent an hour on the treadmill every day, watched what she ate, and doted on him as though he were the last man in the world. Even worse, she believed every word that came out of his mouth. Men and women alike would often tell him how lucky he was to have such a wife—beautiful and devoted.

They passed under the gray shadows of the Memorial Bridge; Lincoln sat on his throne to the left. Thousands of dead lay in Arlington Cemetery to the right. Drake passed a rusted Ford pickup belching blue smoke, and then eased back into the right lane. He shot a soft look at his wife. She rarely ever said no to him—but even steak and eggs for breakfast got tiresome after a while.

He eased back into the left lane.

"I'm excited to spend some time in New York," she said, hands folded in the lap of her peach-colored dress. It suited her complexion and overly sweet temperament.

"Seems like a bad time to me," he said. "I should swing by the office and pick up some papers. We're running early and I'll only be a minute."

"Hart," she said sighed. "I'm so proud of what you're doing, but can't you take this one night off and just enjoy the wedding? There are going to be so many important people there."

"This move that you and I are taking," he said, looking across at her. "It's the single biggest thing we've ever done, Kathleen." He'd learned a long time before that if he wanted her buy in to something, he just had to talk about it as if it was a joint project between the two of them. He studied the tiny lines around her trusting brown eyes and wondered if she'd feel the same way if she knew how he felt about Julia Sanborn's legs.

He didn't love either one, but at least Julia was exciting. Kathleen was not a bad person; she was just boring. He'd admitted that to himself shortly after they'd met in college. But her father had the contacts in local politics to help him get started. Kathleen was far from homely and had produced two strong, healthy sons. She was, more than anything, comfortable.

His heart fluttered in his chest as he they shot past the sign announcing Reagan National Airport ahead. The Potomac River stretched off to their left. To the right was the Roaches Run Wildlife Sanctuary lagoon, a long tidal pond built when the city fathers had been dredging gravel to construct the Pentagon. The sight of it sent a shiver down both legs.

Pressing on the accelerator, he looked at his wife

again, studying the tiny hairs on the nape of her neck. She didn't deserve the lot he'd dealt her. . . .

"Hart, why are you driving so fast?" she said, wringing her hands. "You're scaring me."

"I'm sorry, sweetheart," he said. "My mind was elsewhere. . . ."

He clutched the steering wheel until his knuckles turned white.

"Shit!" he spat, swerving into the right lane to miss a slowing furniture truck.

Kathleen was thrown sideways by the move. "Hart, slow down!"

"I can't," he said through clenched teeth. "The brakes are gone."

Behind them, the dark blue Suburban wove in and out of traffic, struggling to keep up. A line of traffic lay a quarter mile ahead, slowing almost to a standstill. Drake cut the wheel sharply to the right, skidding the BMW sideways. He jumped the curb and careened down the grassy embankment. Drake aimed the long black sedan between the largest trees. Thick brush scraped and clawed at the sides of the car. Saplings the size of Drake's wrist slammed at the undercarriage, hewn down by the momentum.

They hit a small rise before the water, launching them into the air in a long, agonizing arc. The BMW hit the water in the vehicular version of a belly flop, slamming Drake and his wife hard against leather seats. Air bags deployed from the dash as well as the sides, pinning them backward.

Stunned by the sudden impact of the fall, Drake struggled to make sense of up and down. Frigid green water rushed into the car. The half-deflated air bag confused him and made it difficult to locate his seat belt. Pockets of air hissed and gurgled as the car settled with astonishing speed toward the bottom of the gravel lagoon. He knew he needed to get free, but he couldn't get the stupid air bag out of his face. He hadn't counted on the air bag. He had a job to complete. . . .

Water covered his chin and then his mouth. In a moment of panic, he screamed for Kathleen, blowing a volley of bubbles and wasting precious air as the lagoon invaded the last bit of space inside the sedan.

As always, she heard his call and came to him.

Fighting her way past the flaccid air bag, Kathleen Drake reached for her husband's lap and popped loose his seat belt. The eerie glow of the dash lights played off her auburn hair as it floated around her face. She tugged at his arm, pulling him toward her open door and safety.

On the way out, he spotted the shimmering silver bubble of an air pocket in the corner of the car, near the sun visor. Holding tight to her hand, he pushed upward, gasping for a lungful of air before ducking back down beside her at the door. Her tugging grew more frantic as he braced his feet on the car's frame, holding her down.

The water wasn't more than seven or eight feet deep and the surface beckoned.

He drew her close, smiling in the near darkness. She smiled back, trusting him completely. Grabbing a handful of hair, he slammed her forehead over and over against the exposed doorpost, before shoving her back into the passenger seat. A flurry of bubbles erupted from her mouth, forming a silent O of shock and terror.

Lungs on fire, Drake held tight to the frame of the

car. Kathleen tried to claw her way past, eyes wide, pleading. He kicked brutally at her face and chest, forcing her to stay inside the car. A thin trickle of bubbles streamed from the corner of her gaping mouth as her struggles ceased. He ducked back inside for one last frantic look. She could not survive now that she knew.

He had nothing to worry about. She floated peacefully, arms outstretched as if to embrace him. A thin trickle of blood trailed from her broken nose in the murky green water. Brown eyes gaped open, staring directly at him as if they'd always known his secrets.

Drake broke the surface gasping and choking. Two members of his protective detail had worked their way down to the water's edge and stripped off shoes and suit jackets to dive in after him.

"Kathleen!" he sputtered and croaked in what was hardly an act as he tried to catch his breath.

A black agent named Norton pulled him into the shallows and passed him off to a partner before sloshing into deeper water to go after the woman they called "The Missus."

"We'll get her out, sir," he yelled over his shoulder before diving into the blossoming circle of bubbles.

The athletic young officer surfaced a short time later with Kathleen in tow.

Sirens wailed forlornly in the distance as Drake stood on the bank shivering with someone else's suit coat over his shoulders. The four members of his Secret Service detail worked frantically to revive the sodden lump of flesh that had been his wife of over twenty years.

For one terrifying moment he thought Norton might

succeed in bringing her around. In the end, the earnest officer looked up in between rescue breaths and gave a solemn shake of his head. Water dripped from the end of his nose. He kept up his efforts but knew it was over.

Drake fell back against the grassy bank, landing on the seat of his pants. His protection detail would assume he'd collapsed out of grief for his dead wife. Instead, a wave of nauseating relief flooded his shivering body. Events had fallen perfectly into place. Driving off the road had been more exhilarating than he'd imagined. As an added bonus, he'd lost his dear wife. No one would question him too deeply about why he'd lost control of the car.

He would now be seen not only the leader in a crusade against those who would harm the United States, but a widower whose beloved companion had been murdered by those very subversives he had in his sights. The naysayers in the military and elsewhere would be silent now or risk the wrath of public opinion.

Hartman Drake took a deep breath and willed his body to calm. He scanned the trees on the side of the bank, wishing his mentor was there, to see how well he'd done. He thought of his youth and the man who had seen his genius and saved him from a life of starvation—a man who had taught him the one true way and brought him to America for a mission far greater than he'd comprehended at the time. Dr. Nazeer Badeeb, his longtime friend.

Their impossible plan was finally coming to pass. The president and vice president would not survive the evening. As the newly elected speaker of the House of Representatives, Drake was poised to take the reins.

CHAPTER SIXTY-FOUR

Laurel, Maryland

Julia Sanborn held her rhinestone-encrusted Coach purse under her arm. She pressed the key fob to unlock her car door with one hand while she talked to her sister on the cell phone with the other. The gray street outside her apartment was deserted. Her heavy heels echoed on the grimy pavement as she sashayed out from her second-story walk-up like she owned the world. Spits of rain clung in tiny droplets to the shimmering black of her pixie-cut hair.

The fob didn't work, so she unlocked the Mitsubishi sedan with the key.

"I know, I know," Sanborn yelled into the cell phone as if she was deaf. "I got bills to pay, you know. He'll just have to, like, get that through his head or else I'll show him I mean business. . . ."

She tossed the handbag into the passenger seat and hiked up her short skirt to maneuver her legs in behind the wheel. "I know. . . . I know. . . ."

She stuck the key in the ignition and turned it, but

nothing happened. She kept talking while she tried again. "Can you believe it? I mean, like, I have the pictures to prove it. . . . No. . . . Of course I'm naked in the pictures. . . . Of course we are. Yeppers. . . . I know, really. . . . I'm tellin' you, he's, like, some kind of stud. . . . No, you can't see the pictures. I told you, I'm naked too. . . ."

She turned the key. Again, nothing happened.

"Listen, sis, I'm gonna have to, like, call you back. Can you believe this? My damn car won't start. Yeah, really, I'll just get him to buy me a new one."

Sanborn ended the call and put the phone on the seat beside her purse. She tried the key one more time. Not even a click. "Come on." She smacked the steering wheel with both hands. "Why does the bad shit always have to happen to me?"

At that moment, the dark form of Mujaheed Beg rose up from the backseat and looped a thin twisted cord around the delicate skin of Sanborn's throat.

"Because you are greedy, my dear," he grunted as he fell backward. The cord crossed behind her neck, terminating in two hardwood handles he used to jerk it tight.

Sanborn's eyes slammed wide in the rearview mirror. Gaudy fingernails clawed frantically at the biting twine.

Beg would have used the piano wire, but he knew from experience that such material would cut through the woman's flesh like soft cheese. With so much yet to do, this was no time to find himself awash in blood inside the close confines of the car.

He nodded in satisfaction as Sanborn tried to honk the horn. Good for her. But he'd disabled that along with the battery. Her back arched. Feet pedaled against the floorboard, kicking blindly. Pinned back in her seat there was little she could do. Beg himself knew of no way to defend against such an attack—but he was smart enough to check the backseat before he got into a car.

The beauty of a garrote was the silence of its simplicity. There were no screams to raise the alarm. If applied correctly, by the time a startled victim opened her mouth, the unforgiving cord had already crushed the windpipe and pinched both carotid arteries. Her brain denied oxygen and blood, Sanborn fell unconscious in seconds. Beg held his grip for two full minutes, humming "Treat Me Nice" under his breath. Sweat from the exertion of the killing beaded along the dark lines of his forehead and dripped from the end of his nose.

Sanborn died with her eyes open, her once bright face purple and taut with terror.

Beg rolled the thin cord around the two grip sticks on either end and stuffed it back in the pocket of his loose jacket. He shoved the dead woman so she toppled over into the passenger seat, her arm trailing into the floorboard on top of a Wendy's hamburger sack. Grabbing her purse so the incident would look like a robbery, he walked quickly down the shadowed street.

A block away he ducked down the alley behind a CVS drugstore. Earlier that day, while Sanborn had been away, he'd taken an envelope containing the illicit photos of her and Drake from under her mattress. In her purse, he found the thumb drive that was surely her backup. For a blackmailer, she was highly unsophisticated.

Beg snapped the thumb drive into an adapter on his

smartphone and scrolled through the contents. He shook his head at the woman's stupidity. The files weren't even password protected. The metadata showed the photos had been printed twice—that accounted for the set mailed to Drake and the set he'd found hidden under her mattress.

He scrolled through the photos again, looking at each one carefully. He was glad he'd killed Sanborn without spending any time with her. She was a whore and he had no use for that sort of woman.

He took the thumb drive out of his phone and dropped it to the pavement, crushing it beneath his heel. His mind wandered to the jasmine scent of Veronica Garcia as he dialed Badeeb's number. She was a woman he would soon spend some time with. His crooked mouth perked at the thought.

Badeeb picked up. "Peace be unto you," he said. The sound of him exhaling a lungful of cigarette smoke fluttered on the other end of the phone.

"And to you," Beg said, pressing on with business lest the doctor spend the next ten minutes on their greeting. "I took care of the problem with the photographer." He was careful not to use Hartman Drake's name on an open phone line.

There was a long pause. "Cleanly, I trust."

Beg shook his head, sighing. "Of course," he said. There was no truly clean way to kill another human being. "In any case, your man is free to pursue his goals without her interference."

Chapter Sixty-five

7th Fighter Squadron
Langley Air Force Base, Virginia

Tara Doyle leaned against a flat, diesel-powered aircraft tug and watched the weapons being loaded onto her aircraft. She toyed with a crescent wrench while she sipped a can of Pepsi. It was against hangar protocol to drink soda this close to the aircraft, but the two airmen loading ordinance were more interested in stealing glances at her chest than anything she might be doing to bend the rules.

It was still hours before her flight, but she'd already donned her olive drab Nomex flight suit. Normally loose, it was known as a *bag* by those in the business. Tara had found one a size too small that showed off the round swell of her buttocks. A full-length zipper ran from the crotch to the neck. She unzipped it down to her belly button and tied the long sleeves around her slender waist to keep it up like a pair of pants. Her metal dog tags dangled on a chain over the chest of her skintight T-shirt, drawing attention to the fact that she'd worn no bra. She wanted the airmen's focus anywhere but their job.

Tracy, a chubby kid with a mop of dark hair that pushed Air Force regulations, drove the weapons lift. He sat idling next to the aircraft, a load of bombs partially under the plane. The F-22 had to be loaded from the opposite side in order to clear the open bay door. Arlow stood beside his partner, scratching his buzz cut and pursing baby-face cheeks as he looked over the paperwork.

Doyle dropped the wrench on the deck of the tug and walked over to sidle up next to him. Men reacted in one of two ways to such direct attention. Arlow didn't disappoint her. He gulped, looking her direction, trying—and failing—to keep his eyes off her breasts.

She threw her head back to drain the last of her Pepsi. It exposed the delicate lines of her neck and tightened the shirt against her body. She let her left arm drape over the top of her head, exposing the small tuft of dark hair under her armpit. Her real mother had never thought to shave there and Tara vowed not to bow to the vain American custom. It had made her the object of derision during gym class growing up. Air Force flight surgeons raised surprised eyebrows every year during her physical, but never actually asked anything. She was happy to be an outcast. It made her remember what the Americans had done to her father and brother . . . and the way they'd defiled her mother before they'd cut her throat.

Whether or not the young airmen found an unshaven woman attractive, they were certain to find it exotic—and in her experience, that was all a man needed to become hooked like a fish. Tara gritted her teeth behind a tight smile. Her chest shuddered with a mix of excitement and revulsion.

"Something wrong, Airman?"

"Nope." Arlow shook his head, blinking as if to clear something out of his eyes. "I . . . I mean . . . you're goin' out hot tonight. . . . By that I mean your airplane, ma'am. . . . I don't mean you personally. . . ."

"Calm down, Airman. I know I'm the queen of West Texas bitches—but I don't bite. . . ." Her smile turned coy, perking up on one side. It made her physically ill, but she knew how to play a man. It had even worked on Dr. Badeeb, many times.

Arlow swallowed hard and looked over his sparse mustache to consult the clipboard in his hand. "I got you down here for a full complement of four-eighty cannon rounds. I get that." The M61A2 machine gun fired at a rate of a hundred rounds per second, giving her roughly five one-second shots.

Airman Arlow continued. "You got two Slammers and two Sidewinders. I get that too." He called the AIM 120 and the AIM 9M/X missiles by their nicknames. "What I don't get is the GBUs. I've never loaded out live bombs for an over-watch run on home soil."

Tara pitched the empty soda can toward a fifty-five-gallon oil drum used as a trash barrel. She purposely missed and it clattered to the gleaming white hangar floor.

"I know," she said, bending over slowly to pick up the can. She felt like her suit was about to split. She could feel his eyes on her.

"Weird, huh?" she said. "They got Speedo running air-to-air tonight during the big soiree. I'm working air-to-air and air-to-ground. I suppose the big heads that think all this up are worried about waterborne attacks on the island—especially with all the talk of moles and traitors on the news."

Arlow shrugged, his eyes locked on Tara's white T-shirt. "Makes sense, I guess." He was from a little town outside Houston and though he blanched every time she got near him, she knew he considered his fellow Texan an ally. "Anyway, we're loadin' the stuff written on the orders. It's just odd, that's all. He tossed the clipboard on the seat of the aircraft tug. "Eight GBU 39s coming your way, ma'am. . . ."

He pulled on a pair of gloves and went to help his chubby partner finish the load-out.

The GBU 39 SDB or Guided Bomb Unit/Small Diameter Bomb weighed just two hundred and fifty pounds. Its lethality radius was roughly the size of a tractor trailer—not particularly large considering the awesome firepower of the F-22. Doyle had already programed the guidance systems to home on four specially designed transmitters—strategically placed. They were accurate enough to fall within fifteen meters of their intended destinations—and for human targets that would be close enough.

Tara arched her back against the tug, closing her eyes to prepare herself for the next move.

Flying "slick," in stealth mode, the Raptor was literally wrapped around its weapons system. All four missiles and eight bombs were tucked in the aircraft's belly, out of sight behind the bomb doors. Speedo would check his own bird, but leave Tara to check her ordnance. The captain who had forged her orders was one of them. That left Airmen Arlow and Tracy as the only loose ends that might show up in the short term.

"So," she called out, looking at her watch as they finished affixing the last load of four bombs to the mounting carriage on the starboard side of her aircraft. The late shift would be arriving in less than an hour. "I need to go over some inventory with you boys back in the storeroom. . . ."

The storeroom, with row after row of head-high shelving units stocked with aircraft parts and fluids, was a favorite place for squadron members to hold clandestine meetings. People went in looking intense and emerged flushed and pensive. Tara had never met anyone back there herself, but knew well enough what was going on.

She threw her head in a saucy tease and began to walk toward the gray double doors beyond the tool racks. She'd let her flight suit slip, showing a thin line of pale belly skin below the hem of her T-shirt. When she glanced over her shoulder, both Arlow and Tracy followed as though they had ropes through their noses. She patted the slender fillet knife inside the thigh of her suit and gave a long quiet sigh, smiling. It was all too easy.

First she would kill these witless men. Then, very soon, she would rain down death on the very heads of those who believed they were the most powerful people on earth.

Chapter Sixty-six

Governors Island, New York

There was a good deal of grubby work yet to be done and Nancy Hughes hadn't yet changed into the navy-blue dress she'd wear to watch her only daughter tie the knot. She'd had her hair done that morning, but wore a pair of faded jeans that were comfortably big in the hips and a red Texas Tech Red Raiders sweatshirt. She looked up from where she stood behind the small mahogany table at the threshold of the three-story brick home known as the Admiral's Mansion.

The weather had turned out on the chilly side but clear—perfect for a wedding—and she'd left the front door open in an attempt to air the mustiness out of the old manor house.

She situated the white taffeta guest book between two Montblanc fountain pens held upright in marble stones shaped like eggs. With all the politicians in attendance, the expensive pens were sure to "run off," as her mother would say, before the night was over. Still,

Jolene wasn't going to get married again anytime in the near future. No detail was too minor.

Nancy had eloped to keep her daddy from killing young Bobby Hughes. That was long before anyone thought the skinny boy from across the tracks would amount to anything at all, let alone the vice president of the United States. She would never admit it out loud, but this wedding was as much about her as it was her daughter. It had to be perfect. And now security that rivaled a meeting of the United Nations General Assembly threatened to turn the whole thing into a circus.

For the last day and half Governors Island and its surrounding waters had become a spewing fountain of activity.

The two-hundred-and-ten-foot U.S. Coast Guard cutter *Vigorous*, bristling with a twenty-five-millimeter chain gun and fifty-caliber deck guns fore and aft, prowled the Buttermilk Channel between the island and Brooklyn, New York. The hundred-and-sixty-five-foot Algonquin class cutter *Escanaba*, down from Boston, lay just off Liberty Island. A half dozen orange and gray USCG fast-boats, each also armed with a fifty-caliber machine gun mounted on the foredeck, patrolled upper New York Harbor and the entrances to the East and Hudson Rivers. These vessels, along with as many NYPD patrol boats, enforced a two-thousand-foot mar-sec standoff, keeping any other boats away from Governors Island.

A virtual army of Secret Service, Department of State Diplomatic Security agents, and NYPD secured the concrete docks and dilapidated redbrick industrial buildings on the Brooklyn side. Three hundred more from the same agencies locked down Battery Park and the entire southern tip of Manhattan. The Brooklyn Battery Tunnel that ran underwater adjacent to the island, connecting Manhattan and Brooklyn, had been closed for the day. The Secret Service Uniform Division manned a series of checkpoints at the Governors Island Ferry dock, ready to double-check the guest list for those arriving by water. Each guest, no matter his or her rank or standing, would be required to pass through full-body scanners like those that caused all the brouhaha at airports. Heads of state would arrive by helicopter and would be exempt from such scrutiny, though their staff members would be scanned at the security checkpoint in the center of the island, under a large, circus-like tent set up in the wooded park beyond the helipad.

Spotters with binoculars watched from virtually every rooftop. A heavy thump of helicopters shook the bluebird-clear sky. Navy and Air Force fighters streaked overhead, rattling the floor-to-ceiling windows in the historic mansion. Nancy felt as if she was on the deck of an aircraft carrier rather than setting up the final details of her only daughter's wedding. She'd have to call Bob and see if he couldn't pull some vice presidential strings and quiet the sky down a few hundred decibels.

Nancy stepped out and leaned against one of the Doric pillars on the full-length front porch to rest. Jolene would arrive in four hours; guests would start showing up an hour after that. Oh, for a few minutes with her feet up before they all descended upon her. It was unladylike, but she scratched her back against the column, sure some of the flaking white paint had rubbed off on her red sweatshirt.

She caught Special Agent Doyle's eye and gave him

a grin. He stood post, ramrod straight in his dark suit, at the corner of the porch.

"Sorry, Jimmy," she said, sliding up and down like a bear against a tree. "I really hate that you get to see me absent my good Southern manners.

"The United States Secret Service sees nothing—and everything," he said, returning her grin. "But if it's any consolation, Mrs. H., everyone scratches their itches."

"For what it's worth, Jimmy," Nancy said, "I'm glad you're the one assigned to this. Feels safer having you here."

She looked up to see Amanda Deatherage standing on the brick walkway. Her mouth agape, she stared up at the sky.

"Are you all right, dear?" Nancy said. Her wedding assistant seemed to grow more agitated at each pass of the military jets.

The girl's head snapped around as if she'd been slapped. "Yes . . . ma'am," she stammered, a hint of something sullen in her eyes. Her hands trembled slightly as she wrapped blue and yellow ribbon around the black barrels of two heavy antique cannons on either side of the brick walkway.

Mrs. Hughes nodded warily, unconvinced. "Have the flowers arrived?"

Deatherage smoothed a large ribbon into a bow at the muzzle of a cannon. "They have," she said. "I took care of them myself. I picked the best ones for the vice president and the president since he'll be the guest of honor."

"My daughter is the guest of honor." Nancy Hughes glared. She was too exhausted to suffer the girl's foolishness. Still, it wouldn't do to make an enemy of her today. Nancy softened her tone. "You were correct to pick a good one for the president, dear."

"Thank you, ma'am." Deatherage brightened. "I'll take care of putting them on myself so they don't get mixed up with the ones for the groomsmen."

Agent Jimmy Doyle raised a brow, dark eyes flitting back and forth from Nancy to the girl.

"I want you to take care of the photographer tonight," Nancy said, hoping to give the witless girl something to keep her mind occupied. "When President Clark comes through the receiving line, I'd like to capture that moment. Could you see to that?"

"Oh, yes, ma'am," she said. "It would be my honor." Deatherage gave her a long smile, then turned back to her duties.

What a strange girl, Nancy Hughes thought. She wouldn't be staying on after the wedding. That was a certainty.

Chapter Sixty-seven

Manhattan
Chinatown

"You should have let me kill the Cuban woman," Beg said, walking briskly beside his boss. His mouth was set in a tight line as if he'd just eaten something unpleasant.

"She is hospitalized and helpless." Dr. Badeeb held a glowing cigarette in front of him as if to ward off the press of people on teaming sidewalks of Canal Street. "Hardly a matter that requires someone of your skill. I have sent a competent man to take care of that problem."

Beg ground his teeth like a predator deprived of a favorite piece of meat. He'd been looking forward to learning more about the lovely creature that was Veronica Garcia . . . before he killed her.

He suddenly found the crush of the city extremely annoying. Tourists jostled by, mouths agape at the sheer press of foreign humanity on American soil. Beg walked dutifully beside his employer, waving off the persistent Chinese women offering their knockoff goods with a whispered buzz of: "Handbag-handbag-DVD-DVD-handbag . . ." Finding them bothersome as blowflies, Beg had to press back the urge to kill all of them with one of the colorful pashmina scarves that hung by the dozens in every other tourist and T-shirt shop.

"I need you to strangle Li Huang," the doctor went on, as if reading Beg's thoughts and throwing him a bone. "The Pari School has been compromised. Who can say where the Americans will come with their questions? She knows far too much."

Beg had expected the order to murder the doctor's wife for some time. He found it interesting that Badeeb had prescribed the method for her death. Those details were customarily left up to Beg and the Mervi found himself a little put out by such micromanagement.

"Do you suppose they are aware of your plans?" Beg said, musing. "The Americans . . ."

"No one is aware of my complete plan," the doctor grunted, drawing back his cigarette to take a drag before holding it out again. "Not even you. That said, Li Huang knows far more than she should know. I grew careless with her."

"Of course I will do as you wish, Doctor." Beg glanced at his watch as he walked. "I mean no disrespect, but I should have been the one to see to it Tara Doyle follows through with her mission."

Badeeb stopped suddenly, causing the flowing crowd to pile up behind him like water caught on the back side of a dam, before pouring sullenly past on both sides. He glanced up at Beg, nodding.

"Perhaps," he said. "But once she is in the air . . ."

He shrugged. “There is a point when she is out of our control.”

The odor of garbage, car exhaust, and cigar smoke mixed with day-old fish and musky, overripe fruit. If Beg closed his eyes, he could imagine he was in Urumqi, Samarkand, or any other large Central Asian city. When he opened them, the sea of yellow cabs reminded him he was in New York.

A cold breeze blew, swirling bits of litter from sinister alleys and clattering dungeon-like basement stairwells.

“Let us return to the issue of my wife.” The doctor took one last drag from the stub of his cigarette before tossing it to the gutter. “I am loath to give such an order,” he said, eyes sagging with exhaustion. “But times, they are very strange, causing those we care for to do strange things.”

“Indeed.” Beg nodded, glaring at a lanky Chinese woman hawking perfume. She had a mole on her eyelid that he found extremely off-putting. He suddenly found he wanted to kill her as well.

Badeeb’s searched his jacket in a fluttering panic for another cigarette. “If pressed,” he said, “I fear Li Huang might let the cat from the sack, so to speak.”

Beg stopped in his tracks, thought for a moment, then resumed his pace. “The bag,” he said. “You mean to say she would *let the cat out of the bag*.”

“Precisely so,” Badeeb said. “In any case, the sooner you get to it the better.”

“When?”

“Tonight. At once. Now.” Badeeb glanced at his watch. “Our plan has begun to unfold as we speak. I would consider it a personal favor if she were dead within the hour."

Beg took a deep breath, picturing the old woman waiting patiently in the cramped apartment for her husband to return.

A devout Hui Chinese Muslim, Li Huang was responsible for the deaths of many in pursuit of *sheng zahn*, the Chinese word for jihad, and of her husband's dreams. She had been a faithful wife and deadly coconspirator with the doctor for over fifteen years. Deadly or not, there would be no sport in strangling her. It would be like dispatching a venomous spider. She was dangerous, but no match for the heel of his boot.

In a near panic for a cigarette, Badeeb doubled his pace and shoved upstream through the crowd toward a magazine stand at the corner of Mott Street. Beg knew the Pakistani owner kept a good supply of Badeeb's favorite Player's Gold Leaf.

The old man wasn't there, having left the shop in the care of a slender boy in his early twenties, likely his son.

"Peace be unto you," Badeeb launched into the lengthy formalities of his pious greeting, right palm to his heart.

The boy leaned forward, both hands on the counter. He looked as though he was having trouble stifling a yawn.

Two more customers formed a line behind the doctor as he spoke.

The boy rolled his eyes.

"Yeah, yeah, whatever," he said in a dismissive New

Jersey accent. "Do me a favor and just tell me what you want. You're holding up the line."

Badeeb slammed the money for two packs of Gold Leafs on the counter. He spun on his heels, ripping into the foil of one pack as if it contained the antidote to some horrible poison.

"His father is a pious man," the doctor seethed. "But the child is an infidel. After you strangle Li Huang you should come back and kill him." He flicked open his metal lighter, putting a flame to the cigarette. "His death would be most welcome."

"Very well," Beg said, following the doctor east on Canal Street.

"Very well, indeed." Badeeb puffed away on his glowing cigarette. "So much hinges on this night. Plans are falling into place better than I ever imagined they could. In any case," the doctor said as if he were actually going to be part of the immediate action, "let us go see to strangling my wife. Maybe that will cheer me."

Beg followed, his mind floating to the mysterious face of Veronica Garcia. Killing the old woman, the street vendor with the mole on her eye, or even the young infidel at the cigarette stand would be little solace for missing the chance to catch another glimpse of the beautiful Cuban and treat her to the taste of the wire of his garrote. Soon, she would be dead at the hand of a rank amateur and he would never have the opportunity. Such a waste.

CHAPTER SIXTY-EIGHT

Georgetown University Hospital
Washington, D.C.

Ronnie Garcia's mind was awash with disjointed memories. An incessant beeping to her left set her nerves on edge. The smell of antiseptic and a lingering odor of chicken broth set her stomach doing sickening flips. Her back ached, and she was sure someone was sitting on her chest. Oxygen flowed into her nose through a tube looped over both ears.

Her eyes fluttered slowly. She blinked, allowing the sterile white walls, the television, the lumps under the sheet that were her feet, to come into focus. She found it difficult to swallow and nearly cried from relief when she found a Styrofoam cup of ice water on a rolling table by the bed.

Visions of icy stone mountains and roaring motorcycles flashed across her mind. Jericho Quinn . . . she'd thought he might be there when she woke up. She remembered the orphanage, the boys, the sickening impact to her back, and then searing pain as she realized she'd been stabbed. The sensations of not being able to draw a breath, of utter helplessness—of drowning in her own blood—all came roaring back. She could recall snippets of Quinn working frantically to save her life. She needed to tell him something, something she'd heard just before. . . .

Her eyes flicked open, fully awake.

"Tara Doyle," she said out loud. "*The queen of West Texas bitches*. She's one of them." The F-22 fighter pilot was a mole.

The television was turned to CNN, but the volume was down. The ticker across the bottom read *Breaking News . . . Governors Island Wedding.* Ronnie used the remote to turn it up. A dapper reporter with gelled hair and a black tuxedo spoke into the camera.

". . . Clark and the First Lady will be arriving within the hour via the Marine One helicopter. Now, Rene, we haven't seen the vice president or Mrs. Hughes yet this evening, but since it's their daughter getting married tonight, we're pretty sure they're already on-site. And FYI, Rene, this wedding is shaping up to match Prince William and Kate as far as royal nuptials go. It could be the largest gathering of world leaders and celebrities we've seen in the U.S. since . . . well, I can't remember when. . . ."

Ronnie's heart monitor went crazy as she reached for the telephone beside her bed.

Tara Doyle flew the most advanced fighter aircraft in the world. The wedding had to be her intended target.

Ronnie knew she couldn't simply call in and report

the threat. Doyle could have too many accomplices in high places. If the call was somehow received or even intercepted by one of the moles, Garcia might inadvertently move up the time line and put more people in danger. She had to talk to someone she was absolutely certain could be trusted. She beat her head against the pillow, racking her brain.

Ronnie had a good head for numbers, but realized she'd never actually called Quinn or Thibodaux. They'd always called her. She punched in the first number that came to her head.

"Three-five-four-three," a male voice said. He had a familiar Virginia twang.

"Director Ross, please."

"She's not available. Who shall I say is calling?"

A vision of CIA Deputy Director Marty Magnuson, walking through the food court and shooting his coworkers in the head, flashed before Ronnie's eyes. She hung up. How could she know who to trust?

She dialed information and got two more numbers.

"White House switchboard, may I help you?" It was a woman, polite, but all business.

"I need to speak with Winfield Palmer."

"Mr. Palmer is unavailable. I'd be happy to take a message."

"When would he get the message?" Ronnie bit her lip.

"Monday morning."

"It's important I speak to him right away. Could you have him call me?"

"I can certainly give him the message—on Monday morning."

"Maldita sea!" Ronnie cursed. "I have to talk to him."

"Ma'am, with all due respect, I get fifty calls a day from people who *have* to talk to someone here. Is this a matter of national security?"

"Yes, yes," Ronnie said. "It is."

"It's always a matter of national security," the woman said. Ronnie could almost hear her eyes rolling. "I suggest you hang up and dial nine-one-one."

Ronnie slammed down the phone. She fell back against the pillow, catching her breath before dialing the next number.

"FBI."

Ronnie clenched her teeth. It hurt her pride, but had to be done. "I need to speak with Director Bodington on an urgent matter—and please don't tell me he's unavailable."

"Well," the voice came back. "It's Friday afternoon. He *is* unavailable."

Ronnie wanted to scream. Her words spilled out in a breathy stream. "I can guarantee you he'll want to talk to me," she said. "I'm . . . one of his informants. . . ."

"Yes, ma'am," the operator said, his voice cracking a little. "I can get you an on-call agent."

Ronnie hung up without another word and pressed the call button at the side of her bed for the nurse. She was very near to tears, and that alone was enough to piss her off.

A bright-eyed brunette with a round, freckled face opened the door a few seconds later.

"You okay, dear?" she said, checking the heart monitor and oxygen output.

Ronnie nodded, willing herself to calm down so the nurse didn't decide to medicate her. She had to get word to someone about Tara Doyle, but after all that had happened, she didn't know who to trust.

"I'm fine." She forced a smile. "Woke up from a bad dream, that's all."

The nurse, whose name tag said Beverly, lifted Ronnie's wrist and checked the IV taped to the back of her hand. "Think you could eat some soup?"

"Maybe," Ronnie said, wanting to appear compliant. Her head was still loopy from the pain medications they were giving her. "Have you got my cell phone anywhere?"

Beverly shook her head. "Nope," she said. "You didn't have anything like that on you when they brought you in."

"Who brought me in?"

"Not sure, sweetie," Beverly said. "I just came on duty a couple of hours ago. I'm glad you're feeling better though." She leaned in, whispering even though no one else was in the room. "Listen, I don't know what you did, but you seem like a nice girl. There's a plainclothes cop standing outside your room. If you want, I can ask him to come in and answer all your questions."

Ronnie brightened. Maybe it was Quinn. "Dark hair, heavy five o'clock shadow?"

"No," the nurse said. "Sorry."

"Did he give his name?"

Beverly shook her head. "Sorry. I can ask him if you want. Looks kind of mean, though."

Why would a cop be sitting outside her room?

Could she trust him? She kicked herself for not memorizing Palmer's cell number.

"No," she said. "I'll be okay. I just need some rest." Ronnie swung her feet off the edge of the bed as soon as Beverly shut the door behind her.

"You can do this, chica," she whispered, pausing long enough to let her head stop spinning.

She winced as she peeled back the sticky tape holding in her IV. Stumbling, and using the bed rail for support, she rifled through the drawers, settling for a cotton ball and piece of tape to stop the weep of blood from the back of her hand.

Thankfully, she found some clothes hanging in the closet—faded jeans, a black cashmere sweater, and a pair of Nike runners. She shucked off the thin, backless gown and ripped into the unopened packages of socks and underwear. Somebody was looking out for her.

Gingerly, she reached behind her back to touch her wound. She was surprised to find two more bandages, slightly larger than the first. Of course, the doctors had had to go in and repair the damage. One of the incisions was wet with blood from her exertions. She shrugged. Couldn't be helped. She'd probably just pulled a stitch.

Tara Doyle, the "Queen of West Texas Bitches," had to be stopped. And since she couldn't trust anyone, Ronnie would do it herself.

She'd just zipped her jeans when the plainclothes cop walked in on her. He had blond hair and a wild, street-hardened look on his face—not much different than the boys in the caves where she'd been stabbed. He wore a white dress shirt with an open collar. A navy-blue sports coat covered the swell of a pistol on his belt. Ronnie had never seen him before, but there was something vaguely familiar in his eyes.

"Oh no, no, no, young lady," he said, walking toward her with a raised hand, as if he was directing traffic. "You're not going anywhere."

Chapter Sixty-nine

"Can you put her down in the ball field?" Quinn said into his headset. Thibodaux sat across from him, strapped in to his seat forward of the cargo bay on V22 Osprey.

The pilot, a balding man with smiling blue eyes, turned to glance over the shoulder of his green Nomex flight suit. "I can set her down in the middle of Times Square if you want me to." His name was Jared Smedley, an Air Force Academy squadron mate of Quinn's. Smeds had gone on to flight training after the academy, graduating at the top of every class he took. He'd been a flight instructor for the last three years and had been brought in from the Eighth Special Operations Squadron at Hurlburt Field, Florida, to fly overwatch and rescue during the wedding. He gave a thumbs-up to his copilot, a waif of a girl with a blond ponytail hanging out below her flight helmet. She returned the gesture.

He had the swaggering confidence of a pilot and the skill to back it up. Quinn had always found it impossible not to like the man.

Capable of straight or vertical flight, Smedley's aircraft, the tilt-rotor V22, made insertion possible in areas like Manhattan and Governors Island.

Quinn's Bluetooth earbud chirped. He moved the boom mike of his headset away and tapped the device. It was Palmer.

"Homeland Security facial recognition just got a hit on an NYPD security camera on Mott Street. Looks like the doctor is buying cigarettes at a newsstand. I'm sending a still to your phone now."

Quinn took the BlackBerry off his belt.

"Who's the guy with him?" he asked, turning the screen to show Thibodaux.

"Look at that mop," Thibodaux scoffed. "He's Elvis's evil twin."

"Don't know," Palmer said, an edge to his voice that Quinn could feel. "We have intel that Badeeb's wife is hiding out in a flophouse off Bowery. Looks like they're heading to meet up with her."

"Roger that," Quinn said. "We're about to touch down at a ball field in lower Manhattan. It'll take us about ten minutes to get there on the bikes—"

Dust and leaves flew outside the windows as the huge rotors began to lower the Osprey onto the center of the baseball diamond. One of the two crewmen in the back told them to stand by and activated the lowering mechanism on the ramp at the rear of the bird, giving them a quick exit with their bikes.

Quinn stood from his seat along the bulkhead, working to release the straps on Mrs. Miyagi's candy-apple-red Ducati 848.

"Don't forget, Jericho," Palmer said. "We need to

take Badeeb and his wife alive. See who the other guy is. Do me a favor and try to keep from killing him."

"If at all possible, sir." Quinn nodded.

"Make damned certain it is possible," Palmer said. "I'm pretty sure the president will go against my advice and come to the wedding no matter what the Secret Service or I say. He keeps reminding me that the terrorists have won if they get to dictate where we do and do not go. . . ." There was a sudden blip on the phone—another call. "Hang on a minute. . . ."

Quinn and Thibodaux sat, geared up and ready, on their bikes. The heavy rear ramp lowered the last few inches with an agonized hydraulic whine. Dust and litter swirled into the back of the aircraft as Palmer came back on the line.

"Jericho? You still there?" His voice was breathless, heavy.

"I am," Quinn said, feeling a rise in the pit of his stomach.

"Jericho," Palmer said. "It's about Garcia."

Chapter Seventy

Tara Doyle wiped the airmen's blood off her hands and threw the wad of paper towels in the trashcan. A swatch of red painted the chest of her flight suit and the V of her neck. She didn't bother with that. The smell of blood helped her focus on the matters at hand.

Her entire life, at least from the time she was nine years old, had been lived for the next few hours. The years of study, the decades of pretending to love her adopted family, to care for this country of dogs—it all led up to her actions this one night.

"I will cut the throat of the whore that is the United States of America," she chuckled out loud to the cavernous hangar. "With one of her very best airplanes . . ."

Walking toward her jet, she had a fleeting thought of Jimmy. He'd been a toddler when her American parents had taken him in from the Indian reservation in Montana, too young to know she too was adopted. A good confidant—he'd caught her crying on so many occasions and come in to console her without once asking her why. She shook the thought from her mind. None of that mattered now. He was one of them, nothing more than a means to an end, someone to vouch for her citizenship and make her background more believable. She had to remind herself of that. Jimmy Doyle deserved to die like the rest of them—

"Major Tara Doyle, YOU ARE UNDER ARREST!" A muscular Air Force OSI agent wearing khaki 5.11 pants and a black ballistic raid vest stepped from behind the wheels of a nearby F-22 Raptor, Sig Sauer pistol at high ready.

Doyle spun, fillet knife in hand, but Ronnie Garcia rose up from her hiding spot behind the aircraft tug and hit her in the face with a crescent wrench.

The queen of West Texas bitches fell like a sack of wet sand. Garcia winced from the exertion, gritting her teeth against the searing pain in her back.

Moments later, the brightly lit hangar swarmed with OSI agents in black vests and thigh holsters. Everyone present had personally worked with Quinn and, for one reason or another, had his complete trust.

"We need to get a copy of the weapons load-out," Garcia shouted. "Whoever signed for this payload of bombs is in this along with Doyle."

"Got two dead in the back room," an agent who'd been a year behind Quinn in the Academy yelled from across the open hangar. He stood at the door wearing a pair of blue nitrile gloves. "They got their pants around their ankles and their throats cut from ear to ear." The agent shook his head. "It's a mess."

Garcia, still holding the wrench, looked down at the

smear of fresh blood across the front of Doyle's flight suit. "You really are a bitch," she said.

One of the agents, a tan Colorado native named Judson who'd spent time in Iraq with Quinn, knelt to roll a moaning Doyle onto her stomach so he could handcuff her. He looked up at Garcia as he closed the cuffs with a ratcheting zip.

"You better sit down," he said. "You look pretty pale."

Maybe it hadn't been such a good idea to come along considering what she'd been through. But she was just stubborn enough that whatever the cost, she wasn't about to let a couple of holes in her back keep her away from something this big. In truth, Garcia thought she might be sick to her stomach at any moment.

"I got her," a beefy man with mussed blond hair said as he took off his navy-blue sports coat and draped it over Garcia's shoulders. The sleeves of his white button-down were rolled up to reveal a black octopus tattoo on his forearm. "Let's get you back to the hospital, young lady. My big brother would never forgive me if I let anything happen to you."

Garcia swayed on her feet, slumping into his arms.

Two Quinns . . . it was almost too much to fathom.

Chapter Seventy-one

Quinn gunned the Ducati, shooting over the lip of the Osprey's metal ramp. As he was accustomed to the longer travel in the GS's suspension, the 848 jarred his fillings, landing with a stiff thud on the hard-packed soil of the ball field. His spinning tire gained traction almost instantly. Thibodaux, not to be outdone, revved his big GS Adventure, coming up even with Quinn on his right.

Palmer had briefed Quinn about the raid on the F-22 hangar at Langley. It calmed him some that Bo had been there to help look after Garcia.

That left the loose ends of Badeeb and his unknown acquaintance to clean up.

"We're en route to Chinatown now." Linked to Palmer via encrypted cellular, Quinn spoke into the mike inside his helmet.

"Outstanding," Palmer said. "The problem is, with this sleeper jet jockey out of the picture, the president is determined to attend the wedding."

"That's not a good idea, sir," Quinn said, splitting

traffic to cut between two lanes packed full of bumper to bumper yellow cabs. "There has to be more to this than a single pilot. What about the brother?"

"He's clean. Got several extended relatives from the reservation in Montana who vouch for him. Even has a couple of baby pictures and a footprint on his hospital birth record."

"Still," Quinn said, downshifting to shoot around a moving van. "It doesn't pass the smell test. A target as ripe as that wedding has to have two shooters pointed at it."

"I'm painfully aware of that," Palmer said. "I even used your little ditty on the boss—'see one, think two.' I'm afraid he remains unconvinced."

Quinn swerved sharply, countersteering around a puttering delivery boy whose bicycle was piled head high with takeout boxes from a Chinese restaurant.

"Understood. We'll be at the newsstand where Badeeb bought cigarettes in less than a minute. I can already smell the fish shops. . . . I'll call you when we have something."

"Tally ho, beb," Thibodaux's voice came across Quinn's earpiece, as they turned the bikes out of the honking, chaotic traffic of Bowery and into the cramped and twisting alley of Doyers Street. Gaudily painted green, yellow, and red brick buildings with rusted, zigzagging fire escapes rose up on either side of the narrow pavement, giving the place a kaleidoscope-tunnel-like atmosphere.

"See the guy with the cigarette under the neon sign?" Jacques pointed with his chin as he rode. "He look like our Pakistani doc to you?"

"Roger that," Quinn said. His eye caught the movement of another dark figure striding purposefully through the door of a yellow six-story brick halfway down the block. He only caught a glimpse, but the upswept pompadour of black hair and the sure movements told Quinn this was the Evil Elvis in the photograph.

Badeeb stood in the grimy shadows under the tattered sign of the hand-pulled noodle shop. Even in the dim light, his oval face shone with perspiration. Twin black pebbles stared back from an enveloping haze of smoke from the cigarette that hung from his lips. He seemed oblivious to a couple of motorcycles, intent instead on the man who'd just disappeared into the yellow building.

"You got Badeeb?" Quinn gave an almost imperceptible nod of his helmet.

"Matter of fact I do, beb." Thibodaux rolled on the gas and tore down the narrow street. Just before he reached Badeeb, he extended his left arm like a jousting knight—directly at the startled doctor.

The cigarette fell from Badeeb's lips a split second before the armored knuckles of the Cajun's huge right glove obliterated his nose.

Quinn grabbed a handful of front brake, squeezed until he felt the back end lighten, then pushed forward with his legs to bring the bike onto its front wheel in a sort of reverse wheelie known as a *stoppie*. Rolling on the front wheel, Quinn used his body weight to throw the back wheel around, executing a snap hundred-and-eighty-degree turn. It was a move he'd practiced with his brother hundreds of times on a slew of different bikes. Bo called it their patented "going-the-other-way maneuver."

Quinn hit the gas as soon as the little red Ducati's rear wheel settled back on the pavement. Smoke flew up in a whirring rooster tail while the tire found its grip. As his head whipped around he watched the door to the yellow brick building swing shut behind the dark Elvis.

Chapter Seventy-two

Mujaheed Beg paused inside the building, sniffing the stale air. He hadn't lived this long by rushing headlong into things—not even simple jobs like strangling old women. For this, he would use his old friend, the wire garrote. At least that would bring some enjoyment. He'd not been able to employ it on the congressman's mistress—too much blood. Such a thing wouldn't matter in the dark, cage-like atmosphere Li Huang called home. Residents were unlikely to notice a dead dog rotting in the hallway of such a place, much less a little blood on the stained wooden floor.

People hacked and coughed behind low walls up and down the narrow corridors as if the place were a tuberculosis ward. The strangled gurgles of a dying woman would draw no attention at all. Under the sullen light of a dusty hallway bulb, any blood that made it under the doorway would be hard to identify until long after Beg was gone. In any case, most, if not all, of the rabbits in this warren of rooms were illegal aliens and were highly unlikely to call the authorities—even to report a murder.

A long stairway gaped upward to the Mervi's right. The chattering riot of a Chinese game show, sirens from police dramas, and dramatic dialogue of historical romances tumbled down from the black hole above, mixing with the sour smell of human confinement. It was early enough in the evening that most of the inmates—that's how Beg thought of them—were still out working the sidewalks or stuck in a basement sweatshop sewing the sleeves on clothing for American consumers so they could proudly say they bought products made in the U.S.A.

Halfway down the smoky hall, an old man with wisps of gray hair like moldy cotton candy squatted, backlit by a grimy window leading out to the fire escape. A hotplate of boiling noodles and fish bubbled on the floor beside him. Like the rest of the place, he reeked of day-old alcohol and sweat.

Li Huang's wooden door was just beyond the old man, under an exposed row of radiator pipes that ran like monkey bars across the stained ceiling.

Beg put a hand inside the pocket of his jacket, feeling for the wooden handles and reassuring coil of sharp wire. He walked past the old man, considering whether he would have to kill him or not on the way out. The old man was bony and frail as a stalk of drought-parched wheat, and such a thing wouldn't be hard.

Li Huang normally stayed at one of the Badeebs' much more comfortable homes on Long Island or in Pennsylvania. Out of an abundance of caution—and to get her in a place that he could more easily have her killed with no link to him—the doctor had asked her to hide in this horribly filthy hotel used by Chinese Snakeheads to hide their illegal human cargo until they paid off their debts.

State prison inmates had larger accommodations. Each room was barely six by eight feet, topped with chicken-wire mesh in a halfhearted attempt to discourage thieves. Devoted to terroristic jihad—she called it *sheng zhan*—Li Huang had readily traded her middle-class home for this wretched place that smelled like a restaurant trash Dumpster—all for the sake of keeping her dear husband's plans safe.

And now that same husband had sent a very deadly man to kill her.

Beg knocked on the flimsy, hollow-core door, feeling more of a rush than he'd anticipated. Perhaps it was the fact that he had shared tea with this woman dozens of times while he'd discussed plans with her husband.

The door creaked opened a crack to expose one rheumy eye and the glint of charcoal hair.

Knowing that she would surely have a weapon, Beg didn't wait to be invited in. The door gave easily to his weight and Li Huang fell backward in the tiny room, slamming her head against the edge of the wood two-by-four frame that made up her simple bed.

Li Huang flailed out as she fell, knocking over a rickety bedside table and sending a ceramic reading lamp crashing to the bare wooden floor.

Trembling fingers reached up to touch the knot where her head had struck the bedframe. They came back red with blood. Narrow eyes flitted back and forth around the room looking for a nonexistent escape route as Beg slowly took the wire garrote from his pocket.

He grasped the wooden handles in each hand. Li Huang was a proud woman. She would not be a screamer as some were. He could take his time.

Staring up at him, her nostrils flared. Her tongue flicked against her lips, snakelike.

"Why?" she demanded, though the stricken pain in her eyes said she already had her answer.

Beg shrugged. There was no need to explain.

"My husband sent you?" Cold realization flushed across her face.

Beg bounded forward without speaking. He grabbed a handful of hair and jerked her away from the bed. Instead of fighting back, she threw a hand to her throat. Beg couldn't help but shake his head. Such a weak defense would do precious little good against the unforgiving wire noose. This would be over much more quickly than even he had anticipated. The doctor was right, he thought, as he zipped the razor-sharp wire tight. She did smell like old fruit.

Chapter Seventy-three

Quinn left the Ducati at the curb and sprinted up the short concrete stoop. He didn't have to look back, trusting that Thibodaux had already sacked up Dr. Badeeb.

Removing his helmet, he gripped it in his left hand as he pushed open the door. Having the Arai gave him a good cover story if someone stopped him, and it made for a formidable weapon if he had to whack someone in the running lights without killing them.

Once inside the door he entered a dim lobby with chipped tile. The rusted mail cubbies along the wall to his left were covered with old bits of tape displaying the numbers of the rooms—but no names. A long staircase ran up to a dark hallway to his right.

Moving by instinct over intellect, Quinn padded quickly up the stairs, right hand covering the butt of his Kimber. The cry of a squalling baby met him at the top. Cell-like rooms lined the wall to his left; chicken wire covered the dusty windows facing the street on his right. The cloying desperation of the place reminded him of his time in the fake PRONA prisoner-of-war camp in SERE school.

The only other soul in the hallway was an old man squatting beside a boiling pot. Quinn raised an eyebrow in the universal sign for: "I'm here to help if you want it."

The old man sat back on his haunches, heels flat on the floor as he stirred the steaming soup. He said nothing, but his watery eyes flicked up the dark hall.

A strangled cry two doors down confirmed the dark man's location. Quinn had heard the sound all too many times before. It was woman—and she was dying.

Bounding past the boiling pot of fish, Quinn shouldered his way through the door to find his target, full Elvis pompadour hanging low across his brow from his exertions with the thrashing old woman in front of him. Li Huang had thrown a boney hand to her neck, but the thin garrote wire had already bitten deeply into the exposed flesh. Blood spilled from the terrifying wound as if from a fountain. The front of her tan cotton blouse glistened dark red.

The killer looked up with a start. He bared white teeth and tossed his head to get the hair out of his eyes. He gave a sudden yank on the garrote, severing one of the woman's fingers and giving the deadly wire more access to the vital arteries and windpipe. The finger landed with a sickening thump on the floor next to her trembling leg, its manicured nail clicking against the wood.

Quinn swung his motorcycle helmet like a war club, connecting with evil Elvis's forehead. The man staggered backward, releasing his grip on the garrote so it slipped off Li Huang's neck. He sprawled against the low wooden bed with the weapon, glinting with fresh blood, dangling in one hand. Quinn dragged the injured woman toward the door. She slumped against the wall, clutching her neck with both hands in a vain attempt to stem the flow of blood.

Elvis bounced back from the bed, regaining his feet in an instant. Pressing forward, he flicked the wooden handle of the garrote at Quinn like a whip. He pushed the fallen lock of black hair out of his face and stood breathing for a long moment, lip twitching into a half sneer. A heartbeat later, he sprang, rushing forward and causing Quinn to regret not shooting him as soon as he'd entered the room.

Both men tumbled backward, out the flimsy door and into the narrow confines of the hall. They crashed into the chicken-wire wall in a writhing heap, pulling the wire away and exposing dusty, distorted glass of one of the floor-to-ceiling windows. The soup man abandoned his hot plate and scuttled into the dark recesses of the corridor.

Quinn used his opponent's momentum against him, grabbing a fistful of cloth at both shoulders and hauling him face-first into the glowing red coils of the hot plate. He yowled in pain as the element seared his cheeks, branding him with concentric circles. The pungent odor of scorched flesh and singed hair filled the hall as he rolled away, reversing directions quickly to come after Quinn again. As they crashed together, he stomped on Quinn's injured foot as if he sensed the weakness.

Riding on waves of nauseating pain, Quinn was barely able to keep from vomiting. Somehow, his hand caught the warm wood of a garrote handle. He flailed with the other, connecting with the opposite handle that the dark Elvis still clutched in his fist. Locked in a clench around the deadly garrote, they stood face-to-face, gasping, close enough Quinn could smell the soapy scent of the oil in his hair.

Quinn cursed himself again for not shooting the man in the first place. He felt himself fading. Exposure to extreme altitude, cold, torture, and lack of sleep piled on in a relentless scrum of crushing fatigue.

Dark Elvis sensed the lapse of strength and reacted with instant fury. He shoved forward with powerful legs, driving Quinn backward toward the hazy light of the fire escape window.

Fighting dizziness, Quinn leaned in for a split second, remembering his jujitsu instructor's credo: *When pushed, pull*. He wanted to be certain his opponent was fully committed. Without warning, he gave way, pedaling backward to bring the evil Elvis with him. Quinn's fists shot in and upward, crossing in front of the surprised man's throat before looping the taut wire up and over his head of slicked hair.

Quinn let his right leg collapse under his butt as he used his opponent's momentum to drag him along. Rolling backward on his shoulders, he planted his left foot in the other man's gut, throwing him in a forward somersault over Quinn's head.

Glass shattered, raining down on the combatants as the force of the dark man's momentum propelled his body through the chicken wire and out the window.

Quinn gripped the ends of the garrote, feeling the sudden heavy tug as his opponent's weight slammed against the wire. The handles suddenly grew light in Quinn's hands. He rolled to his side, fearing the wire had broken and expecting to continue the fight.

Instead, Dark Elvis's head landed in the dim hallway with a sickening thud, black eyes squinting, fallen pompadour sulking across a furrowed brow. His body lay in a heap outside the broken window on the rusted fire escape grating.

Pounding footsteps brought Thibodaux bounding up the stairs, pistol extended and ready in his beefy hand. He slid to a stop, staring in slack-jawed disgust.

Quinn pushed himself up on one knee, blinking and wincing in pain from his throbbing foot. "Where's Badeeb? You didn't kill him, did you? We're supposed to see what he knows."

The Cajun sighed. "Sucker swallowed a little magic coward pill before I could even unass my bike. NYPD is sacking up the body." He tipped his gun barrel toward the severed head. "Anyhow, you got no room to chastise me. I guess the King's not gonna do much talking either." He did a passable Elvis impersonation, complete with quivering upper lip. "Thank you, thank you very much."

"No, he's not talking." Quinn struggled to his feet, using the wall for support. "But maybe someone else will.

A red smear followed on the wooden floor behind Li Huang where she had dragged herself to the edge of her bed. Dark, arterial blood seeped between the gaps of bony fingers clenched at her neck, ebbing and flowing in time with the weakening beat of her heart. Her lips had gone a chalky blue.

Quinn knelt beside her. "We have an ambulance en route." He took a piece of QuikClot gauze from the black Cordura wound kit in his pocket and applied it to her neck. Even as he worked, he knew the injury was too great to save her.

"My husband . . . responsible . . . for this," she croaked. The glistening gray white sheath of her windpipe was visible through the sagging wound, moving when she spoke. ". . . faithful . . . to that . . . dog . . . fifteen years . . ."

"And yet he wanted you dead," Quinn said, slowly shaking his head. This woman had surely been a party to the deaths of untold numbers of innocents. It was difficult for him to muster much sympathy. "Why?"

". . . hate him," she gasped.

"I believe I can save you," Quinn lied. "But you have to tell me what you know."

"Too late . . ." Her voice came in ragged whispers, like the worn-out remnants of a sobbing cry.

"Your husband ordered you murdered," Quinn said, keeping firm pressure on the old woman's wound. "Are you going to protect him after that?"

"It is a girl," Li Huang whispered, lapsing into Mandarin. "She will kill them all."

Quinn shot a glance at Thibodaux, nodding. "We took the girl into custody," he said, following the woman into her native language. "Before she could get in her airplane."

"Not Tara . . ." The old woman shook her head. The move was slight, but enough to start the wound bleeding again in earnest. "Tara was . . . insurance. . . ."

Her eyes fluttered, dimming.

Quinn held her chin with his free hand. "What is her name?" he asked, still in Chinese. "This other girl? Where is she?"

"Vice president's wife . . . new assistant . . . they will kill your president. . . ." The old woman tried to swallow. "Could . . . I have . . . water?" Dried saliva flaked white at the corners of slack lips.

"They?" Quinn asked, his face just inches from the dying woman.

"There . . . is a man. . . . He . . . he . . ." She coughed, drawing a series of rattling breaths. "What time is it?"

Thibodaux looked at his watch. "Just after five," he said.

A wan smile crossed Li Huang's sallow face. "It does not matter anymore." She shook her head for the last time. "You are too late—"

Chapter Seventy-four

Quinn laid the old Chinese woman's lifeless body on her rude wooden bed. Shaking off the hollow pit of abject fatigue, he reached in the pocket of the Transit jacket for his phone and glanced up at Thibodaux as he punched in the number for Palmer.

The big Cajun stood, staring down at the gaping wound in the old woman's neck, jaws loose again as if he might be sick. "I don't reckon I was ever around a people so keen on cuttin' one another's heads off. . . ."

"Do me a favor," Quinn said.

"Huh?" Thibodaux looked up as if from a trance.

"Get Smedley back on the horn. Ask him to get his Osprey here on the double. We have to get out to that wedding."

"She said, 'he,' " Thibodaux mused. "Got any notion who 'he' is?"

"Could be anybody," Quinn said, waiting for his call to connect.

Thibodaux grunted his agreement and went to work.

"Dammit," Quinn spat. He got the fast busy signal

that told him something was going on with the cell tower handling his call. He pressed redial but heard the same rapid series of beeps.

"Mine's not going through either." The big Cajun met his gaze. "I'm gettin' zip."

"Then we'll deliver the message in person." Quinn was already trotting toward the stairs.

Thibodaux still had the cell phone pressed to his ear as he ran beside Quinn. His face suddenly brightened. "It's ringing." He handed Jericho the phone.

Smedley picked up on the third ring. His phone was connected via Bluetooth to his Lightspeed headset and the lawnmower thump of the V-22's Rolls-Royce engines was barely audible in the background.

"Smeds," Quinn said. "It's me, Copper. Where you been? Your phone wasn't working."

"Just dropped off a load of Castle Guards at the venue," the pilot said, referring to the Secret Service detail. "The place is swarming with those sunglass-wearin' dudes—and I gotta tell you, they all look like they're itching to shoot someone."

"Yeah, well, me too, Jared," Quinn said. "Me too. So where are you now?"

"Setting down at the heliport by the ferry terminal. Why?"

"The moles must have a cell phone jammer on the island," Quinn mused, as much to himself as Smedley. "I can't get through to Palmer and your phone was in-op while you were over there."

"Want me to get a message on the military frequency?" the major asked. "It was working fine."

Standing at the Ducati now, Quinn paused to sort his thoughts. He was hurt and exhausted, dead on his feet.

It was moments like this when he couldn't afford to make snap decisions. But it was one of the great paradoxes of his life that in moments like this, snap decisions were all he had time for.

"Do you have someone on the ground out there you can trust?" he asked. With an unknown number of moles infiltrating the government, sending out an open message could have deadly consequences.

"I trust all my guys," Smedley said. "Without a doubt."

"Okay then." Quinn paused. "Think for a minute. Do you know Tara Doyle?"

"Sure," the pilot shot back. "I'd heard of her."

"Did you trust her before today?"

There was silence on the line. "Roger that." Smedley gave a long sigh. "From now on I don't trust anyone."

"I hear you," Quinn said, twirling his open hand in the air above his head as he spoke, signaling Thibodaux to get ready to go. "I need you to get your bird over here as quick as you can."

"The ball field where I dropped you off?"

"No time for that." Quinn threw a leg over the Ducati. "It may already be too late. We're just around the corner from Canal and Bowery. What do you need for clearance?"

"You gotta be kidding me," Smedley almost shouted into the phone.

"Aren't you the one that said you'd set her down in Times Square if I asked?" Quinn said.

"That's cocky pilot bullshit and you know it," Smedley said. "I can't be held accountable for stuff like that."

"Come on, Smeds. You know you're itching for a reason to do this. What's your wingspan?"

"I need thirty yards, give our take, just to have a few inches on either side. Fifty would be better."

"Canal and Bowery should work then," Quinn said, giving at best, an educated guess.

"Traffic in Chinatown is murder any time of the day."

"Just bring her in," Quinn said, starting the Ducati. "When the taxis see your giant gray pterodactyl swooping down on them, they'll scoot out of the way like a bunch of canaries."

CHAPTER SEVENTY-FIVE

Quinn rode up over the curb with a healthy bounce and stopped beside one of the gray lion statues in front of the HSBC bank building when the tilt-rotor Osprey thumped in from the south.

"This is gonna be a tight fit, beb," Thibodaux said, pulling in beside him and flipping up the visor of his helmet.

Quinn clenched his teeth, willing the Osprey in. There was no room for error, but Smedley was as good a pilot as there was—and though he talked a tentative game, he was fearless. "He can do it."

The major brought his bird in fast and low, screaming in at well over a hundred knots just above the brick fortress of tenements known as Knickerbocker Village. Keeping the Manhattan Bridge on his right, he didn't flare until he reached Confucius Plaza.

Two helmeted crewmen in green Nomex flight suits craned swiveling heads out each side of the aircraft, guiding the pilots down through the maze of light poles, neon signs, and electric wires. Trash, dust, and road grit whirled under the cyclonic effect of the two thirty-eight-foot rotors. Metal trash cans toppled and rolled down the street. The blue and yellow cloth umbrella on a hotdog cart vanished in the whirling gray cloud.

Deafening vibration and flying debris activated car alarms up and down the street for two blocks. Taxis and delivery trucks crashed and squealed attempting to back out of the path of the descending aircraft. A traffic cop in a bright yellow vest stood in tight-lipped awe. He squinted, leaning into the wind with his hand holding down his hat.

The Osprey's rear ramp yawned open as Smedley settled her expertly in the middle of the intersection, now deserted as if it had been swept clean. The crewmen waved Quinn forward and the two men gunned their bikes into the darkness and relative quiet of the cabin.

Quinn ripped off his helmet, still straddling the Ducati. One of the crewmen handed him a headset that was attached to a wire on the wall.

"Now that's what I call some slick flying." Smedley craned his head around in the cockpit, grinning at the adventure of it all. "Don't I even get a thank-you?"

"You should thank me for giving you the opportunity." Quinn said. "When else would you get to make good on your pilot bullshit?"

CHAPTER SEVENTY-SIX

Governors Island

Amanda Deatherage waited less than ten feet behind the receiving line beside the fat iron cannon where she'd tied the bow earlier. Perspiration beaded on her upper lip.

So far, the president had been trapped on the far side of the lawn talking to an endless parade of foreign dignitaries who wanted a piece of his time. Mrs. Hughes and the vice president stood to the right of their daughter. The groom, the secretary of state, and the national security advisor stood beside them, shaking hands and chatting brightly with well-wishers as they came through the line.

They were all so handsome and arrogant—and doomed.

Amanda knew full well Mrs. Hughes thought her odd and erratic at best, but she'd gained the hag's trust and that's what was important. She hoped her quirky behavior would mask any last-minute jitters.

Shadan was somewhere in the crowd watching her,

making certain she followed through with her assignment. She'd never met the man—she'd heard his name for the first time when Dr. Badeeb explained her mission. It would be her honor to kill the president and vice president. Shadan, he explained, would be there to assist if needed. He would have a second detonator if anything were to happen to her.

Deatherage knew the man was really there in the event she changed her mind—but that was something that would not happen. She'd come too far, seen too much, to back out now. She owed it to her parents to seek vengeance against the lie that was America. Death was not something to fear. It would be welcome. She had tasted gall for so much of her young life; her martyrdom would come as a sweet reward.

Since taking the job as personal assistant, Deatherage had made it her norm to wear baggy, ill-fitting clothes. Mrs. Hughes expected her to look disheveled. The canvas vest now strapped to her chest held nine thin blocks of plastic explosive and a full ten pounds of evenly placed BBs and sheet-metal screws—all soaked in rat poison to hinder wounds from clotting. Dr. Badeeb had assured her the device would obliterate anyone standing within fifteen feet and maim dozens more who stood within the blast radius. Her loose dress and frumpy jacket hid everything better than she could have imagined.

Security was everywhere—Secret Service, Diplomatic Security, Foreign protective agents, NYPD, and some Amanda couldn't name. But none of them would be able to stop her now.

All that remained was for the president to walk across the lawn and pay his respects to the bride and groom. At that point he would be close enough to the vice president. Then Deatherage would take two steps forward and the face of America would change forever.

The service itself hadn't taken nearly long enough in Nancy Hughes's estimation. A matter of such importance should linger awhile before being over. She consoled herself with the fact that they could stand in line and gloat for a good while, showing off their now-married little girl.

Helicopters whumped above the trees and fighter jets roared overhead, higher now so as not to deafen the guests, but still too low for Nancy's taste. She shook hands with the foreign minister of Japan, a guest of Melissa Ryan's, and apologized for the racket.

Secret Service agents milled among the throng of guests and myriad waiters and waitresses moving in to work the crowd with silver trays of champagne and hors d'oeuvres

President Clark and his entourage stood in a loose gaggle at the far end of the front yard, opposite the cannon. Toby Braithwaite, the playboy British prime minister, bloviated like the parliamentarian he was, hogging the president's attention as if it were his day instead of Jolene's. Nancy wanted a photo of the bride and her new husband with the president. And now the stupid Brit wouldn't turn loose of him.

Special Agent Jack Blackmore with the Secret Service loitered directly behind his protectee, head on a swivel, looking for any abnormality in a sea of guests. Other agents on the POTUS detail, all in dark tuxedos to fit in with the crowd, took various positions around the yard. Some faced inbound, keeping an eye on the guests. Two dozen more faced outward, watching for oncoming threats.

Sonny Vindetti stood directly behind the vice president with Jimmy Doyle. Six more agents assigned to the VP detail stood in front of the receiving line. Each wore the regulation skin-tone earpiece for the radio at their belt. Their eyes scanned each guest on the way down the line.

Melissa Ryan looked ravishing, Nancy thought, in her dark blue Burberry wool suit. Even at her son's wedding, the top two buttons on her white silk blouse remained alluringly open. Winfield Palmer stood beside her, looking dapper but uncomfortably cramped in his tux.

"Heads-up," Nancy heard Sonny Vindetti's voice behind her as he spoke to his team of agents.

President Clark had, at long last, disengaged himself from his conversation with Braithwaite and now strode quickly across the lawn, his team of agents in tow.

"Longbow is on the move," Vindetti said into the microphone at his lapel, using the president's code name.

POTUS was finally on his way and Nancy would be able to get her photo.

"Amanda, dear," she said over her shoulder. "It's time. Would you be so kind as to bring the photographer around?"

Chapter Seventy-seven

"How do you know who you're looking for?" Smedley said as he brought the Osprey from Battery Park over the south tip of Governors Island. He'd received clearance to land in the center of the island, in an area the Secret Service and the NYPD had set up as a joint receiving point. He deviated from his flight path to fly directly over the wedding party.

"I'm hoping I know when I see them," Quinn said. "You have a FLIR onboard?"

"Sure," the pilot tapped the console. "But what good will thermal imaging do with that crowd?"

Quinn went forward to look at the color screen. People, generally warmer than the surrounding air temperature of late evening, showed up in various shades of yellow and red on the forward-looking infrared system. The cooler ground and foliage ranged from light blue to purple. Quinn concentrated his search in the area around the vice president and his wife and it didn't take long to find what he was looking for.

Behind the reception line was the form of a young

woman. Her arms and head glowed red, but her chest was baby blue as if she wore something heavy under her clothing that didn't let her body heat escape.

"That would be Mrs. Hughes's assistant." He tapped the screen with his finger. "I'm willing to bet she's wearing a suicide vest!" Quinn looked up to get a clear view out the front window. "And the president is walking straight for her."

Quinn racked his brain. "Fly straight at them, Smeds—and if you have a spotlight, see if you can light up the girl. We need them to see who we're focusing on—and hopefully get the president to cover."

The pilot looked up, nodding grimly. "You know they'll probably shoot us down?"

"Not this low, beb," Thibodaux offered. "They'll be afraid our flaming wreckage would land on the big boss."

"You have about ten seconds before the president makes it across the lawn," Quinn said.

"Roger that," Smedley said throwing the Osprey into a dive. "What are you going to do?"

Quinn had punched the button to open the rear ramp and was already running back toward the strapped Ducati. "I don't know," he yelled over his shoulder. "I'm making this up as I go along."

Nancy Hughes looked up as a thunderous roar filled the evening sky. She glared at the vice president. "Bobby," she hissed. "I thought we agreed to kee—"

Her voice was drowned out by an approaching aircraft that looked like a plane with upturned propellers. It swooped in over the wedding party to hover just over treetop level—lower than the roof of the mansion. It was close enough she could make out the strained looks on the pilots' faces.

Trays of food and drinks flew from the hands of the staff. Folding chairs, caught in the mini tornado, were tossed around like rag dolls. The aircraft began to work its way even lower, settling between the trees as if to land on the front lawn and crush half the guests. The tremendous force of whirling wind blew open suit jackets, exposing agents' weapons. The women who wore more skimpy gowns had them literally ripped from their bodies.

A blinding beam of light burned from the nose of the aircraft, cutting the dusky evening haze to point directly at the bride and groom.

"Mr. Vice President!" It was Sonny Vindetti's voice. The Secret Service agent grabbed Bob Hughes's shoulder and tugged him backward toward the mansion. "Sir! I need you to come with me! Now!"

"Nancy!" Hughes spun away from his would-be protector, reaching out with both arms in an attempt to shield his wife from unseen dangers.

President Clark ran amid a tightly packed mob of his agents, bent at the waist, to a waiting armored limousine that had been rolling silently over the grassy lawn, following his every move.

Hand over her hair against the horrific wind, Nancy turned just in time to see Jimmy Doyle running to intercept Amanda Deatherage. The girl's ridiculously long jacket had blown up around her face. Her loose dress was pressed to her body by the downdraft, exposing what looked like a bulky life vest underneath.

Blinded by the tangle of cloth, Deatherage screamed with rage, clawed at her face to clear her vision.

"BOMB RIGHT! BOMB RIGHT!" Jimmy Doyle screamed above the melee. He hit the girl with the full force of his body, knocking her behind the huge iron cannon.

A split second later, Nancy Hughes was knocked off her feet. Every molecule of air seemed inexplicably drawn away, vanished. She felt a tremendous heat, then pressure, as if someone had hit her in the chest with a baseball bat. She was vaguely aware that her daughter lay on top of her—and the world was eerily silent.

Quinn and Thibodaux rode off the back ramp moments after the explosion. Smedley was able to bring the Osprey within five feet off the ground—still a tall order for the sporty Ducati's suspension.

The wedding party looked as though a huge bowling ball had come through and knocked everyone to the grass. Quinn knew the Secret Service would be in reactive mode, bent on egress with their charges more than stopping to face an unknown enemy. The countersnipers, on the other hand, would be back to their scopes in no time, scanning from their rooftop perches to stop all signs of threat.

Two crazy men deploying from a V-22 Osprey, dressed in black on screaming motorcycles, would certainly qualify.

After an explosion people generally do one of two things—lie still to protect themselves or try and get away. It is a rare hero who moves toward the blast zone while debris is still falling—or someone with something more sinister in mind.

Quinn saw the waiter in the white waistcoat at the

same moment the Ducati gained traction. The sight of him sent a chill of cold recognition coursing through Quinn's body, renewing the ever-present throbbing pain in his foot.

Picking his way through the mass of dazed and injured toward where the vice president lay unconscious beside his wife, was the unmistakable bald head and black eyes of Military Interrogator First Sergeant Sean Bundy.

Quinn planted his right foot and gassed the throttle. A rooster tail of grass and dirt spewed into the air as the little 848's Testastretta engine spun the back tire. Deafened by the previous blast, Bundy continued on a direct path for the vice president, his right hand behind his thigh as if he carried something.

Quinn bore down on him, ignoring the shouts of Secret Service agents as he sped past. They threatened to shoot, but the bike was fast and there were too many innocents in the way.

Bundy's face snapped up as the Ducati loomed at him, missing by inches. Quinn, oblivious to the pain it would cause him later, bailed off the motorcycle at speed, catching Bundy's head in the pocket of his chest and shoulder as he flew by.

Quinn ducked and rolled, relatively protected by his helmet and armored Transit Leathers, taking Bundy with him. He used the other man's body to break his fall.

All the pent-up rage from the previous interrogation rushed back into Quinn's veins. The humiliation, the threats to his wife and daughter, the bone-crushing pain of the amputation—he'd never wanted to kill anyone as badly as he wanted to kill this man.

The pistol that Bundy had been hiding flew out in front of them as they tumbled, landing three feet from the Echo's outstretched hand. His left arm was twisted grotesquely backward, making it look as if it had two elbows. Facedown in the dirt, he crawled forward, lunging for the gun with his right hand. Black eyes seethed, intent on violence.

And violence was just what Quinn gave him.

Rather than shooting, Quinn drew Yawaraka-Te, the Japanese dirk he wore in a scabbard along his spine. Rolling forward, he planted the chisel tip of the blade square in the back of Bundy's hand, driving it down with a satisfying crunch through muscle and bone, pinning him to the ground.

Bundy screamed in agony as he flopped and thrashed like a trapped fish. The more he moved, the more he injured his trapped hand on Yawaraka-Te's gleaming blade.

Panting, Quinn raised both hands high over his head. He prayed that would be enough to stop the approaching Secret Service agents from shooting him in the back.

Thibodaux rode up with Palmer on the rear seat of his BMW about the time the agents got Quinn into a full prone position. The national security advisor shooed the agents back and told them to see to the screaming bald man with the Japanese sword pegged through his hand.

"You okay, l'ami?" Thibodaux said, whistling under his breath as he helped Quinn to his feet. "I ain't gonna be the one to tell Mrs. Miyagi about her bike. . . ." He leaned in closer. "Let me pass you some advice. I don't know if you know this, but you can't fly."

Quinn rubbed his shoulder where it had struck Bundy's head. "This is the guy who cut my toe off," he said. "He must be one of the moles. He would have been helping that idiot Fargo in order to sow hate and discontent among the country. When Fargo happened to go after me with his personal vendetta and I was just returning from Central Asia, Bundy really did have some questions he wanted me to answer for Badeeb." He looked up at Palmer. "What about the president?"

Palmer shook his head. "Your stunt with the Osprey worked. Jimmy Doyle identified the girl with the suicide vest a half second before she detonated. He was able to push her back behind the cannon before she blew."

Quinn breathed sharply. "Did he make it?"

"Poor son of a bitch saved dozens of lives . . . including mine," Palmer said. "A handful of guests on the other side of the cannon were injured by shrapnel, but young Agent Doyle and the girl were the only ones killed. Bride and groom are shaken up, but still capable of a honeymoon once the shock wears off."

Palmer sighed, his eyes drifting over the aftermath of the explosion. The entire area was already a sea of flashing blue and red emergency lights. "I wonder how many more are out there."

"Well, sir," Quinn said, glaring at the heaving form of Sean Bundy. "Put me in a room with this guy for a few hours. I feel confident he has a story to tell. . . ."

EPILOGUE

Washington

Ten days later

Late October brought sapphire skies and the crisp days of an Indian summer that reminded Quinn of Alaska. Evening joggers and bicyclists ran and rode under the last few tenacious leaves that clung to oaks and sycamores along the wide paths of the Mall.

Quinn pulled the new gunmetal-gray BMW Adventure into a curbside spot on the park side of Third Street, just down from Madison. The lighted specter of the Capitol dome rose up through the shadows to the east, beyond the Grant Memorial.

He was happy for the warmth of his Transit Leathers and happier still that Ronnie Garcia felt well enough to go for a motorcycle ride. She sat behind him, taller on the raised pillion seat of the GS, long arms wrapped around his waist, chest pressed tight against his back.

His right foot still ached from Bundy's crude torture, but periodic acupuncture treatments from Mrs.

Miyagi helped him deal with the pain. And, if Quinn was anything, he was a fast healer.

Kim and Mattie had returned to Alaska after Win Palmer saw to it that Navy SEALs removed the threat against them by storming Sheikh Husseini al Farooq's mountain redoubt in eastern Afghanistan. Even with the sheikh dead and the danger gone, the wall Kim had thrown up remained as impenetrable as ever. She may have given up on Quinn as a husband, but he'd convinced her to give Mattie her own cell phone. As least he could have some semblance of a relationship with his little girl.

Camille Thibodaux had been released from the hospital but ordered on bed rest for the remainder of her pregnancy. Jacques was all too happy to take the time off and spend it keeping his boys out of her hair.

Investigations subsequent to the Governors Island blast had revealed five more moles who had been patients of Dr. Badeeb in their youth. Among them was a precinct captain with the NYPD and the Air Force major responsible for approving Tara Doyle's load of ordinance for her F-22.

American Special Forces had fought October blizzards to accompany CIA paramilitary officer Karen Hunt back to the Pari School, high in the Wakhan Corridor of Eastern Afghanistan. Along with a stash of Vietnam-era U.S. Army uniforms, they found the charred remains of nine adult men and seven boys ranging in age from five to fourteen. All the boys had been shot multiple times before they burned in an apparent explosion within the mountain. Karen found the body of Sam, the boy who had befriended her, in an ice cave a half mile from the school. He, along with eleven other children, had been strangled and left to rot, presumably because they were too softhearted to carry out the doctor's planned jihad against the United States.

Quinn felt Ronnie shift behind him, taking off her helmet. Her long hair tickled the back of his neck as she shook it free.

"So," she said, "after all that, the queen of West Texas bitches was only the backup plan?"

"Yes and no," Quinn said. "According to Bundy/Shadan, Amanda Deatherage was the one with the primary mission to blow herself up at the wedding. Badeeb thought Doyle would be shot down too quickly if she started with Governors Island. But with all the military overwatch tied up there, she'd have a virtual free rein with her F-22 over downtown Manhattan. The plan was for her to drop half her bombs on Times Square, then finish up over the panicked crowds at the wedding after Deatherage blew herself to pieces. Dr. Badeeb was a man who liked to control every detail. Shadan could see to it Deatherage followed through, but once Tara Doyle was in the air, they would have no tether to her. She would become a loose cannon."

"An attack over Times Square . . ." Ronnie whispered. "She would have killed hundreds. And if the president and vice president had both died at the wedding . . ."

"That would leave the speaker of the House next in line."

"So," she said turning to look at the Capitol dome. "You think he's in there?"

Quinn nodded. "I do. As the new speaker, he's

moved from his basement office to a ritzy suite off the rotunda."

"Did Shadan give you anything you could use on him?"

The media had reported that Sean Bundy had been among those killed in the suicide blast at Governors Island. In actuality, he was being held off American soil in a secret facility outside Parham Town in the British Virgin Islands.

Quinn shook his head, still gazing at the lighted Capitol dome. "To tell you the truth, I'm not sure Bundy knew he was involved. Badeeb was awfully good at keeping his operations compartmentalized." He shot a glance over his shoulder to look Garcia in the eye. "But Drake's a mole. There is zero doubt in my mind. I pulled a copy of his wife's autopsy. Cause of death was drowning, but she had bruising and scraping consistent with being kicked in the face."

"You think Drake killed her?"

"I do." Quinn nodded. "The sympathy from her death gives him a load of public support. If Deatherage had been able to follow through and kill both the VP and the president, Drake would have waltzed right into the Oval Office. As POTUS, he could do untold damage to the stock markets, our national defense, homeland security . . . you name it."

"So, there he sits," Ronnie sighed. "A terrorist, two heartbeats from the presidency."

"Yeah, well, I'm working on that," Quinn mused.

"I'll bet you are," Ronnie chuckled, rubbing her cheek softly against Quinn's shoulder. "You know, I'm not sure I ever really thanked you for saving my life."

Quinn turned to catch another glimpse of her face. The subtle odor of jasmine wafted toward him. "We're even then. I was just returning the favor," he said. "Speaking of you saving my life, I wonder if they'll let us back in Cubano's after I tore up their men's room. Something spicy and ethnic sounds pretty good about now."

"It does, does it?" Ronnie nestled herself even tighter against his back, thighs warm along his hips. The buzz of her breath in his ear made him heady. "You know what I wonder? I wonder what the elevation is in Washington, D.C."

Quinn shrugged, holding back a grin. "Not much above sea level, I guess. Why?"

"Oh, I was just thinking how you told me once you weren't likely to have much resolve against my advances at elevations below ten thousand feet. . . ."

"Resolve . . ." Quinn nodded his head slowly as he thought, lost in the enveloping warmth of this supremely beautiful and capable woman. "That's an interesting ques—"

The phone at his belt began to buzz. He picked it up, sighing when he saw the caller ID. It was Kim.

Ronnie patted his belly and gave him a playful squeeze. "Who is it?"

"Doesn't matter," Quinn said, more resolved than he had ever been in his life. "Let's talk some more about these advances of yours."

He returned the phone to his belt and let it ring.

ACKNOWLEDGMENTS

A book like this would not be possible without the assistance of many people so much smarter than me.

First, I need to thank my bride, Victoria, for listening and plotting and critiquing . . . and pestering me to sit down and get to work.

My editor, Gary Goldstein, and agent, Robin Rue, are two of the easiest people to work with that I've ever even heard of in the business.

Though I own and ride a BMW GS, I often turn to riding buddies when I have a question about such things as the physics and techniques of stoppies, wheelies, and flat track racing. The folks at ADVrider.com provide a great resource to keep Jericho well mounted on interesting bikes in interesting locales. Sonny Caudill, Scott Ireton, and Gary Picoult have proven to have a wealth of knowledge when it comes to all things motorized on two wheels.

On occasion, I've had the opportunity to work alongside agents from Air Force OSI and the U.S. Secret Service. Due to the nature of their work, none of them want to be thanked by name. So: You know who you are—and I am in your debt.

My martial-arts sensei, Jujitsu Master Ty Cunningham, was an invaluable help in walking me through the nuanced dynamics of real-world unarmed conflict. Thank you, my friend.

Finally, I really should thank my barber, Linda, for spreading the word about Jericho Quinn. She's the best public-relations representative a guy could ask for.

And again—I've said it before, but it bears repeating. The folks in this line of work are bound to find some tactical errors in these pages. All (I hope) are by design. The last thing I want to do is write a how-to primer for the bad guys.